Trident P

THE Silk WEAVER

'Suffused with mist and semi-light, Warnock's book portrays the
period's fervent nationalism, its prevalent fear of betrayal from
both without and within; she shows the population's blind need
for heroes and mirrors the complexity of the nation's hopes and
fears through a few poignantly intimate relationships'.

Ellen Beardsley, *The Irish Times*

'For all its deft recreation of late 18th-century Dublin, the real
strength of The Silk Weaver lies in its vividly-drawn characters –
the eponymous Huguenot hero, his good-natured Dublin
employer, the sinister government spy who appears only through
his letters, and a bevy of strong women, including a wife, a
fiancée, two lovers, a demented mother – and in the twists and
turns of its plot, which interweaves fictional and historical
situations with the same kind of thoughtful skill which is evident
in the design of the Warnock garden'.

Arminta Wallace, *The Irish Times*

'The mysteries of silk are woven seamlessly into the narrative
which is interspersed with a fine parody of the letters of Francis
Higgins . . . Warnock's research is meticulous and her evocation
of late eighteenth century Dublin is masterly . . . she displays an
ability to introduce period detail without overwhelming the reader
by fact'.

Gillian Somerville Large, *The Irish Independent*

GABRIELLE WARNOCK spent her childhood in Cork and Kilkenny, studied at Trinity College, Dublin and subsequently lived in England and the US. Returning to Ireland with her husband and two sons, Gabrielle began submitting short stories to the Irish Press. She has had many stories published in Irish newspapers and some have been broadcast on RTE. She was a winner in the Listowel Writer's Week Short Story Competition in 1980 and of a Hennessy Award in 1981. Her first novel, *Fly in a Web*, was published by Poolbeg Press. Having successfully completed a law degree at UCG, Gabrielle returned to writing. In her spare time, she and her husband are creating a magical garden in most inhospitable terrain on the edge of the Burren.

THE *Silk* WEAVER

Gabrielle Warnock

TRIDENT PRESS

First published in 1998 by Trident Press Ltd
2-5 Old Bond Street, London W1X 3TB
Tel: 0171 491 8770 Fax: 0171 491 8664
in conjunction with
Trident Media (Irl) Ltd
Station House, Clifden, Co. Galway, Ireland
Tel: 095 22024 Fax: 095 22068

1 3 5 7 9 8 6 4 2

Copyright © Gabrielle Warnock 1998

The author asserts her moral right
to be identified as the author of this work

A CIP catalogue record for this book
is available from the British Library

Designed and typeset by Johan Hofsteenge

ISBN 1 900724 26 X

Printed and bound by ColourBooks Ltd, Dublin, Ireland

Cover: The Custom House (a detail) by James Malton
(engraving), Private Collection/Bridgeman Art Library,
London/New York
Credit: The Stapleton Collection

ACKNOWLEDGEMENTS

I am indebted to Tom Bartlett of UCD for directing me to the letters of Francis Higgins ISPO 620/18/14 and for his article *Select documents XXXVIII: Defenders and Defenderism in 1795* IHS xxiv. no.95 (May 1985).

I must also, I regret to say, confess gratitude to the informer Francis Higgins himself. His letters were a marvellous source of information and inspiration.

For those who are curious to find out more about the silk trade, I recommend the following:
G.L. Lee, *Huguenot Settlements in Ireland*, Longmans, Green and Co., London and New York 1936
J.J.Webb, *Industrial Dublin since 1698 and The Silk Industry in Dublin*, Maunsel, Dublin and London 1913
Luther Hooper, *Hand-Loom Weaving Plain and Ornamental*, John Hogg, London 1910

I found the following two books indispensable:
Thomas Pakenham, *The Year of Liberty*, Hodder and Stoughton, London 1969
Marianne Elliott, *Wolfe Tone, Prophet of Irish Independence*, Yale University Press, New Haven and London 1989

The lines quoted in the letter on page 143 are a translation of an old Irish poem by John Montague. The lines are reproduced with the permission of Faber & Faber.

For Jeremy, Seán and Keith.

We are all Adam's children but silk makes the difference.
Thos. Fuller (1654 – 1734) Gnomologia (1732) no. 5425.

ONE

Wheneas in silks my Julia goes,
Then, then methinks, how sweetly flows
That liquefaction of her clothes.

Next when I cast mine eyes and see
That brave vibration each way free,
Oh, how that glittering taketh me!
Robert Herrick

Space in the chilly upper warehouse was filled, not, as might have been expected, with bales of silk; instead of silks, the warehouse accommodated an empty warping machine and, more importantly, a drawloom on which was stretched a twitching warp, its four thousand silk threads inescapably connected up to the controlling monture of leashes, many-eyed mails, hanging lingoes, comberboard, the overhead pulleys, tailcords and simple.

The warehouse, though cold, smelt strongly of sweat. The warp did not dance without effort. Standing to one side of the loom, close to the simple which stretched like a vast and copiously-stringed instrument from the floor up to the tail cords high above the loom, the drawboy, an elderly man, sweated profusely; dark veins rose thick and muddy as rootlets in his pale neck and forehead as he pulled, held, and released a succession of lashes. Each pulled lash drew down certain of the two hundred and fifty cords composing the simple; these cords in turn activated the tail cords, which rolled on their pulleys, to hoist the leashes through which the warp was threaded. The drawboy's initial action thus put into progress a series of interconnected reactions, which eventually culminated in the raising of a particular sequence of strands in the warp, while the rest remained lying flat, creating a shed through which a shuttle carrying the weft could be passed by the weaver.

1

The drawboy grunted and sweated and (with the assistance of a two-pronged wooden device thrust behind and before the drawn down cords of the simple) manipulated the strings; but his was not the real power. His task was almost mechanical. So long as he continued to pull the lashes in their correct sequence then the pattern would be drawn up, line by line, on the warp. The result was predetermined. Anton Paradis, the weaver, who now just threw the shuttle from side to side and treadled two lines of tabby weave between each line of the pattern, was the real controller of events. It was the weaver who had spent two weeks draughting the design with immense precision onto ruled paper, and tying up the four thousand-threaded warp to correspond with that design. He had himself drawn the threads individually through the eyes of the mails and on through the teeth of the reed. It was he who had threaded the tips of the lingo-weighted, mail-eyed leashes through the holes of the comberboard, he who had connected the neck cords to the pulleys, he who had stretched the tail cords from the pulleys to the far wall, he who had hung from each tail cord a further cord to create his highly-strung simple. It was the weaver who finally, in accordance with the minutely draughted design, had tied the cords of the simple together in overlapping groups, each group secured by a single lash and delineating a line of pattern upon that squared paper. Each lash was tied to the guiding cords in a sequence which even the drawboy would have had difficulty in misinterpreting. Paradis had trusted no one else to translate accurately to the loom the design which had been given to him by the silk merchant. He had even rolled the warp himself.

The weaving had begun at seven o'clock that morning, and Danno could see that the preparation had gone well. The accuracy was absolute and a perfect rendering of the paper pattern of diminutive harebells, grouped together in three-stemmed clusters, on a striped background, was appearing in silk on the loom. The harebells themselves were being woven in variously textured silver metal threads which gave to each flower, to each unopened bud, to each linear leaf, a reality so intense that it seemed, lacking their self-proving presence, as if both the colour and the size of those other harebells, those ones which drew their existence from the earth, must be mistaken. The sprigs of flowers lay scattered on their striped background, poised (Danno thought) for gathering. The stripes, a double width of cream, divided one from the next by a single width of deep rose, were of fine Italian silk. Danno could tell that Anton was pleased with the cloth for he had heard, as they mounted the stairs, the raucous sound of the weaver attempting to sing in a key above the natural height of his own voice, one of those French religious songs to which he was so attached.

The impact of the cloth and its pattern on the more outraged of Daniel McKenna's two visitors was minimal. Daniel McKenna, silk merchant of repute, but of declining fortunes, was not surprised. Although Anton, contrary to usual practice, wove so that the pattern appeared face up, very little of the finished fabric, even had his irate visitor bothered to look, was visible on the loom and gathering roller. But the drawboy could surely not be ignored? Daniel (Danno to his friends and to some who erroneously imagined themselves to be such) glanced briefly at his second visitor. From the tart smell of his visible sweat to his grunting effort on the lashes, the drawboy was invasively present; while the weaver's precariously warbling French hymns must, Danno thought, if heard, have been startling enough to intrigue. If the second visitor had noticed anything she did not confide her observations to Danno. How could she? The fulminations of the first visitor did not allow for interruption. This visitor (well-known to Danno from their mutual adherence to the cause of the United Irishmen) was intent on obtaining satisfaction concerning the serious complaint he was still laying before the silk merchant as they entered his warehouse in which the two workers were temporarily lodged for the weaving, at a specially mounted loom, of the silk-striped, silver-flowered tobine which Danno had commissioned from Anton for his own personal use.

"My wife . . ." Oh, he was a very self-important man was Marvin Sweetman. A man of tasteful possessions, one of the most tasteful of which had to be his wife. It was imperative that the wife of Marvin Sweetman, the undoubtedly self-respected attorney, should be exquisitely attired at all times. All things owned by him must reflect, without fail, his good taste and his good standing in Dublin society. That was why Marvin Sweetman had gone to Daniel McKenna in the first place. The quality of McKenna's materials was said by many to be unsurpassed in Dublin, and he was, by Dublin standards, innovative. One could be patriotic without suffering for it when one dealt with McKenna. One did not have to encase one's wife in poplin stiff enough to support a sleeping sentry upright. But McKenna had let him down. "My wife was humiliated."

Marvin Sweetman and his wife had attended a ball at the Castle, dressed, as requested by the Viceroy and his wife on their invitation, in Irish-woven fabric. His own particular strain of patriotism had been signalled by the wearing of Irish-made white machine-knit silk stockings, but, more specifically, by the wearing of an ornate waistcoat of green silk brocade, with matching brocaded buttons, the brocade for which had been bought from McKenna's shop below. About the brocade, the visitor had no complaint. His wife's lutestring of midnight blue and gold (she had refused the wearing of the green; green, she had claimed, did not suit her complexion), also purchased downstairs, was quite another matter. The material had been sold to them as an exclusive piece of silk.

"Perhaps, Mr. McKenna, the meaning which you attach to the word exclusive is different to the meaning I have always understood the word to convey?"

Sweetman's mechanism was running down. He had begun to repeat himself. He was a decent man, Danno knew, but much afflicted by pomposity. They had already agreed, before entering the warehouse itself, that exclusive held the same meaning for them both. Danno McKenna had brought his visitors upstairs so that they might together (Sweetman had unfortunately insisted) enquire of Anton, the weaver of the blue and gold lutestring, whether he might not be able to shed light on the unhappy fact that at the Castle Ball, another lady had appeared, dressed in an identical blue and gold lutestring, woven from a pattern supposedly exclusive, not only to the McKenna firm, but also to the web of material woven by Anton himself, and sold subsequently, in its entirety, to Marvin Sweetman's wife.

Sweetman's wife (with whom Danno had no previous acquaintance) did not give the impression of a woman easily humiliated. She was not humiliated now, most certainly. She looked quite entertained. She was standing by the loom of that damned Frenchman, and she was admiring his work. "Beautiful," she commented to the now silent weaver, before turning to the silk merchant. "My husband," she said, as though she had read Danno's thoughts, "was so humiliated on my behalf that any humiliation I might have suffered myself would have been redundant. I therefore took the only possible role left to me that I could see . . ."

"Which was?"

Danno, engaged to a young girl of impeccable niceness and with a fortune capable of propping up his ailing business, was in love. Well, love was what he preferred to call it. A politer way to describe the indecent surge of desire which had afflicted him quite without warning when Sweetman's wife had stepped down from the carriage in front of her husband ten minutes earlier. Danno, despite the suitability of his fiancée, was nevertheless prone to such disloyal surges. He considered himself uniquely fickle, and coped as best he could. The choice of fiancée was his mother's and was not to be faulted, save in the matter of a want of affection for the girl on Danno's part. Affection, he had been assured, would grow with increased acquaintance; so far it had remained stubbornly stunted. Well, in matters of family fortune, one could not afford to seek out the indulgence of romance. As Tone, his darling, banished Tone, would have said, "Tis but in vain for soldiers to complain." One did one's duty and took pleasure where one could. And now the angel was speaking again . . .

"Why, to rise above the embarrassment of course."

She seemed on the verge of a laughter, held in check, Danno was sure, only out of deference to her husband's solemnity. As though this assured creature could possibly allow herself to be humiliated by such a trifle.

"In fact," she continued in a voice airy with self-approval, "so far above it did I rise that I confess, I never noticed the departure of my innocent rival, though I am told (by my husband) that she stayed no more than half-an-hour. Indeed, if anyone required compensation, it must be that unfortunate lady whose night was so obviously curtailed by the incident."

It was only chance misfortune that he had not seen her before. It suited Danno to serve, on occasion, the women who came to his shop. He liked to gather up their comments, assess his stock through their eyes. The habit shamed his mother, while his fiancée insisted that the practice would have to stop once they were married. She could not bear, she said, the humiliation of being married to a shopkeeper. Danno did not intend to indulge her sensitivities, though he had not said so in so many words. Better that she should marry first and repent afterwards than that she should repent too soon. But thoughts of his fiancée were inappropriate to this occasion. It seemed quite cruel that chance should have denied him any previous sighting of this gorgeous creature. And to find her married to Marvin, that most staid of Protestant men! A man with a much-declared, but suspect, zeal for justice. It was well-known that Marvin Sweetman was apprehensive of the consequences of justice. He thought that Catholics should be encouraged, but not indulged. He was afraid of what Catholics would do if given too much power: not educated Catholics of course, not Catholics like Danno. But there were so few Catholics like Danno. Marvin was afraid of the hordes: whiteboys, ribbonmen, defenders. He was terrified of the whole hostile mass beyond the Pale. Even within the Pale, Goddamit. And yet, because he was a decent man, his sense of justice was offended by the disabilities under which Catholics laboured. Marvin was prepared to advocate parliamentary reform and if that had, in all decency, to include giving Catholics the vote, even seats, then Marvin could not ignore the insistence of his conscience. But now that Marvin's demands had been partially realised, his conscience could not suppress the rising to the surface of an occasional, traitorous desire for the continued failure of the rest. His attendance of meetings had grown sporadic in recent months.

He and Danno differed radically. Danno's aims were serious, but his heart was light. This lightness of heart camouflaged his resolution, whereas Marvin's heart, more burdened with apprehension than his aims could properly bear, misled by its outward sobriety. It was insupportable that someone so solemn should not be sincere.

Sweetman regretted having brought his wife. Danno could see that. Remarking testily that they did not have the entire day to waste, Sweetman pointed to Anton. "Is that the man?" he asked sharply.

Danno nodded.

"Anton. He's my best weaver. French."

"Good God, I didn't know there were any Huguenots left in the Liberties."

"There aren't. Not really. Anton and his wife are accidentals. The results of an unsuccessful experiment in Co. Cork."

He was reluctant to allow this interview to take place. If Anton *had* dealt dishonestly with him regarding the pattern, Danno did not want to know. Knowledge procured so publicly would force disciplinary action, and Danno could not bear to jeopardise his relationship with Anton in any way. To say that Anton was his best weaver was to give no inkling of the man's importance. He was indispensable, not only to the business, but also to Danno's personal need to have about him beautiful silk. Only Anton could translate the old, intricate designs which Danno intermittently presented to the weaver. If Anton had *not* dealt dishonestly with the pattern, then Danno risked offending the weaver by making the suggestion in the first place, and the relationship was in equal jeopardy.

Sweetman's wife sensed the silk merchant's discomfiture. She also sensed the weaver's increasing animosity. They were speaking of him in his presence as though he had no ears.

"French!" she exclaimed, without letting her husband speak any further. She smiled at Danno and would have included the weaver, could she have caught his attention. "Well, that explains so much, because, in truth, though the two dresses seemed superficially to be made up from identical material, the other dress was, in reality, much inferior; which fact, while not noticeable to my husband, was immediately obvious, not only to myself, but also to others. The second weaver, most obviously not as skilled as this weaver here, had simplified the pattern to match his ability. Two colours, at least, were missing, and the silk itself was of such poor quality that by lamplight it seemed as dead as ground glass. I think it was their differences more than their similarities which caused my poor reflection to retire so precipitately from the field."

It was, Anton thought bitterly, typical of his wife to take such shoddy shortcuts. Oh, she was capable enough. She was almost as capable as himself if the truth be admitted. But she cut corners where she could. She had no intrinsic respect for the silk which she wove. She abused it. She treated it as no more than a commodity with a high economic value. When she worked for an inferior mercer, she used inferior material, or she worked more loosely with expensive material. A man such as Thomas Reynolds, for instance, would be incapable of noticing the difference. And why, his wife reasoned, should one waste the best silk on a man with no eyes, a man with no feeling in his hands? Anton had not given the pattern to Charlotte. He had brought home the design to draught it onto ruled paper. A copy of his draught had been taken. He did not have the authority to withhold it from her. One could not be said to give what one was not capable of withholding. Anton continued to weave, throwing the shuttles from side to side, banging each line of weft tight with the reed. He no longer sang, but he gave no indication that he was aware of the conversation which was taking place.

"From the quality of this man's work," Letitia Sweetman said, turning to her husband who had now quite lost his brief control of the scene, "it is quite obvious that the other silk was not produced on his loom. And since Mr. McKenna is above reproach," she bowed briefly in Danno's direction, "then it can only be that the design was pirated. I have heard that there are spies sent around the city to examine the finished silks of their rivals and make copies of the best. You wouldn't believe the skulduggery. The weaver can be blamed only for weaving a piece of silk so magnificent that it was bound to be copied." She spoke directly to her husband, while allowing her voice to rise a touch higher with indignation. "Some of my friends say that the only safeguard is to buy, not from the shop itself, where the silks are open for all to see, but from the mercer's warehouse, or directly from the weaver's loom. A web such as this, for instance," and she touched a single harebell lightly, but covetously, with a finger, "has perhaps been seen by no more than the five people now standing in this room."

The drawboy was included in the count of five. Drawboys were much less visible than weavers. Anton, changing neither the expression of his face, nor the tempo of his weaving, noted the unusual sensibility.

She was clever. Undoubtedly, she was clever. She had guided her husband so subtly in a direction advantageous to them all. One could scarcely quibble at the fact that the direction was particularly advantageous to herself. Danno smiled. The performance deserved no less. She saw his smile and allowed him, by a glance held for the fraction of a second, to be aware that she had seen.

Marvin Sweetman moved ponderously into the opening created by his wife. "And so . . . well now indeed, and so . . . yes . . . well, perhaps Mr. McKenna, taking into account the distress caused to my wife, and the fact that she will be unable to wear that dress again for fear of meeting its double, and given that one would not wish for the disaster to be repeated with a substituted material, though of course, the fault may not be yours in the first place and . . ."

Poor Sweetman. Danno was pleased to notice his fellow patriot's embarrassment now that it came to the point. Not that he was ever a clear speaker. His contributions at meetings were equally long-winded and confused. Things to be interrupted as soon as possible, if they could not be prevented from starting in the first place. Danno decided to help him out.

"Mr. Sweetman," he said, patting the roller indicatively with his hand, "the least I can do to make amends is to present to your wife, when finished, this web on which Anton is currently working. And I shall take it upon myself to have the silk made up into a dress of any pattern that your wife should desire, the fittings to take place wherever she pleases. The matter shall have my personal attention."

Now that the offer had been made, Marvin Sweetman was even more embarrassed. He stood there, red and tongue-tied, unable to formulate a reply which didn't sound either too apologetic or too ungracious. Again his wife came to his rescue.

"What a generous offer!" she exclaimed. "The amends are so much in excess of the damage caused, that you would only think it petty were we to refuse."

Danno had expected no other response. Thus easily, the silver-sprigged tobine, which had been intended as a gift for his fiancée, was given away.

As Danno was handing Mrs. Sweetman into her carriage, she hesitated for a moment, her hand deliciously resting on his arm, to tell him that they had a mutual friend.

"Mr. Tone and I acted together in a private production of 'The Way of the World'. Before I met Mr. Sweetman. One of Congreve's plays. Do you know it?"

Danno nodded his assent.

"He was Mirabell and I played Mrs. Millamant. He talked of you a great deal. I think you were his hero from amongst the Catholic faction. He claimed that you were, if possible, more radical than himself. He also said that while your wit might not be so glittering as Mirabell's own (and I think that Mr. Tone intended me to understand Mirabell and himself as a single being when he made that remark), your friendship was unique in its warmth. He had every intention of introducing us, but then he was forced to leave the country. I met Mr. Sweetman and . . ." She shrugged her shoulders and smiled at Danno, who, in his aroused state, saw the smile as wistful, if not positively rueful.

Inside the carriage, Marvin Sweetman leaned across towards the open door. "Step up, my dear! Step up! The arrangements can be made some other time. It's far too cold to linger out of doors."

There had been a girl! Now that she spoke of the play, Danno recalled Tone's enthusiasm for his leading lady. In his youthful acting days, Tone had frequently been smitten by his leading ladies. But on this occasion, the acting had amounted to no more than the spontaneous performance of a couple of scenes from the play at the house of friends, sometime between the trial of Jackson and Tone's exile. Tone had been prepared to indulge in some matchmaking on his friend's behalf rather than on his own. He would admit no more on his own account than that had he been a single man, he would have been tempted. He had indeed proposed to introduce them; but by that time Tone had already lingered on in Ireland a year beyond the date on which the order for his deportation had been issued, and the authorities were losing patience. So Danno never met the girl. He could not remember the name she had been known by. Danno was suddenly frantic to know what had been her maiden name, but she had already, obedient to her husband's summons, passed out of his hands and into the carriage, and the question would have sounded too impertinent. He could do no more than promise to contact her as soon as the web was finished, and await her further instructions.

Danno watched the swaying carriage depart in the direction of College Green. Her desirability, noted on first sight, was increased a hundredfold by the fact that their introduction had been previously intended but thwarted. True love denied. An intriguing poignancy was added to Danno's easily acquired ardour.

Up to now, there had been two passions in Danno's life. Silk and politics. Today he had added the foundations, flimsy though they might seem, of a third: Marvin's wife.

***

"She was beautiful, Anton! Wasn't she beautiful?"
Danno had returned to the upper warehouse after the departure of his pacified visitors. He needed a confidant for his emotions.

"I couldn't say." Anton continued to weave, throwing the shuttle from side to side, banging the reed against the weft.

On the other hand, Danno thought, Anton could not afford to take umbrage. Where else would he find employment which did not depend on his wife's generosity? Weavers throughout the Liberties were unemployed. It was being said that something close to famine existed within the Liberties. Families were beginning to starve. The problem was that even the rich were turning to cotton, and where they clung to silk, it was foreign silk they bought. He sold it to them himself. British and Italian silks, silks from Bengal, China and Persia. What else could he do? If he didn't stock what his customers wanted, they would simply cease to patronise him. His employment of the few weavers he did employ was nothing less than charity. And yet, Anton had warned him that he was in danger of being targeted by a militant combination of journeymen weavers, because he sold imported silk. It was vain to explain that but for those imports, he would not be able to afford to employ the number of weavers that he did. He didn't need the weavers. But if the other weavers were no more than an indulgence Danno could not at present bring himself to forgo, Anton was a necessity and Anton was aware of that. He knew that in no other weaver would Danno find a passion for silk that matched his own. He could take any degree of umbrage he cared to take and remain safe.

"Your wife's doing?" Danno said now, resignation apparent in his voice as he admitted this fact to himself.

Anton nodded. He felt no guilt. He took no responsibility for what he could not prevent.

"Has she seen *this* pattern?"

Anton shrugged. The question was ridiculous.

"How could she not have seen it?"

Such an incident repeated could ruin his business.

"Tell your wife," Danno said to the weaver's back, "that should this present design be woven by herself, or by any of her journeymen, no more of her silk will be purchased by me or by my foreman."

Anton nodded again. "I'll tell her."

They both knew how weak the threat was. Charlotte had never been an important supplier to McKenna's warehouse. She supplied Thomas Reynolds, and she supplied Cope, as well as three or four less significant mercers. She did not need McKenna's trade. Besides, Danno employed his own journeymen weavers.

"Have you no authority?" Danno asked his weaver now.

"You know my position," the weaver said defensively. "She is the master weaver. I am the journeyman."

"Yes, but there are ways, surely, in which a husband can compel obedience from a wife? Some men," he added, with bravado, "when their wives grow uppity, they beat them."

The suggestion was ludicrous, and he knew it. Anton was incapable of such violence; but Danno did not suppose there could be any man alive who would dare to do violence to Charlotte Paradis. Apart from the ample deterrence of her own formidable bearing, there was the renowned loyalty of her journeymen to consider. It was said in the silk business that when you crossed Charlotte, you made ten enemies. Danno would not have been the husband of Charlotte Paradis for all the silk in China. Touch her and ten men screamed with pain.

Danno himself could not imagine beating a woman. Though if she had not the defence of prettiness . . . or were she to goad without respite . . . He was joking of course. But there were men who considered chastisement to be their duty. He could easily imagine his fiancée's father, who had insisted on written agreements concerning so many aspects of the forthcoming marriage, inserting an earnest series of clauses regarding supervision of the moral character of his daughter. Occasions on which beating would be inappropriate; occasions on which beatings would be permissible; and occasions on which beating would be not only permissible, but desirable. Danno was ashamed of the incivility of his humour on the eve of his marriage to that irreproachable, if dull, young woman, upon whom he would never dream of laying a finger. He might neglect her and he might deceive her; he would not beat her. Women had so little power, poor creatures; the least one could do was to refrain from keeping them in apprehension of physical abuse. Danno considered himself to be a gentleman of advanced opinions.

There were some who said that Danno might have learned more about running the business bequeathed to him by his father, had he forgotten about being a gentleman and concentrated on the buying and selling of silk, without the profits from which his gentlemanly pretensions were futile. The accusation was unfounded in both its aspects. Contrary to what was said of him, Danno had no desire to distance himself from his trade, and he did not pretend to be a gentleman. He was one. Danno had come to the silk business at the wrong point in that industry's history. It was in terminal decline, and no exercise of Danno's ingenuity could save it. His father, certainly, had been desperate for social status, and in the seeking of it, had done the gentlemanly thing by his son. He had sent his son to France for his education, and would have financed a Grand Tour had it not been for the intervention of the war with France. He had kept his son free of the trade for as long as was possible in the face of his son's ungrateful insistence on learning it in its entirety (and thus discovering the negligent nature of his father's stewardship of the business).

It had been Danno's grandfather who had founded the business, importing for the purpose, from both England and France, machinery and a diverse and skillful workforce. Weavers, warpers, dyers, throwsters had all been lured to Dublin by McKenna's well-calculated generosity. He had been a substantial man in advance of the venture. He died a man of great fortune. At its peak, the business had employed seventy looms. Now, his grandson had ten looms and not enough work to keep them in constant production. Linen had damaged the silk industry. Cotton had doomed it. Being a gentleman (his father's efforts had succeeded to the extent that Danno could be taken for nothing else) did not prevent Danno from understanding the silk industry perfectly. Dublin silk was being smothered by other fabrics and by cheaper, foreign, finished silks. No change of strategy on Danno's part could halt the process.

Danno had another disadvantage, not normally suffered by young men whom their parents (for the best of reasons) strove to distance from their roots in trade. He had a sensuous and artistic devotion to the silk in which he dealt. Armazeens, sarsanets, florentines, florinets; velvets, brocades and damasks; tissues, tobines, tabinets, paduasoys; lustrings, poplins and persians; silks flowered or striped, silks raw or thrown, silks gilded, clouded or fringed. The names and the descriptions trailed diaphanous in his mind, familiar as a litany. In the house in Dame Street, unfashionably (so his fiancée said) attached to the place of business, were collected samples, pieces of silk and books of paper patterns. Old-fashioned silks with vast unlikely flowers and incongruous touches of chinoiserie. Silk strengthened with weft of worsted and silk so fine that through three layers the shadow of a hand could still be seen. Danno slept between sheets of the supplest purple damask, silk woven for his grandfather more than forty years before. What Danno saw as a unique history of his grandfather's enterprise, his mother and his fiancée saw as rubbish, an embarrassment, an obvious pointer to their dependence on trade and a hindrance to their further advancement.

The impending marriage had been arranged just in time. Danno planned, with his wife's dowry, to expand the business. He was going to branch into cottons. But not at the expense of silk. The cotton would help to subsidise the silk. Well subsidised, he could afford to be both more innovative and more selective. He would be able to indulge his own taste to the full. Oh yes, he would marry his fiancée. She would, undoubtedly, become his wife. Nothing that had happened during the afternoon could cause Danno a moment's hesitation. Duty was paramount. But it was obvious that the requirements of duty should not preclude pleasure, else, who would accept duty? He wondered how easily a more intimate meeting might be arranged with the wife of Marvin Sweetman, and to what breaches of fidelity Marvin Sweetman's wife might be enticed?

TWO

Anton Paradis' father, mother and elder brother had been one of sixty families to arrive in Cork in the August of 1765, on board the *Red Head Galley*, invited by one Thomas Adderley, the Parliamentary representative for Bandon. This worthy and public-spirited gentleman had been anxious to introduce the cultivation and manufacture of silk to Inishannon. He was not a novice in business matters; but in this instance, he over-extended himself. Had he been less ambitious, less visionary, his silk industry might have been as successful as the linen industry he had already set in motion. It was the attempt to cultivate the worm, the larvae of the Chinese moth, the *Bombyx mori*, which ruined the venture. Mulberry trees were planted and survived, but the moist climate killed the silkworms. One of Anton's most abiding memories concerning Inishannon was of the stench of Elizabeth Cortey's dying worms, all those thousands of them, rotting in their trays despite the encouragement of the Royal Dublin Society, and her own frantic efforts to save them. The moist climate which killed the worms also killed Anton's mother, five years after the birth of her second son; those of the colonists that it did not kill found the climate depressing and the countryside, after Lyons, inexpressibly dull. Silk had been woven: even carpets. But after twenty years none of the colonists remained. In 1782, Anton's father moved, with his two sons, to Spitalfields in London.

Anton's uncle, Lucien, travelled no further than Dublin, from where, in time, suspecting himself to be dying, he offered, first to Anton's brother and then, on receiving a regretful refusal, to Anton, the hand of his only child, Charlotte, master weaver, in marriage. Degrees of consanguinity proved no obstacle. The chief cause of Anton's hesitation was his cousin's age. She was twelve years his senior. Even then, it was not so much the gap itself, as the relationship that the age difference had given rise to in the past. At the colony in Co. Cork, his cousin Charlotte had, in effect, been his mother; and how could one contemplate marriage with one's mother? One didn't, according to his father and his brother. One reined in one's imagination, one considered the practicalities of one's situation as a younger son in a strange country twice-removed from home, and one accepted the offer with dignified gratitude. Charlotte was an excellent catch to someone with so few connections as Anton. She was not pretty, but who needed prettiness in a wife? Prettiness was more a liability than an asset, and prettiness, his father and his brother had assured him, could be found in any street in any city. Anton had said nothing of his cousin's looks. So much had he always thought of Charlotte as his mother, that it had never occurred to him to consider her looks. He had no wish to consider Charlotte's looks. The possibility of desiring his cousin was obscene. But lust, or the lack of it, was immaterial. Charlotte, said his father, was not so much a woman, as a weaver; a weaver with a flourishing trade.

In Dublin, her position was almost unique. Charlotte had, with perfect legality, served out her apprenticeship to her own father. In a trade confined so exclusively to men that combinations had been formed to prevent the taking on of female apprentices, Charlotte had been tolerated. Her right to succeed to her father's trade, in the absence of male issue, was acknowledged.

Anton Paradis returned to Ireland in 1792, at the age of twenty-one, to marry his cousin Charlotte Paradis, then in her thirty-fourth year. On accepting the offer of his uncle, Anton had imagined, his thoughts spurred on by the haziness of distance and the hints of his father and his brother, that his cousin, under the auspices of his uncle, would gracefully concede her position within her father's business to him. When they met, he had wondered how he could have been deluded by such imaginings. The reality, as he should have expected, was quite different. Charlotte appeared overjoyed to see him. The first thing she did was to take his face between her hands and kiss his forehead. Anton could have wept with nostalgia at the familiarity of the embrace. She was glad, she whispered to him, that it was Anton, and not his brother, who was to be her husband. The preference was genuine; its basis proved, subsequently, to be humiliating. The warmth of his cousin's welcome coloured Anton's mood and allowed him to view his uncle's settlement proposal with equanimity.

Two months in advance of his nephew's coming, Charlotte's father, Lucien Paradis, had retired to bed to forestall death. The ruse had worked. He remained alive and fully lucid. On the night of Anton's arrival, two documents were brought to the bedside of Lucien Paradis. The first was his will. In the presence of his prospective son-in-law (he wished for no misunderstandings) its terms, possibly contestable (though Anton would never have contemplated such an action), were read aloud. Charlotte's father had bequeathed all his effects to his daughter, to be retained by her personally on marriage. Were she to die before her father, the effects were to pass to any issue of the marriage. In the event that she should fail to secure a marriage contract confirming her father's will, the effects were to pass to Anton's older brother. The second document was a marriage contract, drawn up on the basis of the will.

Anton signed, and the marriage took place before he could have second thoughts. Charlotte, master weaver in the place of her now incapacitated father, took the afternoon off for the wedding. One of the journeymen, Malachi Delaney, came away from his loom long enough to give her away; he returned to his loom without shaking hands with either of them. It was not a joyful afternoon. Charlotte herself, dressed with unbecoming girlishness in her deceased mother's wedding dress, seemed nervous, apprehensive, even regretful. Anton felt compassion for both his cousin and himself. The ceremony seemed more a sacrifice than a marriage. He and Charlotte were being offered up to secure the next Paradis generation. The smile which Charlotte gave him when they signed the register was a smile, not of happiness, but of acknowledged complicity in a fraud. If the ceremony was unsettling, the succeeding act was ludicrous. In the bedroom, so uncomfortably close to the room of his bed-ridden father-in-law, consummation of the marriage proved impossible. Anton was, admittedly, well-filled with wine, but wine had never incapacitated him before. It was simply that intercourse with Charlotte seemed an evil act.

The terms of the settlement entitled Anton to full employment in the Paradis workshop, the right to live in the Paradis house for life, and of course, a secure inheritance for his children. It barred Anton from founding a rival business. So Anton found himself employed as his wife's permanent journeyman, with no prospect of ever being able to set himself up in a business of his own. For several months, Anton's affection for Charlotte remained undiminished; but he could not change its nature and the marriage remained unconsummated. Perhaps the most fortunate thing was that Charlotte seemed more relieved than insulted by his inability to copulate with her. It seemed to Anton as though Charlotte contrived to accentuate their past relationship to ensure his continued failure. Anton formed the conclusion that his wife was a woman too delicate to care for sex. In any case, he reasoned, why should she miss what she had never had? She was kind to him . . . on the whole. She teased him, of course, and she despised him. She called him her doll, her lap-dog, her little manling, but she did not humiliate him in front of the other weavers; except for the fact that she would allow him no more authority than the best of her journeymen. Nor did she treat him with anything less than respect in the presence of his uncle. His uncle fretted over the lack of children, but had no inkling of the cause.

***

After eighteen months of marriage, Anton's wife, Charlotte, became pregnant. She was thirty-five years old when she was delivered, painfully, of an eight-and-a-half pound son. Anton's father-in-law was overwhelmed with relief and began to treat his nephew with markedly greater warmth. Anton received the congratulations of each of Charlotte's journeymen. He accepted them. What else could he do? He had no idea who the father was. When he ventured to ask his wife, she would only laugh and say that her husband must surely be the father. He had not cared to risk further ridicule. The baby manifested tantalising likenesses to each of the other journeymen in turn, depending on which journeyman Anton had in mind when gazing on its features. He had been (was being), he supposed, cuckolded. The act of cuckoldry left him undisturbed. He didn't blame Charlotte for taking a lover. He would not have blamed her for not naming him had it not been for his uncomfortable suspicion that all the other weavers, down to the most recently-bound apprentice, could have named the father had they wished to do so.

Even after the birth of Charlotte's second baby, a girl, Anton remained stubbornly amicable towards his wife, despite her increasing hostility to him. She despised him for his toleration, but he could not, in honesty, consider himself to be profoundly injured by her behaviour. The marriage had been an economic arrangement to ensure that the business and its profits stayed within the family. Had the children conceived been his, they would have been the inheritors. The failure to impregnate his wife with his own seed was his alone. He felt little affection for the children, but no animosity. He had predicted the failure of the marriage before it ever took place, but had allowed himself to be persuaded into it. He was in no position to cast unfavourable judgement on its progress.

Charlotte was in an anomalous position. She despised Anton for his tolerance, but as long as her father remained alive, it was imperative that her husband should remain docile. Her father could not be allowed to discover that his grandchildren were bastards. No wonder she had preferred the equable Anton to his brother. She had married him for this very quality. She had been terrified that the arrival of children would drive him out; that he would be too humiliated to stay. But she was disgusted when he made no attempt to leave. Only by the greatest of efforts could she maintain a façade of civility towards her husband convincing enough to fool her father, Lucien Paradis. Anton's cooperation was essential, but she could not resist tormenting him to see were there any limits to his endurance. She swung between cruelty and pacification, unable to comprehend her husband's indifference to both. She didn't realise how easy it was to endure barbs that did not touch the heart. She refused to name the father, until the question ceased to tantalise Anton. Then she told him in the hope of stirring up his jealousy. But there was no jealousy to stir. Without passion, how could there be jealousy?

By the time Anton heard that Malachi Delaney was his wife's lover, it no more than confirmed what he had guessed for some time. "During the day," she had told him provocatively, "he takes an hour to warm your bed for you." Anton didn't care. "At least Malachi is a clean man," he had remarked dismissively. "Have you no senses capable of arousal?" she had demanded, incensed by his indifference. "Are you not even susceptible to shame?"

He had felt no shame at all. All shame was due to Charlotte, as far as Anton was concerned. She had used him as a foil, knowingly, from the very beginning.

He had been curious, though. If, as she had said, their lovemaking took place in her own bed, then surely her father, confined in the next room, must have been privy to the activity of his daughter and her lover? His father-in-law, she had told him, smiling with sly contempt at her hands, had been under the impression for some time now that his nephew was a young man of gross appetite. Her father's admiration for his son-in-law's energy was unbounded. When asked how long she had harboured such feelings towards her father's (now her own) journeyman, Charlotte confessed she had loved Malachi Delaney for years; but Malachi was a Catholic and her papa could not permit her to marry a Catholic. Although his own had been a voluntary exile, her papa could not forgive the persecution of his co-religionists by Catholic France. The crowning (and wasn't the word deliciously inappropriate?) achievement of the French Revolution, in her father's eyes, had been the subjugation of the Catholic Church.

***

Anton was not quite as indifferent to his wife's hostility as he seemed. He understood the underlying threat. The death of his father-in-law, for instance, was a prospect which filled him with fear. Charlotte thought him despicable in his efforts to immure himself in her father's house. He had reduced himself in her eyes to a parasite. He didn't care. He knew of nowhere else to go. He had come to Dublin at her father's request. She was familiar to him, and his uncle, now that children had appeared, treated him with great kindness. He was afraid to leave the familiar. But he was well aware that only his father-in-law's continued existence secured Anton's position. He knew he would be ejected by Charlotte and Malachi once Lucien Paradis died. No placating or dissembling on his part now could save his future.

Meeting Danno McKenna was the saving of him.

The meeting took place by chance. There had been a flurry of public engagements during the winter of 1795, and McKenna, finding his own weavers overextended, had reluctantly placed several orders at the Paradis workshop. Charlotte, whose professional judgement remained sound throughout the turmoil of her private affairs, had presented Anton with the most complicated of the designs, knowing him to be the most capable of all the weavers on the premises. The lateness of the order and the complexity of the design conspired to ensure that Anton's was the last web to be completed. Anton had been reduced to running down Dame Street himself, the web of silk up on his shoulder, close to midnight, on the last possible day for delivery.

When he had reached McKenna's, the shop and adjoining warehouse were deserted, bleak behind their shutters, and Anton was forced to call to the house itself. Danno had been waiting for him. He had insisted that the silk should be rolled out on the hall floor for inspection, despite the weakness of the lamplight. It would be typical of Charlotte Paradis to deliver the worst of the silks at the last possible moment. Danno had been determined not to be gulled. "If it's below par, I won't accept it," he had warned Anton, who had replied with no more than a shrug before flicking the roll of silk so that it lapped over the feet of Danno McKenna, shivered and lay still. Flowered silks were Anton's speciality, and since McKenna himself had supplied the silk, there had been no shortage of material for Anton to work with. What lay on Danno's hall floor that night was almost decadent in the richness of its shading. The weaver had not simplified the demands of the design in any respect. As soon as Danno had seen the silk, he knew that he must procure the weaver. He had never seen such quality in a Dublin silk. He had knelt down on the floor beside the silk, and, looking up at the man above him, had asked was he the weaver. When Anton had nodded, Danno had launched straight in. Such a weaver, he had told Anton, was utterly wasted in Charlotte Paradis' workshop. Not merely wasted. An artist, such as this weaver so clearly was, could only be stultified by the cost-cutting devices said to be used by Charlotte and her journeymen. It was with malicious pleasure that Anton had announced, during a pause in the pleadings of the importunate merchant, that Charlotte Paradis was his wife.

The dumbfounded look on the merchant's upturned face!

Danno had not known what to say. Anton had allowed the silence to develop.

Eventually the silk merchant had risen to his feet and had said, choked with mortification, and looking towards his own staircase for a steady perspective to alleviate the dizziness with which he had been assailed, that he could scarcely ask the husband of Charlotte Paradis to desert his wife's workshop for the workshop of a rival. It would, Anton had agreed, be an improper request. Unless, of course, the offer made was to be so enticing as to convince his wife that her husband's desertion was to the overall advantage of the Paradis enterprise.

On hearing the terms (and they were generous) that Danno had been prepared to offer, Anton had shaken his head a little and had pursed his lips dismissively together. But he had promised, as he shook hands with the merchant on the dark doorstep, to consult his wife in the matter.

Three days later, Anton had started to work for Danno McKenna.

***

Once Anton realised the extent of Danno's need for his skills, he realised that his future was secure, and he ceased to treat his wife so tolerantly. He began to retaliate and for a time, life at home grew more comfortable for him. Of course, the more comfortable he became, the more reluctant he was, despite his new-found security, to contemplate his eventual eviction. Paradoxically, Charlotte's respect for him increased as she grew to fear his ability to jeopardise the stability of their arrangement.

A curious game of brinkmanship evolved between them. The crux of the game was this: Anton wished to negotiate an agreement with Charlotte, prior to the death of her father, that he, Anton, would, after Lucien's death, be entitled to a certain portion of the Paradis business in return for his agreement to vacate the house; Charlotte was determined to allow him nothing. Anton's main tool of persuasion was a threat to reveal the truth to Lucien. However, as they both well knew, should Lucien Paradis become aware of his daughter's deceit, such an agreement would be meaningless, since her father would undoubtedly disinherit both Charlotte and her bastard children, bypass Anton, and the business would pass to Anton's brother. Therefore destroying Charlotte would result in Anton's own defeat. But while it remained essentially in both of their interests that Lucien Paradis should continue to believe that Anton was the father of his grandchildren, there was a point beyond which, if it seemed certain that Charlotte would refuse to come to an agreement, it no longer mattered to Anton whether or not Lucien Paradis knew the truth. The question for Charlotte was whether or not Anton was likely, when that point was passed, to reveal the truth to her father. The brinkmanship involved each of them giving the other just sufficient hope to continue to play the game.

In fact, Anton was not a vindictive man. For Anton, the game had grown to be a diversion. A form of entertainment within the bleakness of their marriage. He felt he was entitled to take some revenge for his former humiliation, but it was not a game that he expected to win. He could not, in all probability, bring himself to betray his wife and her children to Lucien Paradis. Apart from the injury to his wife, how could he bestow such grief on a dying man? Unfortunately, he had managed to convince Charlotte that he was capable of such revenge.

A month before, Lucien Paradis had suffered a stroke which paralysed one of his arms and impaired his speech. He remained lucid, but the doctor had advised his daughter and son-in-law that a second stroke was likely, though not inevitable. A second stroke would almost certainly destroy his powers of speech completely.

Charlotte grew more reckless in her tactics.

In the past few days, Anton (who no longer did any weaving for Charlotte) had sensed an air of menace in the Paradis workshop, as he passed through it both morning and evening, an air of hostility that had never been present before. He guessed that Charlotte had brought the journeymen into her confidence. The move frightened him and for the first time, he felt that he was out of his depth.

***

"You can't deny," Danno remarked to his weaver, as he came to look over the work at the end of the day, "that you're an artist."
It was one of their spheres of disagreement. Anton claimed that his was a trade, not an art. Danno insisted that Anton had raised his work to the level of art.

"I do nothing more than reproduce a given design," Anton said now. "I don't create. I excel in my trade. I admit that. But I'm only like a competent musician following a musical score."

Shimmering beneath the warm, flicking light of two oil lamps, the curved piece of woven cloth visible on the roll seemed poised to yield up shining drops of liquified silk to the touch of a tongue. And what if the silk was to be curved with equally erotic appearance over a thigh, or a breast? Would the tongue be similarly tempted? Danno caressed his upper lip with a silky-smooth finger-nail, and his eyes closed slowly over the images conjured up inside his head. The human body was the perfect vehicle for silk. Even his fiancée, thus attired, could allure. Wheneas in silks . . . He opened up his eyes again.

"There are competent musicians," he spoke from beneath his finger, "and there are musicians who soar. Such musicians are artists. You are an artist."

Anton could scarcely bear to be so admired by Danno. It gave him a disabling sense of obligation towards his employer.

"There's a meeting called for tonight," he told Danno now, reluctantly, as he put on his jacket. The drawboy had already left, so there was no witness to his indiscretion.

He knew he shouldn't be telling the man even that much. It wasn't as though the information would make Danno McKenna change his mind. It only put him on the alert. He was so stubborn. Still, Anton wouldn't have felt right if he hadn't passed on the information. Danno wouldn't be able to turn on him later and complain that he hadn't known the men were serious.

"And what are you going to say at the meeting?"

"It depends on you. I could say you were having second thoughts."

"You could say nothing of the sort. Tell them the truth, Anton. Tell them that Danno McKenna doesn't need the weavers."

"God, but you're an arrogant man! And a fool too! It'll do you no good to underestimate us."

Sometimes Anton had a contempt for Danno and his kind; grown so high above their roots they had forgotten what it was that held them upright. "Without the merchants, silk can still be woven. Without the weavers, the merchants have nothing to sell," he said now.

Danno couldn't believe the naivety of his weaver. It hurt Danno that Anton should regard him as an antagonist, when he was only trying to prevent a catastrophe. Then it occurred to him that Anton might only be saying what he had been told to say. He repeated to the weaver what he had said to him so many times before: "I love my weavers, Anton, as God is my witness, but I'd be saving money if they were out of the place altogether. They're a luxury. It's the selling of the foreign silks that allows me to employ as many weavers as I do."

Anton was dismissive.

"That's only because if you don't sell foreign silks, then another merchant will do it for you. But if all the Dublin merchants ceased to buy foreign silks, then the demand for Dublin silks would rise dramatically."

"And how are you going to stop them all?" asked Danno impatiently. "And if you did stop the selling of foreign silk, what would you do about the cotton? Would you ban the importation of cotton too? And linen? Be realistic, Anton!"

But Anton knew that the idea concerning silk was perfectly realistic. Unpopular, perhaps, but realistic, if the weavers were sufficiently determined to carry out the plans that had already been made. Time enough to worry about cotton and linen then.

Danno sighed. He and his weaver were both admirers of the French Revolution, they were both disciples of Paine, they shared a devotion to silk; and yet Danno McKenna could not gain the trust of Anton Paradis.

"You won't force a solution through combination," he warned. "You'll force your own demise. If the weavers refuse to supply the merchants, the merchants won't be terrorised into shunning foreign silks. They'll buy it in greater quantities. The merchants don't need you. The public don't give a damn for Dublin silk. They despise it. They see foreign silks as a status symbol. Only a government ban on the importation of finished silks can hope to protect the Dublin weavers. It is to the Parliament that you should address your grievances. Backed, preferably, by respected merchants, like myself. Instead of threatening us, you should be wooing us."

Anton was silent.

"Don't raise a combination," Danno pleaded. "The damage to me will be minimal. The damage to yourselves will be enormous."

Anton's father had taught him never to trust the merchants. His uncle, his wife and all the weavers that Anton had ever worked with, agreed. The merchants were the adversaries of the weavers. They had to be. They wanted from the weavers as much as they could get for as little as possible. The weavers wanted the opposite. The weavers and the merchants might at times negotiate accommo-dations with each other, but only for as long as their interests happened to coincide. When the interests ceased to coincide, such agreements always broke down. And who invariably lost out? The weavers. Nevertheless, it was difficult to resist the lure of Danno's warmth. He was the closest thing that Anton had to a friend in all of Dublin. Such a relationship was impossible, of course, but it was difficult to believe that for all his light-heartedness, and his bizarre affection for silk, Danno was no better than the rest of them; Anton did his best to remain aloof.

"Don't underestimate the weavers," Anton said once more as he was leaving. He could do no more to protect Danno. He had his loyalties, and they were not primarily to Danno.

***

Danno shook his head, sighing, as from the warehouse window he saw Anton step out into the dimly-lit street below. The lamp-lighter had done his rounds, but there were precious few lamps for him to light between here and College Green. It was raining and the weaver cringed down into his jacket under the onslaught of raindrops; then he began to run up the street, in the direction of the Castle. Danno turned impatiently back into the room. Had the man no conception of his own vulnerability? He stared at the silver sprigs trapped like flies in the warp. Only a single lamp remained burning, and the silk had grown duller. It was time for Danno to leave. He had an important meeting to attend later that night himself. Before then, he was expected to spend at least an hour in the company of his fiancée and her parents and he had yet to change his clothes, powder his hair and pay his respects to his mother (a duty which could rarely be avoided, given the assiduity with which she attended to all his movements). Danno pitied the weavers. These combinations gave them a false sense of strength. They thought they had the power to influence when in reality they had none at all. Instead, they were threatening to draw upon themselves their own destruction.

***

Anton was, in fact, attending two meetings that evening.

The first, at the *Sign of the Red Cock* in Back Lane, had been called by Danno's weavers that morning. During the afternoon, word had been sent over from the weaving hall behind the shop to Anton and his drawboy. Anton had sent the messenger back to say that he could not attend at the hour suggested, as he had a prior engagement. As he had feared, the messenger returned a short while later. The time of the meeting had been altered to accommodate him. He was ordered, on pain of the payment of a fine, to attend the meeting.

His jacket hung sodden from his shoulders by the time he reached the public house. He walked into their usual room, wiping water from his face with his hands. Naggins of whisky had already been sent for and a dish of fried chops with bread was standing on the table.

"You said nothing, I hope?"

Anton shook his head. Drops of water flew from his hair. "Why would I?" he asked uneasily.

The weavers, by their occupation, were a pale-faced group of men; but the face of the young man who asked the question was particularly and vividly white. Matt Treacy was a sick man. He worked (on those days when he was capable of work) with his mouth carefully averted from the loom, for fear of staining the silk with the sudden scarlet flowers of blood which he periodically coughed up from his lungs. He was nineteen years old and was not expected to last the winter through. Unreconciled to the probability of death, his whole being was gripped by outraged bitterness at the injustice of life.

"You have reasons enough, I'd say."

Some others at the table nodded in agreement. It was suspected, though not proven, that Anton received a higher rate of pay than themselves.

"Ah, leave him be. Didn't he agree to the plan, the same as the rest of us?" It was Peadar Howlin, the conciliator, who spoke. He shifted up the bench, and patted the empty space beside him. "Hang your jacket over by the fire, Anton, and put your arse down on the seat here." Peadar used soft, foolish words to placate. It was his way.

"Easy enough to agree," remarked another man, leaning forward to peer around the bulk of Peadar the weaver as he spoke. "Easier still to make yourself scarce when the action takes place."

Not only was his relationship with Danno McKenna regarded with suspicion; Anton was also distrusted for his relationship to Charlotte Paradis. If their planned agitation should fail, failure wouldn't destroy him the way it would the other weavers. He had a wife to work for. Whatever about the rumours, she was not only his wife; she was also his cousin. He would not be left to starve. He had it too easy compared to the rest of them. They were wary of him. He was too comfortable to be a true and urgent radical.

"Well, he's here, isn't he?" said Anton's drawboy, and his voice was aggrieved.

"Coerced," said Liam, the man on Peadar's far side.

Liam was the most forceful of the weavers who worked for Danno. Indeed, he was one of the most forceful weavers working in the Liberties. He was articulate, literate, and had the ability to rouse others. Despite the fact that Danno had reduced the number of weavers to ten, he was unable, for lack of demand, to keep them fully-employed. They all (apart from Anton) worked sporadically. It was Liam who, during the last slack period, had threatened to choke the merchants and their pampered clients with their own silk. He had expressed the desire to wind skeins of it around their necks: to thrust it in swatches down their throats. He was the agent provocateur in this affair. He had been the spokesman for the delegation which had called upon Danno to cease stocking foreign silks. When Danno had protested that such a move was impossible; that were he not to accommodate the whims of the rich, those whims would be attended to by his rivals, Liam had decided to agitate more widely. He had contacted several groups of weavers in the city, and Danno's rivals had been approached by delegations like his own. A few weavers had refused his invitation to agitate. The weavers in the Paradis workshop said that they had more work than they could handle. They were not prepared to put their work at risk for an ill-founded adventure. (Their response had given Liam further grounds for questioning the sincerity of Anton Paradis.) All the delegations were rebuffed by the merchants they approached. None had been rebuffed with the courtesy afforded to Liam's own delegation by Danno McKenna. Liam called a meeting of the delegates while they were still smarting from their receptions. The merchants, he had told the weavers, could be forced to change their minds; and he had outlined to them a plan of action, the tactics of which went far beyond anything that Danno might have envisaged.

Anton had been brought along as part of Liam's own delegation. Liam distrusted Anton so much that he had been determined to tie him in to the combination from the very beginning. He had assumed that only duress could command Anton's loyalty.

"The coercion was unnecessary," Anton said stiffly now, referring to the order which had been passed on to him during the afternoon. The threat of a fine had annoyed him; he resented

Liam's assumption that his loyalty depended on coercion. Worse still, Danno also assumed that he was not his own man in the affair. Despite his weaver's protests to the contrary, Danno continued to profess a belief that Anton's presence on the delegation, and his subsequent stance on the question of foreign silk, had been dictated by others.

Liam ignored Anton's interruption. "Don't let us down, Paradis. A man with so many conflicting loyalties as yourself should take particular care to show where his first loyalties lie. If McKenna gives any indication of having been forewarned, you'll be blamed, however much you protest your innocence."

"McKenna knows nothing," Anton insisted. He was growing uncomfortable. It wasn't of any importance, but he wished he had made no mention of the meeting to Danno.

"It would be viewed as a great act of treachery on your part if McKenna was able to take any steps to protect himself in advance of the action. And if you were not to participate with the greatest of enthusiasm, you might end up an unfortunate casualty of that action."

He was no longer being coerced; he, the unflinching supporter of the French Revolution, was being threatened.

"Anton is sound." The old drawboy spoke up in his favour once again. "He didn't say nothing to Mr. McKenna. I was there, wasn't I?"

Anton nodded his appreciation at the drawboy.

"It would be foolish of Anton to be less than fully on our side."

Was it his fault that Danno McKenna was besotted by his talent and had made his admiration so obvious? Was it his fault that Danno had an understanding and love for silk quite exceptional in a merchant? Was it his fault that the merchant was an engaging young man from whom it was difficult to withhold trust? Anton believed, despite his constant efforts to keep a proper distance between himself and the silk merchant, that in Danno he had come upon that rare thing: a merchant for whom the quality of the silk and the preservation of silk weavers was of paramount importance. Was it his fault that he was unable to persuade the other weavers in the McKenna workshop of Danno's good faith, and that his very attempts at persuasion had increased their distrust of him?

"Have you talked to him again?"

Anton nodded. He had asked to be allowed to put the weavers' case once more. Permission had been granted, though he had been warned to have a care for his tongue. He had been forbidden to say anything of the tactics to be used. "He thinks we can bring no influence to bear worth speaking of. He thinks we should petition Parliament. He has no idea of our intentions." Then Anton remembered Danno's injunction. "He said I was to tell you that Danno McKenna doesn't need the weavers."

Liam was nodding his head approvingly, and was about to say something, when Anton added, "Perhaps if he were to be given some hint?"

"No hints, you stupid bugger!" shouted Matt, with one of the sudden upsurges of ill-temper to which his condition had made him prone. Then he began to cough. He continued coughing until blood began to ooze out between the fingers which he held so tightly over his mouth. He stumbled away from the table. With his back to them, he spat into the fire, and they all heard a sizzling, followed by a singing, as the expelled blood burned dry in the embers.

"Matt is right. The slightest hint and you can kiss goodbye to the entire operation," Liam said, leaning past Peadar once again.

"But . . ."

"Kiss it goodbye," Liam repeated, shaking his head, and staring with incomprehension at Anton.

Matt returned to the table. His face was sweating, and there were traces of glossy blood around his lips as though he had recently bitten into some living beast.

Liam, unintentionally, closed his eyes. "If word got out, the warehouses would be as unassailable as nunneries."

Only Matt had the stomach to laugh. He couldn't see how he looked. The others waited, horrified, for the laughter (slight as it was), to bring on a further bout of coughing. Matt remained calm. But he had grown suddenly feverish and the episode had exhausted him; he lay his perspiring head down on his crossed wrists and began to shiver. "So, no hints," he whispered into the circle of his arms.

Peadar stretched a hand across the table to stroke the young man's damp hair. "Best go home, Matt," he advised tenderly.

By the time the meeting was adjourned, the date and the hour of the operation had been provisionally settled, subject to the agreement of delegates from the other groups. Each man from Danno McKenna's workshop knew what was expected of him, none more particularly than Anton.

"You do me an injustice," he protested to Liam as they were leaving the public house. "I am a weaver and my loyalties lie with weavers."

"You'll never get a chance to prove otherwise," Liam assured him.

"You have no grounds for doubting me," Anton shouted after him angrily, as Liam set off running towards Thomas Street. Whether or not he heard, Liam, his jacket cradled over his head against the drizzle, made no reply.

"Damn him," Anton muttered. He looked back at the clock which could be seen inside the open door of *The Red Cock*. He was already late for his second meeting. He began to run himself, his boots slap-slapping through the puddled streets.

As he ran, he repeated to himself the catechism he had committed to memory only two weeks before. 'Are you concerned? I am. To what? To the National Convention. What do you design by that cause? To quell all nations, dethrone all kings and plant the Tree of Liberty in the Irish lands. Who commands you? The French Defenders will uphold the cause and Irish Defenders will pull down the British laws.' And what was it the password was? Oh yes. 'Elishimorta.' As a newly-committed Defender, he would have to recite that catechism once again tonight.

THREE

෴

... *I am sorry, Dear Sir, to Communicate that Working Tradesmen and Manufacturers, are set on by the Committee, to Institute Republican Clubs, under the name of United Irishmen – where an oath of secrecy is first tendered.*

... *The caution now used by the RCC almost precludes any information. I should humbly advise that persons might be obtained to join such clubs and lodges (in City and Liberty) as members – to give an account of their proceedings.*

Thursday night (undated).

Out of letters from Francis Higgins, Stephen's Green, to Secretary Clarke, the Castle.

Pansy, Danno's fiancée, was not pleased to hear that the tobine, intended as a gift to her, had been purloined by a customer. In her view, her fiancé had allowed himself to be blackmailed into parting with the silk by an opportunistic act of cunning (a verdict with which Danno could only, with unexpressed admiration, agree). On his own admission, he had not even attempted to save the silk for Pansy. Pansy naturally felt herself belittled. She was not impressed by Danno's claim to have sacrificed the silk, knowing one could only ask such sacrifices from those to whom one was closest. She had been insulted by her fiancé. Tears were brought into play; questions concerning the depth and the sincerity of his love were raised. Danno spent the hour inventing expressions of remorse suitable for the occasion. These fictions were grudgingly received, and the atmosphere throughout his visit was dense with offended feelings. Another tobine, more sumptuous than the last was promised. This promise, made towards the end of the hour, led to a partial easing of tensions, though doubts were expressed as to the value of such a promise in the light of what had just occurred. Pansy declared that she would not consider the newly-pledged tobine safe until it had been delivered into her own hands (whenever that might be, given the length of time a silk took to weave, and the minor importance that Danno seemed to attach to his fiancée's expectations).

Pansy's reluctance to forgive him annoyed Danno. He could concede that if she had known the pleasure with which Danno had given away the silk, and the thoughts which he harboured towards the newly-intended recipient, then her reluctance would have been understandable; given her lack of knowledge, the reluctance was churlish. His fiancée had shown a pettiness of spirit with which he had no patience.

***

By the middle of January, 1797, rumoured sightings of French ships off the coast no longer had the power to terrorise or excite. It was clear by then that General Hoche's ill-fated expedition had returned ignominiously to Brest, without a single French soldier having been put to shore in the wilds of West Cork, and that it was not about to reappear.

Why the fleet should have set forth for Ireland at such a treacherous time of year was anyone's guess. The failure of the expedition was undoubtedly disappointing; but the rousing thing was that it had appeared at all, and in such force (between fifteen and twenty-two ships had been reported anchored off Bantry Bay and it was rumoured that as many again had gone astray). The people of Ireland had, for the first time, been given solid proof that theirs was a cause deemed worthy of assistance by the mightiest of their enemy's enemies. The numbers of sworn United Irishmen and Defenders soared.

It was during that euphoric week at the end of December, when the French were definitely known to be anchored in Bantry Bay, that Anton Paradis first swore, in his distinctively accented English (an accent believed by some of his Dublin associates to be French, but which was, in fact, the irrepressible intonation of County

Cork), to plant the Tree of Liberty in Irish soil, a tree unmistakably identified in his mind as a mulberry tree. As a Frenchman he could hardly do less. Besides, if someone did you the courtesy of inviting you to become a Defender, it didn't do to risk offence by refusing the invitation, however reluctant you might feel in your heart. He was approached on the grounds that when the French arrived in Dublin, who would both the French and the Irish need more than Anton? Someone who could interpret not only what both sides were saying, but even what both sides were failing to say, and why. His potential use to the Defenders increased as rapidly as the imaginations of those recruiting him flourished. For the first time since coming to Dublin, Anton found himself in a position of popularity.

***

Anton would have turned round and left *Nelligan's Ale House* if it hadn't been for the fact that so many people had already seen him. He couldn't believe his bad fortune. Sitting between the man who had sworn him in a couple of weeks before, and the weaver who had recruited him to the organisation in the first place, was Malachi Delaney. There was Anton, attached, for the first time, to a group of people who not only tolerated him, but who had actually courted him for some of the very differences which caused him to be regarded with suspicion; and that bastard, Delaney, had to turn up.

Malachi was the first to speak. "Well, well. Would you look at what the cat threw up. Paradis himself. How are the children, Paradis? Growing more like their father every day, I have to say. Paradis, are you not pleased to see me? We know one another," he added inconsequentially to the others.

Each morning, as Anton passed through the Paradis workshop on his way to work, Malachi Delaney asked him how the children were. He never failed to add that they were growing more like their father every day. Up to four days ago or so, the response provoked around the workshop had been equally unfailing in its hilarity. Since the change of mood amongst the Paradis weavers, the tenor of both the remark and the response had undergone a radical transformation. There was menace in the remark, and menace in the responding silence. The menace of the remark, repeated here so casually, amongst people for whom (apart from the weaver who was acquainted with them both) it had no significance, was enhanced.

"Paradis' wife is my mistress . . ." said Malachi, "Or should I say, master?" he added, when satisfied that the remark had shocked. He began to laugh. "I love to do that. Lord how I love to do that. If you could only see your own faces! I gave the bride away, and then I made her my mistress. That's good for a laugh too, isn't it, Paradis?"

Anton stared at his tormentor, his face tight and unsmiling.

"Paradis is French, you know," Malachi explained to the others. "He doesn't always get the joke."

"Why don't you shut your damned mouth?" Anton asked, and then he sat down. "You drink too much, Delaney," he added.

"You two know one another, most obviously." The man who had conducted Anton's initial swearing-in ceremony began to speak, and then he sighed. "Apparently you have your differences; this is unfortunate. You would never have been brought together had it been known. Listen to me carefully, for I shall say this only once: whatever your private disagreements, here, we are on the same side, working for the same cause. We live for one another. We are prepared to die for one another. And now, let us join hands"

Each of the nine men collected around the table put forward their right hand. The hand of the newest member, which turned out to be Malachi himself, was placed at the bottom. Anton's hand was next, and he placed its palm, without resistance, on top of the hand of his wife's lover. A flesh tree of hands grew upwards from the table-top.

"Are you concerned?" their leader asked.

"I am," each man replied simultaneously.

"To what?"

"To the National Convention."

"What do you design by that cause?" Anton saw that the leader had closed his eyes.

"To quell all nations, dethrone all kings and plant the Tree of Liberty in the Irish Lands."

Malachi Delaney was looking at him as they both gave their responses. Anton closed his own eyes for protection.

"Who commands you?"

"The French Defenders will uphold the cause and Irish Defenders will pull down the British laws . . . Elishimorta."

The men were still intoning the final response when Danno McKenna walked into the room with a companion.

***

A man from Belfast, an opinionated man with long-established links with both Defenders and United Irishmen, going by the name of Johnny Little, had come to Dublin some months earlier to warn that the Defenders in the south were far more politicised and volatile than the Dublin branch of the United Irishmen allowed for, and that if the southern United Irishmen failed to harness them, it would soon be found impossible to do so. The Dublin branch of the United Society was, so Johnny Little from Belfast had said disapprovingly, too exclusive, too inward-looking. It had failed to give leadership to a discontented and potentially fiery mass of people. He had also (in a voice of most patronising solemnity) warned the Dublin society against any hint of condescension in its approach to the Defenders. The warning had been heeded and contacts were being made. It was a slow process. Defenders, clandestine and amorphous, were difficult to identify; and when identified, were reluctant to enter negotiations for fear of treachery.

The cell of Defenders that Danno had been asked to address that night was, according to the man from Belfast who accompanied him, typical of the cells which abounded in Dublin. The Defenders might not have articulated their aims as carefully as the United Irishmen (and there was still, as Johnny Little informed Danno McKenna, disagreement concerning the aims of the latter), but they certainly knew what they hated. The Defenders were good at hating. By contrast, the United Society, in its Dublin form, was, in the view of Johnny Little, too genteel. It needed an infusion of hatred.

"I'm not afraid to hate," Danno told Johnny Little defensively. "When something demands hatred, I will hate."

"The men you are meeting tonight would like to hear that from a United Irishman. Whether they will believe you . . ." the man from Belfast shrugged dismissively.

"Do you?" asked Danno.

"I imagine you'll have opportunities to prove yourself right or wrong in the next few months." From the tone of the Belfast man's voice, Danno gathered that a Dublin silk merchant was not expected to pass the test. "I think we're all about to be confronted with things worthy of hatred."

Johnny Little had an irritating prophet-like quality to him. It stemmed, Danno supposed, from an overweening belief in the truth of his own pronouncements. He was a worthy man and his cause was undoubtedly good, but Danno's initial cordiality had turned to dislike in less time than it took the two of them to walk from McKenna's shop to the tippling house in Dirty Lane in which the meeting was to take place.

Danno McKenna might not have been his companion's superior in many things, but he had this advantage over him: he knew that any cell containing the two men that Danno recognised as they entered the back snug of *Nelligan's Ale House* could not be described as a typical Dublin cell.

It had not occurred to Danno that Anton might be a Defender. Still less had it occurred to him that Anton would be a member of the very group of Defenders which he had been asked to meet with a view to discussing the closer cooperation of the two organisations. On seeing Anton he was unable to conceal his surprise. But if he was surprised to see Anton, then he was astonished to see Malachi Delaney in the same room. Anton might have told Danno little about his private life, but it would be a silk merchant of unnatural aloofness who was unaware of the rumours concerning Charlotte Paradis and her chief journeyman, Malachi Delaney. There was a spell-binding incongruity attached to the sight of the two men, seated at the table, with their hands entwined, apparently joined in fervent prayer.

For Anton, the evening was acquiring nightmare dimensions. He had closed his eyes to avoid the gaze of Malachi Delaney. He opened them to the sight of Danno. He stared at the silk merchant and the silk merchant's companion in bemused misery. Danno's appearance in that particular public house could not have been a matter of pure chance. It was not a public house in which people like Danno McKenna came to drink. Anton believed himself to have inadvertently drawn the silk merchant to the tavern, thus destroying the confidentiality of his own particular cell, by exposing its members to outsiders. He feared that Danno had trailed him from the first public house to the second public house, in the hope of easing out of his weaver some information concerning the proposed combination of his own discontented men. What would Anton's companions think of him now? Anton could imagine how Malachi Delaney would make use of the incident to heat their suspicions. McKenna was a man of honour (Anton knew that, but how could he persuade his new colleagues?); but even if McKenna could be trusted to forget the people he had seen, what of the man with him? Anton hadn't seen him before. Dublin crawled with Castle spies and informers who attached themselves like parasites to unwitting hosts like Danno. He hadn't been a Defender long enough to recognise the man from Belfast.

"Anton," Danno said finally, by way of greeting. There was, by then, no way of concealing the fact that they were acquainted with one another. He thought it better to acknowledge the weaver openly.

"Sir."

Anton, with hanging head and concealed eyes, acknowledged the silk merchant with manifest reluctance. Considering he was here by invitation, Danno thought his weaver's embarrassment excessive.

Danno did not greet Malachi Delaney, and Delaney, in turn, gave no sign of knowing the silk merchant.

The cell leader was on his feet. After discovering that the two new recruits to his cell were bound in mutual dislike, he was the more easily disturbed by this further breach of security. The cell was threatened by every uncalled for recognition. Anonymity was the key to security.

"Mr. Little," he exclaimed. "This should not have occurred. Someone has slipped up."

Danno could not decide from the inscrutable demeanour of Johnny Little whether or not he had known of the relationship between Danno and his weaver, Anton. Was this bringing together an error, or deliberate policy on the part of the Belfast man? Little was sufficiently cunning to be operating a concealed agenda within the one which he chose to display.

"If they hadn't met before, they were going to meet now," Little said casually. "What's the difference?"

The leader was infuriated by the indifference of Little's reply. "The rest of us will be no more than faces to your friend." Despite his anger, the leader kept his voice low. The meeting was taking place in a private room, but who knew what lurked beyond the door. "Faces without facts. But this man," and the leader pointed to Anton without naming him again, "has a face, a name and a history. His safety has been endangered by this encounter."

The men around the leader were nodding their agreement. The mood was sullen. Danno wondered would the meeting be terminated without further discussion. He had not expected such a crude performance from Little. He decided to intervene before the man did more damage.

"I consider your fellow Defender to be my friend," Danno told the leader. He realised that he should not have greeted Anton by name and he regretted the mistake, "and I can imagine no circumstances in which I would be induced to betray him. Nevertheless, I appreciate your fears." He spoke directly to the leader. The others seemed so completely under his sway that it seemed necessary only to influence the leader. "But there would only be a danger if I was your enemy. This, I can assure you, is not the case. We are all working for the same cause. The liberty of the Irish people. I have come here this evening as a suitor."

One of the men at the table gave a laugh, quickly stifled by the surrounding silence. Danno, who hadn't expected any independent response, was encouraged. He continued. "I freely admit it. I have come to court the Defenders on behalf of the United Irishmen. Our intentions are honourable. We are looking for marriage."

"Well," said the leader slowly. He had taken note of the stray laughter and, being a leader of skill, wished to capture it, not kill it. "Since you're here, I suppose there's no harm in hearing your proposals."

The trouble was, he had very little by way of obvious inducement. Danno realised that what he considered these Defenders to need they might not know they wanted. In the view of Danno and those who had sent him, the Defenders were in urgent need of strong, central leadership. Such leadership could only be supplied by the United Irishmen. Danno believed fervently that it was in the interests of both groups to amalgamate. There were Defenders in nearly every county; they had infiltrated the army, the militia and even the yeomanry; they enjoyed a popularity unknown to the United Irishmen. But it was the very wideness of their support and the vagueness of their aims that posed the greatest danger. Without strong leadership, there was a danger of sporadic local risings sparked off by local injustices. Neither side could rise successfully without the support of the other, but it was feared that the Defenders were too volatile, too diffuse, too diverse in their ambitions, to be contained. It was best to be honest. "We are afraid," he said bluntly, "that the Defenders will rise too partially, too soon and spoil our chances of success."

Danno and Johnny Little were still standing up. Danno sensed Little's fury. Little thought that Danno had wrecked his opportunity. The leader stared at Danno without speaking, judging him. Finally he gestured them to a space at the table.

"Sit down," he said and his face had lost maybe one layer of suspicion. "If you're that honest, we may be able to talk."

Johnny Little, looking openly taken aback at the leader's response, said that he had to leave. He had other business to conduct that night. He wished them luck in their meeting and left the room.

Danno sat down. He was glad Little was gone. He had felt inhibited by his disapproving presence. No introductions were made; none were sought. There was further silence. No one was going to assist Danno.

"We think that the United Irishmen and the Defenders should combine," he said. He continued to address the leader, since it seemed that no one else within the group was authorised to speak. "You want to know what we can offer. Well, I can tell you that we are well-organised and we have a recognised leadership. We are in the confidence of some of the most influential families both here and in England. We have access to persons of the highest importance in France. Above all, we are on the same side. But I don't believe it's a question of what either side can offer. It's a question of securing the liberty of the Irish people by all the means at our disposal. We need one another equally."

"I have a point to put to you," said the leader, picking at his ear with a fingernail. He did not seem impressed by Danno's speech. "You say you are well-organised, and that you have the ears of the most powerful in France." He paused long enough to look at his nail and to flick a piece of burnished yellow wax onto the floor. Then he continued. "If the United Irishmen are so well-organised and have such advantageous connections, how is it that the arrival of the French fleet took them so much by surprise that they were unable to take any advantage of it? Not so much as a green banner pegged up on the shore down in Bantry. Nothing to show the French that they were expected. Nothing to encourage them to disembark from their ships. You say that your organisation is afraid of a premature rising. Well, my organisation doesn't believe that the United Irishmen are capable of rising. You say we need one another equally. I don't believe so myself. You need us because you've lost face over this French disaster; you should have been ready and instead, the Government knew of the French arrival before you did. You have seen the people flocking to join the Defenders in the aftermath of the French appearance and you know that we will rise without you. You are afraid of losing your share of the new Ireland. And even if such a rising should fail, you know that in the eyes of the people it is better to rise unsuccessfully than never to rise at all."

Danno had not expected such eloquence. It would be dishonest of him to pretend otherwise. He had expected something far more incoherent, more unfinished. He could see that the man's interpretation of events was persuasive and that it was probably the interpretation most widely believed. Danno knew, nevertheless, that the leader was wrong and that he, Danno, was right. A premature rising by the Defenders would ruin their chances of a successful rebellion. Reprisals by the British would be so savage that the spirit of rebellion would be quenched for good. But Little was right; condescension was inappropriate and must be guarded against.

"The French came sooner than promised," he said. "That was unfortunate. The important thing to realise is that they came at our direct request."

Danno was unaware that it been his friend Tone who had succeeded, by skilled and patient diplomacy, in securing the offices of one of the most renowned of the young French generals (rivalled only by Bonaparte), a fleet of 43 ships, and approximately 16,000 French troops; nor did he know that Tone, now adjutant-general in the French army, had been on board the *Indomptable*, an 80 gun ship-of-the-line, one of the ships which had actually succeeded in reaching Bantry Bay. Danno did not know that on Christmas day, while he was exuberantly celebrating the arrival of the French in the company of his less-overjoyed fiancée and her family, Tone, trapped on board the *Indomptable* by the appalling weather, was writing, 'I see nothing before me, unless a miracle be wrought in our favour, but the ruin of the expedition, the slavery of my country and my own destruction . . . I have a merry Christmas of it today'.

"They would not have come had it not been for the tireless efforts of our agents. And they will come again. They have assured us that they will return."

"When?" The tone of the leader's voice was both challenging and cynical.

"The spring perhaps, or failing spring, the summer." Danno didn't know, and his voice reflected his uncertainty. He saw the men around him glance at one another, and he forced assurance back into his voice. "It is imperative that we should not rise in advance of their arrival."

"The mood of the people is for rebellion now. That mood may change and the opportunity will be lost. Arms are being amassed. There are pikes hidden throughout the Liberties, and I don't doubt but that the same is happening throughout the countryside."

This information tallied with information received by others in the Society. If the Defenders were to be believed, their supplies of pikes and men were virtually inexhaustible.

"What about firearms?" Danno asked. He was told that they were low in firearms, but when Danno tried to ascertain what low meant, the leader grew coy. Nevertheless, Danno was left with the impression that, compared to the arms available to the United Irishmen, caches of arms held by Defenders were extensive.

"The people are ready now," the leader repeated. "Summer may be too late."

"A second coming by the French will be sufficient to rouse us all again."

"Perhaps rebellion on the part of the people would convince the French that it was worth their while to return. The lack of response to their first coming may have given them cause to doubt our sincerity."

"They know the reason," Danno said urgently. "We had no warning of their arrival. Besides, however prepared we had been, the French had no intention of landing. Half the fleet never reached Ireland. Many, when they reached the coast, were blown back out to sea by storms. But I can assure you of one thing: had the United Irishmen been primed to rebel, and had the French failed at the last minute, as they did, to land, we would have been able to contain our men. Can you make the same claim? Have you that much control over your followers?"

The leader shrugged and made no reply. Danno replied for him. "I'll warrant that there are cells around the country that are answerable to no-one only their own leader, and it's those leaders who are setting the agenda. Not you, or anyone like you."

"So, are you saying that you have a leadership with no followers, and that we have the followers but no leadership?"

"Precisely," Danno said without hesitation. There was no reason for hesitation. The leader's question insulted them both as much as did Danno's reply.

Nothing was being written down. No minutes were being taken. No traces were to be left of this meeting.

"If I was to admit to there being any truth in that statement, and I'm not saying that I do so admit, how can you have any confidence that the United Irishmen would be any more successful in reining in the allegedly uncontrollable masses?"

This was where things could become treacherous.

"If the two societies were to amalgamate, we would expect the Defenders to swear the oath of the United Irishmen."

A murmur ran round the table like fire along an oiled string.

"Equally, we would swear ourselves in as Defenders," Danno added quickly.

The murmur died away. The leader looked surprised.

"It has been done," Danno told them. "Defenders throughout the country have taken our oath. In certain parts of the country, where the Orangemen are rife, it is felt that membership of the United Irishmen gives added protection. There is," Danno said, "a difficulty concerning that offer. A condition, if you like . . ."

The second murmur flared more quickly.

"Some of our members are concerned over the outbreaks of sectarianism with which your organisation is associated. You know our policy. While they can see, in certain cases, a justification for what is labelled sectarianism, our members could not associate themselves to an organisation which had a sectarian element in its oath. Equally, our members question whether your members would be sincere in their adherence to our aspirations to a society allowing equal freedom to all its members regardless of their religion."

"Oh!" The leader looked relieved.

"What about the accusation that the Defenders are sectarian?"

The leader looked wounded.

"As you must be aware, unless your acquaintance is of the most trivial, we have here in our own cell, a man who is not only a Frenchman; he is also a Protestant."

But how long, Danno wondered, had Anton been a Defender? Had he perhaps been recruited for the occasion? Had they intended to get rid of him again once this meeting had taken place? That could hardly be done now, given the relationship which had been exposed between Danno and the weaver. He was being unduly cynical, he knew; but even if Anton's recruitment had been genuine, Danno did not believe, as Little had insisted, that this was a typical cell.

There were those of the United Irishmen who said that if it was sectarianism that best roused the population, then sectarianism was a legitimate weapon to use. Besides, what was seen to be sectarianism only appeared so because the religious divisions so exactly matched the divisions of society. Of course, there were Catholics of property and Protestants with none, but by and large, the Protestants had, and the Catholics had not. Sectarianism would wither away once justice prevailed. And even if it refused to die, there was time enough to worry about bigotry once the country was out of the hands of the British. Danno did not agree.

For now, he hid his scepticism as best he could.

"Indeed," he said, "I was immediately aware of the significance of my friend's presence in terms of what it said about the attitude of this particular cell."

"I don't deny that sectarianism exists," the leader admitted. "But equally, there are cells which have no truck with it. In Dublin city, a cell such as ours may not be untypical. In the country, well, who can say. Conditions are different in the country as you know."

"Are you saying that the men in your cell would have no difficulty with our policy?"

The leader nodded unhesitatingly and Danno was inclined to believe him.

"In that case," said Malachi suddenly breaking into the conversation, "He should have no difficulty in accepting the policy of this cell."

It was clear that the other members of the cell were shocked by the intrusion. Malachi ignored them. "If you really want to ensure his loyalty, swear him in."

The others stared at him with open animosity. But the leader contemplated Malachi with interest: so did Danno. Malachi had pre-empted Danno's own offer with his suggestion. Why?

"Swear him in as a Defender?"

"Yes. If he wants to create links, he'll be willing."

"His willingness to swear a Defender's oath would prove nothing. The more engaged in deceit he was, the more willing he would be to swear."

"I am, nevertheless, willing," Danno interrupted, "If your oath is one I can, in conscience, swear to."

"Anton will vouch for him." Malachi smiled maliciously at Anton.

"Well, Anton?" The leader looked at the weaver enquiringly.

"I've never known him dishonest," Anton admitted, raising his head for the first time since Danno's arrival. After he had spoken, he dropped it again.

***

Anton was no less cynical than his employer. If it were not for his nationality (no longer such an obvious asset since the retreat of the French fleet) Anton might also have been afraid that he had been recruited especially for the occasion. To impress Danno McKenna. As it was, he knew that he had not been recruited for his mere patriotism. If he was the Frenchman, what, Anton wondered, was Malachi's role? Was Malachi an ardent patriot? Anton didn't know. He had never been in a position to speak of patriotism to Malachi Delaney. Malachi certainly wasn't here with Charlotte's blessing.

Or was he?

Charlotte was terrified of revolution. The Paradis family owned several houses in the city of Dublin and an estate in County Wicklow. Charlotte had been outraged by the arrival of the French fleet and by the government's lack of preparation. Only the weather had prevented the complete annihilation of the gentry (Charlotte saw herself as such by virtue of her property) at the hands of the French and the swarming Irish peasantry. The government had abandoned them. Not only did it take an unconscionable amount of time for news of the appearance of the French to reach Cork city, but in the ten days that the French lingered on in Bantry Bay, not a single soldier reached Bantry. The town was left to the defence of four hundred apprehensive militia, and who knew but that the militia might have greeted the French like blood brothers, were the French actually to have landed. What would Charlotte think were she to discover that she was harbouring a Defender in her own bed? But even as Anton considered and discarded the possibility of telling her (within this cell of Defenders, there could be no deeper betrayal than the betrayal of a brother Defender), it occurred to him that she probably already knew. Charlotte was devious enough to seek the protection of both sides. She might not want the men of no property to take control, but if they should succeed, what better than to have one by her side?

The oath had been examined by Danno and had been found fitting. Anton found the ceremony which followed this examination distressing.

It was not right that he and the silk merchant should be joining hands in an oath of brotherhood. Merchants and weavers could not, in the most normal of circumstances, swear brotherhood. And how could he swear brotherhood to the man who, no more than an hour before, he had sworn to destroy? And yet the hands built up, one upon another: McKenna's hand on the table, the hand of Malachi above it, then his own. The flesh tree was erected and the oath was chanted. Danno and his weaver swore to plant the Tree of Liberty in Irish soil.

**

Before they left the room, Malachi came over to Anton and held out his hand. "Since our aims are the same, we must attempt civility. We are brothers, whether we like it or not."

Anton took the hand cautiously. This was the third time this evening that he had touched Malachi's hand. Were Malachi to cease tormenting him, Anton would have no quarrel with Charlotte's lover. He had never denied Charlotte's right to some sexual satisfaction. But Malachi's attitude had forced the growth of enmity. Anton did not trust this proffered hand. The gesture was for the benefit of others. It did not offer true reconciliation.

One humiliation Anton did not have to undergo. While Danno and the leader were still engaged in conversation (no reciprocal oaths had as yet been taken by the Defenders), Anton slipped away from the meeting. He was damned if he would walk home, exposed to public view, in the company of the silk merchant.

FOUR

Marvin Sweetman had always considered himself to be a tolerant and accommodating husband, but when he came upon his second wife reading *A Vindication of the Rights of Woman*, he felt compelled to protest. He was shocked by the discovery and felt himself to have been betrayed. He was a United Irishman; he had been an admirer of the French Revolution, before its degeneration to terror and counter-terror had damaged it irreparably in his eyes. He still admired its aims. He believed in fraternity, equality and liberty. For men. He had always cherished his daughter and his wives. He had considered them all to be above the conceits of men. His second wife, Letitia, he cherished particularly. She was decorative, sensitive and thoughtful; and she possessed a child-like gaiety, a limpid innocence which her husband found intensely moving. He was not ashamed to admit that he found an intellectual, forceful woman an unsexual thing. The governess, for instance, whom his second wife, Letitia, had hired to teach the daughter of his first wife, Dorothy, was unattractively clever. She was combative. She lacked any sense of deference in the presence of men. She was devoid of sensuality. She was, in almost every respect, the opposite of his own dear Letitia. So much was she his wife's opposite, that he sometimes suspected his darling wife of having hired the young woman in order to accentuate her own myriad charms.

Now he found his wife, sitting in his own library, reading a book lent to her by that very same governess. A book written by another spoiled governess. Worse still, his thirteen year-old daughter was lolling (there was no other word for it) on the sofa, dishevelled, her face flushed with heat, beside her step-mother; and Marvin thought, though he could not be sure, that she had been reading from the book over her step-mother's shoulder as he came into the room. Very worst of all, his wife appeared not to understand his indignation.

He remembered his wife's extreme youth (she was still only eighteen years of age after a year of marriage), youth's suscepti- bility to every new opinion, and he composed himself. It was at times like this that he felt himself to have two children in his charge. The feeling was not unpleasant. Looking at his daughter more closely, he saw that her face, as well as being flushed, was· unbecomingly moist.

"Your forehead, Caroline," he said to his daughter, and his distaste was clear, "is damp. Surely the room is not so warm as to cause such an unnatural outbreak of perspiration?"

Caroline shook her head wordlessly. She was afraid of her father.

Caroline's mother had died when she was seven. Until her father's marriage to Letitia a year ago, all his attention had been focused upon the upbringing of his young daughter. Caroline had suffered an excess of paternal attention. Far from resenting her step-mother as an intrusion, she worshipped her. Who but Mama could have succeeded in drawing her father's attention away from his daughter? She called her step-mother Mama. Her father would allow nothing less formal as a mode of address. Even so, Mama was a compromise. Mother had been his preferred title, but Letitia had ridiculed the idea. She didn't care that the title was to denote her status rather than her age. Only five years stood between herself and her step-daughter. It would be humiliating to have a girl of thirteen addressing her as mother, and she refused to sanction it. At a pinch, since she had to be called something, she might tolerate Mama. The compromise was agreed. Then, using frivolity as a weapon, Letitia and her step-daughter attacked the word. By intonations, accentuations, inflections, modulations, hesitations, the word was undermined, until it seemed, at best, a term of endearment; at worst, it seemed a deliberate affectation. Marvin Sweetman sensed that something had happened to the word, but could not pin-point any particular mark of its deterio- ration. He only knew that there were occasions on which he thought that if his daughter were to address his wife as 'Mama' even once more in his presence, he might lose control of himself, such extraordinary and irrational rage was the word capable of provoking within his heart.

There were things about her Mama that were not satisfactory. On those days when Letitia took notice of her, she felt cosseted; but there was the fact that her Mama was capable of forgetting her existence for days at a time. Caroline knew well that her attachment to her step-mother was not reciprocated with anything like the same depth. There was no constancy to her step-mother's attention. Caroline was also afraid that her father's love for her step-mother was not matched by equal affection on Mama's part.

And now, this afternoon, it seemed that Mama was also capable of rousing her father's temper. Caroline had thought only she could rouse her father's temper so high. Caroline snuggled closely, nervously against her step-mother. She could feel the fast beats of her step-mother's heart. She had sometimes felt her father's heart beat that fast too. It could be beating that way now. She might imagine it, but she was glad she couldn't feel it. She had thought that Mama must be frightened, but when her step-mother spoke, she was laughing.

"Of course her face is hot! My own face is hot as well. Feel it."

She caught her husband's hand and pressed it to her cheek.

"You see? We've been dancing to the music of our own voices. Having been confined to the house so long by rain, we had grown sluggish, hadn't we, Caroline?"

Caroline's head nodded against her step-mother's shoulder. "Yes, Mama," she whispered, without looking up. Her father's arm was stretched above her head, its hand clamped to Mama's warm face. How could Mama act so insouciantly? The tip of Caroline's tongue picked cautiously over her upper lip, gathering up tiny salted drops of sweat.

Letitia pushed her step-daughter to her feet.

"Thank you, darling, for your company. Now go and splash some water on your face before your father turns against us ladies altogether. Then I think Miss Temple is expecting you for a lesson."

"Yes, Mama."

Mama's offer of escape was too tempting. In an effort to appease her father, Caroline ventured a smile, a sad thing which trembled briefly on her lips before fading to nothing. Then she ran from the room. She hoped that he would not frighten Mama. She could not bear Mama to turn fearful. It hadn't happened yet. But maybe Father hadn't used the power.

"Your daughter is charming, Marvin. But too timid. You've done almost too fine a job in bringing her up. Why, when I think how boisterous my sisters and I were as children, and how my father used . . ."

"She is as a young girl should be," her husband said. His hand was still on her cheek, trapped in hers. "She's quiet and she's responsive to the wishes of those around her. But you should not underestimate Caroline. She is as capable of manipulating her father as you are. Look at the way you both have managed to disarm me in the last few minutes." He fondled the skin of his wife's face. "Observe my strong fingers helplessly trapped by your butterfly hand."

Letitia removed the hand. She still held the book in her other hand.

"Have you read this book yourself?" she asked her husband. His answer was as she had expected it to be.

"Certainly not!"

"But, in that . . ."

"One does not listen to the temptations of the devil to prove to oneself that they should be shunned. I rely on the judgement of those I admire to assure me that Miss Wollstonecraft's is a book to avoid. You should have done the same."

"I did rely on the judgement of one whom I admire. She told me that I should read the book."

"The serpent tempted me and I did eat! My darling Letitia, you are condemning yourself out of your own mouth. Did you think of consulting me before you began to read?"

"I did. Miss Temple advised against it. She predicted that your reaction would be as it, in fact, is."

"Our governess and Miss Wollstonecraft are of a kind. Embittered, envious women. Why, I believe that Miss Wollstonecraft was at one time herself a governess. Straight from the ranks of the disappointed. Only a woman unbalanced by envy could have written such a book. We must feel pity for the Miss Temples and the Miss Wollstonecrafts of this world; but we must not allow ourselves to be misled by their jealous tirades against their more fortunate sisters."

To sweeten the harshness of what he was saying, Marvin Sweetman began to stroke the top of his wife's head. Her hair, recently washed, slid silkily in the palm of his hand. But she rose abruptly to her feet as though his hand did not exist and began to speak with rash and uncharacteristic vigour. "Miss Wollstonecraft's reasoning seems admirably balanced to me, Marvin. She is saying that it is impossible to know whether or not women are the equal of men in intelligence until they are provided with an education the equal of that given to men. And she says, furthermore, that if women are given an inferior education, how can they be expected to be good wives and mothers?"

"Oh good heavens, Letitia! Does one need to be conversant with Greek and Latin in order to run a household and teach children the moral precepts of life? Indeed, I imagine that an advanced education for a woman would be a hindrance to a harmonious family life. Such a woman would all the time be preening herself on her learning the way other women preen themselves on their beauty, their musical skills, their artistic endeavours. She would be intolerable to live with, always vying with her husband for the right to have the last word. Tell me, Letitia, have I ever tried to compete against your admirable skill with a paintbrush?"

Letitia had closed her eyes. She stood beside him swaying slightly back and forth. She shook her head in rhythm to her swaying body.

"Of course not. It is because each of us has our own area of special competence. The Miss Wollstonecrafts and the Miss Temples of this world want more than their fair share of what God has divided between men and women."

She might have known that he would bring God in on his side. He always did. The injustices which were so clear while she had been reading *A Vindication of the Rights of Woman*, grew dim while Marvin talked. She knew that they continued to exist, but the certainty with which he refuted them shook her confidence. Confused, she leaned her head against his shoulder. "I love you," she whispered.

"That's my pet," her husband said.

***

Letitia had been shocked by the book. A part of her wished that she had refused to read it. She was the woman so pityingly described. She was the coquette, the child, the dupe of man. She had been frightened by the recognition of herself as an incomplete human being. She was further chilled by the knowledge that, though recognising herself to be that woman, she probably would not change. The prospect was too frightening. Too much of her well-being, too much of her comfort was invested in the person which she now was. It was so easy to please others. All she had gained, she had gained through her beauty and her ability to please. None but a fool would abandon those devices which had proved their worth.

As long as the governess remained she was a witness to Letitia's failure of nerve. Letitia could scarcely bear to be in the company of Miss Temple; she felt that her cowardice was visible. The governess had to go. So Letitia agreed unhesitatingly with Marvin's suggestion that it might be better to dismiss Miss Temple; that whatever about Miss Temple's intellectual abilities and her ability to entertain Letitia herself, her suitability as a moulder of young minds was questionable.

But the departure of the governess was not enough. Before, Letitia had been an innocent; now she was a knowing victim. She had turned collaborator in her own debasement.

Letitia's husband was twenty years her senior. She had been deceived by an outward appearance of youth, combined with a courtship of startling urgency, into thinking him a man whose mind was uniquely vital: a man unfettered by his age. Besides, her prospects had been poor. At the age of seventeen, her beauty had been undeniable; her expectations, as the third daughter of a minor government official, were small. To be courted for love had been an unexpected gratification. She had married Marvin Sweetman willingly. Afterwards she discovered that her husband's vigour masked a cautious spirit in all matters other than love. He had been capable of fieriness only in his pursuit of her.

The intensity of his pursuit was explained by the insatiability of his needs. Letitia supposed that this was what love consisted of for men. His innumerable, brief, bursting couplings gave Letitia no satisfaction; but since she had no expectations, she experienced no sense of deprivation. A year of marriage had not produced a child; it had not even given rise to a pregnancy. Letitia was glad. She feared childbirth. Nevertheless, she pretended a disappointment as being more appropriate. To her surprise, Marvin Sweetman was not anxious to see his wife pregnant. "You're too young," he kept telling her. "Too close to childhood. Your body is still too small to bear a child. Look at the distance between your hips." It didn't stop him plunging nightly in, grunting like one constipated by desire behind her back. He did not care, he said in explanation for this position, for the faces women pulled when making love. He therefore preferred that she should keep her face to the pillow. Letitia did not believe that her facial expression changed in any way while her husband took his pleasure. Why should it? The activity had long since ceased to be painful. It seemed to Letitia that what her husband did behind her back was a small price to pay for the life to which she had been elevated by her marriage.

She found that her husband liked to display her to his friends. He liked her to be admired; he even liked her to be coveted. His friends were mostly of his own age and older. She was still eighteen. It was not difficult to rouse their envy; their envy increased the value of his prize. Dressed in clothes of her husband's choosing, it cost Letitia nothing to flirt with these elderly men (several were older than her own father) now that she knew the void which lay at the heart of flirtation.

***

Letitia had not expected Danno McKenna to be so young. Because he was an acquaintance of her husband, and because (according to Marvin) he was a silk merchant of substance, she had assumed that he would be of her husband's age. Indeed, it was not until she had met him, and had seen how young he was, and how attractive, that she realised this was the McKenna that Tone had spoken of a year or so before. As Letitia had driven home in the company of her husband, it had struck her forcibly that Tone had been right to think of introducing them. Mr. McKenna had admired her. She knew he had admired her.

Letitia was lonely. The governess had gone and Caroline, though sweet (if clinging), was too young to be a friend. There were her sisters, of course, but they were as they had always been. They reeked of the home Letitia had been glad to leave behind. They provided nothing fresh by way of entertainment for Letitia. Besides, they didn't visit much. If they had hoped to find suitors in their sister's house, they had certainly suffered disappointment. Marvin had no friends of Letitia's age. Letitia, therefore, could provide no suitors. They did not begrudge their sister her good fortune, but their own youth was evaporating, and they could not afford to spend their hunting days saving their enviable young sister from her very pampered loneliness.

Had Letitia not been so lonely and so intensely bored, the idea might not have occurred to her. But what else had she to do but invent games? She was eighteen and she was being choked by her own energy.

Upon meeting Danno McKenna and finding him so personable, and so obviously taken by her, it struck Letitia that if her husband was flattered by the envy of old men, then he would be even more flattered by the envy of a young man. And if that was the case, then why should she be condemned to having her thighs surreptitiously kneaded and her breasts brushed by her husband's sombre, middle-aged friends when she might flatter that same husband's pride to a far greater degree by allowing him to discover his prize coveted by a young man? That would surely increase her value in Marvin's eyes, and she was aware that the higher she was valued, the more she was rewarded.

But it wasn't the reward that inspired her. It was the fun which the game promised. She determined that her husband should improve his acquaintance with the silk merchant.

Marvin was reluctant to do so. Since the business with the French fleet, Marvin had grown even warier about his associates. He had ceased entirely to attend clandestine meetings. He had no desire to become embroiled in some fore-doomed revolution; on the other hand, he did not want to become a casualty to the suspicions of his more adventurous friends. On reflection, it seemed to Marvin that a private dinner invitation, issued to someone as influential as Danno McKenna, might be an effective way of assuring their mutual friends of Marvin Sweetman's continued good wishes for the United Irishmen. He therefore agreed with his wife that, to show their appreciation for the swatch of silk so handsomely offered (though not yet delivered), Mr. McKenna should be invited to dinner. Marvin undertook to issue the invitation himself.

Danno McKenna was intrigued by the invitation; he was surprised that it had been issued.

The best that could be said for the move, from Marvin Sweetman's point of view, was that it had not been interpreted by the silk merchant as the initiation of his friend Marvin Sweetman's career as a Castle spy. Danno McKenna did not, as he might otherwise have done, wonder why a man who had been so anxious in recent months to divest himself of his more radical acquaintances should now, when radicalism had grown more dangerous, resume friendship with one of the worst of those acquaintances. Instead Danno McKenna, who had, since that initial meeting in the warehouse, longed for the next one to take place, assumed (correctly) that the wife of Marvin Sweetman had secured the invitation. That Sweetman should not only have acquiesced in the invitation, but should have issued it himself made the man appear so stupid as not to deserve consideration. Besides, Danno intended no lasting harm to Sweetman. He merely planned to make the acquaintance he had formerly been denied; and so, he was now convinced, did Marvin's wife. The charms of Sweetman's wife would not grow less for Sweetman through being shared without his knowledge.

***

She was as light-hearted as himself.

It was perfectly clear to Danno that Letitia (he had discovered her name at last, and a delightful name it was) considered them both to be joined together for the evening in an intimate conspiracy called up specifically to mock, not only the other guests present at her table, but also her own husband. She appeared to think that the mockery was obvious only to themselves; but it seemed to Danno that her intentions were as transparent as his own.

The guests had been deliberately selected as broken objects against which their youth and their beauty must constantly stand out. In the company in which she had chosen to place them, they could be seen as nothing other than a matched pair in a tray of oddments. It was certain that her husband, Marvin, saw them so.

Letitia didn't seem to notice. She seemed crazed to the point of impropriety by a desire for amusement. She had taken him to sit by her at the table and she had, from that moment, engaged him in conversation to the exclusion of all her other guests, including the judge seated on her right hand side. She seemed oblivious to the protocol of the dinner table. She ignored the attempts of the judge to engage her in conversation. Indeed, at one point, she flapped her hand dismissively in the direction of the judge's face. The judge seemed remarkably (and, for a judge, astonishingly) tolerant of his young hostess's rudeness. (How was Danno to know that Letitia had, as little as ten days before, permitted the judge to lie his hand upon her knee for fully ten minutes at this same table?) As for Danno himself, well: could Danno slight his own hostess by refusing to play her game, a game which he very much wanted to play?

She was not perturbed by the news that he was betrothed. Indeed, the information encouraged her to flirt with even more abandon.

"Perhaps I know her," she suggested, but when Danno mentioned Pansy's name, Letitia shook her head.

She was enchanted by Danno's confession that the silver-sprigged silk had been originally intended for Pansy.

"Oh, but how wicked of you," she exclaimed delightedly. "You should never have done such a thing had you been my betrothed. I should have killed you had you tried to soothe a customer with my silk."

Danno rather thought he heard the judge (who, for lack of conversation, had grown very drunk) murmur some lines from a common, back-street ditty on the pleasures of being murdered by one's darling love. He ignored the interruption, and so did Letitia.

"Were you my betrothed," Danno assured her, "You would have no cause to kill me."

"Poor Pansy," his companion murmured without pity.

Letitia herself was drinking claret with abandon. She was gorging on it. Her lips were dark-stained and her eyelids had grown heavy over her shining eyes. She leaned towards him and her silk (that elegant lutestring of blue and gold which had been the subject of the unfortunate imitation), straining across her breasts, took on new lights and shadows. For a moment, she couldn't recollect what it was that she had been about to say, and she stared at him with sleepy, drunken eyes. Her lips had fallen open and her breath escaped, wine-scented and entrancing; her mouth presented itself as the entrance to a dark, inviting hole.

"Do you know," she whispered to him and his nostrils bathed sensuously in her breath, "that there is not a single man in this room who does not desire to bed me? And that if they did not desire to bed me, then my husband would fear (quite properly) that his property was deteriorating in value?"

My God! Had anyone heard? Danno glanced down to the far end of the table. Marvin Sweetman was looking at them both and he was smiling genially enough.

"Look at me," Letitia insisted, with drunken insolence. "Look straight into my face."

He did so, obediently. While he gazed at her face, she turned her eyes to watch her husband, and her mouth smiled at him. While she watched Sweetman, she spoke to Danno. "The fact that you are looking at me with such blatant admiration has given my husband more pleasure (you should see his face now!) than you can possibly imagine. These old men are one thing. Mere youth would be enough to make them drool; but that a young man so handsome as yourself should want what Marvin Sweetman has increases my value ten fold. Your admiration confirms his good taste and his good fortune."

"Look at me now," Danno urged her. "I have a question which deserves your attention."

Danno had ceased to care whether or not their conversation was being overheard by the other guests. He recalled a fifth century mosaic that he had once seen at S Maria Maggiore in Rome. Moses, Aaron and Joshua are shown protected (apart from two still-dangling feet) by a cloud suspended from the Lord's hand. The cloud resembles an oval bubble of glass, and stones, thrown by the mutinous children of Israel, are bouncing harmlessly off its side. Despite the impropriety of their conversation, Danno felt that he and Letitia were protected from attack by such a cloud. He suspected that the thought was blasphemous.

At his request, she ceased to look at her husband. Her eyes, Danno saw now, were almost green. He could not remember their colour in daylight. She tried to raise her eyebrows in expectation of his question, but the effort of coordination was too difficult.

"What if this young man were to take, or even to borrow, your husband's property?"

She giggled.

"It would be rendered valueless. A broken vase; a ripped silk. That wouldn't do. That wouldn't do at all."

"But what if the damage to his property went undetected by your husband?"

She shook her head, frightened. Then she said, pertly, cajolingly, "Poor Pansy! First you give away her silk; now you seem prepared to offer yourself as well! She should take better care of her property. She should take lessons from my husband, whose care for those things under his control never fails. My husband is most assiduous in minding his belongings. He never mislays them."

The judge belched and Letitia eyed him with disgust.

"The judge has drunk too much," she said severely to Danno. "When you are refilling our glasses, don't give him any more." She moved closer to Danno and tilted her head in the direction of his ear. "The judge, you know," she whispered confidingly, "has no idea of where to stop. Only last week he tried to push his hand between my thighs when we were seated just as we are tonight. I felt his hand burrowing into the mounds and layers of material like a nesting rabbit. Indeed, a ring on one of his fingers caught in the front panel of my skirt and tore the lace. However, I retained my composure throughout."

"Do you mean to say you allowed him such a liberty?" Danno was shocked.

His companion shook her head and it lolled heavily from side to side. "By no means," she said, and she had begun to giggle once again.

Danno hoped that she was not about to become hysterical.

"You haven't poured us more wine, Mr. McKenna. You are neglecting your duties. Avoid the judge's glass. The judge, as I have said, does not know where to stop. No, no. While fully in possession of my composure, I removed a small brooch from the bodice of my dress, and I stabbed the offending hand with the pin. He let out a quite involuntary shout of pain, which he was forced to ascribe to a sudden attack of gout. I believe I must have drawn blood, for I found traces of blood on the front panel of my skirting. This week, he has made no attempt upon my leg."

Her head fell suddenly, and her forehead tipped his shoulder. "Oops," she said. "You won't, Mr. McKenna, feel obliged to stab my forehead with a pin? The touch was accidental. I believe that wine collects in the head and weighs it down. My head invariably grows heavier with claret."

Marvin Sweetman called suddenly from the far end of the table, "Letitia, my darling. You are forgetting yourself. You were going to offer pots of chocolate in the drawing room to the ladies."

An elbow leant on the table and she was propping her head up with her hand. "Damn the ladies," she murmured at the tablecloth. "Always, at every turn, ladies appear, waiting to be taken away before the most exciting scene. The ladies must not be over-exposed. I suppose you will discuss politics now. While we talk of . . ."

"Letitia!"

"Yes, yes, sweetheart. I was just saying a last few words to Mr. McKenna here." She raised her head with difficulty from her hand. "Oops," she said again, and winced. "Perhaps, Mr. McKenna, you might take my arm as far as the dining room door?"

"With pleasure."

"Yes. I could well imagine."

As the entire tableful of people rose to its feet for the departure of the ladies, Danno advised his companion that she might be better served by coffee.

"Chocolate is such a rich drink."

"You don't think I'm drunk, Mr. McKenna, do you?"

"God forbid, madam. But coffee is less filling to the head."

"Perhaps."

Supported by his arm, she seemed steady enough. The other ladies followed with interest close behind. When he released her arm, she tottered and leant against the frame of the doorway.

One of the ladies pushed forward.

"She needs to lie down, Mr. McKenna. Poor darling. These young brides. They never do realise what it is that's ailing them. Here, let her take my arm instead and we will call for her maid to put her to bed. Plenty of rest, my pet," she said to Letitia, patting her white face. "That's what you need. Plenty of rest and nothing too testing on the stomach."

"Bed," Letitia murmured, nodding her head agreeably. "They all want to go to bed . . ."

"You see, she's half-asleep already, the little dote."

The women encircled their hostess and removed her from the dining room. Danno shut the door behind them. He was smiling. He had caught sight of her face between the shoulders of two women. She was close to throwing up, he knew, and yet she had attempted to wink at him.

They thought that she was pregnant.

It was possible, of course; she could be both pregnant and drunk. But if she was pregnant, it certainly had not affected her capacity to drink more than the judge himself, and her present indisposition was the result of drink, not pregnancy. She had been, when Danno thought about it, almost fanatic in her desire for enjoyment. Ladies of any breeding did not drink as she had drunk that evening. What had possessed her to violate the rules so emphatically?

Danno did not see his hostess again that evening, and the gentlemen joined the ladies for only a short period in the drawing room before they all took leave of their host.

Danno was the last to depart, detained by the staying hand of his host.

"I think you found my wife charming, Daniel," Marvin Sweetman said to him, his voice a trifle disturbed, as they stood together in the emptied hall. "You monopolised her attention."

Sweetman was in a quandary. Pride fought with jealousy in the man's voice.

"I can't remember when I have been better entertained," Danno said cruelly. He made no attempt to conceal the enjoyment he had gained from the evening. If Sweetman needed confirmation that his wife was admired, then he should have it, even if the confirmation should bring apprehension in its wake.

"Nothing satisfies me more than to see my wife give pleasure to our guests," Sweetman said, before adding repressively, "But you mustn't turn her head with an excess of attention."

"Your wife is so beautiful, Sweetman," said Danno, "that you may as well order the birds to cease their song as attempt to prevent admirers from surrounding her." Then he added, for the joy of tormenting Sweetman further, "your wife is a prize that doesn't fall to many. I envy you your good fortune in acquiring her."

Sweetman's face was a mosaic of conflicting emotions.

Marvin Sweetman's dilemma amused Danno. Its heart was so sordid. It was essential for Sweetman's enjoyment of his belongings that others should want what he possessed. So, he displayed his belongings; but then he worried about their possible theft. A pride which begat fear. Such was the price for Sweetman of possessing a desirable object.

Danno decided to try his host further still, but upon a different subject.

"You were encouraged by the French attempt, I trust?" he said.

"Who was not?" his host replied cautiously.

"Oh indeed, it is difficult to find a soul who did not welcome the event. The people whose opinions are most difficult to ascertain are those who, like yourself, no longer attend our meetings. I naturally assume that you have the most honourable of reasons for your recent absence and merely take this opportunity, since so few are offered, to seek your valued opinion."

"Robust times, Mr. McKenna, and the courts are busy. My time is not my own. I fear the society will see even less of me in months to come. My support is in the practical sphere. The defence of our fellow patriots."

A hypocrite of subtlety. He had neither given nor withheld his support. Poor Sweetman. He was a well-intentioned man. He couldn't help his cowardice; it was, like his possessiveness, endemic to the man's nature. You could no more order the birds to stop singing than . . . Danno sensed laughter rising. He must cease his teasing forthwith. "I shall tell our brothers that you are working at the very coalface of the cause, Sweetman," Danno said, clapping his host soundly on the shoulder. "And now, I must go. Please give my compliments to your wife, and my good wishes for her speedy recovery."

The most disappointing aspect to the evening was that, because of her indisposition, he had failed to make another assignment with her. He had to further their acquaintance. She was quite the most interesting young woman he had ever met. In fact, he hadn't passed so amusingly irreverent an evening since Tone's departure. Doubtless, the source of her interest would turn out to be entirely superficial; but he had to admit that his attention was, for now, entirely hers.

***

It was also Letitia who made sure of their third encounter.

Two days after the dinner party had taken place, she simply arrived at the shop, in the company of a young girl, and asked to be shown the silk. She wanted, she told the assistant, to be shown the silk by Mr. McKenna himself; if he was not at home, she would be quite happy to wait until his return. Her day, she said, was her own.

Danno was, in fact, in his own house, closeted in an upstairs room with two United Irishmen. They had been studying a report of rumours, gathered by one of their minor agents on a recent trip to Bordeaux, of a further invasion planned by the French for April. Despite their desire to believe the report, not one of the three had any confidence in the agent.

On being told that a customer insisted on seeing him, to the point of occupying his premises until he should return, Danno reluctantly brought the meeting to a close.

"My apologies, gentlemen. In this economic climate, a dissatisfied client will take precedence over the very revolution! Which I do not, despite our friend's assurances, expect in April."

Leaving his visitors to see themselves out, he hurried around to the shop.

Letitia sat waiting on a stool. In the distance, Caroline was trying on hats, gazing with pleasure at her changing reflection in a pier glass.

"Mr. McKenna," Letitia exclaimed, sliding from her stool and extending her hand to Danno. "I must see my silk! I woke this morning, and I thought to myself that I could not bear so much as another day of unconfirmed speculation on its progress."

"Mama! Mama! Just look at this!"

Caroline came coquettishly down the length of the shop, her excited face shadowy beneath the brim of a silk-trimmed straw hat.

"Mama?" Danno said to Letitia. "Good heavens, madam, but your indisposition has borne fast and strange fruit!"

She gave him a brief and shameless glance of amusement. Her eyes remained green in daylight. Then she turned to study the progress of the girl towards her. Caroline had been temporarily transformed into a girl of poise and allure. Letitia gave a sudden laugh of pleasure, and clapped her hands together in a gesture of genuine admiration.

"Caroline, you quite out-do me. You look ravishing."

Caroline flushed with delight. "Do you really think so? You are not just saying what you think I would like to hear? Does it suit me?"

Letitia nodded. "It suits you so well, that it would be akin to removing a finger from your hand were we to leave this shop without that hat being firmly attached, by its own ribbons, to your head. Don't you think so, Mr. McKenna?"

She put out her hand and drew the younger girl close.

"Caroline, darling, this is Mr. McKenna: your father's friend."

"And yours, I trust," Danno said. He bowed briefly at Letitia, before holding out his hand to Caroline. "A pleasure to meet you, Miss Sweetman. And if I shan't be accused of pressing a sale, I must endorse your Mama's praise. The hat suits you tremendously well."

"Shall we see the silk now?" Letitia asked with sudden impatience.

So abrupt was the interruption, and so urgent was her tone that Danno could almost have believed that a desire to see the silk formed her sole reason for visiting his shop.

She raised his spirits almost immediately by asking, quite unnecessarily, for his arm to mount the stairs to the warehouse.

Caroline, still wearing the hat, and still trying to glimpse her reflection, twisting her head this way and that, in every pane of glass they passed, trailed dreamily along behind them.

"Once a wish comes to my mind," Letitia confessed to Danno, glancing slyly sideways at him while she spoke, "I burn until it is fulfilled. The greatest disappointment is when (as is so often the case), the anticipation surpasses the fulfilment."

"I disagree," said Danno quickly. "I think that the greatest disappointment occurs when the anticipation is not completed by fulfilment." He stood still on the stairs. Constrained by the pressure of his arm upon her hand, she stood beside him. He looked at her. "I hope," he said, "that you suffer neither type of disappointment concerning any wish which I have it in my power to grant you."

She pulled her hand away from his arm, and lifting her skirts, ran up the last three steps.

"Let me see the silk," she cried in agitation, without turning around, "and we shall soon know!"

He smiled. She was becoming enmeshed in her own game.

The viewing of the silk was hardly of great benefit to her. The roll of finished material had grown fatter, but no more of the pattern was visible than had been visible before. It made the visit seem all the more pointedly the result of a desire to see him.

"Oh well," she said, after no more than a minute or so. "That's it then. When will it be ready?"

"Three days," the weaver said without looking up. The drawboy smiled at her through the strands of the simple. But like certain stars, the drawboy's light was variable. This time, she didn't see him. "Do you like it, Caroline?"

"Mmm. It's pretty." But Caroline was still engaged in her own reflection which she had discovered quite clearly in the windowpane. She thought that in her hat she could be mistaken for sixteen.

Danno was glad not to linger in the warehouse.

If Johnny Little from the north had thought to cement an alliance between the different social interests by forcing political links between particular employers and their workers, he had misjudged badly. Mind you, had he asked Danno's own opinion in advance, Danno would not have guessed that the result would be so catastrophic.

He and Anton had hardly passed a civil word since the night of the Defenders' meeting. Anton had accused his employer of treachery; of trying to undermine the unity of labourers and mechanics by infiltrating an organisation which had never been intended for men of his rank. "You're not afraid that a rising of the Defenders will fail. You're afraid it will succeed and that your own heads will roll in the aftermath." He was being ridiculous and Danno had told him so. But pointing out the obvious had done no good. Anton had said he was entitled to some respite from the presence of his employer. He was under his thumb all the day. Why should he be forced to consort with him at night as well? Danno felt that the very silks in their bales wilted in the bitterness of the atmosphere. He wished that he had never attended the damned meeting in the first place.

Back in the shop, Letitia dismissed her step-daughter.

"Wait in the carriage, Caroline. I wish to discuss the payment for your hat with Mr. McKenna. It is a gift from me to you, and such a gift should be priceless in your eyes. Don't you agree?"

Caroline had already grown hesitant. "Perhaps I don't deserve such a hat. My father might believe that I had taken advantage of your generosity to . . ."

"Oh Caroline, don't worry so! How could your father possibly think such a thing of a creature so undemanding as yourself?"

"But . . ."

"I shall tell him you needed it. I shall tell him I was embarrassed to travel abroad with you for the shameful state of your hats. I shall . . ."

Caroline had begun to retreat, giggling to the door. But at the door, her face grew anxious once again. "You will? You won't forget?"

"This very evening," Letitia assured her.

"Does your husband keep so firm a hand on your conscience as he does on the conscience of his daughter?" Danno asked when Caroline had gone to the carriage.

"I do not have my step-daughter's natural timidity," Letitia replied. "Nor do I have her excess of conscience. I am not, however, immune to embarrassment."

She put out her hand for his, and drew him with her to a private corner of the shop. There, looking quite anxiously into his face, she said, "Mr. McKenna, did I behave disgracefully the other night?"

"Yes," he replied.

She put her hand up to her mouth. "My husband intimated as much."

"If, that is" Danno continued, "by behaving disgracefully, we must include the fact that you deprived me of the desire for any other company but your own throughout the entire evening."

"You are trying to soothe me."

"Perhaps," he admitted.

"I thought to please my husband, you know. He likes to see me gay."

"Then you must have pleased him."

"He said I behaved like a whore."

"I doubt, in that case, that your husband has much experience of whores."

"Do you?"

She would always ask the extra question. One could never be bored with such a woman.

"No," he said.

"Well then . . ."

"But enough to know that yours was not the behaviour of a whore. I am disappointed in one sense, though."

She looked at him quickly. "What?"

There was plainly some reply she did not wish to hear. He wondered what it was. "I am disappointed by the fact that your attention to me was all to please your husband. That leaves me humiliated. I had hoped that a part of your performance was for my benefit."

"I see." She flushed, but more, he thought, with relief than with embarrassment.

"You certainly succeeded in fooling me at the time. You had me quite mesmerised by your attention."

The flush had spread no further, and was, indeed, beginning to diminish.

"Perhaps you owe me the kindness of your undivided attention for the duration of an afternoon to make up for your mistreatment of me?"

"I couldn't possibly!"

She answered mechanically, as though she had been expecting the suggestion.

Others, perhaps, had made similar propositions. Yet Danno thought he had an advantage over any of those others. Danno thought that Letitia had found herself unexpectedly drawn to him and was struggling with unfamiliar sensations.

"So," he pressed, "the humiliation of a guest counts for nothing?"

"What of Pansy?" Letitia asked, and there was a touch of desperate gaiety to her voice. "Think how upset she would be were you to take another woman driving in your carriage." (So, she had already placed the forbidden assignment: within a carriage.) "Surely your humiliation is minor in comparison to the hurt you might cause your betrothed?"

She was doomed, Danno was sure of it. Her imagination had escaped its normal bounds. It was beyond retrieval.

"How can I think of Pansy in your presence?" he asked with sudden harshness.

She stepped close to him. "And what becomes of me in Pansy's presence?" she whispered close to his ear.

He looked down at her face so near to his neck. He was actually trembling. Was she aware of the danger of the game she was playing? He shook his head very slightly from side to side, never taking his eyes from her face. "Oh that, my dear Letitia, has been presenting me for some time with an entirely different problem."

She turned her head away. It seemed she could not bear the new intensity of his look. She was, he realised quite suddenly, driving him mad. "Since I met you," he told her in a low voice, "your face has not been absent from my mind."

She was drumming a foot, encased in its black leather boot and its red silk stocking, on the floor.

"I shall come to collect the silk myself," she said suddenly. "In three day's time."

"Alone?" he asked.

She shrugged and would not meet his eyes. "Quite possibly," was all that she could bring herself to say.

FIVE

"I am, Dear Sir, pleased to inform you that I have managed, after several vain attempts, to obtain the services of one Malachi Delaney, a respectable weaver, a tenant from one of my houses in the Earl of Meath's Liberty. He is, after much persuasion, prepared to pass himself off as a member of one of these abominable clubs and to render me, on those days when he delivers to me the rents collected from his fellow tenants of the house in which he has a room, an account of their proceedings and composition. He declares himself ready to make this sacrifice for love of King and Government, and for the prevention of bloodshed. He is, nevertheless, very apprehensive for his own safety. He talks of there being not less than five Committees of Silence formed for the purpose of dispatching those who turn approver or who threaten to give Evidence for the Crown. He has, because of his apprehensions, laid down several conditions for his employ: firstly that his name be kept inviolably secret (you will, Dear Sir, remember, therefore, that you never heard the name Malachi Delaney from me); secondly, that he will never give evidence before a court or committee of inquiry; and thirdly, that a sum of money, sufficient to provide for his immediate escape and relocation in some foreign country, should be paid into his hands before he will pass on any information. Knowing that he has already attended one meeting of banditti and desperadoes, and believing his contention that what he has gleaned from that one meeting alone makes him an informant of the greatest importance to the government, I have taken the liberty of assuring him that such a sum will be forthcoming within the next week. If we are not to lose his services, this promise must be kept without prevarication. Few of those offering their services to the Crown would have suffered the indignities and humiliations suffered by your good, loyal and uncomplaining servant.

I have as you know, Dear Sir, rendered you copious acts of friendship and service, without receiving in return the least favour or situation

71

from Government. I now implore you, for the love of God, to honour that friendship by putting in a word for me with those in whose power it is to reward constancy such as mine."

* * *

Anton was glad of the excuse for a quarrel with Danno, and he was magnifying it deliberately. It was true that he had been annoyed by Danno's appearance at the meeting; and it was equally true that he distrusted any political mingling between the workers and their employers. At some point, their political ends would diverge and trouble would ensue. Nevertheless, he recognised Danno's sincerity. Danno had told him that, had he been consulted, he would never have agreed to meet with a cell in which Anton was already a member. Anton, who, in retrospect, was far more worried by the recruitment of Malachi Delaney than by the appearance at the meeting of his employer, believed him; but he chose to pretend an angry scepticism concerning all of Danno's motives. It allowed him to keep his distance from his employer; and it kept at bay any desire to warn Danno further of the impending action by the weavers. Danno had ignored Anton's earlier hints. He had insisted on dismissing the power of his weavers to hurt the industry. Let him look out for himself.

Anton was bitter all the same. His loyalty lay with the weavers, but his affection lay with Danno. The action in which he was being forced to participate was going to wound that friendship irreparably.

This afternoon, shortly before the arrival of Danno and that woman, another message had arrived from the workshop. The date had been agreed with the delegates from the other combinations. The action would take place exactly as scheduled. Anton was deeply disappointed. He had hoped that negotiations would prove so long and arduous that the weavers would have lost their urge for action before any could take place.

When Letitia Sweetman had asked how soon the silk would be ready, his answer had provoked a sudden chill in his own heart; and when Danno had come running back up the stairs after her departure, too elated by the possibility of conquest to be silenced by Anton's new hostility, Anton could hardly bear to listen to his employer's insouciant plans for the seduction of the hapless young woman on the day that she came to collect the silk. In three day's time, the action would have taken place. He would deny his employer's ability to consider seduction, even of such a woman, on that day.

The Paradis weavers fell silent while Anton walked through their workshop that evening. Malachi, he noticed, was not at his loom; nor was Charlotte. He was glad. Malachi himself, it was true to say, had grown friendlier under the constraints of their enforced brotherhood. He had even gone so far as to say that he'd never thought Paradis would have the guts to join a revolutionary organisation, and that maybe he had underestimated him, though that remained to be proved. The sheep, Malachi had said, would be separated from the goats soon enough, once the revolution started. And it had been Malachi himself who had waylaid Anton on the day following the meeting, and had extracted from Anton a promise (for what, Malachi had added, such a promise was worth) that Charlotte should not be told of her lover's adherence to the cause of Irish liberty. Anton had demanded and received a similar promise in return. Still, he did not trust Malachi. In conversation with the weaver who had recruited him, Anton had discovered that, in the case of Malachi's recruitment, it had been Malachi who had made the first move. Anton wondered why. Public civilities between the two men extended no further than a mutual acknowledgement of the other's existence each time they passed. The other weavers were under no such constraints; he wished them a good evening, but no one answered. It frightened him that they should be so hostile to one as harmless as himself. Anton believed that on the day Lucien Paradis died, the Paradis weavers (with or without the assistance of Malachi Delaney) would turn on his son-in-law and whip him from the house. The living quarters were on the first floor. Anton was glad to reach the safety of the stairs.

Only the newly-acquired Caitlín was in the kitchen.

73

"The other two are above with himself," she told him, in those tones of contempt which she invariably employed, when talking of the master weaver and her lover to Anton.

On his return from the McKenna workshops, before his wife and her chief journeyman climbed the stairs to Lucien Paradis' bedroom to give to him a meticulous account of the day's business, it was Anton's habit to drink a glass or two of wine with his father-in-law. Tonight, he was too late; his wife and her lover had forestalled his arrival. The closeness of Malachi Delaney (despite his disabling Catholicism) to Lucien Paradis did not cause Anton to fear exposure at Malachi's hands. Lucien Paradis, were he to discover that his son-in-law was a Defender, was capable of ejecting him from the house, but Anton was not unduly concerned. Malachi knew (at least, he had to assume) that any unfavourable disclosure of Anton's activities would provoke the immediate disclosure by Anton of the true parentage of Charlotte's two children; so much as Malachi might be tempted, he could not afford to take the risk. Between Charlotte, Malachi and himself, all moves were blocked. A stale-mate existed.

Caitlín looked at the weaver. "You seem tired, sir," she said. "Why don't you sit down here with me a while and I'll rub your shoulders for you."

The offer from the child (she really was no more than a child) was most enticing. It was one which had never been made to the weaver before. Between the weaver and his weaving wife were no such kindnesses. "I suppose," he said warily, sitting down, "that with Charlotte above, it would do no harm."

"You'd hear her on the stairs," Caitlín assured him, beginning to massage his shoulders with undulating movements of her hands. "Though I'm doing no more for you than she should be doing herself."

He was silent, and Caitlín wondered nervously had her comment been too forward. She need not have worried. Anton had closed his eyes and was no longer listening. It hardly mattered what she said. She slipped her hands under his long, brown hair, and danced her fingers up and down his neck. "My dad used have terrible trouble with his shoulders," she told him, "and Mam was forever at us to give him a good rubbing. He'd just carry on weaving with us all taking it in turns to knead his poor fat back like a piece of dough. But it didn't stop him hanging himself in his own pulleys."

Anton's head dangled as loosely as the head of a freshly-hanged man. Her hands wound sensuous as silk around his neck. The words she spoke floated unnoticed above his head.

Caitlín had only been in the Paradis household a month. She adored Anton unequivocally, for he was, without exaggeration, her saviour.

When her father had committed suicide, the family had broken up. Her mother had gone, with the two youngest children, to live with a sister and her husband, a carrier, in Wexford town. A brother, who worked sporadically for McKenna, had begged Anton to find work for his sister. "She'll be on the streets otherwise," he'd said, "and she's only sixteen and still sweet with innocence."

With Caitlín standing at her brother's side, a dark blue ribbon (which matched the colour of her tear-glazed, apprehensive eyes) threaded through her dark brown, curling hair, her worldly goods filling no more than a small leather pouch which hung from one wrist, how could Anton have refused? But what was he to do with her?

In the end, what else could he do, but bring her home to his astonished wife and her equally astonished weavers. It was the sheer audacity of his move which astounded them all; it was so uncharacteristic. That the befriending of a homeless girl (a strikingly pretty and well-formed young girl) could have been propelled by charity simply did not cross their minds.

Whatever about her sweetness, Caitlín's innocence could hardly have remained intact in the Paradis house. Being Anton's protégée (and protégée was not the word the weavers used) immediately classified her as the enemy of Charlotte and the weavers. She was not offered the possibility of a position of neutrality in the house. (Had she been offered such a position, she would have rejected it.) But her hostility stayed well-concealed beneath a perversely dense mask of innocence. She was deeply offended by what she discovered, and Anton (as a result of his own charity) experienced the pleasure of having an ally in the house for the first time since his arrival. She was filled with a wonderful, righteous indignation at the deceits being perpetrated upon innocent parties, and her indignation was balm to Anton. Had it not been for the absolute nature of her devotion to Anton, she could hardly have been restrained from going to Lucien Paradis (that poor, deceived old man) and denouncing his daughter as a whore and his grandchildren as bastards. But such was her devotion to Anton that his wishes were unquestionably her command. For his sake, she ignored the deceits around her. Her behaviour to her mistress, if Charlotte *was* her mistress (Charlotte did not consider herself to be so), was exemplary and Malachi was scarcely aware of her existence, so silent was she in his presence. But on those days when Charlotte Paradis took her journeyman upstairs to her own bedroom, Caitlín left the house, unable to bear witness.

Two reflections gave Caitlín great comfort while simultaneously arousing her indignation: the first was that her mistress was far too old for Anton (by the look of her, she was old enough to be his mother); the second was that if Anton had been happily married, then Caitlín could not have allowed herself to indulge in many of the fantasies which constantly filled her mind. The indignation aroused by these two reflections concerned the ability of the master weaver to reject a man so beautiful in body and mind as Anton.

Anton, because he was deriving too much pleasure from the girl's attentions, rose to his feet abruptly, startling Caitlín, who had spent the last few minutes silently fondling the young man's neck, her own eyes closed, her breathing gathering pace. Contrary to the assumptions of the weavers, Anton had not brought home a companion for his own bed. It was Caitlín's overwhelming desire to be just such a companion, but Anton was scrupulously bound in his own mind, by the terms of his own charity, to refrain from any sexual advances upon the young girl who had been thrust upon him.

"I must pay my respects to my father-in-law," he said, while something within his groin shivered uncontrollably on.

Caitlín looked at him, disappointment plain upon her flushed face.

"You won't find the company upstairs so nice," she said, putting her hands up to her cheeks to cool them down.

"I know," he told her. And Caitlín felt her face heat up again around her hands, at the tone of his voice and the sight of the smile which accompanied his words. She was, she knew, in a bad way over Anton Paradis.

Anton never entered his father-in-law's bedroom without anxiety. There was always the fear that this would be the day on which the second stroke had taken place, and that the annihilation of Lucien Paradis' wits would be complete. But tonight, his wife and her lover were with her father and Anton could not go in. His excuse for escape from the beguilements of Caitlín had been false. He did not intend to join them. It was within that room of Lucien's that the most sustained of pretences had been enacted over the years; and one avoided what hypocrisies one could. Instead, he stood listening outside the door, bathed in the stale air which had long since overflowed from Lucien Paradis' room to permeate the entire upper landing. Even the sound of his wife's voice inside the room did not allay the fear. He could hear no sound from Lucien Paradis himself. Not until he heard for himself that slurred and hesitating French voice, calling upon his daughter to refill his glass, was he satisfied that Lucien Paradis had survived another day.

Barely had Anton reached the seclusion of his own room (her children now slept with Charlotte; Anton slept alone), when Charlotte came out of her father's room, with the journeyman close behind her. From within his room, Anton watched Malachi, the journeyman, pin his wife against the wall. He watched them kiss silently within earshot of Lucien Paradis. They both looked old, and their gesture was so poignantly defiant that Anton was momentarily filled with pity for the two of them. They went down the stairs, and Anton lay on his bed. He was tired. Perhaps he should just leave, and let the old man draw what conclusions he wished. But he knew he wouldn't leave. He had acquiesced initially in the deception for Charlotte's sake. He maintained it now for the sake of the dying Lucien Paradis. He had seen the charade this far; he couldn't abandon it so near the end.

***

Dear Sir, were I less devoted to serving my King and His Ministers, I should be tempted to withhold my own services in the hope that such a withholding might gain for me the swift attention afforded to the good weaver, Malachi Delaney. Yesterday, I called upon the Castle and

your office, hoping for news concerning my own request, but was told
that you were too busy to see me. I was, however, comforted by the
note delivered to my house by your own servant, in which you assure
me that you have, despite the pressures on your time, made representations on my behalf. I am most grateful to you for your great kindness.
I fear, Dear Sir, that your ceaseless labours on behalf of the Government,
will bring you to an early grave, and must urge you to guard your health
in these turbulent days.

I must now divulge to you the most extraordinary information passed on
to me by the weaver (a man, by the way, not given to exaggeration). It
seems that he has been, through his own subtle machinations, sworn into
the very same cell as that attended by the husband of his employer, the
masterweaver and Frenchwoman, Charlotte Paradis, herself (the weaver
assures me) an indisputably loyal supporter of his Majesty's Government.
The husband, Anton Paradis, is, according to Delaney, a most rebellious
character: a Paineite, a Democrat, a fomenter of Combinations. He married
his own cousin, a woman old enough to be his mother, for her money and
her business. The relationship between the husband and the wife is so bad
- the children of the marriage are rumoured not to be his (though Delaney
does not believe the rumour himself) - that the husband (our Defender)
now works for none other than Danno McKenna, the silk merchant,
with whose name I know you to be most familiar. As if this information
of itself was not interesting enough! But it turned out to be the mere tip
of the iceberg! What I am about to tell you now quite confirms a warning
given by me some time ago to your good self; namely that the poor misguided
tradesmen and manufacturers of the City and Liberty are being actively
recruited by the United Irishmen into their dastardly cause. Delaney
had been in the meeting for no more than ten minutes, and was engaged
in the swearing of an oath (a copy of which I enclose for your perusal),
when who should walk in, accompanied by one of those confounded Belfast
radicals, but Danno McKenna himself. Delaney says that though
McKenna and Paradis pretended a great surprise and annoyance at
the sight of one another, it was quite obvious to him that the two were in
conspiracy together. However, the curious upshot of the meeting was that
McKenna took the Defender's oath, while not one of the Defenders
agreed to become a United Irishman.

In answer to a question you put to me in your note of this morning – I do not see how Delaney could be persuaded to give evidence in court. He is far too cautious of his own skin to take such a risk. For now, as I am sure you will agree, McKenna is far more useful at large and exposing his innermost secrets to the attentive Delaney. I shall send you further information as it comes to me, Your obedient servant . . ."

***

They had chosen a night when the moon would be new, but even had it been as fat and as glistening as a force-fed goose it would have shed no light, for cloud completely covered the sky. It was easy enough for the nine, dark-clothed men to remain invisible between the meagre puddles of light shed by the street lamps near McKenna's premises. Conditions could not have been better.

Only one of Danno McKenna's weavers was missing.

Anton Paradis had worked feverishly and irrationally all that day on the silver-sprigged tobine intended for the seducible Letitia Sweetman. If it was only finished, he could remove it from the warehouse. He feared its contamination by events, as though it were a living thing. He knew there was no reason why the silk should be in any physical danger; it was not, after all, a foreign silk. Nonetheless, Anton continued working until his drawboy refused to draw down another lash. He was beat, the drawboy said. He was entirely beat, and even stopping when they did, he said, he'd be hard put to it to turn out again in the night. But maybe that was Anton's intention, he'd added, smirking with his own humour? To wear the pair of them out so much that, let their consciences dance jigs on their eyelids as they would, he and Anton would sleep through the whole shenanigans. But Anton had told his drawboy dourly that he would have no chance to fall asleep, for his conscience would not be dancing alone. She would be partnered by apprehension. There was nothing like apprehension, Anton had promised his drawboy as they were locking up the warehouse, to keep the mind alert.

"See you later, then."

They might have been arranging to meet for no more than a drink, from the drawboy's cheerful tone of voice. Anton had been unable to bring himself to reply.

It was when Anton had been slipping the key of the warehouse into his pocket that he had nearly betrayed his loyalty to the weavers. It had taken him all his strength of mind to force himself to walk past Danno McKenna's door. The presence of that key in his pocket had filled him with so much shame. Six months ago, Danno had trusted his weaver, Anton, with one of the two keys to the warehouse. Tonight, his weaver would abuse that trust.

As Anton had walked away from temptation, he had thought with contemptuous pity of the silk merchant. His contempt had helped to harden his resolve. God, but McKenna was a poor, silly bastard. Because Anton had made no further mention of the dangers of combination, Danno had presumed that the crisis, whatever it was, had passed. The weavers were prone to bouts of anger, which surged and died for no apparent reason. He hadn't even troubled himself to ask if his presumption was correct. (Anton could not bear the possibility that Danno had refrained from asking questions out of pity for the weaver's torn loyalties. Such an act of friendship was impossible to contemplate in the light of what he was now preparing to do.) It had seemed to Anton that in the last few days, McKenna had been uncommonly distracted by this new love of his. He had been too distracted to notice the uncanny peace in the workshop. Such peace should have alerted him to the impending storm.

Anton had been relieved by McKenna's negligence. Anton had been afraid that, had Danno asked, he would not have been able to restrain himself from issuing a warning. As he had walked on stiff, reluctant legs, beyond McKenna's door, he knew he had been saved only by McKenna's own inattention; as he had walked away, he had thought that nothing could induce him to return that night.

But when the weavers gathered silently in the McKenna yard, Anton was there. Poor Matt Treacy was the missing man. He had gone to bed three days before and was not expected to rise again.

Liam Cronin congratulated Anton on his presence. "I was afraid," he admitted to the Frenchman in a low voice.

"I told you where my loyalty lay," Anton said, his own voice low, and lacklustre with weariness. "Why would you not take my word?"

Liam touched him lightly on the shoulder. "I can see I was mistaken."

Peadar Howlin was aware that Anton was present only because he, Peadar, had gone to fetch him from his house.

He had arrived in advance of the time that Anton had been due to leave, to prevent his belief from being proved. Mick's young sister, Caitlín, had been so relieved to see Peadar. She knew, through her brother, of the weavers' intentions. "Thank God you've come," she'd said to him at the door. "He's in a terrible state." She had shown him into the kitchen, "Look at him," she'd whispered. "He's been like that all evening. Won't say a word." It was midnight, and Anton had not retired to bed; but he had not been dressed to go out. He had been slumped on a stool near the fire, with the stunned appearance of a man no longer in command of his own actions. His wife, the master weaver (who thought the proposed action misguided, and who had warned Anton that the promised action by other groups would fail or be, at best, sporadic), had retired long since.

Anton had eyed the intruding weaver with animosity, and when Peadar had asked him was he ready, Anton hadn't stirred.

Peadar had shouted at him to get to his feet and Anton had stared at the weaver resentfully. "He's my friend," he'd said dully. "McKenna is my friend."

Peadar had shaken his head. "Not McKenna. He only cultivates you for your skill. Your friends are waiting for you."

Anton had risen reluctantly to his feet. He was close to tears. "I don't know who is the better friend: McKenna or my fellow weavers. But I know who would make the worse enemy. I'm joining you as a coward, not as a loyal friend."

Caitlín had gone over to Anton, and had taken his hand in hers. "You're no coward, Mr. Paradis," she had told him vehemently. "You're a fine man. It's no disgrace to suffer pain for doing your duty." Her own father was one of the silk merchants' victims; he had been without work for five months when he hanged himself. But there had been no need for Caitlín to make mention of her father to Anton. The clarity with which she saw his duty, and her placid assumption that he saw it as clearly himself (however sharp the accompanying pain), had filled Anton with borrowed certainty and he had accompanied Peadar without further ado.

The shop and the warehouse in which Anton so frequently worked alone were on opposite sides of a courtyard. Although it was simpler to reach the warehouse from the shop by crossing the courtyard between them, an indoor route led round three sides of the courtyard between the two buildings. Because Anton possessed the key to the warehouse, the weavers could, by this route, gain entrance to the shop without having to break their way in. This suited the workers very well, as they were particularly anxious not to be detected. Theirs was to be an operation of far greater subtlety than usual. The main workshop, on the fourth side of the courtyard, stood detached from either building and could not therefore be entered without force. But the weavers had no wish to destroy their own work. They planned no breaking of machinery, no firebombs, no physical injuries. The carrying of guns had been banned.

Throughout the city, small, orderly groups of weavers, acting upon the same instructions, were assumed to be meeting with similar stealth outside other retail premises.

A dog in a nearby house had begun to bark, disturbed by something, disturbed by the men themselves perhaps. Another dog began to bark in response to the first dog: then a distant third, like an echo.

"Jesus, Paradis, open the damned door will you?"

They were all as jittery as fleas.

It was too dark to see the keyhole. Anton fumbling with the key, dropped it and it landed with a sharp report on the door-step. The others, crowded behind him, cursed him. He crouched down to pat around the step with hurried, flat-spread hands. He could feel nothing but the smooth stone. The others began to mutter uneasily amongst themselves.

Liam came to crouch beside him. All his suspicion had returned. "This isn't what you would call a tactical delay, is it, Paradis?" he whispered, his words rapid and his breath rank. "You're not waiting for someone, are you?"

"You'll just have to hope for the best, Cronin."

He was here, wasn't he? What more did he have to do?

Shifting backwards, Anton knelt, painfully, on the missing key.

Once inside, they felt no safer. They wanted to get out again as soon as possible. They stumbled through passages, unfamiliar and endless in the dark. At length they reached the main shop. One man saw a shining eye in a corner and gave a scream of terror. It was the mirror in front of which Caroline had first tried on the hat. They all waited, unmoving, for some reaction to the scream. Nothing happened. Eventually, Liam allowed himself to whisper, in a voice that shook with nerves, that the sooner they got down to the job, the sooner they'd be out of the place.

It didn't take long for the men to destroy Danno's entire stock of English silks. A single, elongated stab wound sufficed for each bale of silk. Silk sighed and gaped beneath their knives. A half turn of each bale concealed its damage. Late as it was, people were still passing up and down Dame Street outside the shop. The men inside could hear them, but they could see nothing, for the shutters were bolted across the front windows. Those outside sounds were unnerving, and the men worked swiftly and edgily in silence. Each knew precisely what needed to be done; no further instructions were required. In half an hour, by the light of two candles (reluctantly lit), the job was finished. Apart from a dusting of frayed threads on the floor, there was nothing to alert the casual eye to the complete destruction of £3,000 worth of stock. The damage would not be discovered until the first bale was pulled from its place. The Irish silks remained untouched.

Anton had done what was required of him. With Liam working by his side, he could have done no less, but Liam's absence would have made no difference. The unlocking of the warehouse door had already completed Anton's betrayal of Danno McKenna. He was beyond redemption by the time he stabbed his first unresisting silk.

The closer they came to completing the job without detection, the edgier they all grew. By the time they had retraced their footsteps as far as the warehouse door, they were ready to run like a great clattering of pigeons out of the trees. And it was at the door that they discovered what had been the most dangerous mistake of the night. The door had been left open. Even the most careless of McKenna's hired watchmen, touring the courtyard, could not have failed to see that open door.

No one would admit responsibility. There was no need. They all knew who was to blame. Anton Paradis had opened up the door, had stood aside to let the others pass through, and had then entered the passage himself, closing the door behind him. Or so he swore now.

Only Caitlín's brother Mick claimed to believe him. "I heard the door close," Mick insisted stubbornly, but the others dismissed his claim. He was too much in Paradis' debt to be worthy of belief. Not even Peadar Howlin believed Anton, though he, at least, believed that the door had been left open by accident. The rest saw a failed conspiracy.

"You must have given McKenna the wrong night, you bastard!"

The cloud had broken up enough for the others to see that Liam had his hands at Anton's throat; Anton's fingers scrabbled at Liam's hands.

"You were to be taken with the rest of us, I suppose. To lull our suspicions. And we were to swing, after you had sung your song. What did McKenna pay you for the information? Or was payment not to be made until afterwards? Have you ruined your own chance for reward?"

Anton's head shook frenziedly to and fro.

"Maybe he only gave him the wrong hour," the elderly drawboy suggested nervously. His weaver had been accused of disloyalty too many times; finally the drawboy had succumbed. He had glimpsed true betrayal behind the open door. "Maybe McKenna's coming yet. We should leave while we can. We always know where to find Paradis."

He began to run, and most of the others followed suit. The noise of their shoes rang loud and careless in the cobbled courtyard.

Peadar, terrified by the noise, and afraid for Anton's life, tugged frantically at Liam's arm. "Come on, Cronin. We'll be caught if we don't leave now."

"Leave him alone, Liam! You'll kill him! I tell you, the door was closed when we came in. Someone else opened it."

"The dawn will be on us, Cronin."

And indeed, dismal night was beginning to give passage to dismal morning.

Together, Mick and Peadar succeeded in detaching Liam from Anton. Anton, who could no longer stand up without Liam's hands supporting him by the neck, sank, gagging, to the ground.

"Look what you've done to him. An innocent man, and you've half-killed him."

Bending down, Mick pulled Anton up over his shoulder.

"He'll live," Liam said contemptuously. "So long as he doesn't show his face round here in the morning."

"He has to. We must all turn up," Mick said. "It was agreed. We must behave with perfect normality. Those were your very words."

"That was for our own protection. He needs no protection from us."

"He is an innocent man. And tomorrow he has our protection."

"Can we, for the love of God," Peadar interrupted, "leave this courtyard before it's too late?"

As soon as the thin moon began to disappear behind the next band of cloud, they ran across the courtyard.

***

Anton did not go to work the following morning.

His neck was bruised and swollen, but that was not his reason for staying at home; he was, despite Mick's assurance of his personal protection, afraid of the other weavers, but that was not his reason for staying at home; he was staying at home because he could not face Danno.

During the morning, Caitlín swathed his neck in a succession of cool, damp bandages.

At lunchtime, Peadar and Mick called by. Peadar was crying.

They told him the weavers had all been sent home.

"Dismissed?"

They didn't know.

Half way through the morning, McKenna had come to the workshop door with the foreman by his side. McKenna had the look of a man betrayed. He spoke to no one. He asked no questions, he gave no explanations:

"He just told us to get out."

"And then he left."

The weavers had been too frightened to remain on the premises without permission.

Since they had agreed to feign innocence at all times, Liam had made a formal protest to the foreman supervising their departure. He had stated that the weavers were leaving because ordered to do so by Mr. McKenna; but they failed to understand the reason for their dismissal. He felt, he had said, that they were owed an explanation. The foreman was to tell Mr. McKenna that the weavers would return to the workshop at their usual time the following morning to receive just such an explanation.

The foreman had not been reticent in his reply to Liam, and the weavers had left without more ado.

Liam had wondered where Paradis was. He thought that his absence only went to prove his guilt.

"He intends you harm, Paradis," Peadar warned as he and Mick were leaving.

"Hasn't he harmed him enough already?" Caitlín demanded, pointing to the bandaged neck on which only the day before her fingers had danced so airily. "Without the least cause."

Mick looked at his sister and wondered was she still a virgin. "Have a care, Paradis." he warned. Anton, observing the look, wondered to what the warning referred.

"I will," he said, his voice still hoarse. "I certainly will."

The attempt to bring the silk merchants to heel had turned out very much as Charlotte Paradis had predicted. Support for the McKenna weavers had been almost non-existent.

By nightfall it was clear that only two other silk merchants had suffered damage; in one of the two cases, the agitators had been ambushed within the warehouse by the militia, and the greatest part of the damage had been caused by the bleeding of a bayonetted and dying weaver into several swatches of silk.

"Out of work, brother Paradis?" Malachi asked maliciously as they passed on the stairs that evening. "Reduced to living on your wife's charity once again? I hear McKenna is a ruined man. His weavers have a strange view of persuasion, it seems to me, if they imagine that by destroying a man's business they will make him more amenable to their point of view."

But Anton knew that he was the one weaver who would not lose his job. McKenna would not be able to let him go. This very fact would only serve to confirm the conviction of the other weavers that between Paradis and McKenna there existed at best, an agreement, at worst, a conspiracy.

***

But when he joined the other weavers at seven o'clock the following morning in the half-light outside the locked McKenna workshop, it was Anton who was the first to be dismissed.

Danno McKenna stood before his weavers and told them he was a ruined man. One of them muttered that McKenna didn't know what ruin was and there was an angry humming of agreement.

"A starving weaver is a ruined man, McKenna," Liam shouted.

"Well then, you'll all be ruined with me unless you can find work elsewhere, for I can't afford you." Danno wasn't shouting. He had long left anger behind him. "You weavers were my luxury for the maintenance of which the English silks were a necessity. You destroyed the silks that were keeping you."

"You'll recover, McKenna." It was Anton who dared (reluctantly) to speak, imagining himself to be the most likely of the weavers to be listened to. Danno stared coldly at him. "And while you are recovering, we . . ."

"Get out, Paradis." Danno spoke, and his voice was icy with contempt. "That you should turn up here this morning defies belief. The others I might forgive. I was never misled into seeing them as anything other than what they are. But you!"

He drew close to Anton. "I thought you were my friend," he whispered, and tears spilled from his eyes. "But only a man to whom I meant nothing at all could have done what you did."

"I warned you," Anton whispered desperately in return, and he was crying himself. "Again and again. You wouldn't listen."

"It was such a particularly vicious act of vengeance."

"We were all in it together."

"Yours was the hand, Anton. Yours was the killing hand."

Danno turned and walked away across the cobbles towards the back entrance to his shop.

"All of you, get out," he shouted back to them over his shoulder, his voice thick with tears. "There's nothing for you here. Nothing at all."

It was the heat of the moment. It must have been the heat of the moment. It was not possible that he could have lost Danno's friendship.

All through the day, Anton walked, lamenting, about the streets of the city. His spirit was entirely filled with grief. His mind was stuporous with misery. He ate nothing and he drank nothing and was hardly aware of the people moving to and fro about him. He had always questioned the very existence of friendship between himself and his employer; it had taken its withdrawal to show the weaver how essential its presence had been for the well-being of his soul.

Not until the late afternoon did it occur to him that however betrayed Danno felt, he needed his weaver still. Only Anton could complete the silver-sprigged tobine. Without the completed tobine, the silk merchant possessed no lure with which to tempt Letitia Sweetman beyond discretion. He still had the key to the warehouse. Danno had forgotten to take it from him. Anton sprang along the pavement, with swollen neck and swollen eyes, banging his knuckles together with overwrought excitement. He knew what he would do. He would go at once and he would extract the drawboy from his squalid quarters in the Liberty; and he would complete the tobine that very evening. It would be a gesture of reconciliation that Danno would be unable to resist.

The drawboy was very reluctant to accompany Anton. He did not want to be seen walking in the company of the suspect weaver. He feared the consequences of discovery should they be found trespassing on McKenna's property; but the madness in the weaver's eyes made him fear something worse should he refuse. There were, he conceded reluctantly, no more than three hours' work left to do on the silk; and the lady had been so anxious for it. At length, he agreed to come. He did refuse to walk beside Anton. He said that they would only draw suspicion on themselves. So they walked down Dame Street like two halves of a severed horse, the drawboy twenty paces ahead of the weaver.

Afternoon light was disappearing. Once again, Anton fumbled for the keyhole.

"I did close the door behind me the other night," he said suddenly to the drawboy who stood nervously beside him. The weaver's voice was far too loud for the place they were in.

"Sssh," the drawboy whispered.

"But I did. I know it."

"I believe you," the drawboy told him. It seemed best to profess belief.

A lamp had been left burning at the foot of the stairs. Even in his heightened state of excitement, Anton noticed that touch of carelessness and thought that Danno really couldn't do without him. Anton never left the premises without checking that all the lights were quenched.

As they climbed the stairs, beyond the light cast by the lamp below, Anton observed new light spilling through the cracks in the door at the top of the stairs and he knew that Danno must be in the warehouse. Anton's heart rose. By gestures, he indicated to the drawboy that he should remain below. In the absence of the other weavers, he would be able to talk to Danno, explain himself, clear up misunderstandings. Danno would have cooled down by now. He only had to see the unfinished silk, to know he could not do without his weaver. He might, even now, be considering how he might best approach a reconciliation.

Anton reached the top of the stairs and opened the door quietly. There he stopped, and went no further, immobilised by what he saw.

The unfinished silk had been cut out of the loom. The simple had been shredded, the warp had been severed from side to side and the silk itself had been torn from the roller. That was a shocking sight; but it was not that sight which caused Anton (once he had recovered himself sufficiently) to stumble hurriedly backwards from the room, without bothering to close again the door so recently opened.

He had guessed correctly. Danno was in the warehouse. But he was not expecting Anton. Writhing on the floor near the loom, oblivious to the entry of the weaver, and naked but for pieces of slashed silk with which they had defiantly decorated themselves, were the panting silk merchant and the woman he called Letitia.

SIX

Their meeting had begun so inauspiciously. When Letitia, contrary to her own sense of caution, did appear, not only had Danno's mood of romance, as his weaver had predicted, quite evaporated; he had forgotten that any assignment, however tentative, had ever been made.

The weavers had disguised the damage with great skill. On that slack, mid-week morning, it had not been until the sample book was being updated for dispatch by messenger to the house of Sir Thomas and Lady Fitzpatrick, when the shop had already been open for more than two hours, that the damage was discovered. An assistant, snipping narrow strips of material from the newest rolls of silk, had, noticing the dusting of frayed threads scattered on the lower rolls and on the floor below, grown suspicious, and had tipped over the bale from which he had just taken a sample. He had seen, with horror, the gaping slash like a vast eye-socket from which the eye itself had been plucked. Rolling over, with increasing frenzy, bale upon bale of silk, the distraught assistant had quickly discovered the full extent of the damage.

Danno had been sent for.

What Danno had found most unnerving had been the chilling restraint of the attack: its precision and its silence. It demonstrated an organisation and control which had never been evident before. Damage had been inflicted so efficiently. Destruction of the English silk had been the objective; no other destruction had taken place. The recreation of a semblance of order to conceal the damage had been the final touch: somebody's insufferably brilliant conceit. Danno had suffered before; his high standing had never given protection, in periods of sluggish trade, from the haphazardly catapulted stones, the blazing, flying fireballs of pitch, the shredded

91

silk. But this had been an assault of a different order, an assault which was the result of cool premeditation. That the destruction would rebound upon the weavers themselves the more resoundingly for its very effectiveness was later to strike Danno as rather cruel.

On that morning Danno was incapable of such generosity of spirit. On that morning, his heart as precisely severed as his silk, and as superficially concealed, he had felt his premises to be contaminated by the presence of the weavers. He could bear to confront them, with their deceitful, frightened faces, only because he could not wait for them to be gone. It had cost him immense effort to speak even those two words of dismissal; the effort required of a priest who is called upon to exorcise devils. It was in such a light that Danno saw his weavers on that morning.

The departure of the other weavers had compelled Danno to consider Anton. Their disappearance had made Anton's continued presence a source of greater contamination still. It was required that he too should be dismissed.

The confrontation had been almost too much for Danno to undertake. Not until the afternoon had he been able to summon up the courage to mount the stairs to the warehouse. The silence as he had climbed the long flight upwards had been what had most attracted Danno's attention. It was not just the absence of song. It had not been a day on which Danno would have anticipated song from his weaver; but the loom had also been silent. He had known before he had entered the room that Anton too had suffered a failure of courage, and that knowledge had given Danno a tiny, glinting stone of comfort. That stone had been shattered when Danno had opened the door and had realised the derisible naivety of his own assumption.

Anton had failed to come to work that day because there had been nothing for him to do. The silk, so nearly completed, had been cut from the loom. The finished cloth had been wrenched from the roller and had been split right down the centre from end to end, like a freshly gutted, still sleekly shining animal. Its two halves lay in circling coils upon the floor. Danno had knelt down on the floor by the split and distorted silk. Lowering his head into the coils, as though making placatory obeisance to some maltreated deity, Danno had begun to weep.

It had been then that Danno had erroneously recognised the truth of what Anton had always insisted and Danno had so emphatically denied. It became clear to the weeping Danno that Anton had been right and that he had been wrong. Anton was not an artist. Had the weaver been an artist, he could not have destroyed his own creation. Unless his hatred for the merchant was greater than his love for his creation. The more Danno reconsidered the weaver in the light of what he had found, the more monstrous the weaver grew in Danno's mind. When Danno recalled how hard Anton had worked on the previous day to complete the silk, it seemed to the merchant that Anton had been indulging himself with a game of chance. Anton had been prepared, if it could be finished by night fall, to reprieve the silk. But the game had been no more than an entertainment - a means of lending purpose to that final day's weaving; for without the challenge, why should Anton have woven a single line of the pattern? It never occurred to the kneeling Danno, distractedly looping the silk around his arms and neck, that anyone other than Anton could have inflicted such a wound. It was the action of a man intent on destroying a friendship. Danno had rocked on his heels, recalling all those occasions when he, Danno, would not permit the friendship to be killed by lesser wounds. He had nursed it instead with unnatural care. Had he allowed the friendship to die sooner, then he might not have had to face this irreversible declaration of enmity.

The sound of Anton's voice at seven o'clock the following morning, from the midst of the anxious weavers, had shocked him. He had not observed the presence of the Frenchman. He had not expected him to be there. He had not believed the weaver capable of such insensitivity. He thought the weaver no better than a dog drawn back to his own sick.

Most painful to bear was Anton's apparent surprise. He seemed genuinely taken aback to discover that Danno should, in the first place, have expected more of him than of the other weavers; that Danno should, secondly, consider his uncalled for attack upon his own silk (Danno guessed this to be the case, since no other Irish silk had been touched) to be more reprehensible than the damage done collectively to the English silks, seemed equally to take the weaver by surprise.

Looking through his watery eyes at the pliantly watering eyes of the weaver, Danno saw no understanding. He could find nothing of significance: only that mechanical imitation of his own tears.

***

Letitia knew, as she stepped from the hired sedan, that she was going beyond what was safe. In her outward actions she might as yet be committing no folly; but by her journey, she had succumbed to the inward lure of sensations never previously experienced. She had been fully aware, as she had sent a servant to call for the sedan, that it would have been considered wiser, given the extraordinary capacity of these new sensations to ignite both her imagination and her body, to have remained at home. Within the confines of her own house, untended, such sensations would eventually have faded and died. But Letitia did not intend to let such sensations die. It seemed to her that the wilful surrender of sensations so buffeting, so shockingly encompassing as these, would be a folly greater than any other.

On her last visit, she had at least taken the precaution of bringing Caroline with her. This time, she was alone. On the last occasion, she had informed her husband, at breakfast, of her intended inspection of the silk. This time, she had kept her plans a secret.

By the time Letitia discovered that the shop was closed, the sedan, so airily dismissed, was too far away to be recalled. A notice on the bolted door apologised to customers for any inconvenience. Stocktaking, the notice continued, was in progress. Letitia stood abandoned on the pavement, protected from the cold by a cape and matching muffler of beaver fur (the gift of her devoted husband), flushed scarlet with mortification. Her position was humiliating. Three days ago, she had been so rash as to commit herself to the possibility of calling upon Danno McKenna today. She had compromised herself by even so tentative a commitment. Now, having completed her folly by arriving, she discovered herself to be of so little significance to the man for whom she had allowed herself to burn (astoundingly) for many days, that he had forgotten their agreement.

Had there been transport to hail, Letitia Sweetman would have hailed it. She would have returned to her home. In time, the demise of those troublesome emotions would have taken place. Her safety could so easily have been assured. But for the length of Dame Street, as far as Letitia's eyes could see in either direction, no transport in which a lady could travel was to be seen. Instead, she decided that she would collect the silk directly from the weaver. There was no reason, she thought defiantly, why she should deny herself the pleasure of that silk (though its possession, she feared, would, in all likelihood, serve only to aggravate those sensations which she must now do her utmost to suppress). By collecting the silk, Danno McKenna would, she knew, realise that she had come. But he would also know that she had gone and that she would not be returning.

An archway between the shop and the McKenna house led into the courtyard. Letitia was relieved to reach its seclusion. A lady, alone, was such a conspicuous thing. On the far side of the empty yard, the door to the warehouse was open.

Half way up the stairs, her courage nearly failed her. What, she suddenly thought, if Danno McKenna himself should be there? How, in such circumstances, would she be able to acquit herself with dignity? But the same thought which made her hesitate, simultaneously urged her forward. For if Danno McKenna was there, how could she bear to leave without seeing him? She continued to climb the stairs, her heart beating with anticipation.

The room was empty.

Letitia's reaction on seeing the ripped silk was similar, in some ways, to Danno's own reaction on the previous day. She ran across the room and knelt down, sinking her knees into her own cast-off fur cape, beside the silk. When Danno entered the room shortly after her, she had gathered the injured pieces into her arms and was crushing them to her face.

From a window in his own house, he had seen her cross the courtyard and had been shamed by the fickleness of his mind which had allowed him both to forget their appointment and to wish, on observing her determined passage towards the ruined silk, that she had not come. Her appearance signalled an effort too immense for him to contemplate. She would be injured by his failure to remember. There would be poutings, flouncings and resistance. She could be won round; they could always be won round. But cajolery in such a cause could not be easily sustained without the accompaniment of desire, and today, Danno lacked all desire. A romance which had seemed overwhelmingly urgent no more than two days before was, today, of no account. It was only by chance that he had seen her at all. He was tempted to do nothing. She would see the destruction; she would ooh and she would aah; and then she would leave. By her behaviour, Letitia Sweetman had promised an affair of interest; but the entire episode, now unavoidably tainted by Anton's treachery, was probably best forgotten.

It was with the greatest reluctance that Danno had followed Letitia. He would make the most formal of apologies to her, promise her a piece of silk comparable to the piece destroyed, and find her a cab with as little delay as possible. Manners compelled him to do that much.

Her response was so unexpected. There was no pretence of injury: no pouting or flouncing. She made no attempt to flirt. Instead, lowering the silk from her face, she looked up at him and there was great pity in her eyes.

"Your very step on the stairs," she told him, "sounded wounded."

He looked at the silk trailing over her shoulder and round her neck. "You've had a wasted journey," he said.

"Perhaps," she said. While she spoke, light ran, like drops of water, along the folds of flimsy silk which trembled round her vibrating throat. "Is this the only damage?"

Danno described, briefly, the state of his stock. "They've brought me close to ruin," he told her.

"Why?" she asked him then.

"Why did the weavers take the action they did?"

Letitia nodded, and a curled feather, protruding upwards from her hat, waved like an insistent question mark. "Surely their objective was not your ruin?"

Pansy had not asked that why; she had asked a different why. Pansy, having stated that hanging was too good for the weavers (a comment made, independently, by his mother), had asked her fiancé why he had not already instituted legal proceedings against the men.

Her papa, she had said, was concerned by his attitude. Mr. McKenna's reluctance to proceed, her papa had said, denoted a worrying weakness of resolve. Their motives for the destruction they had wrought were of no interest to Pansy and her father. It was the weavers' speedy punishment which concerned them. Pansy's father, Danno had deduced from his conversation with the daughter, was having second thoughts about the soundness of his proposed investment. He was worried that by allying his family to the McKenna family, he might be throwing good money after bad.

When he had laid out before her the weavers' grandiose and witless notion that they might, by a concerted action, force the silk merchants of Dublin to cease their purchase of English silks, Letitia's sympathy for the weavers' predicament was intense. Indeed, she seemed as sorry for the weavers as she had initially been for himself. She described their action as akin to the action of a starving animal reduced to feeding off its own leg.

She had continued to kneel on the floor while they spoke. Now she put her hand up and pulled Danno down beside her. She wound coils of wrinkling silk about their wrists.

"This is not an English silk," she said, stroking the silk which bound their hands together. "Why was this destroyed? And who destroyed it?"

"The weaver destroyed it himself."

She shook her head in disbelief. "Not the Frenchman. A thing so painstakingly created as this could not have been destroyed by its own creator."

"He was punishing me," Danno said, "for daring to presume that a friendship existed between us." This had become the only possible explanation for a destruction, otherwise so wantonly inexplicable.

"Did friendship exist?"

"I thought so." Danno shrugged, and their joined wrists shifted. "Obviously, I was mistaken."

Letitia wondered could anyone resist his friendship? She recalled the zeal with which the weaver had worked. The intensity of his concentration. She could not say that the weaver had loved Danno; but she was sure that his work was done with love. She did not believe that the weaver could have hated Danno enough to destroy his own much-loved creation.

"I think the friendship did exist. I think that the friendship between you and — what is his name?"

"Paradis."

"Your friendship aroused jealousy. One of the other weavers destroyed the silk. Not Paradis. Paradis was being punished for crossing forbidden lines. There is always," she added, "someone ready to punish those who cross forbidden lines."

She thought of the clear, dark line drawn for her by her husband. She could arouse, but must not be aroused. Before she met Danno, the line had been invisible. She had been unaware of her own weakness (Marvin, she had discovered, saw such sensations in a woman as weakness), so the line had never been called into play.

She began to unravel the silk which linked them together.

"You know I didn't come here to collect the silk, don't you?" she asked Danno. "And yet, you say my journey has been wasted."

Her voice was regretful and her words were without artifice. Silver harebells glinted between her fingers. Her eyes looked directly at his face.

Danno was unnerved by her lack of dissimulation. She had led the conversation between them at the dinner party. Here, she had taken the initiative again, refusing to play by the recognised rules, and Danno found himself floundering in uncharted and quaking territory. She now sat carelessly on her beaver cape, her knees poking her skirts upwards to a webbed V shape. Festive harebells lay scattered and vibrating about her arms, her breasts, her neck. His interest had been aroused, but events were moving at her dictation, not his. She was making no pretence of relief. She had come here to make love. She had found a chaos sufficient to spoil the chance of such an event taking place, and she was bitterly disappointed; the disappointment showed.

Danno heard the sound of horses in the courtyard below. He rose to his feet and went, tugging at his waistcoat, to look out the window. He began to laugh. He turned back to look at Letitia, stranded, like a person left behind amongst the debris from a picnic.

"Pansy has arrived," he told her. "With her mother. For tea. The mistake is mine. I issued the invitation this morning." It was, he knew, a visit of great strategic importance. The persuasion of the family which stood between Danno McKenna and ruin that his was a connection still worthy of pursuit. That Pansy's father was not (though invited) of the party, seemed a good sign. There was a trusting informality attached to the visit of two unguarded women.

Letitia gazed up at him from the floor. She made no attempt to rise to her feet. Danno was entranced by her refusal to capitulate to curiosity. She must, he was sure, be tempted to view her opposition.

"But you, McKenna," she said, and she spoke without stirring an inch, "have a prior engagement which you can't escape. I am here."

Letitia thought of him always as McKenna; it was a name with urgency in its syllables.

She was right. He could not escape. She had him captured. Had Pansy looked up from the yard below and beckoned to him, he could not have obeyed the summons. He watched Pansy and her mother negotiate the cobbles, pass under the archway and turn around the corner, out of sight. Their close presence lent a wicked piquancy to the occasion. He listened to the silence behind him.

When he turned back, Letitia, undressed as far as her shift, was, with seemingly perfect composure, removing her shoes.

Letitia had remained seated because she was incapable of rising to her feet. She had been in terror that he would leave. From the time he had arrived, she had been in terror that he would leave. She was both fascinated and frightened by the disturbance of her own body in his presence. At first, she had made no effort to control it. Now she believed that it was beyond her control. Much as she had longed for a glimpse of Pansy, she had not trusted her legs to support her upright. Without some relief, she did not see how she could bring herself to go home. Had she been asked to leave, she doubted that she could have obliged. She saw his face, and knew that she would not be called upon to do so. What she had come to do would be done.

The floor of the warehouse was dusty, and the air about them was raw. Clots of dust lodged in their hair; winter skin crept uneasily in the piercing cold. But Letitia said she had to see him and to feel his skin on hers. (She had never seen her husband's body in its entirety; nor had he seen hers. He wore a nightshirt which he raised to no greater height than was demanded. Hers he lifted likewise.) So they undressed completely, kneeling face to face. Sensations which she quite expected to die beneath his scrutiny instead grew more intense. Her belly was in pain for wanting him to put his hands upon her body. But he wouldn't touch her. He was looking at her and he was smiling, but he wouldn't move a hand to touch her.

He wanted to see what she would dare to do. She had led him this far. Let her make the next move too. Her husband, she had said the other day, had described her as a whore. Danno thought now, looking at her half-closed eyes, her hands which, in lieu of his own, had begun to caress her own breasts, that she had the impatience of a whore, but with this difference: whereas the whore was impatient to be finished, Letitia Sweetman was impatient only to be started. As he watched, she moved one hand from her breast and began to knead her own belly with her fingers. Her eyes were now squeezed shut and her teeth were clenched with pain. She was so engorged by desire that she was in danger of bypassing the object of that desire to achieve her own relief.

The situation appealed irresistibly to Danno's sense of the ridiculous. While his fiancée awaited (no doubt with increasing impatience) his arrival for tea, he was kneeling naked, with an erection as hard as jade, on a warehouse floor, watching a woman humiliate herself for want of him. She would, he was sure, come to regret her behaviour. Afterwards they always did. For now, she was quite abandoned to sensation. Well, if he were not to die from an excess of contemplation, he must engage.

She should want him, Danno thought afterwards, but surely not that much. Perhaps he should have felt flattered. Instead, he was intimidated. What had been exhilarating while it occurred, was, in retrospect, ominous. She had exhibited too much abandon. Her enjoyment had been too intense. She had not shown a moment's restraint. Her entire body had been in thrall to sensation. Writhing beneath him on her bed of beaver fur and shredded silk, she had shown such unseemly pleasure, with her kissing, her moaning, her biting and her licking: and words. She had spoken words far too specific to be safe. She had articulated her desires; she had cried menacing words of love; and she had repeatedly and rhythmically panted out the name McKenna. Danno thought, with some heat, that she had shown herself to be an unparalleled libertine in her behaviour. The episode had not corresponded to any sexual experience previously encountered. It had been, Danno feared, an experience to be compulsively resought. He was in danger of becoming trapped in an affair unresponsive to the normal controls.

(Danno was not aware of how deep his own absorption in pleasure had been. Neither he nor Letitia had heard the entrance and retreat of Anton Paradis.)

And now, instead of indulging in post-coital tears and self-recrimination, she was dressing and insisting, most outrageously, that she should be introduced to Pansy.

"I wish to meet your fiancée."

She was as drunk with sex now as she had been with wine at her own table. He watched her cram her hat on top of her disarrayed curls. The angle was not as it had been when he had first seen her that afternoon. He stepped close to her and adjusted it.

"Out of the question," he said.

"Why?"

When she and Danno entered the drawing room, it was obvious to the waiting ladies that the carelessly-dressed Letitia Sweetman was agitated by some emotion. Her cheeks were coloured by a high, feverish sheen and her voice, when she spoke, was afflicted by a most unnatural tremble.

Afterwards, even when she was aware of the cause of the young woman's agitation, Danno's mother expressed surprise at its extent. The loss of the silk was undoubtedly a disappointment; but it was scarcely a calamity sufficient to cause such ferment, particularly when Danno had offered so generously (and so foolishly) to have an identical one woven ("woven by whom?" Letitia had enquired) in its place. Not that she knew Mrs. Sweetman in normal circumstances, and a degree of hysteria was common amongst young married women. Nevertheless, Mrs. McKenna had wondered to her son Danno whether poor Mrs. Sweetman might not be in the early stages of consumption. Danno had agreed that Letitia Sweetman might indeed be in the grip of something devastating. "We must pray that her condition was not contagious," his mother had remarked. "Indeed," her son had agreed drily.

"She was devastated," Danno told the assembled and fractious ladies now, as he stood at Letitia's elbow. "I persuaded her that she should rest for half-an-hour before attempting the journey home."

"I am burdened by delicacy," Letitia announced, leaning deliberately against Danno and fanning her face with a hand. As her fingers fluttered to and fro before her eyes, she glimpsed minute filaments of silk snared in the claws of her diamond ring. She would like to have drawn the fact to Danno's attention. He was attempting to detach himself from her. She pressed closer still. "Mr. McKenna was forced to attend upon me for an hour or more before I was fit to travel even the width of the courtyard below. I sincerely hope, Miss Pansy, that your fiancé shows to you an attention at least the equal of the attention shown to me, the most insignificant of his customers. My fear would be that he might so exhaust himself in the satisfaction of his customers, that there would be little left to offer to those deserving most. He is excessively conscientious in the performance of his duties."

"I think you need not worry on my behalf, Mrs. Sweetman," Pansy said, looking with dislike at Letitia.

"Of course. It is presumptuous of me to question the capacity of a man so generous as Mr. McKenna. The reserves of such a man are infinite. His ability to give could never cease."

The atmosphere was growing uneasy under the influence of Letitia's lush, but suspect, praise, and Mrs. McKenna interrupted abruptly. "Your praise, Mrs. Sweetman, is causing my son's ears to burn. It would be kinder to desist. Would you care for some refreshment? Some chocolate, perhaps?"

"A chair for Mrs. Sweetman, Danno," Pansy said to her fiancé. He was still, despite her papa's qualms, hers to direct. She wondered whether this excessive courtesy of her fiancé towards, as Mrs Sweetman herself had admitted, a customer of no importance, was another instance of what her papa had identified in Danno as a dangerous weakness. "She seems incapable of standing unsupported." Her voice was filled with distrust and she smiled a marble smile. Mrs. Sweetman's legs might be wilting, but her tongue most certainly was not.

Letitia allowed herself to be escorted to a chair, the only empty one, which was positioned between Pansy and her mother and had been intended for Danno himself. His fingers pinched hard and warningly into the flesh of her upper arm as they crossed the room. She recollected where the fingers of that hand had so recently been, and she suppressed with difficulty an urge to laugh. A moment later, the same hand (unwashed) clasped one of Pansy's hands as Danno bent to kiss his fiancée on the cheek, and despite her efforts at self-control (the suspension of breath, the hand which flew upwards to clutch with desperation at her twitching mouth), Letitia broke into shrieks of laughter, laughter for which, on the spur of the moment, she could invent no reasonable explanation. The sight of Danno withdrawing his lips abruptly from his fiancée's face served only to increase her hilarity.

She was aware, helplessly, that she was disgracing herself and that departure was the only appropriate move left to her.

"I think, perhaps," she gasped at Danno, through recurring and apparently senseless peals of laughter, laughter which had, by now, acquired a nightmare relentlessness, "that I had better go home as soon as possible. The afternoon has been too bizarre to assimilate."

As Letitia was about to rise to her feet, tears of mirth (or had they by now become tears of embarrassment?) still trickling down her fiery cheeks, Pansy suddenly shot forward in her chair to stare at something on the shoulder of the beaver fur.

"Good gracious, Mrs. Sweetman," she exclaimed, pointing with her finger, "whatever is that on your fur? It looks for all the world like the slime left after the passage of a slug across grass."

Letitia craned her head sideways to peer in the direction of the pointing finger. Her shoulder appeared perfectly clear to her.

"I can see nothing," she said. She had begun to hiccup in the wake of her laughter.

Pansy's finger came closer.

"There," she said impatiently. "Almost under your chin."

As Letitia pulled her fur away from her neck to see its shoulder the more conveniently, Pansy's finger was smeared by the offending substance. She withdrew it with a small cry of disgust,

103

rubbing frantically at it with her thumb, and, subsequently, with her mother's handkerchief.

"Who rubbeth now, who froteth now his lippes

With dust, with sond, with straw, with cloth, with chippes . . ."

The fur was matted with cold semen.

The substance which Pansy was, like the lovesick Absolon in retreat from his humiliating night time encounter with the arse of the carpenter's wife, so urgently trying to remove, not from her lips, but from her finger, was (in Pansy's case) her own fiancé's seminal fluid.

Not that Pansy knew its nature.

Her mother, the inflexibly lady-like, but curious Mrs. Roche, peering closely at the fur and sniffing, knew at once, but found the knowledge so unbelievable that she ignored the evidence of her nose and eyes.

"Mrs Sweetman leaned against a snail, perhaps, and crushed it?" she remarked doubtfully. All the unpleasant eruptions of nature were, at heart, she decided, as she continued to stare and to sniff, so similar.

Letitia, whose laughter had precariously subsided, did not dare to look at Danno as she said, "Mr. McKenna, could you, perhaps, come with me to the street and call me a sedan? I really feel quite overwhelmed by my afternoon. A ruined silk, a ruined fur. I must leave before my reputation itself comes under attack."

Around her, the ladies murmured faintly (far too faintly) in protest.

"No chocolate, Mrs. Sweetman? No tea?"

Mrs. McKenna only asked the question because she was sure of the answer.

Letitia could not bring herself to admit that the encounter had been a mistake. She leaned against the hall door and indulged herself in paroxysms of laughter.

"You were insupportable." Danno told her.

She pointed at the stain and Danno himself, unwillingly, began to laugh with her.

"When have you last been so entertained?" she challenged him. "Has your mind not been distracted from your troubles?"

"Your behaviour in the presence of my fiancée may have done nothing but increase them."

"She has no right to exist in that capacity," Letitia said with a sudden burst of impatience. "How can you contemplate marriage to so prim and humourless a young woman?"

"One could tolerate a great deal worse than Pansy Roche for the securing of a lesser fortune. She is pretty and I am told that she is entirely loveable."

"Pansies tied by a ribbon in a posy are also pretty things," Letitia said dismissively.

"But a posy doesn't come with a fortune attached."

"A Pansy valued by the guinea."

It was detestable to be jealous of what one despised. Pansy's proprietary air had been unbearable. However ludicrous her assumption of authority over her fiancé might have seemed in the light of what had taken pace between Danno and Letitia, it was grounded in the unassailable fact of their betrothal. After she, Letitia, had gone, McKenna would return to his fiancée. Pansy would ridicule their departed visitor and McKenna would say nothing in her defence. He might even come to agree. Letitia was afraid now. She had probably intimidated him by her recklessness. She had represented herself as entertainment at too high a price. Her action had probably only served to make him value his fiancée's dullness more highly. He would look at his pretty, docile Pansy and consider himself to have had a lucky escape from detection.

"Will you be able to behave more circumspectly before your husband?" he asked her now, and his apprehension irritated her.

"You're afraid, aren't you?"

He nodded without hesitation.

She laughed. Now that she was due to leave his presence, she was terrified. However meekly she carried herself, how could her husband possibly fail to detect that momentous events had taken place in the course of her afternoon? The fact that Danno considered her incapable of concealment caused her terror to increase. Her laughter was an heroic effort to appear insouciant.

Danno saw no reason to deny his apprehension.

"I find no entertainment in the notion of duelling with an outraged spouse," he told her coldly.

"Oh, such timidity!" She flicked a finger stingingly against his cheek and smiled without sympathy when he winced. "I had thought you a much worthier playmate than that, McKenna! You need have no fears. Your demise is not imminent."

Even were her husband to guess an assignation, she would never betray the name. And were he to discover the name, it would not be by means of a duel that Marvin Sweetman would seek his revenge. He was not a fighting man. He would be too afraid for his own life to call a rival to a duel.

Danno was piqued by her tone of contempt.

"Are you afraid of nothing?" he challenged.

"I was afraid of dying without living," she told him, surprising herself by the unexpectedness of her response, "But now I no longer have that fear."

"It meant that much?"

"Yes," she said, without dissemblance.

"Why me?"

"You appeared," she said, "at the right moment."

Sometimes her humour cut too close to the bone. Such a remark, made without the tremor of a smile, could disconcert the unprepared.

"Fortunate for me," he said. "Unfortunate for any whose chance, apparently equal to my own, was foiled by my fortuitous appearance."

"Exactly," she said. "Who can guess the powers of those who failed to appear?"

When she had left, the fear that she might have meant precisely what she had said tormented Danno unbearably and made him immune to the influence of Pansy's comments concerning the shocking Mrs. Sweetman. He sat beside Pansy. He looked at her while she talked, and he did not see her. (While Pansy's comments grew more strident the less notice her fiancé took of them, until she had to be hushed sharply by her mother, Danno's mother was at pains to explain to the visiting ladies that her son was not himself. The loss of silk preyed deeply on his mind.) Danno's mind was completely occupied by Letitia. The idea that she might have responded with equal passion to any personable young man who happened to appear at the right moment was so outrageous. If any young man would have sufficed, who was to say that he could not be dislodged by some fresh suitor as easily as dust by sneezing. The idea that she might use men as easily as he was accustomed to using women was most unsettling. This uneasiness whetted his desire more surely than any declaration of immoveable devotion could have done.

***

Letitia thought the notion outrageous herself.

It nevertheless remained a possibility, hypocritical to deny, that another young man could have aroused in Letitia sensations just as uncontrollable as those which happened to have been aroused by Danno McKenna. He had appeared at an opportune moment. But suppose he hadn't come? Suppose someone else had appeared in his stead? What if love were at the mercy of no more than chance? Marvin would say that nothing happened by chance. Everything was either the work of God, or the work of the Devil. But what if he was wrong? Their marriage, he said, had been ordained by God. She found that difficult to believe. It had taken place for such worldly reasons. She could accept the wisdom of calling upon God to bless their marriage precisely because it had not been ordained by Him. Why, she wondered defiantly, as she swayed inside the closed sedan, dampening her handkerchief with her tongue and rubbing at the matted fur which lay across her knees, should God have been so perverse as to provide her with a body capable of such astonishing passion only to marry her off to a man who could not arouse it?

SEVEN

There were people that Marvin Sweetman wished he had never known. Danno McKenna was a good example of such a person. He, Marvin Sweetman, was probably one of the most progressive Protestants you could find in the City of Dublin. For the sake of his own progressive principles, he had alienated many of his former friends, and had ruined any chances he might have had of furthering his career through Castle favours. Now it seemed that he was to be vilified by the United Irishmen as well.

As far as he was concerned, it was the aims of the United Irishmen which had changed. His principles had remained the same. He had supported (fearfully) full emancipation for Catholics; but within the existing framework. It appeared that his fears were fully justified. Parliamentary reform was no longer a sufficient goal for the Catholics. The hasty recall of that fool Lord Fitzwilliam (who, on taking up the appointment of Viceroy, had so airily and so unjustifiably promised full emancipation to Catholics) was still, two years later, being used by the now clandestine United Irishmen to substantiate claims that so long as the British connection remained to prop up the Protestant Ascendancy in Ireland, Irish Catholics would never be emancipated. However, it was being said in some quarters that absolute separation had always been the aim of the United Irishmen. It certainly had not been Marvin Sweetman's aim. He would never have joined an organisation professing such aims.

But who was going to believe him now? Certainly not his former Protestant friends; while today, in the Exchange Coffee House, he had been approached by a friend of McKenna, a man he hardly knew, and had been accused of suffering a failure of nerve. It seemed that the entertainment of one of their number to dinner was not sufficient to quell their suspicions; or perhaps it was that Danno McKenna had done nothing to persuade his colleagues of

Marvin Sweetman's essential goodwill. How far was his entertainment of McKenna supposed to go before McKenna would deign to show his appreciation?

The man at the Exchange had argued so cajolingly. He had assured Marvin that separation was not the aim of the United Irishmen.

"The aim (which you claim to subscribe to) is Catholic Emancipation," he had whispered soothingly to Marvin, bending solicitously over him, while tapping on the table top with Marvin's coffee spoon. "If emancipation is only to be achieved through separation from Britain, then separation must be sought. But in such circumstances, separation is no more than the necessary means to an end. Your principles should not be affected."

He had said other things.

"I'm not prepared to pursue my principles through illegal means," Marvin had whispered back eventually, stiffly and reluctantly. It had been more than he had wished to admit, but it had been clear that the man, who had remained on his feet throughout, nudging periodically at Marvin's thigh with his knee to make a point, had not been about to leave without a reply. Marvin guessed that he had been sent and he had wondered if McKenna had been told. McKenna's friend was not a man in whose company Marvin cared to be seen. "I should not be harassed for that," he had added. "Nor should I be suspected of treachery for being prepared to go so far but no further. I am an administrator of the law. In my view the legal means have not yet been exhausted. Emancipation will come. It may take longer than anticipated, but . . ."

"I'm surprised you're not in the uniform of a Yeoman," McKenna's friend had said to him contemptuously before turning on his heel.

Marvin believed that Danno's friend had lied to him. He believed that separation was now (and perhaps had always been in the eyes of certain of the founders) the primary aim of the United Irishmen.

He had been shaken by his encounter. He knew that he had been goaded into admitting too much. He had gathered from the conversation that it was not possible to withdraw honourably. Anyone who withdrew became a threat. The more engaged one had been, the more information one possessed, and the greater the threat one posed. The further the United Irishmen ventured beyond the limits to which Marvin had been prepared to go, the more his loyalty was likely to be eroded, and the more likely it was that he could be persuaded to disgorge all he knew to the government.

Marvin was frightened, because by believing their own analysis, they forced him to act in accordance with it. Believing him to be a threat, they could best secure his silence by disposing of him. Unless he could find a way to convince them of his goodwill, he would be forced to look to the government for protection; and the government would not protect him without reason. He did not want to become an informer, God knew; but still less did he want to die a fool.

***

Letitia had chosen a fortunate day on which to betray her husband.

Despite the lateness of her homecoming, he had been later still. This was the first piece of good fortune of which Letitia herself was aware. He was out at a time when he would normally have been at home. His absence allowed her time to soothe her flushed face and to wash from her body the incongruous odours of love. Back within the confines of her house, she found herself frightened by the ease with which she had jeopardised her own comfort. It had been no more than a game, she reminded herself desperately, as she dressed for dinner: a trivial game, a game not worth repeating. Real life lay safely within marriage. She would take no further risks.

Her second piece of good fortune was that any agitation Marvin Sweetman did notice in his wife (and he was capable of noticing very little) he presumed to be felt on his account.

In fact, she found him ridiculous. It was his own fault that she should find him so. He had concealed from her so thoroughly the depth of his commitment to radical politics. Now he wished her to believe that his life was in danger because of these very commitments; that people like Danno McKenna would kill him for his failure to go one step further.

"They want me to back revolution."

It was ludicrous. He could not expect her to believe that anyone saw Marvin Sweetman as a potential revolutionary. For the second time that day, Letitia found herself called upon to suppress an inappropriate surge of laughter. On this second occasion she was more successful, though her eyes grew tear-filled with the effort. Those gleaming eyes gave to her face an air of great sympathy. Marvin, she could tell, was comforted by her demeanour.

"Surely they know you better than that?"

They were alone in the sitting room. He laid his head down on her shoulder and began, unexpectedly, to fondle one damask-concealed breast. She lost all desire to laugh. With great effort, she prevented herself from shrinking back from his touch.

"They assume that those who are not for them are against them." His breath blew warm and damp on her bare collarbone while, beneath his lolling head, her neck grew sticky with his perspiration.

"But that's unfair!" she exclaimed, as his sweat trickled slowly down her skin. "Instead of denouncing you, they should be praising you for having dared to accompany them so far. I should have thought that your temerity must have greatly exceeded their expectations."

His hand was beneath the damask now, kneading insistently at her partially-exposed bosom. He had never behaved in such a way before outside the bedroom. Her sympathy, it seemed, was overwhelming him. He was losing all sense of propriety. She expected her breast to ooze out between his hot fingers. She found his attentions repulsive. Then she recalled the desperation with which her own hands had moved over her breasts that afternoon, her complete abandon, and was struck by the incongruity of her condemnation of her husband's lack of propriety within his own house, towards his own wife. She began to giggle hysterically.

She could have chosen no more effective weapon. Marvin removed his hand from within her bodice as swiftly as though it had been touched by fire, and sat up straight. He glanced nervously towards the door as he did so; in fear, Letitia supposed, of having been surprised by a servant. Once planted, she thought with relief, such fear would keep him from any further advances in such public terrain.

"There is some humour to be salvaged from my situation? Something I've missed?"

He detested laughter at his own expense.

She shook her head. "I'm so sorry," she gasped. "Tickles! You touched a sensitive spot."

"Oh, for heaven's sake!"

Letitia shrugged and moved further away from him.

"Such childishness."

"I'm sorry," Letitia said again. "Such reactions are beyond my control."

He sighed and, for want of anything better to knead, began to knead his scalp with both his hands. "They're putting me in such an impossible position, Letitia. I don't want to bring harm to anyone. I just want to be left in peace by both sides." He began to cry.

Letitia saw for the first time how someone so harmless, so apparently well-meaning as her husband, could pose a threat serious enough to warrant his destruction. It was not her husband's sincerity which was in doubt. It was his courage. They had never mistaken him for a revolutionary. They feared him as a coward.

"I saw Mr. McKenna today," she said suddenly, and her mouth grew dry around the words.

"Why?" he asked suspiciously. "Why today?"

McKenna was capable of using a wife to trap her husband; without her ever being aware of having been so used.

"My silk," she replied with ease. "It was to have been ready . . ."

"But wasn't?"

He sounded excited.

She shook her head.

"And won't be," she said flatly.

She knew what he had been about to ask of her. Marvin too was capable of using a wife; of that she was quite aware.

McKenna was a man whose courage she would not doubt. McKenna, she also recognised, was a man who would not hesitate to kill a man who threatened his cause. He was a man to whom she did not believe she could bring herself to appeal on her husband's behalf. If her husband was a genuine threat, then men like McKenna were his target. She could not ask McKenna to trust Marvin Sweetman. She did not trust him herself.

"My poor Marvin," she said, and her pity for the frightened, tear-stained man beside her was genuine. Fear was as corrosive as the most gripping of diseases. Looking at him, she saw how a person could die of fear alone.

"McKenna likes you," he whispered to her from his end of the sofa. "You charmed him at our table. You could speak to him on my behalf. He would listen to you."

She shook her head hastily. "I have no cause to meet him."

"Create one," he pleaded, stretching his arm out to touch her.

"But he'll think . . ."

"He'll think whatever you believe it is necessary for him to think. Why this reluctance?" Marvin spoke sharply now. "No impropriety endured for my sake can fail to be forgiven. You have no cause to hesitate."

She looked at her husband in astonishment. "Are you actually proposing me for a whore to save your skin?"

"It would never come to that!" He looked uncomfortable as she continued to stare at his reddening face. "I doubt indeed t'would ever come to that! McKenna is a gentleman and certainly my one-time friend. He would not do injury to a friend by violating his wife. Besides, I trust your skills. You are capable of extracting what you want on your own terms."

Letitia stood up.

"I think," she said coldly, "that fear has warped your judgement. What you propose is quite impossible."

She was already in the hall when she heard him shout out after her: "If you loved me, such a proposal would not be impossible."

She returned as far as the doorway.

"I believe it would make no difference," she answered quietly.

It was true that she did not love him. But would she have made such an admission had it not been for the afternoon's events? And had she been asked to prostitute herself on her husband's behalf to any man other than Danno McKenna, would her anger have been so intense?

She lay on her bed, afraid that he would follow after her. He did not come, but her fear did not subside. She knew that he would come that night. Before this afternoon, she had not considered how she might cope with her husband's legitimate attentions. It had not occurred to her that she might no longer be able to face them so equably.

There was a knocking at the door. Oh God, she thought. Oh God. But it was not Marvin. It was Caroline. Caroline had heard her father shouting at Mama and Caroline was afraid.

"My father is angry with you."

She stood by Letitia's bed, biting her lip nervously. She had a small weal on her lower lip from nipping continuously at the same place with her eye tooth. It was a habit which her step-mother had been unable to cure her of.

"Yes, darling. But you don't have to worry. His anger will pass."

"He didn't punish you?"

Letitia laughed. "No, sweetheart. Of course not!" Caroline's worries were sometimes so refreshingly childish.

"He used to punish me when I angered him."

"Well, naturally he did. You were a child then, and children have to be punished. You know that."

"Yes."

She looked so apprehensive.

Caroline had certainly inherited one trait from her father, Letitia thought cruelly. She had inherited his cowardice. Letitia was immediately ashamed of the thought, and sat up on her bed to hug the girl hovering so nervously beside her. "But he won't punish me," she said firmly, and then she added, laughing, "And he won't punish you because he's angry with me."

"No?"

"Oh Caroline!" Letitia exclaimed impatiently, giving the girl a shake. "Don't be so ridiculous." Then she kissed her step-daughter's pale cheek. "Now go to bed before I get angry with you myself."

"I could sleep with you," the girl offered, her voice bright and high with tension. "I would be company, should Father remain angry."

Letitia shook her head. "I'll see you in the morning, Caroline," she said firmly. Caroline left the room reluctantly. Sometimes her step-daughter's timidity wearied Letitia immeasurably.

It was comical, Letitia thought, while waiting for Marvin to appear. She had been given permission to seduce the man she had just seduced, and with whom she had already, she feared, fallen in love. But she found herself quite unable to use this permission to her advantage. She could not mislead Marvin into thinking that she was seducing McKenna on his behalf. She knew she would not plead for him and she could not allow him to believe himself, falsely, to be safe.

She had to see McKenna again; she could not stop herself from seeing him. But it was more important than ever before that their meetings should be concealed from Marvin.

EIGHT

❧

Dear Sir, I fear that the Government has gauged the intensity of my devotion to the Crown only too well. It is known that I will serve just as loyally without as with reward or any hope of it. But oh, Dear Sir, do you not think it is too cruel that I should be taken advantage of thus, when all about me, the most despicable of brigands line their pockets amply with the Crown's gold, in return for the merest crumbs of information? I can only hope that what I am about to pass on to your good self will soften even those most obdurate hearts?

My good weaver has been in touch with me again, on a matter which he described to me in advance as being of some urgency (though not so urgent that it could not wait until a further sum of money had been placed directly in his purse by me). I shall put the story before you and leave you to judge its urgency for yourself. There has been a tremendous falling out between Mr. McKenna, the silk merchant, and his French weaver. From being the closest of friends, they have become the deadliest of enemies. You may ask how such a sudden change has come about. It seems that the Frenchman, angered by some imagined injustice perpetrated upon the weavers by their employer, fomented a combination amongst the weavers against McKenna. His fellow-weavers took up the struggle with more enthusiasm than the French man had bargained for. As a result, McKenna is said to be a ruined man. Contrary to the Frenchman's expectations, he was not forgiven for his part in the destruction (who but a Frenchman could be so conceited as to expect forgiveness in such circumstances?). Instead, he was dismissed without compunction. My informant (whose name must at no time be mentioned as the source of this information) believes the Frenchman to be bearing a grudge great enough to be of use to the Government. He believes that if the Frenchman were to be picked up and charged with being a Defender that he would be prepared to divulge much interesting information concerning his erstwhile employer, and to back up his accusations in court, in return for very little by way

116

of clemency. However, my informant believes it to be essential that the Government acts with speed. He fears the Frenchman plans to leave the country. I leave the matter to your discretion, my Dear Sir, and would remind you only that the Frenchman's wife is, and always has been, a loyal supporter of the Government. For this reason, my informant begs that any arrest made should take place at some distance from the Paradis establishment.

I am, Sir, your Devoted Servant . . .

***

Anton actually felt better once he had seen the destruction wrought upon the silk. What he had seen not only explained Danno's behaviour towards him; it also gave him hope that the friendship could be salvaged. It wounded him that Danno could think him capable of such an act of personal hatred, yet he could not blame Danno for his conclusion. He had committed the other acts of abuse without demur. He followed Danno's reasoning. In a way, who else but Anton could have committed that final, uncalled for, act? To whom else could it have had such meaning?

Anton was entitled, by the terms of the marriage settlement drawn up by his uncle, to work at the Paradis workshop. Should orders be in short supply, Anton was entitled to take work at the expense of any weaver in Charlotte's employ. Anton was not, however, a fool. When he was dismissed from Danno's workshop, no weaving was offered to him in his wife's workshop; he did not press his claim.

He pined, whether as an artist or as a craftsman, for his work. The loom in Danno's warehouse was his own, but he dared not send for it for fear that Danno would oblige. As long as it remained there, Anton felt that the chance of reconciliation still existed.

In his wife's kitchen, where he spent most of his time, Caitlín assaulted him with love. He resisted her assaults heroically.

"Why?" she asked him in despair.

"Decency," he told her. "There's been little enough decency in this house."

"Do you not want me?" she asked.

"That's not the point. I am your guardian. I cannot despoil what I have been set to guard."

Her brother, it seemed, had more control over her destiny than Caitlín herself.

"But what if I want you?"

That, apparently, was not the point either.

"In the circumstances, you cannot be said to be a free agent."

"You should have been a lawyer, Mr. Paradis. You have too many arguments for such a simple dispute."

He was quite unreasonably chaste, but Caitlín did not lose hope entirely. His circumstances, she could see, were about to change. When that change took place she would, she was sure, secure him as her lover.

Caitlín thought that Lucien Paradis was drawing closer to death. She gave him no more than a month. She had, she said on the day she made this pronouncement to Anton, an eye for such things. "And so has Charlotte," she added. "She's afraid you'll do something rash."

"I know."

He sighed. He did not want to talk of Charlotte. He had more important things on his mind. There was a cell meeting that night. He was frightened to go and he was frightened to stay away. What if Danno was there? He wanted to see Danno alone; but so far his courage had failed him. He was so afraid that what he said might make no difference. Danno might accept Anton's assurances concerning the silk, but still find the friendship beyond revival.

Caitlín knew nothing of the meeting. She understood a different apprehension from his silence.

"Get out before they drive you out," she told him.

He heard the urgency in her voice and recalled their conversation. She was right. He should leave. They might not wait for Lucien's death before they turned on him. After tonight, his future might appear more clearly.

"Would you come with me?"

It was the furthest he was prepared to go in impropriety.

"What other choice do I have?" she asked provocatively. "You tell me I'm not a free agent in the matter."

She caught his hand suddenly, and pulled it up to her face. He allowed it to lie limp in her own hand, and she drew it lingeringly across her cheek.

"My skin is soft, isn't it?" she remarked to him. "Don't waste time, Anton. Such softness does not last long."

***

He would speak to Danno. If necessary, he would kneel to Danno. He would not cease from his pleadings until their friendship was restored. Anton was determined, as he walked to the meeting, that the night would not pass without the first move being made. If Danno was not at the meeting, then Anton would call upon him at home. If Danno refused to see him, then Anton would kneel upon the very doorstep until Danno took pity. He would lodge there for as many days as were required.

But Anton never reached the meeting.

Close by the Castle gate, he was arrested.

He was given no reason for his arrest. They locked him into a cell and allowed his fear to grow. At intervals, grey food, and water clouded with dirt, were passed wordlessly through a hole in the door. The same hand which passed him the filled plates hung through the hole, waiting for the emptied receptacles of earlier meals. At first, Anton had returned the food untouched. Then he realised that food returned came back, older, but otherwise unchanged, the following day. He changed his strategy; he created of his uneaten food small neat mounds around the edge of his cell. Silky-furred rats with long, bare tails, came to feed unhurriedly on the waste. Anton guessed that he had succumbed to a familiar and recurring pattern. The cell smelt foully of his own bodily waste (far too copious for the amounts of food and liquid that he consumed) which lay, unemptied, in an open bucket. Lice multiplied in his hair and in his new, young beard. They laid eggs in the seams of his clothes, in the cracks of his skin, and on his eyelashes. He was forced by itch to tear at his skin with his nails until it bled. Sometimes, he would caress his scabby arms with his hands and would recollect the softness of Caitlín's briefly

119

touched face. Her warning, so flippantly given, that such softness would not last for long, haunted him now.

Did Charlotte know where he was? And if she did, had she taken any steps to secure his release, or was she content to let him lie? Once, he could have relied on Danno's help; now Danno would be unaware that he was missing. Danno would have attributed Anton's absence from that meeting to cowardice. Of all those outside who knew him, only Caitlín could be relied upon to seek him out; but Caitlín was only the daughter of a dead journeyman. She had no influence.

Being unaware of the reason for his arrest, he couldn't settle on any plan either for his own defence or for the protection of others. Who was he supposed to be protecting? Weavers who had dared to combine? Fellow Defenders? And what was he to be accused of, in either capacity? As he grew weaker and more fearful, the ability to concentrate deserted him; then his memory itself began to fail. He knew that there were names which must not, under any circumstances, be mentioned, but he couldn't remember what any of those names were. And if he couldn't commit the names to be forgotten to memory, then how could he ensure against their being inadvertently blurted out if they floated unexpectedly to the surface of his mind with no warning attached?

He suffered thus for thirteen, or possibly fourteen days. (In the twilight of his cell, the count quickly grew uncertain.)

At the end of this inexactly-determined period, Anton was taken from his cell by two guards and was led upstairs and along a corridor which was unpainted, to a corridor which was not only painted, but whose floor was covered in thin, darkly-patterned carpeting, to a closed door. One of the guards opened it and stepped inside, saluting. While the first guard said loudly, "Mr. Paradis, Sir," the second guard pushed Anton into the room from behind. The first guard saluted a second time, skirted round Anton, and left the room, closing the door behind him.

Anton was left alone, in a plushly furnished office, with two unknown men who faced him from behind a large desk of walnut and green leather.

The two men, one fat and one thin, had such cultivated voices. They spoke gently in accents akin to that of his former employer and former friend, Danno McKenna (one name he remembered, at least), and their faces, as they viewed their prisoner, were filled with concern. Anton was humiliated to stand before them, stinking, his skin torn open by the frantic scratching of his own fingernails, while they talked to him so courteously.

"My dear Sir, we had no idea you were here." The thin man spoke in a voice wrung by guilt. "No one bothered to tell us." He stared at the scratching Anton, sighed and shook his head with regret. "There are so many prisoners these days. It's difficult to keep track. The most terrible oversights take place with distressing frequency; yours is by no means the worst. There was a poor chap up here last week, standing just where you are standing now. Mind gone completely. Couldn't get any sense out of him. He just drooled and stared. He'd been lost in the system for nearly a year. He's back with his family now, but . . . and his arrest, you know, had come about through the malice of a man he thought his friend. But that's the way it is these days. One soon finds out, in times of turmoil, how cheaply one's friends can be bought."

During his friend's apologetic speech, the fat man had pressed a scented handkerchief to his nostrils. He spoke from behind its folds.

"But still. At least we discovered Mr. Paradis in time."

"We must ensure that he doesn't get lost again."

"We would offer you a chair, Mr. Paradis, but unfortunately, we have none here that are not upholstered, and . . ."

"I understand," Anton whispered. He had not spoken for two weeks and his voice was unstable.

"We should have given you time to clean up, but, having discovered you, we were so anxious to speak to you, I'm afraid we selfishly put our own convenience first."

"I'm sure Mr. Paradis understands our anxiety," the fat man said consolingly to the thin man. "He knows our need for information in these treacherous times."

The thin man nodded. "Reliable information," he added enthusiastically. "But I can promise you, Mr. Paradis, that as soon as we're through here, you will be permitted to bathe and change your clothes. Fresh clothes of your size have already been chosen."

"We should send for a meal," the fat man interrupted, removing the handkerchief from his nose for the sake of clarity. "Mr. Paradis looks quite emaciated." He replaced the handkerchief and took a noisy breath.

"How kind," Anton whispered, and his eyes filled with tears.

"The least we could do, dear Sir, to make amends." The thin man's voice was fruity with kindness. "The least."

Anton found it difficult to remain on his feet. His body was much weakened by his period in gaol. He hoped the interview would not last long. He did not wish to embarrass these people by falling to their floor when the chairs about them remained empty; though indeed, had they offered him a chair, his own good manners would have forced him to refuse. "What can I tell you?" he asked, looking earnestly from one man to the other.

"A great deal, we hope," said the thin man, and a smile severed his face.

Never before had Anton found his own smell repulsive: but he did now. Within the cell, its intensity had been masked by the greater intensity of the waste bucket; here there was no camouflage. He would die if he was returned to his cell without a bath; he would die if he was returned to his cell. He wanted to oblige these two well-meaning men, but they were giving him no help. "I can think of nothing you might wish to know," he said and he burst into tears. "I don't even know why I'm here!"

It was apparently the wrong comment to have made. The atmosphere changed at once.

"It's amazing," the fat man remarked to the thin man, "how often the same, unimaginative ploy is used. And by men from whom one hoped, if not for truth, at least for some well-executed invention."

The thin man had picked up two quill pens in his hands. He pumped the shaft of the smaller quill impatiently up and down inside the shaft of the bigger quill. "Come now, Mr. Paradis. Let us be serious." His voice was raised and all warmth had disappeared from his face. "Let us by-pass these tiresome preliminaries. Your membership of a subversive organisation is not in doubt, either to you or to ourselves. We want the names of your fellow members."

The two guards had re-entered the room, as if on cue. They stood, one on either side of Anton.

Anton shook his head confusedly, tears still spilling from his eyes. He could not believe that their concern had been no more than a pretence. He had not expected deceit from such refined men. He was no more than a weaver of silk. These were the men who wore such silks. He was desperate to give what assistance he could, but they were asking him to reveal the very things which had disappeared most firmly from his mind. At last he remembered something. "My brothers," he said with a tremulous smile of relief. "They were all my brothers."

To a degree, his interlocutors remained gentlemen. Gentlemen of higher refinement would have left the room. But the fat man did go so far as to turn his head away from certain sights, while on those same occasions, the thin man pressed his hands together very tightly and appeared to pray.

They were convinced that pain could revive the memory.

Over a three day period, they tried their best to do so. Under their direction, the two guards crushed Anton's hands, his weaver's hands. They broke his toes, one by one. They burnt his genitals with lighted tapers. They extracted (with difficulty) two nails from the broken fingers of his right hand. Anton's memory did not improve. When they finally told him that it had been Danno McKenna who had betrayed him to the Castle, the name no longer meant anything to him, and the lie served no immediate purpose. "The bastard," he mouthed, as one would mouth of any traitor, but the information was incapable of moving him to any act of revenge. McKenna had vanished from his mind. Knowing his cowardice, Anton's mind had taken steps to protect its information. In the end, he defeated them. They were all too exhausted to continue. He was returned to his cell. Another month, it was felt, would make him more amenable. They were, privately, astounded by his tenacity. Neither had thought him capable of such bravery.

In his cell, burning with pain and fever, his hands cradled in his armpits, his toes setting to grotesque shapes, Anton hovered somewhere between living and dying and tried desperately to remember names. Nothing came to him.

The second loss of Anton was genuine. He had not been forgotten, but other, more pressing, matters had taken priority and he was not recalled for questioning as soon as had been intended. Instead, a bureaucratic error occurred. Six weeks after that first interrogation, Anton, still alive, and balanced awkwardly on his newly aligned toes, was sent accidentally, with a batch of other prisoners, before an examining magistrate who, under the protection of the Insurrection Act of 1796, dispatched Anton, as a disorderly person, untried, to the fleet.

**

Danno did know where Anton was.

Caitlín had come to him to look for Anton. The weaver had gone out to seek Danno's forgiveness, hadn't he? So that was where he must be. When he was not to be found there, she stood before Danno and accused him of having driven Anton away without a hearing.

"He never arrived," Danno told her gently. He had not been told of Caitlín. He had no idea of what importance she was to the weaver; but Anton's importance to her was undeniable. And then, because he needed to know, he asked did Anton deny having ruined the silk?

"Anton destroy his own work? How could you think such a thing of him?" she asked Danno contemptuously. "Do you not know him at all?"

Her conviction shamed him.

"My judgement has been gravely disturbed," he admitted, and then he added defensively. "Besides, what Anton did do was unforgivable."

"You don't believe that," she told him shortly, then she clung onto his arm. "Find him, Mr. McKenna," she begged. "Please find him. He's heartbroken for the lack of your friendship. It's your imagined hatred that he's hiding from."

It had not occurred to Caitlín that Anton might have been arrested. She was ignorant of his political involvement.

But Danno knew quite well where Anton was. He also thought he knew who might have put him there.

When he asked was Charlotte Paradis looking for her husband, Caitlín looked at him. "What do you think?" she asked.

A couple of days later she informed him that Lucien Paradis had suffered a second stroke. He was still alive, but was no longer capable of speech. Malachi had moved into the house. She, Caitlín, had been told to leave. Still Danno kept his suspicion to himself. There was no point in revealing a suspicion unless he could gain some benefit from the revelation. Confronting Malachi Delaney would not release Anton. Therefore, it was better that Malachi should continue to think himself unsuspected. Instead, Danno (not guessing the vulnerability of his own position) tried himself to have the weaver released.

Had he known it, his efforts (and they were tireless) worsened Anton's plight. His interference merely served to confirm the closeness of the relationship between the two men to the authorities. His only deed that could definitely be said to have been to Anton's benefit was his employment of Caitlín as a serving assistant in his greatly depleted shop.

Eventually, Danno was told of Anton's proposed transportation. It was the first confirmation he had been given of Anton's continued existence. Up to then, he had not even been sure that Anton was in prison. A warder, for a substantial bribe, divulged not only the fact of the transportation, but also let Danno know the date on which it was to take place. Because the bribe had been so substantial, he was generous enough as to warn Danno against making any further enquiries. "Your friend was meant to swing," he told Danno. "He was not intended for the fleet. The mistake has so far not been discovered." The warder refused to take any messages, written or verbal. Nor would he carry any food. "Don't press me, Mr. McKenna," he warned. "Any attention given to your friend places him in jeopardy."

The warder said nothing of Anton's injuries. A man with such injuries as his had little chance of surviving the rigours of the fleet; but there was no point in distressing the man's friends unnecessarily. Best to let him be gone and forgotten about.

Danno could not afford not to believe the warder.

He told Caitlín nothing until the day that Anton was to set sail out of Dublin Bay, in a prison ship, bound for that section of the fleet which lay at the Nore. He could not have trusted her to refrain from action. The best he had been able to do was to hire a small boat in which he and she tipped and rocked on a cluttered sea, a sea churning with the small wakes and cross-currents of a hundred other hired vessels which circled the anchored prison ship. From within their flimsy containers, the women (it was mostly women) mourned the imprisoned, invisible men. The men were leaving. The bulk of them would die at sea. The women engulfed the still unmoving ship with sorrow. Loud and plaintive as the calls of seabirds were the cries with which the women buried their still-to-be-drowned men. Listening, Danno thought his heart might break, split in two by the piercing bitterness of the sound.

Once, Caitlín ceased to weep and, with her hair curling tightly in the damp, salty air, stood upright in the boat, and moved towards its edge with the air of one determined to walk on water. Danno caught at her coat and pulled her back down beside him.

"Anton was reprieved from the noose," he told her. "He is meant to live. Wait for him."

"He'll die out here," she said, gesturing at the delicately frolicking sea about them. "The noose might have been kinder." She began to weep again.

The atmosphere about them was too laden with despair. He was sorry they had come.

While Danno rowed back to shore, Caitlín lay against his knees, her face pale with unhappiness and the unaccustomed motion of the boat. Water slopped about her feet.

"I loved him," she whispered to Danno, as though Anton was already dead.

"I loved him too," Danno told her bleakly. Retreating from that formidable, silent ship, he was too desolate to give her hope.

***

Anton, lying with two hundred others in a poorly-ventilated hold for forty men, deep within the ship, heard no murmur of his public wake.

***

Contrary to the quite legitimate expectations of the warder, it was Anton's injuries which saved him; his injuries and the fact that he was joining the Navy in a period of extraordinary ferment.

Certain naval officers at the Nore were, towards the end of April, 1797, feeling apprehensive about their continued safety on board their own ships.

A blockade of the Dutch fleet at Texel was planned, under the command of Admiral Duncan. But by the time Anton joined the *Conqueror* (a ship of sixty-four guns, which lay waiting at the Great Nore under orders to join the main squadron of the North Sea Fleet at Yarmouth), the fleet at Spithead was in the grip of a mutiny. In the eyes of some, the Spithead mutineers were being pandered to. Negotiations were being permitted between the ringleaders and the Board of the Admiralty itself. It was feared that if the men's demands were to be successful, the discontent would spread. Mutiny would become the order of the day. Amongst the officers at the Nore, there were conflicting views on how best this should be prevented. The choice was between a reign of terror and one of pacification.

It was Anton's good fortune to be assigned to a ship in which all officers of influence leaned towards pacification.

Not that they greeted his arrival with any enthusiasm. It was difficult for any of his officers to understand why a man so crippled as Anton should have been dispatched to the Navy. They considered his arrival to be an insult of even greater than usual proportions, perpetrated upon the Navy by an insensitive government. The Navy was the dumping ground for many misfits whom the Government would not dare send to the Army; but up to now, not even the worst of the dross imposed upon the fleet had been deprived of the normal use of hands and feet. If they could have rid themselves of him, they would; but by the time his inadequacy had come to their attention, it was too late.

Amongst the Irish sailors on board the *Conqueror*, Anton had already become a mascot.

The ship's doctor, O'Hara, into whose care Anton first fell, was an Irishman. In his bouts of sobriety, O'Hara viewed the Frenchman as a hero. The doctor was susceptible to the appearance of heroism. Other people's heroism filled the doctor with yearning admiration and violent, but short-lived, resolutions for his own rehabilitation. He spoke of the Frenchman with enthusiasm. Within the confines of the ship, his was an influential opinion.

O'Hara didn't see how he could fix Anton's hands, though.

"I'm a weaver," Anton had said, holding out his foetally-curled hands to the doctor. "I have to be able to weave."

The doctor had shaken his head. "You're a sailor now," he had told the French man flatly. "Your weaving days are done."

"He's no sailor," remarked the doctor's assistant, staring at the cup-shaped hands. "Unless his hands were to be used as rum measures."

"Short of breaking them again, there's nothing I can do," O'Hara told Anton. He was holding one of Anton's hands in his, attempting to open out the fingers. They would not yield to his pressure. Anton drew his breath in with the pain of the doctor's efforts. It was as though the hand had been fired to a new shape.

"Then break them," Anton said without expression.

"And even then, there's no guarantee which way they'll set a second time."

"Break them," Anton repeated.

Afterwards, Anton thought he could not have repeated the order for a third time.

By the time Anton had been rendered sufficiently drunk for the job to be done, the doctor was in no fit state to do it. He was as drunk as his patient. It was left to the assistant to climb up onto the wooden operating table, kneel on Anton's wrists to hold them steady, and hammer each finger flat to the wood to the accompaniment of the screams of a man who would be a weaver, against all odds. At the sound of such screaming, the doctor laid his head down on his arms and wept with supportive abandon.

The assistant had done a good job. A job to be proud of. He had taken precautions very similar, had he known it, to precautions taken by the guards who had originally broken Anton's hands. The assistant wished the patient to survive; so too had the guards. By placing a thick wad of linen beneath the head of the hammer, the assistant had for the most part (like the guards before him) avoided breaking skin. With luck, the hands would not grow putrid.

Afterwards, it was the assistant who bound each finger to a wooden splint with clean linen and then, to guard against the senseless rage of pain, bound the patient himself to the table that he might not undo the assistant's good work.

By the time Anton was fit to rise again, he found himself at the mercy of a large group of unwanted and devoted followers.

For officers determined on pacification, the return of such a man to His Majesty's prisons was quite impossible; he could not even be quietly let loose on shore (a move which would have been welcomed by Anton himself). The men wanted their mascot. Here was a Frenchman, a Protestant, an agitator; a man who had maintained silence, under torture, to protect the identities of his Irish friends; yet he continued to resist, quite vehemently, the label of hero. The combination of unlikelihoods was irresistible. The *Sandwich* might boast the services of Richard Parker, a released debtor, as their chief renegade and proffer him as the natural leader of a mutiny; but the crew of the *Conqueror* had Anton. They did not intend to give him up.

Anton was terrified by their adulation. He felt that, like his hands, he had been broken down and remoulded by others. He was their creation, approximating only vaguely his reality. The names he had forgotten had returned to him now. He knew that if he could have remembered them at the time, he would have passed them on to his interrogators. He would have done whatever was necessary to save his hands.

He also knew that not one of those that he recalled would have recognised the sailors' new creation.

***

When mutiny finally did break out, and Parker was set up as the "President of the Fleet", Anton Paradis, his fingers spread out like the spokes of a fan, found himself one of two delegates representing the mutinous crew of a ship he had joined two weeks before.

NINE

૨૦

Danno was in mourning.

Not only was Anton gone; he had gone without Danno's forgiveness. He could not look to Caitlín for comfort. He had told her that Anton would be back. He could not disclose his own despair. He longed to confide in Letitia, but to put his heart at risk in such a way was out of the question. The wedding was in sufficient jeopardy as it was. In fact, his heart had already succumbed, but he refused to take notice of its clamour. He continued to mourn alone for the loss of the weaver: an artist, a friend.

Pansy found him quite beyond comprehension. She was beginning to fear that her father was right and that Danno McKenna lacked certain attributes essential to a man determined on success. That he should be pining for one surly French weaver when Dublin was awash with weavers! Pansy would have pined more sincerely for a dog. At least a dog would not have had such ingratitude as to turn around and bite the hand that had fed it with such unfailing generosity.

Pansy made the mistake of saying as much to Danno; and then she accused him pettishly (and accurately) of preferring his weaver to his fiancée.

He had barely sufficient will to deny the charge and Pansy grew more fractious still.

"But why should I be surprised to yield my place in your affections to a weaver? Why, I've seen you treat that insufferable Mrs. Sweetman with more animation than ever you treated me!"

Danno assured his fiancée that she could never yield her place to the weaver. He did not add that she could not yield a position never held. As for Mrs. Sweetman's charms, which Pansy seemed to fear so much: she should rest assured. The two women were incomparable.

It was the minimum that Danno could have said by way of reassurance; and he said no more than that.

It was Danno's mother who brought her son to his senses.

"Only Pansy," she told her son, having spent a trying afternoon attempting to console her son's tearful betrothed, "lies between you and the debtors' gaol. Not only that, but the poor child has had the misfortune to fall in love with you. And now she is consumed by jealousy which you are doing nothing to alleviate. Were you to tell the poor, gullible dear with sufficient sincerity, what I have already spent the afternoon repeating to her like a parrot-trainer, namely, that you love her to distraction, then our future might not appear quite so bleak. I am too old, Danno my dear, to take to poverty."

So Danno lied to his fiancée. It was the first occasion on which he had found such a task difficult to perform. It was not just that his heart was not in the performance; it was also that he found himself unaccountably pricked in his conscience. He felt, for the first time, predatory; he felt that way because, also for the first time, he saw his fiancée as a victim. That she should be willing made it the more poignant. He attempted to soothe his conscience by recollecting that he was, after all, intending to marry her. She would find marriage itself an excellent substitute for love. It was not as though love had ever been contracted for by either side. So that to pretend to love her now was no cruelty, but an act of kind deceit on his part, the act of a charitable gentleman; and, as his mother had assured him, the act would become like second nature to him the more he practised it.

She was so easily convinced, poor Pansy; and was capable of so little love herself. To Danno, it seemed impossible that Pansy's frail passion should be classified, along with the passion of Letitia (and that of Caitlín for the absent Anton), under the same heading of love. Danno did not believe that Pansy understood the meaning of love; and it made her all the easier to deceive.

To save the rest of the weavers, Danno committed one further deception for which he hoped Anton, alive or dead, would forgive him. Pansy's father, misinformed by Pansy herself, believed that the weaver transported to the navy without trial had been the ringleader in the trouble at the McKenna premises. He was also under the impression that the arrest of Anton Paradis had been at the instigation of Danno himself. Danno did not correct his future father-in-law's erroneous impressions. To do so would not have been in the interests of the business. The decisive action apparently taken by Danno restored him in the eyes of Pansy's father. A loan from the future settlement was made available to the silk merchant. The weavers came quietly back to work. Plans for the wedding were resumed.

Fearing the ability of love to unsettle such delicate arrangements, Danno resolved to resist all attempts by Letitia to see him. None were made, and he believed himself more unsettled by her silence than the sight of her could possibly have made him. He was struck by the poignancy of his own sacrifices: forced to pretend love to one woman, whilst forgoing known pleasures elsewhere. He was as much a victim of this damn marriage as was Pansy herself.

He had other concerns. The British Navy was in the grip of a full-blown mutiny. What more perfect opportunity could there be for a French landing? But the French did not appear. This failure by their allies to take advantage of British disarray was a cause for Irish bitterness. Danno was not immune from such emotion. He even began to question French sincerity. Such doubts made him susceptible to the suggestion that there could be no more perfect time for a rising, with or without the French.

***

. . . I have determined, Dear Sir, not to describe to you in this letter my grave pecuniary difficulties. I will not let it be said that I was reduced to begging of the Government. I shall only confess to you, good Sir, that the word 'grave' is not misused as a description of the financial problems facing a man who daringly presumes to think of himself as your personal friend.

My informant, the industrious weaver, tells me that the Frenchman slipped through your fingers. 'Tis great shame that such a mishap (if mishap it was) should have occurred; though I imagine that Paradis could have been easily retrieved had his evidence been of sufficient importance. I did not say it to him, for fear of discouraging further disclosures, but Delaney may have over-estimated the Frenchman's value. Delaney continues to attend the meetings of those dastardly rogues at Nelligan's Ale House. In recent weeks, the members have been more agitated than usual by the French failure to arrive. There is a kind of millennial fervour to this Irish belief in the second coming of the French; however, it is a belief held (as is common in all such movements, whether religious or secular) more strongly by some than by others. This time, the mutiny was to be the catalyst for the French; but the French have not bestirred themselves. The men meeting at Nelligan's Ale House could, without exaggeration, be classed as sceptics. They believe, frankly, that the French can no longer be depended upon to arrive. They believe that by continuing to wait for French assistance, an opportunity more perfect than any that has yet arisen or may be likely to arise in the future, is being lost. They are angered by the timidity of leading United Irishmen. Where before they feared that the people were uncontainable, now they fear that if a rising does not take place soon, the people will lose heart and will prove impossible to stir when (if ever) the time is judged to be right. Dread of pitch-cap and triangles is having its effect.

Most interesting of all, Delaney believes that Danno McKenna, formerly a passionate advocate for the necessity of French assistance, is being won round (through despair of the French) to the idea of rising alone. Given his position within the United Irishmen, this makes him a convert of most dangerous dimensions. Unfortunately, I have not been able to persuade Delaney to give evidence; nor will he divulge the names of any other member of the cell. He is convinced that either action would be more than his life was worth. I do not doubt his judgement. I can see that there will come a point when his freely-extracted confessions will be worth more than his highly-purchased information. For now, however, I feel that to arrest him would be akin to killing the goose that lays the golden eggs.

Before I seal this letter, I must tell you that I am pursuing (with great delicacy) a gentleman who has been, up to now, well-placed within the United Irishmen. This gentleman, shocked by the organisation's lurch towards the politics of revolution, finds himself in the unhappy position of knowing too much about an organisation which he now wishes to quit.

While his only desire is to fade back into obscurity, those from whom he wishes to separate himself doubt his goodwill. So much so that he believes his life to be in danger from his former friends. He fears being compelled by the threat to make the move he most wishes to avoid; he fears being compelled, through motives of self-preservation, to seek protection from the Castle. He realises what such protection would cost, and he finds it a cruel irony that the distrust of these former friends should force him, against his will, to fulfil their expectations of him. Is not this a nice dilemma for me to play upon? I am, as you can imagine, full of sympathy, advice, and counter-advice. I do not believe that his conscience will survive his fear.

I am, Sir, Your devoted Servant . . .

***

She had obviously gone too far.

There could be no other reason for his silence. Had she frightened him away by the unseemly urgency of her love-making? Should she have dissimulated? If so, she had misjudged him. Letitia was furious for having exposed so much desire to one who subsequently chose to humiliate her with silence. Perhaps he had not been frightened. Did he perhaps think that a woman so forward as herself could be relied upon to come to him? If this was his belief, then it was uncomfortably close to the truth. She was determined that she would make no further advances.

At the end of a month, she was near to hating Danno McKenna. She wanted him so much, and he seemed so unworthy of such desire. He had made no attempt to see her. She was humiliated to find her mind so completely at the mercy of their two bodies.

But when Letitia finally called upon Danno, it was not at the dictation of desire. She went reluctantly and with a sense of great foreboding.

Marvin no longer ventured outside without pistols and small-sword; and a manservant also bearing pistols. He rarely invited friends to the house now. He no longer knew who his friends were.

Besides, he was afraid of being seen with the wrong friends by his new enemies. He trusted few people, but his wife he continued to trust. She might have all but admitted that she did not love him; she might be showing a new and disturbing reluctance to welcome him to her bed; but it never occurred to Marvin that he could lose his wife's loyalty. Nevertheless, he chose to exclude her from a series of conversations which took place in their house sporadically over a three week period, between himself and an unannounced visitor, who came and departed on each occasion in a closed sedan. He was sure of her loyalty; he wished to retain her respect as well. He could have taken no action more certain of arousing Letitia's suspicion.

There were women who would have applauded his decision; there were those who would, at least, have condoned it; Letitia, he knew, fell into neither category. Marvin knew that were his wife to be a party to those conversations, she would condemn his decision as treachery.

She did.

What was more she knew, from the outset of that first, almost inaudible conversation, that treachery was his intention: once his conscience had been pacified. He demanded much of his visitor. Approval for his treachery was not enough. He required a denial that treachery was taking place. Once the visitor understood his host's requirement (and this understanding came about in the course of the third visit), it was easily provided. From the adjoining room where she stood warm in the slanting evening sun, with her ear pressed to the party wall, Letitia heard the visitor woo her husband's conscience. He was so skillful. In the fourth and final conversation, he converted her husband's proposed treachery into a selfless act, an act carried out for the greater good of society; an act not contrary to conscience, but dictated by it. By its close, her husband had agreed to betray his friends (including Danno McKenna), and was at perfect peace with himself. The visitor's triumph was not complete. He could not persuade Marvin to give court evidence. But by the end of the final meeting, Letitia felt that her husband's agreement to that one outstanding request was only a matter of time.

That night, her husband's lovemaking was more vigorous (and therefore more short-lived) than it had been for weeks. On the following day, three soldiers in plain dress discreetly joined the household staff.

Letitia had no quarrel with her conscience. Her initial step was clear. Her husband was a traitor. Either she warned Danno McKenna of the danger he was in, or she allowed McKenna to be betrayed by her husband. There was no question of which action she would take; but the clarity of her course did not make her task any more palatable.

***

This time she arrived in a hired carriage with the damp, velvet curtains drawn close around the open windows. The air inside the carriage was warm and musty. Letitia wore a dress brought with her from her father's house. She could no longer wear clothes given to her by Marvin. Upon deceiving her husband, she had been ashamed to wear his gifts; now she felt contaminated by them.

She remained within the carriage while the driver summoned Danno. She was terrified by her duty. She who had deceived her husband must now denounce him to the man by whom he had been deceived. What she called denouncement, many would describe as an unpardonable betrayal of the man to whom she had sworn obedience. Were her action to be exposed, she would find few supporters. The society in which she moved would ostracise her, while pardoning her husband. No, they would not pardon him; they would find no sin to pardon. They would praise him; Letitia they would call a strumpet, a scarlet woman, a Papist's whore. Considering all this, her duty remained plain.

When Danno knocked on the door of the carriage, she opened it up and held out her hand. "Get in," she said. "Quickly."

He had expected to see Pansy.

Letitia could not have arrived on a worse day. It was a day of the utmost importance to Pansy. She was coming to choose materials for her wedding trousseau and she was already late. Unpunctuality was one of Pansy's affectations. She thought a little capriciousness pretty. He had been much in Pansy's company of late, acting the part of a lover with all the sincerity of one as financially distressed as he; he had come to know her foibles tediously well.

Danno climbed reluctantly into Letitia's carriage, knowing his weakness.

She looked at him, her face pale in the stifling heat of the carriage. "I had to come," she said nervously.

"I can't . . ." Danno interrupted, slamming the door behind him. He was gazing at her face in the dim light as though it might disappear before his eyes.

The carriage began to move. Danno stopped abruptly in mid-sentence. "Where?"

"Neither can I," said Letitia haughtily, turning her face away. She was here to save his life and he didn't even have the courtesy to let her speak before attempting to banish her from what remained of it. The driver had been ordered to drive to Ringsend. The curtain, undulating gently with the ambling movement of the carriage and the faint stirring breeze through the window, grew blurred before her eyes.

" . . . live without you," Danno finished. It was not the way the sentence had been meant to end; but it was the truth. As God was his witness, he was sure it was the truth.

Letitia turned back to face him. "Don't lie, McKenna," she told him coldly. "Pansy may expect such artifice. I do not." Then, with effort, she contrived a small and mocking smile. "Though it is the very least you could have said, I know, if you were thinking to save my face."

He shook his head wordlessly. There had been an element of gallantry in the sentiment; but it had not been empty gallantry.

"You needn't fear. I am not engaged in your pursuit, McKenna."

Yet he was in her carriage, heading God knew where.

"Why then am I being abducted?" he asked lightly and attempted to take her hand in his. She would not allow it. He was not, it seemed, to be permitted to take advantage of his abduction.

Quite without warning, she began to cry. It occurred to Danno (a thought which was to be a source of continuous, retrospective shame to him) that Letitia was about to disclose a pregnancy; and he thanked God that a marriage existed to conceal the impropriety. He did not dare to touch her.

She controlled herself sufficiently to speak.

"My husband has become an informer."

She could put it no less bleakly than that. Even so short a statement nearly defeated her powers of utterance.

Most bitter for Letitia to accept was the realisation that Marvin's treachery came as no surprise to Danno. It had been anticipated. She had married, willingly, a man from whom nothing more than cowardice was expected by those who knew him well. She had seen no baseness, but that did not excuse her; she had looked for none.

Danno could even find room for pity. "Poor Marvin. What a cruel reward for his bravery."

"What do you mean?"

"He followed his conscience into far more frightening terrain than a man as timid as Marvin should have to confront."

Letitia was angered by Danno's compassion. Such softness was dangerous. "His conscience has been diverted to easier paths," she said sharply. "He will not find betrayal hard."

Then she realised that Danno had been delivering her husband's obituary.

"How can I return to him now?"

"You must."

"I have betrayed him," she whispered. Her mouth had grown dry with fear. "Even traitors can be betrayed. He trusted me. I breached that trust. I must confess the breach."

"And alert him?"

She laid her head down on his shoulder, and closed her eyes. She would have liked to sleep.

"Some betrayals are necessary," he told her gently.

"I overheard the government agent say just such a thing to my husband," she whispered back to him.

"Truth can be used by the devil himself, Letitia."

"How can I live with him and not confess?"

"You have deceived him before for no more than your own convenience. Now you're deceiving him to save lives."

"At the cost of his own."

He was her husband. She despised him; but she could not promise silence. She kissed Danno on the neck; he began to stroke her hair.

"My husband," she told him, her voice dreamily slow, "wished me to win for him your protection. By whatever means proved necessary. The duties of a wife are wider than one could imagine."

"And what was your response?" he asked quietly.

"I refused. I was afraid that I might not be able to bring myself to plead on his behalf."

"Why?"

"I knew that if pushed he would betray you all without hesitation. I could not bear to plead for such a man."

She raised her head to kiss his lips. She was crying again and the tears ran down to their lips. Danno tasted their salt in his mouth. She could not promise silence, but he knew now that she would not speak.

They continued to travel towards their destination. Within the sedately swaying carriage, they rocked in each others arms. He kissed her eyelids while she traced the pattern of his ears. She ran her tongue around his lips and he played with his fingertips upon her flute-like neck, while their bodies shivered with desire.

She withdrew reluctantly from him. She had been forced by her husband's treachery to call upon Danno McKenna. She had come for no other reason.

"This is too easy for you, McKenna," she said. "You're taking advantage."

"Are you not taking advantage too?"

Perhaps the journey was a gift. Not a reward for duty done, but an unexpected gift. She resumed her intimate exploration of his face.

Their mouths were damp and swollen, their faces flushed, their eyelids heavy when they stepped out, blinking, into the dazzling, mid-afternoon sunshine by the river at Ringsend. They had decided, for safety, to return to town separately. The driver had been dispatched to hire a horse for Danno.

"I must see you again, Letitia."

He should not admit that he loved her; and he could not contemplate the abandonment of his marriage to Pansy. He must be realistic. Neither the admission nor the abandonment would serve any purpose. His freedom would not increase hers.

She nodded, bleakly. She knew the most she could expect. Even now, in this first ecstasy of feeling, she could see the desolation plainly. The greater portion of her life intolerable but for the anticipation of those snatched occasions of clandestine love. Each meeting foreshadowing a parting.

He put an arm around her shoulders, and they leaned against the carriage, looking to the river, while the horses shuffled between the shafts and the seagulls screamed like humans hanging from the points of spears.

"It is no comfort to think that most people live much smaller lives than this," she said, as though such a comment had been made by one or other of them. "It does no more than increase one's sense of waste."

Danno thought of how he had spent his recent weeks. The effort he had expended in the simulation of love. His mind recoiled from the thought of the effort still to come. The existence of Letitia eased nothing; it only caused the wooing of Pansy to grow more shameful.

The road on which the carriage was parked stretched long and straight. In the distance, a horse paddled doggedly through a shimmering mirage. The driver was returning with Danno's mount.

Danno began to kiss Letitia's sun-heated hair. He was defeated by his own sense of approaching loss. "I love you," he murmured, as though, said so softly, the words might be taken to be no more than a continuation of his kisses: tender, ephemeral, passing.

***

That evening, Marvin's visitor came again.

The Chief Secretary's industrious correspondent had judged that, touched judiciously, his subject was ripe to fall. Not at once, of course. He did not expect the fall to be coincident with the touch; but he sensed that it was time for the touch itself to be given. The fall would not be too distant. The government agent (he styled himself thus) was proud of his manipulative skills.

He revealed what up to now he had kept hidden from Sweetman (and from the concealed Letitia) for fear of striking prematurely; namely that, according to a most reliable source, a rising was planned. At first, Marvin was dismissive. Letitia heard him ask were the French expected; and then she heard him assure his visitor that without the French, the United Irishmen would make no move. It was the agent's reply which made her blood run cold; his naming, quite suddenly, of her lover. For men like McKenna, she heard the agent say, the French were no longer to be relied upon. McKenna was prepared to rise without the French.

Letitia sank to her knees before the wall. The voices followed her ear.

She heard her husband refuse to be the instrument of McKenna's death. He would not, he could not, give evidence against McKenna in court; a man to whom he had offered the hospitality of the dinner-table. There must be others, less intimate, who could finger McKenna. How could he? His refusal held firm that night; but within the protests, both Letitia and the government agent could already hear the plea to be shown how such a betrayal could be absolved.

***

A letter was delivered to the Paradis workshop, addressed to Caitlín. Charlotte accepted the letter on Caitlín's behalf. She didn't recognise the handwriting, but from its markings, it was plain that the letter had been written by a member of the fleet.

"Either he's dead," she remarked to Malachi as she cracked the seal, "or Anton's moved up in the world and has a clerk to scribble his intimacies."

"Unless his spell in prison has caused him to forget his letters."

Lucien Paradis had died, and his daughter Charlotte had mourned his passing with true sincerity. She had loved her father. His death had been, nevertheless, a relief. She need no longer fear the whims of her husband; his sudden desires for recompense; his talk of a just share. Who would willingly recompense a man for his own inadequacy? She had been frightened by his air of instability in those last weeks before his disappearance.

Malachi, now, was so dependable. A man of his word. He had promised that Anton's disappearance could be arranged, and that was what had happened. One day Anton was there, hanging idle around the Paradis house, flirting with that sly, pussy-faced young girl; the next day he was gone, Malachi could (would?) not say where. He had been able to assure her only that Anton was not dead by his hand. (How could Malachi know what might have happened to the man in gaol?) Not until Anton's impressment (how else could one describe the dispatching by magistrates of untried men to the fleet?) had been confirmed, had Malachi told Charlotte of the initial arrest; and then he made no confession of his part in that affair. Charlotte did not inquire. So long as she knew nothing, she could pretend her own and Malachi's innocence.

There were hysterics, of course, from the girl when Anton first was missed; which were easily enough dealt with by dismissal. Charlotte had no idea where the girl was now; nor did she care.

It was the hysteria of Charlotte's own young daughter which had been more difficult to counteract. The four year old Marie pined for the man she believed to be her father. She still pined. No matter that Anton had been as poor a father as he had been a husband; he was, it appeared now (quite unaccountably), a person of importance to Marie. Before the disappearance of Anton, Marie had been very attached to Malachi. She had not known he was her father. (To keep the matter secret from Lucien Paradis, his grandchildren could be no wiser than himself.) Since the disappearance of Anton, and the subsequent disclosure of Malachi's true relationship to her, the child's affections had changed. She avoided Malachi, who now, since the death of the old man, lived in the house; she viewed him with suspicion. She would not honour him with the name Papa unless threatened by the whip. She linked him with her father's (not-to-be-called-father) disappearance.

Well: it seemed he was too inadequate to write his own love letters. He had to employ a scribe.

Charlotte first read the signature at the bottom of the letter: *"Charles Hawkins (one-time strolling actor) for Mr. Anton Paradis."*

She turned back to the beginning and began to read the unfamiliar script . . .

Caitlín, my darling: In taking upon myself your guardianship, in disallowing the blossoming of love, I assumed myself your moral superior. I know now how much your inferior I really am. Why, oh why did I not listen to you? You were right. You were always right. To you the central truth of existence was always obvious; that in the midst of life there is ever death. You never relied upon the future. You saw that the present was the only certainty. What a posturing fool I was. If you knew the anguish I have suffered for your skin unkissed, your body uncaressed, you would know only a fraction of the torment I have undergone. Caitlín, darling Caitlín; I never told you that I loved you and the omission has me almost destroyed. They broke my hands and my feet in prison; but I broke my own heart knowing how I must have broken yours . . .

Charlotte paused. The voice was uncompromisingly that of Anton; apologetic, self-abasing. Yet Charlotte had tears in her eyes which she had to wipe clear before she could continue. His hands! Had it really been necessary to break his hands?

I am well-cured of belief in a future now. I was dispatched without trial to the Navy. A mutiny, already existing in other parts, has spread since my arrival to include my own ship, The Conqueror. I have been appointed, for ill-founded reasons, a delegate for that ship. I am, in other words, a leading mutineer. God help me, Caitlín, but hanging is the only end that I can see to this affair. McKenna's revenge is turning out far sweeter than he could have imagined.

Caitlín, my beloved, I never wanted to be anything more than a weaver of silk. Write to me. I need your forgiveness before I die. But Mr. Hawkins insists I must not end thus with despair. I must finish instead, he says (he is a man much merrier than myself), with a love poem which he provides from memory:

> The son of the King of the Moy
> met a girl in green woods on midsummer's day:
> she gave him black fruit from thorns
> and the full of his arms
> of strawberries, where they lay.

He says that such a first encounter should be dreamt into the existence of all lovers.

The Post Office to which letters may be safely addressed is: Mr. Pink, the Bear and Ragged Staff.

As soon as Charlotte had finished the letter, she tore it up and threw the pieces to the fire. She was not vindictive. Had the letter contained no more than the sentiments of love, she would have seen it delivered to the girl. But there was within the letter the condemnation of McKenna. Charlotte had no clear knowledge of what Malachi's role had been in the arrest of Anton, but that he had been instrumental was not in doubt. It was therefore a piece of good fortune that Anton should believe Danno McKenna to be the author of his misfortunes. She could not allow the girl to disabuse him.

If his future was to be as he predicted, poor Anton's beliefs were of little account; but one could no more guarantee that the future did not exist than that it did.

TEN

Anton confirmed his heroism once again simply through being one of those mutineers who managed to escape the rope.

The failure of the Nore mutiny was inevitable. To have conceded terms for a second time would have been fatal to the authority of the Admiralty. It would have confirmed the efficacy of mutiny as a weapon of persuasion. A dangerous precedent would have been set. It could not be allowed to succeed. The mutineers themselves forfeited popular support by setting up a blockade of the Thames. This loss of popular support allowed the Admiralty to confront the seamen largely unopposed by public opinion.

Anton, to whom the outcome of the mutiny was obvious, lived through it in a state of bemused terror. The sources for his terror were manifold; but since it was those sources closest to him (his fellow delegates, and his followers) which provoked the most immediate terror, and which therefore dictated all his moves, his terror only served to enhance his performance as a mutineer. Because it was inconceivable that a hero should be afraid, his fear was not recognised as such and was therefore immaterial. Anton's value to his followers was as a symbol. The more pliant he was, the easier it was for each of them to see in him what they wanted to see. He might have been detected for the (reluctant) fake he was, but for one important fact. His most immediate terror was not his greatest terror. Anton's fear of being sent back to await the further attentions of his torturers, in that cell from which he had so accidentally escaped, was the greatest of all his fears. He was therefore one of those most adamantly opposed to surrender. Couched in revolutionary language, his sentiments sounded splendid. It was, Anton insisted, impelled to lie by the intensity of his hidden terrors, better to die at sea than to abandon the principles for which they were fighting.

Anton did not wish to die anywhere; but from the moment of his arrest, there was no time throughout his ordeal, when he did not consider death to be imminent. He held Danno McKenna responsible for his predicament, and he hated him with the particular hatred of a friend deceived. According to the men who had overseen the breaking of his hands and feet, it had been Danno McKenna who had betrayed him. It was not that he trusted their word; but he had no reason to think otherwise. Who but Danno would have dared betray him? Malachi would not have done so, for fear of counter-betrayal by the betrayed. Only a gentleman of Danno's standing could have betrayed with such insouciance, confident of the word of a gentleman to disavow any accusations tossed out by a vengeful weaver. Besides, Danno had thought himself already betrayed by Anton. He would have seen his own action as a justified reprisal. The weavers had been right. The merchants could not be trusted. They were the enemy; they could be nothing else. He, Anton, had been arrogant enough to believe that in Danno he had discovered the exception to the rule.

The collapse of the Nore mutiny began on the 29th of May with the surrender of the *Clyde* and the *San Fiorenzo*. By the 14th of June, only the *Inflexible*, the *Conqueror* and a couple of other ships still held out. On the 15th of June, the *Inflexible* surrendered. So too did the *Conqueror*.

On board the *Conqueror*, the decision to surrender had actually been taken on the previous day. At that final meeting, Anton found himself deserted by all but five of his followers. Out of respect for the obduracy of their former leader's principles, and as a salve for their own faltering loyalty, Anton and his five followers were given the opportunity to escape by those who had voted to end the mutiny. It did not seem right that such a man should be forced, against his principles, to surrender (with death as a ringleader his certain fate), when the rest of them were surrendering only in the hopes of saving their skins. So actual surrender was delayed by twenty-four hours. During the night that intervened, his five loyal followers, with muffled oars slipping delicate as cats' paws in and out of the water, rowed their admired delegate, his scribe (his right-hand man) and the stupefied doctor (whose medical efforts had succeeded in accidentally killing an unfortunate, captive officer two days previously and who was therefore an equal certainty for the gallows), to Feversham. From there, they sailed to France in a fishing vessel.

***

Of the seven men who accompanied Anton to France, and lay with him at a lodging house near Le Havre awaiting the arrival of English-speaking officials who had been summoned from Rouen to interview them, only one (the scribe) expected him to return to Ireland. Yet each of the others, when they thought about it, could see (erroneously) that they should have expected such a move. A price might be on his head, but he was a patriot, wasn't he?

The blood of Anton Paradis might be French, the doctor remarked tearfully (the least sentimental notion moved the doctor to tears these days), when he heard of Anton's intentions; but his soul was Irish. Most definitely, the man's soul was Irish. The doctor himself, what with one thing and another (including the quantity and excellent quality of the wine provided so far at no cost to themselves), thought that his own soul could easily be persuaded that it knew no boundaries. He hoped that Anton would not expect to be accompanied home.

At the far end of the room, near a window in the small parlour appointed to them, Anton exercised his fingers one by one on the notes of a piano while the doctor spoke. This exercising, initially taken up on the advice of the doctor, had become his constant occupation and his hands grew daily more supple. He had never touched the keys of a piano before, and the instrument delighted him. He had a sense of how melodies could be woven from the notes of the piano. He would have been a natural player of Bach. The others had become so accustomed to the sound of the piano that it no longer had the power to disturb their conversation.

Ich am of Irlonde,
And of the holy londe
of Irlonde.
Goode sire, praye ich thee,
For of sainte charitee,
Com and dance with me
In Irlonde, quoted the strolling player softly, mischievously from

where he reclined upon an upholstered chair. He had been listening to the words of the doctor. Three high notes of the piano beat rhythmically to the pace of the player's voice.

"That's beautiful," said the doctor, while the tears overflowed and ran down his florid cheeks (it was the unfortunate loss of his patient which had so unmanned the doctor). "It expresses precisely what I was trying to say of our good friend, Paradis. The patriot who inspires others with his own gaiety."

For a few tumultuous moments, the doctor felt himself reckless enough to accept the invitation expressed in the poem. He would take the arm of Paradis and, to the accompaniment of harpists and pipers, they would dance defiantly through Ireland, rousing the people to unassailable heights of passion and fervour. The English would fall away, defeated by the very gaiety of such an uprising.

The player looked across at Anton who stared, engrossed, at his own moving fingers, and he began to laugh, much more softly than he had spoken. The man might be a patriot and then again (it was not for the player to say) he might not; but he was not a patriot to the exclusion of all other interests. The player, after all, was the man who had written the letter to Caitlín. It was well-known to the player that Anton had heard nothing from the girl in reply and that he was maddened by the silence. No rational explanations would do him. He could only believe in the most melodramatic of reasons: she was dead; she had been married to another against her will; or, worst of all, she had fallen in love with another man, and Anton was quite forgotten. Because this last possibility was the one which Anton feared the most, it was the one which he was most inclined to believe. Patriot bedamned! The man was desperate to reach Ireland because he was unhappy in love.

***

Anton returned to Dublin alone. He came only because of Caitlín.

He could not have stayed away, but he had come back to Dublin dreamily, without a thought to his safety. Had it not been for the insistence of his followers, he would not even have grown the cover of beard and moustache that he now sported; nor would he have bought the wig, which perched upon his head, hot as Hades in this humid, July weather. He was a weaver (and when he flexed his fingers he knew, triumphantly, that he was still a weaver). He had shed the last and most persistent of his followers. He was of no importance to anyone. He was a Defender because he could hardly have refused; he had become a mutineer because his options had been similarly curtailed. He could not believe himself to be of any real significance to any one.

But Anton was a wanted man.

So badly was he wanted that a close likeness to his face had been sketched and printed upon a thousand posters. Beneath the likeness was: the information that Anton Paradis was an admitted Defender and a chief promoter of disaffection amongst the crew members of His Majesty's Navy; a written description, telling the population of Dublin (correctly) that he walked with a limp and (incorrectly) that his hands were severely disfigured; a warning against attempting to conceal his whereabouts; and the offer of a substantial reward for information leading to his arrest. The poster was displayed prominently in taverns, shops and coaches, throughout the city of Dublin.

Anton had been walking for ten minutes before he saw the first poster. He glanced at it as he passed by and wondered (as he frequently wondered) why the faces on posters always seemed familiar; then he forgot about it. He was looking for Caitlín. She would have no reason to be in this part of the city, but yet he hoped to come upon her. It was inconceivable that he should be in Dublin and that she should not sense it and come in search of him. It was not until he came upon the second poster that Anton realised that the likeness was of himself. He stopped and stared at it in horror, and felt, as he stared, the blood fall from his face and the hairs of his beard creep with fear. Then he realised that he was drawing attention to himself by the intensity of his perusal. Anyone passing by had only to compare the face on the poster with the white and terrified face confronting it to know that here was the wanted man for the taking. He walked on. But his whole demeanour had changed. Feeling himself to be conspicuous, he became so through his efforts to render himself unnoticeable. He hunched his shoulders and sank his chin towards his chest; he constantly averted his face from those who passed him by. It was his limp which worried him most; it was that which most caught people's attention. Those who would not otherwise have seen him were drawn by his tilting gait to glance in his direction.

As he made his way along the river, with dipping footsteps, Anton's anxieties multiplied. He grew suspicious that he should have passed unnoticed for so long; he began to look behind him surreptitiously, to see if any of those who had passed him by with apparent lack of interest then paused to glance back. He grew positive that he was being followed by certain of those who walked at his own pace behind him. He even began to suspect that some who had come towards him, and had passed him safely by, subsequently turned around to follow in his footsteps.

Wanted men could not go home. Besides, who at home would welcome him? Only Lucien, if Lucien was still alive. Anton began to sweat profusely as he limped hurriedly towards the Liberties. Caitlín would not be there; he realised for the first time that he had no idea where she might be instead. He realised too that wanted men could not go anywhere in safety. It was the rare friend who would welcome a wanted man into their house. Anton had only ever had one such friend and that friend had turned traitor. Anton was hungry, he was tired and he was afraid. He had a little money. Before he had left the ship, a collection had been taken on his behalf. In France, his remaining followers had insisted that he take it all. They would look to the French for their support. They appeared to think it was their due. It was dangerous to look for lodgings, Anton knew; but it was more dangerous yet to remain at large. He would apply to a respectable house for a room. It would not be the expected move of an unemployed weaver. They would be hunting for him in the Liberties. He turned, and began to limp away from the Liberties again. When he came close to McKenna & Sons, Silk Merchants (retail and wholesale), he crossed to the far side of the wide street. McKenna, should he happen to glance out from his house, would not recognise a distant, limping man, as his former weaver.

Anton passed a dangerous evening at his lodgings, in the guise of a silk mercer from London.

Luckily, he had thought it safer not to diverge too sharply from the trade he knew. This precaution proved to be more necessary than he had imagined. The landlady (a widow) who probably made inquiries no sharper than were customary for one in her trade, appalled him, as he stood exposed upon her doorway, with the relentlessness of her questions. It took him all his courage to stand his ground while she quizzed him with all the intensity of a parent inspecting a potential suitor. He was, unfortunately, her only lodger that night and taking him, at the end of her inquiries, for a gentleman, she insisted, graciously, that he should share her meal. To have refused such an invitation would have invited suspicion. Besides, he had survived her first scrutiny; who knew, but hers might be the safest dining room in the city.

He had been so daring! Afterwards, as he lay shivering with retrospective fright in his bed, he was astonished by his own effrontery. He had taken the initiative. Instead of allowing the red-wigged widow to continue her interrogation over dinner (an excellent dinner, cooked by the widow herself), Mr. Grinsell, the London silk mercer, had, with all the curiosity he could muster, commenced a counter-attack. He had overwhelmed the widow with questions, questions that Anton Paradis, the wanted man, would not have dared to ask, for fear of raising dangerous fancies in the mind of the person questioned.

The earliest and most daring of his questions had concerned the mutinous weaver himself.

"A most extraordinary coincidence has been disturbing me since my arrival here, Ma'am." he began, even before the soup bowls had been cleared. He paused to mop uncertainly at his mouth with a napkin. He still found himself disturbed by all the unaccustomed hair about his lips.

"Really, Mr. Grinsell? And what might that be?" the widow spoke encouragingly. She liked a guest (she called her lodgers guests) who had something to say for himself.

Mr. Grinsell resumed his confidence.

"Well, Ma'am. Before I left London, my father gave me the names of several weavers with whom I should make contact. Most

prominently commended by him was the master weaver
Charlotte Paradis . . ."

The widow raised her eyebrows at the name and seemed inclined
to interrupt, but Mr. Grinsell carried firmly on.

"I find myself in the city for no more than quarter of an hour
when I am confronted with a poster bearing the name Anton
Paradis and information of a most shocking kind concerning his
alleged activities. And then, after that first poster, a perfect
spawning of them throughout the city. Tell me, Ma'am, is it possible
that this vicious desperado could be in any way connected to the
master weaver whom I have been advised to see? I confess I hesitate
to do business there before consulting further. God forbid that I,
in my innocence, should attempt to support an establishment that
is in any way connected with subversion."

Mr. Grinsell dabbed at his forehead which had begun to sweat
with the memory of those terrible posters. The widow offered to
have a window opened on his behalf, but he refused: "A passing
sweat, brought on by the heat of the soup. No more."

The widow was delighted with her guest. His was such an
interesting predicament and who better than herself to advise him?

Mr. Grinsell learnt that his was all too common a reaction. The
Paradis workshops were said to have suffered a sharp falling-off
in business as a result of the Government's poster campaign. Well,
was it surprising, when the man in question was no less than the
husband of Charlotte Paradis? Charlotte Paradis had been forced
by the adverse reaction of her clients to place an advertisement in
the leading Dublin newspaper, condemning the actions of her
husband and disassociating herself and her business from him. But
who would be prepared to rely on such self-interested protests? The
widow's sympathies were entirely with Charlotte. Anton Paradis was
her own cousin, whom she had married to please her father and
his, and look how she had been rewarded! The Paradis name
dragged through the mire by that ungrateful young man who, it
was said, had scarcely done a day's weaving in his wife's workshops
since the day of the marriage, but had taken himself off instead
to work for a rival, a raving democrat if rumours were to be believed
(though he stocked the best silks in the country). But if Mr. Grinsell

was considering doing business with Charlotte Paradis (and there was no reason against it so far as the widow could tell), then he might be wise to avoid the firm of McKenna & Sons.

"When I come to think upon it, Mr. Grinsell," the widow said later, coyly, as she poured more wine for her guest, "you have a look of Anton Paradis yourself. Something about the eyes . . ."

Mr. Grinsell laughed so heartily that he began to choke. When he had recovered sufficiently, he went so far as to agree with her. "Both the execrable Mr. Paradis and myself are Huguenots," he said, tears still streaming from the remarked-upon eyes. "What other comment is necessary? They say that the interbreeding within the Huguenot community outside France has been so profound that with another century of it, we shall all wear the same face and none but our nearest and dearest will be able to tell us apart!"

She thought him quite hilarious. Her remark had not, in fact, been meant in any serious sense. The widow had reached that age when the sight begins to fail. To have seen any of the notices properly, she would have had to squint. Self-interest would not allow her to do that in a public place. She was still not without hope of equipping herself with a second husband but at forty-five, such a commodity was not won without effort.

The widow was sorry when her guest (married, so he had confessed) retired for the night. She hadn't passed such an entertaining evening in weeks. And he was not even sure if he would be still with her the following evening. Once his business was done, it was done, and if the tide and the wind happened to be right, then he would be foolish to stay, much as . . . and Mr. Grinsell had risked an amorous glance at the widow.

During the night, Anton decided to call upon his drawboy.

***

. . . I was to have taken my wife and child out of town for the months of July and August, but could not, for lack of money. My circumstances are most unjustly straitened. My wife is afflicted by boils of a most prodigious nature for which there exists no cure more effective than good country air. A simple remedy, unnecessarily placed beyond my means.

I enclose, for the fourth time, a bill for my expenses to date, and I must insist on payment without further delay. My wife's health, good Sir, is not a cause to be trifled with.

I hope, Dear Sir, that the government knows its business, concerning the Frenchman, Paradis. His silence in captivity (indicated by the fact that no other member of the cell was arrested in consequence of his own) had already proved him loyal. Now the posters, with their description of his transformed physical condition, show his silence to have been unbroken by state brutality; the man has become a hero. Mr. McKenna has already been persuaded to put the case for action to the leadership of the United Irishmen. I have no word as yet of how his case was received; but were the Frenchman to return (which God forbid should happen), I fear that his fellow banditti (including the damnable McKenna) might feel obliged to show themselves worthy of his heroism, whatever the response from McKenna's superiors. I must warn you, Good Friend, that the name Paradis, which the government has brought so unthinkingly (in my opinion) to the attention of so much of the population, could prove a formidable rallying cry.

I am the more concerned by this unnecessary elevation of the Frenchman's status now, because I fear his importance may have been rated too highly in the first place. Some weeks ago the weaver, Delaney, ceased, without proffering any reason, to be a tenant of mine. I was, I confess, surprised. Upon making inquiries, I discovered that he had moved into the house of Charlotte Paradis, wife of our newly-created hero. Furthermore, my fresh informant (his name is of no consequence) names Delaney as the true father of the Paradis children; claims it to be common knowledge. This makes me suspect the motives of our honest weaver in bringing Paradis to my attention in the first place. I do not say that the information received concerning the Frenchman was incorrect; but his importance may have been exaggerated.

Delaney thinks me innocent of his intrigues. (I have need of him yet.) He came to me the other day with a long and woeful face to enlist my support for his employer, the inadvertently maltreated Charlotte Paradis, ruined by the unavoidable association of her own name with that of her husband. I praised him effusively for his loyalty to his employer (I refrained from calling her his mistress for fear my face might fail me) and he cleverly confessed to a touch of self-interest. Her fortunes,

154

he reminded me, dictated those of her weavers. Her loss is theirs. Was there anything, he wished to know, that J could suggest to minimise the damage, for which he felt, in part, responsible? To preserve my mask of innocence, J offered him, with an unparalleled show of generosity, sufficient space in my paper for an advertisement protesting his employer's abhorrence of her husband's affairs and her own innocence of any involvement. J even drafted the words for him. Such was his gratitude that he almost forgot himself. J had to remind him that, being only an employee, he could hardly authorise the insertion of the advertisement without first consulting Mrs. Paradis herself!

As to the other strand in this affair: the gentleman of conscience is being uncommonly stubborn on the final and most important point. He still refuses to give evidence against McKenna in court. He was on the point of agreement when his wife was offered a gift of silk from McKenna. The gift apparently represented the honourable fulfilment of a promise in circumstances where failure would have been no disgrace. McKenna's friend was too affected by the gesture to make any further concessions to me; indeed, he expressed regret for those concessions already made. He is proving more troublesome than J had calculated; his conscience shows unexpected fighting spirit (unless it is merely that his fear has been allayed by McKenna's apparently unabated friendship). J would enjoy the challenge more, were J not conscious that time may be short.

J am, Sir, your Devoted Servant . . .

***

The drawboy was aghast to see Anton at the door of his room. At first he shut the door in the weaver's face; but before Anton had time to knock again, the door opened and he was pulled inside. The drawboy, with tears streaming down his face, took the weaver's hands in his and began to kiss them.

"What did they do to you, Mr. Paradis? What did they do to you at all? Let me look at them. Ah, but they're not too bad, the hands. Not too bad at all. I love you, Mr. Paradis. I love you like a son, as you well know. But you can't stay here. Oh God in Heaven, Mr. Paradis, but did you pass anyone on the stairs? The soldiers say I'll betray you if you come. I have soldiers, gentle-voiced as doves, calling on me day and night. They expect you here. They tell me no one could resist the reward that's out for your capture, especially a starving old man like myself. They laugh when I say I'd rather die. Once they brought food (a beef sandwich it was) and they put it down on the table there. Imagine now, they said, that Mr. Paradis will die if so much as a mouthful of that sandwich passes your lips. And then they left. Two hours later they were back. The sandwich was gone, Mr. Paradis. It breaks my heart to tell you this, but the sandwich was gone. Where is it? they asked. The cat, I said. The cat ate it. But they knew I had no cat. A Judas you'll be, they told me, laughing. No question of it. The Lord knows I'd hate to be a Judas to you, Mr. Paradis. But don't stay here. Don't put me to the temptation."

Anton put his arms around the old man and hugged him closely. The drawboy smelt of silk. "You're no Judas," Anton whispered, in imitation of the drawboy's own frightened undertones. "But I'm not looking for shelter. I only want the answer to one question and then I'll be gone."

"What, Mr. Paradis? What's the question?"

The drawboy's impatience was transparent. The question could not be answered until it was asked and he could scarcely wait for the weaver to leave.

"Where is Caitlín?"

The drawboy knew nothing of Anton's feelings towards the girl; he knew of no feelings to be spared, and the insinuation in his whispered reply was unmistakable.

"She's put herself under McKenna's care. She knows how to look after herself, that one. Living under his roof, they say."

"Jesus," murmured Anton. He leaned against the door with the drawboy still held in the curve of his arms.

The drawboy misunderstood.

"It won't be to my Judas that you are Jesus, Mr. Paradis," he promised from within the weaver's arms. "But have I told you all you wish to know? The soldiers, you see. They rarely leave me alone more than an hour."

Anton nodded.

"I'm going," he said. Then he put his mouth right up to the drawboy's ear. "You're too wise to be a Judas, old man," he whispered, surprising himself by his own cruelty. "Doesn't everybody know that Judas wasn't murdered only because he did the job himself before the others could get to him?"

The drawboy closed his eyes and began to shake his head helplessly from side to side. "God help us all, Mr. Paradis, but we have fallen upon evil times if we are driven to mistrust our own friends."

"There is no worse evil than a friend's betrayal," Anton said by way of reply and he slipped, with the ease of a silken shadow, from the room.

Until then, Anton had not considered revenge.

He had escaped without detection from the Liberties. Now he limped fearfully through unfamiliar areas of the city. It was early evening, but he dared not return to the widow's lodgings for a second night. He should not have gone to the drawboy. The drawboy was incapable of resisting for long the temptation that betrayal offered. The threat of retaliation would not restrain him long. He would hold his tongue a couple of days at most. Once the drawboy talked, Anton's presence in Dublin would be known. All chance of concealment would disappear.

But the results should have been worth the risk taken. Anton had intended, upon finding Caitlín, to ask her to flee with him to France. He had hoped to have disappeared from the country before his arrival had even been reported.

She'd not come with him now; but he could not leave without her.

Did McKenna respect no boundaries? Had the taking of Caitlín been the completion of his revenge? No wonder Caitlín had not replied to his letter. Shame (or McKenna himself) must have stayed her hand. By the end of this second day, Anton was exhausted by fear. His imagination grew irrational. He had misjudged McKenna. Why should he not have misjudged Caitlín too? Why should he not see her as she was obviously seen by others? The drawboy had spoken of her contemptuously, and the drawboy was no more than an echo for the opinions of others. Perhaps she had the contemptible ability of a cat to transfer love (or its likeness) to the one who offered the greatest comfort. Perhaps she had shown the letter to McKenna. Anton grew hot as he imagined them laughing together over its sentiments; their mockery of his misjudged morality. He could hear Danno laughing as he remarked to the woman who lay beneath him that the rewards of timidity are few. He recollected the view he had glimpsed of Danno and the woman, Letitia, writhing so wantonly on the shredded silk; his imagination replaced that woman's barely-seen body with the unknown body of Caitlín. Once, Anton saw himself running a sword from Danno's spine straight through to the floor so far below, pinning the two of them like struggling butterflies to the boards. The sight gave him no satisfaction. He could not bear to see their pain.

Later, as it grew dark and people disappeared from the streets, he hid himself in a coach-house, and his thoughts grew maudlin. He reproached himself for having judged Caitlín too harshly. Was it not sensible for a young girl, abandoned (seemingly for good) by one man, to put herself under the protection of another? What alternative did she have? Her brother, Mick, had seen nothing but the streets. Was it not to be expected that in her gratitude towards her benefactor, she would offer to him what few gifts she had? But only a cad would take such gifts; gifts offered under duress (however artfully the duress lay concealed). Anton had resisted the offer. No matter that he had afterwards regretted his own resistance. What remained important was that he had, when tempted, been strong enough to resist. Danno McKenna had taken advantage. Anton knew the merchant well. He had heard his conquests described so many times. When had Danno McKenna ever failed to take advantage?

Throughout the night, his thoughts monotonously traced and retraced the same ground. By morning, his only firm conclusion was that Danno McKenna must be punished.

He was not a vengeful man. He had no desire to bring upon Danno what Danno had so cruelly brought upon him. He still could not believe that Danno had intended all the consequences of that initial betrayal. Anton imagined that he could still purchase freedom from the consequences of his own political activity by agreeing to reveal, under oath, the activities of others, including Danno McKenna. But Anton could not disclose unprompted what he had kept concealed under torture. He could, however, expose the sexual activities of his former employer; to Marvin Sweetman, the husband of Letitia.

Anton found a public house, in which the poster of himself had been defaced so thoroughly as to be unrecognisable. He called for paper, ink and a quill from the publican. Then he sat at a table on the darker side of the room, to write a letter to Marvin Sweetman.

***

After he had sent the messenger with the unsigned letter to Sweetman's house, Anton began to regret the deed (the lack of signature in itself caused him shame). Sweetman could not let such information lie. He could not fail to challenge McKenna. Suppose Caitlín loved McKenna? Anton was a modest man. He doubted the strength of his own attraction. As he grew calmer, it still did not occur to him to question the drawboy's insinuation. It did not surprise him that Caitlín should prefer another to himself; especially when that other was Danno McKenna. Who could resist McKenna? He had not been able to himself. God knew, he was a loveable man. Anton had loved him. Why should Caitlín not love him too? Any injury to Danno would cause Caitlín equal pain. Why should she be punished for allowing McKenna to seize what Anton had refused?

ELEVEN

The author of *A Vindication of the Rights of Woman* would not have approved. But Letitia herself felt that there was certainly an ironic sense of justice to the way in which the affair had begun. It illustrated so neatly the case of the turning worm. She had been bait set before her husband's friends; a lure to be reeled back by himself whenever he should so choose. He had taught her the game which she had played for his gratification. He had not considered the nature of the bait itself; that it was live, not dead. He had assumed that it was his to throw out, dabble and withdraw as he would. It had never occurred to Marvin that the game might be subverted and turned against him. He still was not aware that this had happened.

In any case, Letitia no longer cared what the opinion of Miss Wollstonecraft might be.

There had been a brief period of time in which she had felt a kinship with the other woman; when she felt that by subverting her husband's game, she had made a radical move towards self-hood which Miss Wollstonecraft might applaud (though the self revealed might not be one of which Miss Wollstonecraft would fully approve). But now she was in the grip of a control far stronger than any she had experienced before. The control which Marvin Sweetman exerted over her was an external thing. He had never taken control of her heart. She had never been in thrall to someone else. She was in thrall to Danno McKenna. She could at any time have ceased to act at Marvin Sweetman's command. She now believed herself incapable of refusing anything that Danno might ask. She adored him; she would lay down her life for him; she would kill for him. Were he to ask her to kill Marvin Sweetman in his bed, she believed that she would do so; but of course, she knew that Danno would not ask.

She kept a curl of Danno McKenna's hair in a locket around her neck. He had given her the locket. She told Marvin that the locket had belonged to her grandmother. But the hair inside, she had said, stroking it gently with a finger, had not come from her grandfather's head. Marvin had been intrigued. An illicit sweetheart? he had asked. Letitia had taken the curl out of the locket and had held it to her cheek. She had shrugged her shoulders. Who could tell, she had murmured, what secrets lay in her grandmother's heart? Then she had returned the curl to its locket. Such a curl, she had said, might be used as a profane symbol for the purposes of love in the way that Catholics were said to use a holy relic to meditate upon God; one would cup the locket in one's hands while dwelling upon the instances of one's worldly passion.

Marvin rarely came to her room now. She had, inadvertently, discovered a way in which to repel him. She had, on one occasion, attempted to replace the actual body of Marvin with the imagined body of Danno. The experiment had been unsuccessful, but the attempt had frightened Marvin. She had faced him; she had closed her eyes; she had groaned and she had writhed (all to no personal avail). Marvin had left her bed unsatisfied. He had remonstrated with her when he next came to her room. Her behaviour had been unseemly, he had told her. It was ugly, it was coarse and he could not but take exception to it. She must desist. She was so apologetic, so confused. She was not quite sure in what way it was that she had displeased him, but certainly, she would oblige him in any way she could. So she returned to her former position, lying on her stomach beneath his dry-skinned body. But she found herself unable to refrain from movement and those sounds of pleasure which so disgusted him. "You excite me too much," she would whisper when he complained. "I cannot help myself, Marvin; it shames me beyond words, but my actions seem quite out of my control."

She felt no pity for him as she drove him triumphantly from her bed with mocking groans of ecstasy.

***

161

Danno had sent a note to Marvin himself: a fresh order of silks had arrived from England. He would like to present a dress length to Mrs Sweetman, in lieu of the silk so wantonly destroyed during his recent labour troubles. If Mrs. Sweetman cared to call to the shop, she could choose from amongst his new materials. Were she to find a silk to her taste, McKenna and Sons would be honoured to fit Mrs. Sweetman for a dress in any style of her choice.

He had to see her; he had also wanted to know the state of her husband's conscience. In the note, he had named a day and he had named a time (which Mrs. Sweetman was at liberty to change should she so desire).

It had not occurred to Danno that the sending of the note would actually affect the state of Marvin Sweetman's conscience. Letitia, listening behind the wall upon the occasion of the government agent's next visit, had heard her husband regret the hastiness of his earlier capitulation, and had known that Danno had inadvertently won himself a reprieve.

This time there was a bed. A mattress had been laid upon the floor, spread with silks of different strengths and patterns; a riotous nest of silks.

Anton's loom lay empty.

Danno could not see the loom without thinking of the Frenchman's hands. By whom had the hands been severely disfigured? Danno had been obliged to display a poster of the wanted weaver in his own shop window. To have refused would have aroused suspicion.

"Will he come back?" Letitia asked. She had seen the posters. Her summer muslin lay on the floor. She sat naked on the bed with her arms, tinged brown with summer sun, wrapped around her pale shins, her knees level with her breasts. Her throat was scattered with tiny freckles.

Danno shook his head. He too was naked and he lay embedded in the layers of silk, his hands behind his head, one leg straight, the other bent and fallen out to the side. Letitia sat in the angle created by the position of his two legs.

"He'd be a fool, wouldn't he? They say that some of the mutineers escaped to France. What better place for Anton?"

"You think he'll return, don't you?"

He tickled the two dimples at the base of her back with the toes of his bent leg.

"There's a young girl besotted by him who thinks he'll come back for her. The arrogance of love. He never wrote her a word. He let her think he was dead; but Caitlín thinks she was loved with a passion the equal of her own."

"And you believe her?"

He was leaning up on one elbow now, and he drew the forefinger of his other hand, with almost intolerable slowness, up and down her spine. Her back unfurled and furled again in agonised response to his sliding finger.

"She would be difficult to resist."

"Have you?"

Her breathing had grown unsteady, and she was writhing like a fish out of water. Watching her was driving him mad with desire.

"She hasn't put me to the test."

"Damn you, McKenna," she breathed and she twisted around to sprawl across his belly.

"For me, Caitlín is untouchable," he mouthed upon her eyelid; but Letitia no longer cared.

Afterwards he told her that his wedding date was set for a fortnight hence. She buried her face in his shoulder to stop herself from crying. "How can you?" she whispered. "How can you love me and marry her?" It was just the question she had determined she must never ask.

He did not know himself. He hugged Letitia's body to his own; his legs were wrapped around her thighs, his arms enclosed her torso with one hand pressed against her buttocks, the other on her shoulders. He was silent. The question could not be answered.

She surrounded him by questions crazed with jealousy:

"With what will you woo Pansy on your wedding night? A bed such as this? Have you seen her naked? Of course not; she's a marriageable girl. Oh God! Oh Danno! What if, naked, she surpasses me? Or what if, in bed, with the candle blown out, you can tell no difference?"

163

He hugged her and he rocked her and he kissed her while she sobbed. She bit upon a handful of silk. She thought if only she might stuff her mouth tight with silk, to stop the words from flowing out; but they continued to flow inexorably on.

What if, alternatively, upon seeing Pansy, he could only prepare himself by thinking of Letitia?

"And if you can do so, through thoughts of me, does that mean that our sexual activities take place predominantly within our own skulls?"

She had forgotten her own inability to substitute the imagined Danno for the actual Marvin. She beat at Danno's chest with her fists as though he were already guilty. "And if you can create me so conveniently," she cried, "will you, perhaps, wonder do we need to meet in the flesh at all?"

He loved her for the intensity of her jealousy. She was burning with jealousy. Her entire body had heated up. Her jealousy was well-founded. He would make love to Pansy on their wedding night, and he knew that he would have no need to call upon an image of Letitia to assist him. He was ashamed that it could be done so easily. He cradled Letitia's hot, damp neck in his hands and he kissed her lips to silence.

"Pansy can't exist in your presence," he whispered guiltily and the words he spoke fell like balm into her mouth.

As they were dressing, she asked him what he would do if he were forced to choose between them.

"The question will not arise."

"But if it did," she pressed.

"I could not live without you," he admitted reluctantly.

It was Caitlín who took Letitia's measurements in a private room at the back of the shop. A length of silk had been quickly chosen. "Who destroyed the web on Anton's loom?" Letitia asked.

Caitlín, encircling Letitia's waist in a loop of tape, shrugged her shoulders. She had her own suspicions, but she was not about to divulge them to a woman she had never met before. Mr. McKenna, Caitlín noted, could not keep his eyes off Mrs. Sweetman. A poor look out for his wedding.

"Mr. Paradis is not short of enemies, is he?" she remarked savagely. "When his friend was so quick to find him guilty." His hands! She could not bear the ruin of his hands. Mr. McKenna (who bore her attack as always, the wonderful man that he was, without complaint) wondered why he had not written. How could he have written to her with broken hands? But still, he was alive! The government did not offer rewards for dead men. She had not expected that much. She looked at the tape. "Twenty-two inches, Mr. McKenna – or no. Wait. You're holding your breath in, Ma'am."

Letitia blushed and relaxed her stomach muscles.

"Twenty-three and a half inches, sir."

Letitia saw Danno laugh as he crossed out one figure and replaced it with another. Rich scarlet, she turned her head away and stared through the window to the courtyard behind. She turned back in time to see him wink at Caitlín. She looked at him with dislike.

"If you'll just raise your arms, Ma'am."

Danno smiled. Oh God. He was looking at her breasts outlined in muslin. She remembered how his tongue had touched her nipples and she closed her eyes.

"Thirty-four inches."

She opened her eyes again and found Caitlín looking at her with the longing eyes of one deprived of a love the equal of the love so remorselessly displayed before her. Letitia touched the girl's face gently with her hand.

"He'll be back for you."

The girl's mouth trembled. She shook her head.

"He should stay away," she said bleakly. He would be back, she knew. "He's a hero now. I don't know how he came to be a hero. He was happy as a weaver. But Mr. McKenna says it had to be so."

She began to cry.

"Why could they not have let him be?" she asked Danno pitifully. "Don't they know that in this country, heroes always die?"

If Anton came to Dublin, Danno hoped that he would stay alive long enough to discover that he was a hero.

There were certain people in the city who would be honoured to conceal Anton Paradis; there were others who would betray him.

But to whom would Anton first reveal himself? He would not reveal himself to Danno. If it would have helped, Danno would have gone through the city, scratching the message, 'Danno loves Anton', on the walls of all the houses in which posters were displayed, in the hope that out of thousands, Anton's eye might have alighted on one or two. But what might have drawn Anton would most certainly have drawn others. What Danno feared was that Anton would reveal himself to those who knew Caitlín, and in so doing, put his trust in those most likely to betray him: the weavers.

"If he comes here," he had said to Caitlín, "Tell me."

***

Marvin himself had urged his wife to keep the appointment with Danno.

"Be sure he understands how highly I esteem his friendship," he had said, and Letitia had replied, with sly honesty, that she would leave Mr. McKenna in no doubt as to the sincerity of her husband's feeling for him.

"That's my girl," Marvin had said complacently.

"Perhaps you should come with me," she had added, knowing that he no longer dared to leave the house.

The letter, which arrived shortly after Letitia had departed, was short and direct:

Mr. Sweetman: I wish to bring to your attention the fact that Danno McKenna has seduced your wife. Whether or not the seduction still continues, I cannot say. I suggest you question Mrs. Sweetman.

The messenger had disappeared before he could be questioned, but it was not difficult to deduce that the letter came from one of McKenna's troublesome weavers.

Marvin Sweetman did not at first believe the contents of the letter. He was misled by its lack of sophistication. It was too nakedly vengeful. The letter made no claim to have been written for Marvin's sake; nor was there any hint of reluctance to perform the task undertaken. 'I wish' was what the informer had written, not 'Would that I were not the one' or, 'I feel it my unwelcome duty'. The informer had not even had the grace to describe himself at the close of the letter as 'a wellwisher'. Marvin, accustomed to gilded truth, read the letter and mistook its simplicity for falsehood.

Besides, the accusation was ridiculous.

It had rained earlier. Marvin Sweetman paced around his sun-stewed, muggy garden pursued by overlapping clouds of fresh-hatched midges. From windows, his course was observed: by militia men; by his daughter. Had Letitia not refused to sleep with McKenna, when by sleeping with him she might have saved her husband? A cheating wife would have jumped at such an opportunity to fulfil her husband's request. His forehead was sweating profusely; midges were drowning in the sweat. Instead, she had been so shocked by the suggestion as to burden him with a sense of shame for having made it.

But what if she had later regretted her refusal? What if his anonymous informant was right in stating that a seduction had taken place, but wrong as to his identification of the author of the seduction? He wiped a hand across his forehead, smearing both hand and forehead with crushed insects. What if Letitia, his darling Letitia, had thought better of her prudery and had thrown herself to McKenna to save her husband? He, after all, had concealed from her his meetings with the government agent, for fear of losing her respect; what if she had concealed the seduction of his enemy for fear of losing his respect?

Marvin Sweetman now understood everything; that hitherto inexplicably lascivious behaviour, for instance, stood revealed. Condemning herself (unjustly, my darling Letitia, unjustly) for a whore, she had taken to acting thus before her husband.

Holding Anton's letter in his hand, Marvin Sweetman wept praise not only for his wife's courage, but also for her shame. While he wept (under surveillance) in what he believed to be the privacy of his first wife's rose garden, Letitia and her lover lay kissing with pained, post-coital tenderness in their silky bed. He began to gather roses (crawling with greenfly) to give to Letitia, tearing them from the thorny bushes with his bare hands.

He had sent her to that man today. Danno McKenna, under the guise of honour, had summoned Marvin Sweetman's wife, with Marvin's own unwitting assistance, to an assignment; and she had gone so meekly, without protest, knowing the sacrifice ahead. Then he remembered that she had asked him to accompany her. He had refused and she had not made the request a second time. His refusal had been an act of desertion. Marvin sat upon a wooden garden seat, the roses drooping from his bleeding hands, and longed for Letitia's return. Midges settled on his damp hair. He was humiliated by the strength of her devotion. He longed to forgive her for a sin so nobly committed.

***

Letitia hated his displays of love at any time; but to find him at his most yearningly affectionate when she had just come from Danno was intolerable.

She had been singing (she could not refrain from snatches of song) when she came into the house. Marvin had been standing in the hall, holding a bunch of wilting, blown roses in his hands. The hall was tainted with their over-ripe smell. Petals had already fallen to the floor. He had apparently picked them especially for her. No sooner had he given them to her than she laid them aside on a chair. "The thorns," she had said, by way of explanation. Her husband looked dishevelled. Dirt was smeared across his forehead, and his hands were scratched. His self-imposed confinement was, she thought, provoking her husband to great oddity.

"Your afternoon?" he inquired hesitantly.

She saw reason for the roses then. She had forgotten. She was expected to be the bearer of good news.

"You need no longer fear McKenna."

Her voice was cold as she lied. The seduction of her husband's conscience by the government spy had released Letitia from any sense of obligation to him; yet the deliberate telling of a lie was hard to accomplish.

He took her hand in his, then raised it to his lips and kissed it. She attempted to pull it back. She could not help herself. It was as though he were (in innocence?) feeding on the remains. He let her hand fall, and then, quite horribly, tears rolled out of his eyes. She put her hand up to her mouth and stared at him.

"Marvin?"

"You were away a long time."

She had been gone for almost five hours.

"There were things which had to be done."

"I know," he said. "I know." And he bowed his head with docility.

He knew of the affair. She was almost certain that he knew, and yet he would make no accusation. He had, it seemed, grown amorous with pain. Or did he know there could be no worse punishment than an unwanted wooing?

The more she attempted to repel him, the more insistent his advances became. He could not be avoided. Where she went, he followed. And there were places where he would not allow her to go. She was forbidden the privacy of her own sewing room. "You must be brave," he told her gently, when she attempted to retire to her bedroom. Not even the presence of Caroline (and Caroline, disturbed by the atmosphere, clung closely to her stepmother) could save her from his attentions. The resurrection of lust made him careless.

In front of his own daughter, he did what he had never done before; he kissed Letitia on the mouth, clasping her head between his hands to prevent her from moving her lips away from his.

"Poor child," he murmured, holding her head inexorably still while she struggled to escape. "Poor child. I understand."

"Your daughter, Marvin!"

Caroline stood white-faced, staring at them. She looked on the point of swooning.

"Caroline, darling!"

The girl said nothing, but continued to stare, horrified, at them both. Her reaction, even to Letitia, seemed extreme. Marvin Sweetman was acting within his rights, and a kiss, even of that degree of passion, should surely not have such an effect on a girl so old as Caroline?

"She should have left." Marvin said impatiently. He still held his wife's head between his hands. His breath, like his roses, smelt over-ripe. "My daughter has a curiosity about the habits of others which she must learn to curb. It vies with her good manners."

Letitia made no further attempt to escape from her husband's embrace. A struggle would have frightened Caroline further.

"It was just a kiss," she told her unmoving step-daughter gently, her face still snared within her husband's fingers.

She was comforted herself by the dismissiveness of the words. They assured her that while there were kisses which counted, there were others which did not.

Marvin abandoned his wife at last.

He approached his daughter and pinched her small, soft chin gently between his thumb and forefinger. "She is a jealous Miss, isn't she?" he asked his daughter, and his voice took on an air of teasing cajolement. "She cannot bear to share her father. She had me to herself too long. She was ever a greedy child. Is that not so, Caroline?"

Caroline nodded her head obediently. "Yes, Father," she whispered.

Perhaps he had been too insistent? Had he been so engrossed in demonstrating absolution that he had taken insufficient account of his wife's understandable sensibilities? When he thought of the bleak way in which she had said that there had been things to do at McKenna's warehouse (dear God, not in the warehouse!), his heart could break on her behalf. How was he to make his forgiveness understood but by persistence? Should he admit to having guessed her secret? The secret she had taken so much trouble to conceal? An admission in such circumstances would seem a cruelty. No. He must allow the realisation to come gradually, soothingly to her, without the need for words. Perhaps an approach by night, without fuss; as though nothing had ever been amiss.

When Marvin Sweetman came to Letitia's room that night, he found his daughter in her bed. She was already fallen asleep, lying on one of his wife's arms.

"What is she doing here?"

Letitia wasn't sure herself.

"She was upset. She seemed afraid to leave me alone."

"Wake her."

Letitia shook her head reluctantly.

"There'll be a scene."

Marvin leaned across the bed and shook his daughter's shoulder. Caroline woke up and looked at her father with reluctant, blinking eyes. He bent down and kissed her on the cheek and felt her shrink away.

"She's jealous of you," he said to Letitia with his mouth still close to his daughter's cheek. Then he straightened up again. "Caroline, if you stay here, you will be punished," he said. "You would not like to be punished in front of Mama, now would you?"

She shook her head.

"Then go, while there is still time. And consider yourself lucky to have escaped so lightly. Were Mama not here . . ."

"Mama, I . . ."

Caroline looked guiltily to Letitia. Letitia nodded.

"You must obey your father, sweetheart. You'll sleep better alone."

Caroline crawled slowly across her step-mother's body.

"Come and be kissed goodnight, Caroline," her father said as she walked towards the door. She came back to stand beside her father and she raised an expressionless face.

Letitia watched Marvin's lips brush lightly over his daughter's mouth and realised that until tonight, she had never seen her husband kiss his daughter.

He was normally so unyielding towards Caroline. It seemed a pity that when he relented so far as to show the child affection, the child should be too much engaged in a fit of the sulks to appreciate the gesture.

"And now . . ." Marvin said, when Caroline had closed the door.

***

She had endured and she had survived.

She had been unable to summon sufficient heart to mock the passion of the afternoon. It had seemed less painful simply to endure him. So she had lain beneath him, crying soundlessly into the sheet below while he had pushed his way with grunting perseverance to a conclusion. Then he had left her, with no more than a whispered goodnight.

After breakfast, she was allowed to retreat, unaccompanied, to her sewing room. She was altering another of the dresses brought with her from her father's house. She wished she could return to her father's house. But such a thing would not be countenanced. She could scarce think of any grounds her father would consider serious enough to warrant a return. He would not hesitate to deliver his daughter back to such a husband as Marvin Sweetman.

Caroline, when she entered the room, was carrying an open book like a shield across her chest. Her eyes were set in purple shadows and their lids were pink and swollen. She was biting at her lip with her tooth and her words, when she began to speak, were hard to hear.

"Did you know, Mama," she asked hurriedly, as though she were delivering a lesson of the greatest urgency, "that each silk cocoon yields about a thousand yards of a continuous double thread of silk; and that twelve strands twisted make the finest thread that can be used for weaving?"

Letitia shook her head and Caroline fell silent.

The girl seemed consumed by guilt. A confession of some kind was clearly imminent. Letitia's heart sank. She wondered did she have the strength to hear it out. Caroline's crimes were always so insignificant; the guilt experienced so disproportionate to their size. Caroline stepped closer to her stepmother, and put the book down on the sewing table. Letitia braced herself.

"I thought he might be here," she whispered.

"Your father?"

Caroline nodded. She put her hand tentatively on Letitia's hand.

"I saw my father punish you."

"Punish me? What do you mean?"

"Last night. Through the keyhole."

"Caroline!"

Letitia snatched her hand away, shaking it as though it had been stung by an insect.

"I should have stayed; but I was too afraid. You must despise me now."

That she should be subjected not only to the father's doglike rutting, but also to his daughter's prurient curiosity was just unbearable! Marvin was right. His daughter suffered from a morbid jealousy. Letitia stared at the girl in silence. She did not know what to say.

She watched as Caroline folded her arms closely across her chest and began to rock to and fro.

Caroline had more to say.

"He used to punish me that way. Until my blood came. When he saw the bleeding, he said that God had taken over my punishment now. And then he married you."

Letitia was frightened. She felt the need to pray, but nothing would come into her pulsing head.

"You don't understand what you're saying," she whispered.

Her sewing had fallen from her lap. She held an empty needle in her hand. Young girls were so fanciful. One Halloween, she had searched in a mirror for the face of the man she would marry, and she had seen the image of her own father.

"You should beware, Caroline," she said, her voice cool. "Have you not allowed your imagination to run riot?"

Dear God, let this be fancy! Her fingers grew white around the needle. She had a great desire to run, with covered ears, from the room.

Caroline had closed her eyes. Only within the protection of such darkness could she bring herself to speak on.

"Sometimes when I heard him enter my bedroom, I would feign sleep; then he would wake me with a kiss upon the cheek. It was always as a punishment for wickedness committed. My sins were so manifold, Mama, that I could not always remember the particular wickedness for which the punishment was intended."

Sunshine was streaming into the room. Beyond the window, birds still sang. Letitia's chest had grown constricted and she could only breath with difficulty.

"Do you think me wicked, Mama?" Caroline opened her eyes to look at Letitia, fearfully.

Letitia could not speak. She shook her head.

"He said I must never tell you, for you would leave should you discover how wicked I was."

On the night of her marriage to Marvin Sweetman, Letitia had known, with a dull shock, that her childhood was over. She had been unprepared. But for Caroline, there had been no childhood at all.

"What age were you, Caroline, when your father first began to punish you this way?"

"I was seven. The punishments began the year my mother died."

Marvin was happier that morning than he had been for weeks. The wife who had won McKenna's silence at such cost had lain so peacefully beneath him the night before; he felt an understanding had been reached. Even the jealousy of his little daughter had been touching. He craved to celebrate the day with some extravagance, though he knew he must do nothing to unsettle a balance so tenuously achieved.

But when he heard the faint sounds of footsteps on the wooden landing overhead, he had to come out from his study. Could they resist the offer of a picnic in the park with strawberries, cream and wine?

He discovered his wife and daughter (almost the height of his wife) descending the stairs on tip-toes. They stopped when they saw him. They were holding hands.

"And where are my two beautiful girls going with such stealth?" he asked, smiling at the pleasingly blurred image that they made in the distance, on the stairs, in their white muslins. "You both look good enough to eat."

Neither made any reply.

After a moment's hesitation, they continued to descend.

When they drew nearer, he could see that he had been premature in his praise. They looked, in fact, quite ill. Letitia passed straight by him by with the vacant air of a somnambulist. His daughter followed, clinging to Letitia's hand.

"I thought," he said doubtfully to their backs, "a picnic. With strawberries. But if . . ." He was frightened by the women. They had reached the front door. Were they going to leave the house without a word?

"Letitia," he said sharply.

She had opened the door and she stood illuminated in the sunlight. Beyond her, a militia man stood guard upon the step.

"A cab, Ma'am?" Marvin heard him ask.

"Letitia," Marvin called again.

It was Caroline who spoke, turning her head to look back towards her father with bewilderment, but continuing to cling to Letitia's hand.

"I have confessed my wickedness to Mama," she told him. "She says we must leave," she added apprehensively. She wished Mama would speak.

Caroline didn't understand. Mama had said that she was innocent of any fault. Indeed, it was Father she had accused of wickedness, though plainly this could not be so. But Mama had spoken so adamantly. And now, instead of attempting to prevent their departure, her father put his hands up to his face and ran back into the study from which he had so recently emerged.

TWELVE

The same French captain who had carried Anton from France to Dublin agreed to carry him back. He was sailing with the dawn tide, God willing. Anton should be on board by midnight.

"You will not expect me to wait beyond my time."

The captain had seen the posters. He would neither betray his passenger (for who was going to reward a Frenchman?) nor extend himself on his passenger's behalf. If Paradis did not appear, the captain would assume his passenger (whose fare was already in the captain's pocket) arrested.

"I'll be there before she sails."

But he would not be on board by midnight. By midnight it would be barely dark, and the final episode of this Dublin odyssey could only be undertaken in the dark.

Anton had concluded that his only course was to return to France. There was nothing but betrayal for him here. Yet he could not bring himself to leave without a glimpse of Caitlín.

The sun, the heat of which had earlier hatched that torment of midges in Marvin Sweetman's garden, continued to shine throughout the evening. Night settled with dangerous, silvery lightness on the city. They were looking for a man, furtive and alone in night-time shadows. It was frightening to walk alone. Outside the gates of Trinity College, Anton flung his arms around the neck of an unknown, drunken student; the two of them staggered unnoticed, in a close embrace, up Dame Street. Close by to McKenna's shop, Anton detached himself from his insensible companion, who continued on, unsteadily, towards the Castle.

The shop itself was boarded up. New, wrought-iron gates had been set into the archway. They were locked, preventing access to the courtyard beyond. Anton stood helplessly at the foot of the steps leading up to the front door of McKenna's house. He remembered that he had been prepared to kneel on those same steps until Danno agreed to forgive him (for a crime not committed). At the time he planned such self-abasement, Danno had already given his name to his Castle friends. Anton spat with ritual contempt upon the spot where he imagined he might have knelt. He had no idea how he might attract Caitlín's attention without rousing the entire household. Besides, he could not even be sure that it was in the house she slept.

There was a woman with a hand-cart and a shovel, collecting horse-dung from the street. He and the drunk had earlier passed her by. He waited until she drew level with him. For a couple of pence, she agreed to hide her cart in the next laneway, knock at McKenna's front door and ask for Caitlín. She was to say that Caitlín's brother was deathly sick; Caitlín must come to him at once.

It was Danno himself who answered the door. Anton, hiding in the laneway beside the stinking cart, could hear the see-saw murmur of his voice. Then the door closed. The dung woman came around the corner.

"The gentleman who answered the door was puzzled by the message," she told Anton. "Said he thought her brother was gone to Wexford; to make hay. I told the gentleman quicker than you'd blink your eye that a lad couldn't make hay when he was dying. The brother, I told him, had come back; to see his sister before he died."

She looked pleased with herself as she took up the handle of her cart. "So wasn't I the great story-teller? I could hear the poor girl inside the house, screaming at the news. She'll be at her brother's side as soon as she can," she told Anton. Then she began to laugh, looking into his agitated face. "Lord, mister! If you are the sickly party, I hope you're not her brother; for you are dying of love, if you're dying of anything."

She accepted a final coin.

"A tribute to your imagination," he said.

It was with hesitance that Caitlín walked down the steps to the pavement and stood beneath the street lamp.

Anton watched her from the entrance to the laneway as she peered up and down the street, trying vainly to see beyond the lighted circle in which she stood. There were no tears upon her skin. She had not believed the message. If she feared for her brother's life, she would be running up the street, with her skirts hitched up in her hands, and the tears flying from her face. Instead, she stood still, watching and listening. Her face was tight with anticipation.

She was looking for Anton Paradis.

The distance was still too great between them. Were he to call her name, he would have to pitch his voice too loud. He did not dare to do it, for fear of who might be standing listening behind the door at the top of the steps. He felt for a coin in his pocket. His hand closed on a French one, he could tell by the shape. Taking it out, he lobbed it in her direction. It landed, with a sharp rattle, a yard short of her feet. She looked down, startled, then bent to pick it up. He saw her turn it over in her fingers. Then she looked up the street towards him. A smile was edging its way out onto her face. He waited. She lingered within the pool of light, turning the coin over and over as she continued to look up the street with that intimate little smile tickling at her lips. Was she daring to tease him? Was she teasing herself, standing there, knowing she was just beyond his reach? He saw her lift the coin slowly to her lips and kiss it; then she began to walk towards him, her figure darkening as it came towards the outer edge of light.

She might be acting falsely, dispatched to gleam and entice beneath the lamplight; if so, she had succeeded. He was enticed. He was incapable of flight. He could not fail to follow her wherever she might wish to lead him.

She saw him before he could touch her. She said nothing. His name could not be spoken out aloud. It was she who touched him first, slipping an arm around his waist and drawing him silently back towards the house. He walked with torpid obedience beside her. She felt his hip rub up and down against her own; he felt her shiver. She had forgotten his feet; she had forgotten his hands.

"Oh, Jesus," he heard her whisper.

It could have been a cry of guilt.

He should have gone while she was still no more than a sliver of substance in the light.

Even when he saw McKenna waiting at the doorway, he could not break away. She had so far abducted his senses that he no longer had the power to save himself. Defeated, he laid his cheek briefly down on her hair.

"McKenna knows?" was all he said, in a voice almost inaudible with despair.

"He said to bring you into the house; like we were courting lovers."

Inside the door, she let her arm fall from round his waist. She had seen his face in the light of the street lamp. Danno, who had been going to embrace the weaver, hesitated and then stood still.

"Anton?" he said gently.

The weaver made no reply. He didn't even look at him. He had eyes for no one but Caitlín. Caitlín moved closer to the silk merchant, so close that her arm was touching his.

The weaver's look was of such abandoned desolation.

"Was it easy, Caitlín?" he asked her bleakly.

She looked at him without comprehension.

He reached forward and caressed her cheek.

Danno gazed rapturously at the silk-weaver's fingers as they pressed with flexible ease on Caitlín's skin. The weaver's hands were not as damaged as had been implied.

"Still soft," Anton murmured. "It hasn't lost its softness."

His fingertips were tippling flames upon her skin. She closed her eyes. It was as much as she had ever been given by him; and then she heard him add: "So McKenna was not too late."

It was too cruel. She had kept faith on the basis of so little. She opened her eyes and looked at his despairing face; then she slapped it hard with the flat of her hand, before pushing past him and running out through the hall to the servants' quarters beyond.

The two men were left alone.

"You succumb easily to rumours, Paradis," Danno said coldly to the weaver. "Though I am pained by your opinion of me, I can understand it; but that you should distrust Caitlín is incomprehensible."

The weaver stood with his hand on his smarting cheek. His eyes were closed. The joints of the fingers, Danno noticed, were discoloured, and the fingers themselves were fatter than they should be.

"Can you still weave?" he asked. He had to know.

Anton gave no indication of having heard McKenna's words.

Anton had not forgiven him. Danno could scarcely bear the knowledge that he had, for several months, remained an object of hatred to the weaver. Danno felt so tender this evening with the smell of Letitia's perfume subdued, but still lingering on his skin. He would like to have put his arm around the weaver's shoulders, but he did not dare. God, but he wished that Anton would answer his question. It was the most important question that could be asked. Was Anton still capable of handling the loom?

"Anton?" he said, and he touched the air above the weaver's shoulder with the palm of his hand. The weaver, sensing the movement of the merchant's hand, shrank away. Danno withdrew his hand.

He must have patience. The weaver had been treated badly. Why should he not expect betrayal from those closest to him? Danno remembered how he had, with far less provocation, believed impossible baseness of Anton. The weaver was smiling into his hand. Danno understood why; Anton knew by his stinging flesh that Caitlín had not deserted him for the merchant. Danno, who believed that a man could survive the loss of love more easily than (having so little himself) the loss of his artistic creativity, saw that, for now, his question would not be answered.

"Who led you to believe that I had taken advantage?" he asked.

Anton's hand still clung to the fading stigmata of love upon his face.

"She was your innocent decoy then?"

Anton's voice was hostile and devoid of affection. Danno looked at the weaver in astonishment. The question implied an expectation too humiliating to countenance.

"Your opinion of me is so low, Anton?" he asked, nevertheless. The question was put to prompt a denial. None came. Instead the weaver's face grew more inscrutable, as ice, thickening, grows more opaque.

"What was your reward for the first betrayal?"

The question exploded within Danno's body like an over-heated crystal ball. Shards pierced all his inward parts without distinction: his heart, his brain, his guts. That anyone who knew him could imagine him capable of such treachery was pain enough; but that Anton, the indispensable curator of his soul, should think so, was insupportable. Shards pierced his eyes and tears as heavy as blood began to fall.

"Betray you? My brother in silk?" he said, his language over-wrought with emotion.

Danno heard contempt in Anton's answering silence. He had been judged and condemned long ago. It seemed that he was no longer worth even the exchange of words. The silence was broken only by the whirring sound of a daddy-long-legs beating along the ceiling.

"Mr. McKenna loves you almost as well as I do myself."

Caitlín had crept back into the hall. She could not keep away.

Anton shook his head. He didn't want to hear truth from Caitlín. He could not bear to believe in Danno's innocence. He could not have been duped into a hatred so vibrant as the one he had harboured towards Danno.

"He is a merchant and I am a weaver," he said dully. The lesson had finally been learnt. "A friendship did exist. I don't deny that there was love between us. But nothing so strong that it could not be repudiated should circumstances demand. Isn't that so, McKenna?"

"He thinks I was the cause of his arrest," Danno told Caitlín. He didn't know how much she had heard from behind the servant's door.

"I know he was," Anton said to her. "I was told by my interrogators."

"You'd believe your enemies more readily than your friends?"

"He had ceased to be my friend. He betrayed me as an enemy; and he's still my enemy now."

Her look was so incredulous. Anton sensed himself ridiculed by it. His belief in Danno's guilt, unnaturally implanted, and unchal-lenged for so long, began to waver. Anton found himself a prey to growing uncertainty.

"Malachi Delaney betrayed you," Caitlín told him, her voice high with the surprise that he should ever have believed otherwise. "And it was a pleasure to him. He never confessed to it, but the whole household knew."

He wished that she would come and hold him round the waist once more. She was standing too far away from him. Of course Malachi had betrayed him. Malachi was a fellow weaver, a fellow Defender; but he was also a naturally treacherous man (as Danno was a naturally honourable man) to whom Anton had been an obstacle. Why would Caitlín not come and stand beside him? She was judging him. He could not bear to be judged by Caitlín. She should be offering him comfort: not judgement. What if she were to find him wanting?

"Even Charlotte?" His voice was pleading.

"Yes, though she pretended ignorance."

Danno's innocence was itself a type of betrayal.

Anton felt himself unhinged by its appearance. The fragile, falsely-based categories of loyalty and disloyalty into which those who surrounded him had been divided, crumbled in the light of Danno's innocence and Malachi's guilt. The merchant stood before the weaver, amidst the silk-laden walls of his own shadowy hall, his face suffused with love and injury. His bewilderment made Anton's belief in his guilt seem all the more outrageous. Anton hoped that neither Danno nor Caitlín might ever be forced to understand the derangement an abandoned soul can suffer; the bitterness that can infest the taunted mind. He thought of the letter he had sent to Marvin Sweetman that afternoon; a letter written in the grip of a jealousy which now (viewed through their eyes) seemed ridiculous. How they would despise him were they to know of it.

"I am a weaver," he said unexpectedly. "If you still need me."

He held out his hands tentatively to Danno, turning them over and back before the merchant's face. He was offering his hands to Danno; in return for the merchant's forgiveness. He could do no more.

It was enough.

Danno caught the weaver's wrists in his own hands. He was afraid to touch the swollen fingers. Slowly the weaver clenched his fists; slowly he stretched his fingers wide. His arms swelled and trembled with effort; tendons tightened beneath Danno's fingers. Caitlín watched with her hand against her mouth. Small joints in Anton's fingers cracked like snapping glass. Sweat rolled from the weaver's cheeks down into his beard.

"It was intended that I should not weave again. But I have outwitted them."

They were damaged, but they were not the hands described in the poster.

"I expected worse," Danno admitted, and he dared to stroke the reddened, shining joints.

"A second breaking was necessary to repair the first."

Anton heard Caitlín moan with pity and his spirits spun the brief upward flight of a fly trapped under a glass.

"But yesterday," he said, "I picked an eyelash from my eyeball with the thumb and first finger of my left hand. My fingers have not lost their dexterity. I believe that they are still capable of drawing the finest of threads through the eye of a mail."

"Sweet Mary," said Caitlín, taking the weaver's hands from Danno.

She was very ashamed. His precious fingers had touched her face and she had not given so much as a thought to their condition. She had been aware of nothing more than the intense burning of her own skin beneath their pressure. She began, feverishly, to examine the fingers before drawing each one, in turn, across her parted lips; as though each might be healed by a kiss.

He watched dreamily, detachedly, as though the hands were not his own.

"Of course, you are more than just a weaver now," Danno told him. "You're a hero," he added, though the notion seemed, in the weaver's actual presence, unlikely. Unlikely, but surely flattering?

He was not prepared for the violence of the weaver's response.

"I'll be no one's bloody hero," Anton shouted, snatching his hands away from Caitlín's fondling mouth.

From upstairs came the sound of Mrs. McKenna's frightened voice: "Danno, Danno, is anything wrong?"

"Nothing's wrong. Go back to sleep."

"I am a weaver," Anton said sullenly then. "I will be nothing else."

Caitlín put her arm protectively round his waist, just as he had earlier longed for her to do. It was such a small ambition; to be a well-loved, assiduous weaver. She could understand the satisfaction of such an ambition fulfilled.

"Leave him be, Mr. McKenna," she said.

Danno looked doubtful. He shrugged.

"He's a hero whether he likes it or not."

Danno was more than doubtful; he was disappointed. He could not understand the weaver's lack of pride. "There are people who would follow you were you to lead them to hell," he said cajolingly.

Anton shook his head wearily. Danno could not have said worse.

"Just a weaver," he whispered, and he threaded his fingers in and out through Caitlín's hair. He had been a hero. He knew what it was like to be allowed an existence only in the imagination of others. He thought that it was still not too late to leave; but he didn't want to go.

"They can't use me if they can't find me. If you want a weaver, Danno, hide me."

Anton saw the merchant slowly nod his head and felt a great relief.

"You have more right than most to be a weaver," Danno conceded reluctantly. Though he knew that Anton could be nothing else, his refusal to accept what Danno most desired (the leadership of a devoted following) was almost beyond bearing. Between being a weaver and leading a revolution, there was, for Anton, no choice. Danno's disappointment was without logic. It was imperative (even for Danno's sake) that Anton be a weaver. But in his absence, it had seemed to Danno that the weaver could quite easily be both.

Why had he allowed his expectations such rein? He, who knew Anton better than anyone else, had created from the weaver (his well-known friend) a soaring, brilliant, multi-faceted creature, irreconcilably at odds with its alleged progenitor. This charismatic creature of his imagination bore no more resemblance to the weaver than did a dog to the flea which happened to live on its back.

"But you did behave with heroism, didn't you?"

The question was accusatory. It sought to lay blame. The tone insinuated that an irresponsible flirtation with heroics had allowed false expectations to take hold.

Anton shrugged. He understood Danno's disappointment. Heroism had been bestowed upon the wrong man.

"It was unavoidable," he told the merchant. "My survival was achieved by means considered by others to be honourable. Are you saying I misled the people by behaving inadvertently with honour? I gave away the names of no Defenders, because no name would come to mind. Was that an offence?"

Danno sighed, while the fabulous creature slunk, defeated, from his mind. Only Letitia was capable of living up to her imagined image; indeed, she sometimes threatened (dangerously) to surpass it.

"I think you underestimate your own courage," was all he dared to say.

"Perhaps," Anton said without particular interest. He was gazing at the net of Caitlín's hair caught between his fingers. "It doesn't matter. Courage is not a quality I desire to prove further."

There was too much talk.

"Are you willing to hide him or not, Mr. McKenna?" Caitlín asked impatiently.

"Of course," Danno said.

***

Where better to hide a weaver than in the warehouse where his own loom was lodged?

It had not been possible for Danno to come up with any plausible alternative. Reluctantly he had led the way to the room in which he and Letitia had so recently made love. The bed had not been cleared away. He had created it himself; he had intended to dismantle it as well. Theirs was not an affair that he had wished to bring to the attention of any servants. He had not cared to risk gossip so close to the wedding.

"A pretty bed for a weaver," Caitlín had commented, eying the tousled silks; and had added slyly: "Haven't you great powers of foresight, Mr. McKenna, that you knew he was coming?"

He could hardly have denied them the bed. They had so obviously been waiting for him to leave.

***

She had not received his letter. Until the posters had appeared, she had not known that he was still alive.

"Charlotte must have read it," she said and she began immediately to mourn. "My letter. I've never had a letter. Such cruelty! She knew you were alive and didn't tell me!"

He watched her cry for the hope she had been deprived of.

He was humiliated by her faithfulness to a man who had given her nothing. How long would she have waited? It was a question which, in the light of his earlier, misguided accusation, he would not have dared to ask.

They lay wound around in the silks that Caitlín had approached with such initial caution.

"They smell of her perfume," she had said with distaste.

And sex, Anton had thought, though did not say. They had used the bed that very afternoon, so Caitlín said. She had not been able to like Letitia. Letitia, she had said, had been too unbearably brimming with love. And had overflowed, Anton had thought. The odour of spent sex clung sharply to the silk.

"I don't want it to be the smell of her perfume that reminds you ever after of me."

"You need have no fears," he had assured her, his lips against her ear, his hands pushing her opened dress down from her shoulders. "My sense of touch has always overshadowed my sense of smell. Besides, I'll have you ever after here before me."

He should have felt guilt; he who had betrayed the lovers whose bed he now appropriated. But no guilt surfaced. He was too engaged too quickly. Caitlín's face was soft, but before they had lain full-length upon the silk, his fingers had found places where the skin grew softer still.

It was a wonder to him that they should now lie grafted together, a sap of warm sweat raised on their skins, while the flushed grey light of dawn leaked into the room and the French captain sailed out from Dublin Bay with the fare of his missing passenger in his pocket.

She had become so much a matter of imagination that her reality had grown questionable. It had been too easy for uncertainty to take hold. By the time he came to hear it, the drawboy's story had really not surprised him. That Caitlín should have taken up with Danno had seemed much more likely than not. The closer he had come to seeing her, the more impossible it had seemed that anyone approximating the creature of his imagination could have had anything more than a passing affection for such an unmemorable man as himself. What would she have had to remember him by?

But there she had lain, snug against his body: her tongue, pink, and stippled like the skin of an unripe strawberry, had licked sweat from his shoulder; her legs had clasped his own between them; and her fingernails had dug deep pits into his buttocks.

It was now, watching her cry for her lost letter (she wished him to recall it for her word by word), that the memory of the letter sent to Marvin Sweetman began to prey on his mind with renewed vigour. Whatever should happen (and maybe nothing might happen at all), it must not be discovered that the letter had come from him. It would be nicer that his betrayal should be known and that he should be forgiven. Probably he would be forgiven. But he could not bring himself to risk the possibility that forgiveness might not be forthcoming. He was loved by Caitlín: and by Danno. He could not allow that love the chance to be withdrawn.

THIRTEEN

At first Danno thought that without Anton, an uprising would not be possible. But by morning, he had realised that the focal point was not Anton himself; it was the idea of Anton which enthralled. Indeed, the appearance of Anton himself could have a dampening effect. To those who had known him before, he might seem too little changed. He had not been a hero then. How could they be expected to see the same man as a hero now? (Danno was not aware of the ability of people to conceal from themselves the obvious, even when it was before their eyes.)

His was a dangerous position.

His plea for action had already been rebuffed by the central committee. Too many influential United Irishmen still felt that the time was not right for revolution; too many thought that revolution could not take place without French backing. By urging action, Danno had made himself an object of distrust. He had shown an unruliness of mind quite out of keeping with the serious nature of revolution. He was told that if his courting of the Defenders threatened to jeopardise the aims of the United movement, then the courtship should cease. Danno had said, to the annoyance of many in the room, that he was glad to hear the movement still had aims to jeopardise; he himself, he had said, was no longer capable of identifying any. As for withdrawal, the advice came too late. He was committed.

Unfortunately, he was no better trusted by the Defenders to whom he had attached himself. It had been suggested, quite unfoundedly, by Malachi Delaney that McKenna was shy of revolution and that the case for revolution had been put to the United Irishmen without sufficient enthusiasm. His plea, according to Delaney, had never been intended to persuade. Danno was not sure why it was that he had roused Malachi's animosity; unless it was that Malachi knew himself suspected of treachery by McKenna and therefore wished to discredit the silk merchant's voice before it could be raised against himself. Unfortunately, Delaney was easily heeded. To the rest of the cell, McKenna was, and would remain, an intruder. Delaney's accusations were made of an already tainted man. Danno would not have dared to suggest to cell members that Malachi had been the cause of Anton's arrest. They would have been enraged by such an accusation, coming from him.

If it was to be discovered by the cell that Danno McKenna had concealed the weaver, he would be charged with cowardice, duplicity and double-dealing. He would have confirmed their expectations of him; and he would be as good as dead.

Certainly, the weaver must not be discovered.

But what if Danno was to appoint himself as the absent weaver's voice?

***

"I have left my husband."

She was standing on his doorstep, with Sweetman's daughter, pale as the new moon, by her side. The carriage in which they had arrived was already turning in the street.

This could not be happening.

He gazed mesmerised over Letitia's shoulder. Pansy's carriage, containing Pansy, her mother, and two small, be-ribboned dogs, was drawing up behind. A picnic had been agreed upon the morning before: in the Park. Strawberries and cream were intended as the highlight. Small chickens had been roasted in the McKenna house. Bread wrapped in napkins lay waiting in a basket in the hall. His mother was to join the party. Pansy was descending from the carriage with one of the dogs in her arms. Her grandmother's ivory fan, borrowed for the occasion, hung by a thin, silver ribbon from her wrist. He saw her squeeze the dog's face against her own. She began to talk to it, admonishing it with her closed fan; she was telling it, most likely, that her little prettums was coming on a picnic and that if prettums was a good prettums, then prettums might be given a spoonful of sugared cream by its own Mama. She had not yet seen Letitia and the girl.

He looked back to Letitia, aghast. She had spilled irretrievably over the edge of her space.

"Why?" he asked, since no other question came so readily to mind.

Down on the street, Letitia's presence had been drawn to Pansy's attention by her mother. Both women hesitated by the carriage, each cradling a dog.

Letitia raised her eyes with effort. The sun was shining, but she shivered like one caught by an unseasonal shower. She was unaware of the presence of other visitors pressing close behind her. She had about her an air of immense tiredness; the air of a bird stunned by a stone. Conscious, but with death in view. Her voice, when she spoke, was bereft of tone.

The words she spoke were clear but made no sense.

"I find I was a substitute for his daughter. No more than an object in which to expend his seed with safety."

He looked at Sweetman's tall daughter. He couldn't remember her name. She leaned against Letitia, and she scratched at the ankle of one leg with the toe of a shoe. She had a spot on her chin and another, more livid, on her forehead. With her fingers, she plaited strands of her long hair together. She appeared younger than her height would suggest. She gave no indication of having understood Letitia's words.

"So you came here."

"Yes."

"To stay."

A picnic had been about to take place; a marriage was arranged; financial transactions had been entered into with the father of his bride-to-be.

"Yes."

Pansy and her mother had retreated to the carriage. Pansy watched him with anxiety through the glass. She was mouthing something at him, he could not say what. Her mother conferred through the far window with her coachman. It struck Danno that he should hurry immediately down the steps. With effort, it might not be too late to avert disaster.

"And his daughter? I am to abduct his daughter too?"

He continued to look at Pansy. Her face grew still behind the glass. She stared back at him for a couple of seconds before averting her head.

"I cannot leave her there. She doesn't even understand the nature of his offence against her. She believes herself properly punished for her own evil."

The carriage was turning where Letitia's hired carriage had earlier turned. Too late, he ran down the steps, waving his hands to catch the attention of the disappearing women. If his gesture was seen, it was ignored.

He stood on the pavement, watching until the carriage was out of sight. Behind him, chickens roosted silently on his doorstep.

***

Caroline no longer thought that leaving home had been a good idea. She lay in the unfamiliar bed, alone in an unfamiliar room and thought that Mama should not have acted as precipitately as she had done. Mama had said they were not safe with Father. But Caroline still could not understand the nature of poor Father's sin. The sins, she was quite sure, were of her own and Mama's making. That they could not be recognised by the sinners did not mean that the sins did not exist. She felt sorry for her father, left alone, not knowing where his wife and daughter were. Mama should at least have told him where they were going.

It was frightening to be in a house where their welcome was so uncertain.

Mr. McKenna had not been pleased to see them, despite Mama's promises to the contrary as they had driven here in the carriage during the morning. The gayest, warmest man imaginable was how Mama had described Mr. McKenna as she had pulled Father's wedding ring from her finger and dropped it on the floor of the carriage. (Father would be outraged were he to discover what Mama had done.) Caroline had been frightened, but had not dared to pick it up. Mama had not been herself. Mama had craved water (her fingers spread-eagled with disgust) with which to wash her hands; it had been as though poor Father's ring had carried some acute infection. In Mr. McKenna's house she intended, Mama had added, to wash her entire body and then to wash it a second time. Though she was not sure that she could ever be entirely clean again. (She

191

had seemed perfectly fresh to Caroline.) Then Mama had said, quite inexplicably, that the punishment devised by Father was meant in other circumstances to be an act of love. That statement had made Caroline doubt Mama's entire judgement.

And Mr. McKenna had been neither gay nor warm. Why should he have been? She and Mama had arrived without announcement at his house; they had spoiled arrangements he had made for a picnic, putting his betrothed so out of countenance that she and her Mama had left without a word; and Mama had made no apology. She had taken poor Mr. McKenna's entire attention as her due and had seemed irrationally displeased by his reluctance to give it to her.

As for his Mama! Mr. McKenna's Mama had refused to acknowledge their presence in the house throughout the day. She must have seen the arrivals; she would also have seen the disappearance (quite unnoticed by Mama) of her son's fiancée. By the time Mr. McKenna had brought Mama and herself into the house, Mrs. McKenna had retired to her bedroom. She did not reappear. She was unwell, was all her maid could be persuaded to say, when questioned by Mr. McKenna. It was obvious that she intended to remain in ill-health until after their departure.

It had quickly grown clear to Caroline that the sooner they went home the better. Mama had made a mistake, but she would be forgiven.

"Father must be expecting our return," she had said to Mama nervously in the early evening.

The sooner they returned, the less angry he would be.

"We have left your father," had been all that Mama would say.

She had not looked at Caroline. It had seemed to Caroline that Mama had been making the statement for the benefit of Mr. McKenna himself; and Mr. McKenna had nodded slowly, as in recognition of an unavoidable truth.

***

It had been a terrible day.

Alone in her room, her mind was sluggish with tiredness and yet she could not sleep; her limbs would not lie still. They could not cease shrinking from the imagined touch of her husband.

Upon the discovery of her husband's corruption, she had come to Danno, in great distress, expecting succour; he had not offered her the least kindness. She believed herself to be wholly forsaken. If he should come now and knock upon her door, she would not let him in.

They had not spoken much, and some of the things said would have been better left unsaid.

During the afternoon, he had asked was there no one else to whom she could have turned? Why had she not approached her father first? When Letitia had said that she had not taken Caroline to her father's house because she had known her father would not take her in, he had asked why not? It had seemed astonishing to Letitia as she had listened to his chilly voice, that only the day before they should have been entwined on silk as creatures inseparable. She had replied, as coldly, that her father would not believe the accusation made against her husband, and Danno had asked, with cruelty, who would?

"No one, if not you."

"Young girls lie. Without being . . ."

Caroline, in the monstrous grip of sins unknown, would probably have agreed.

"She told the truth."

If Letitia had suggested leaving, he would have agreed without demur. He would, she felt, have been happy never to see her again. What she had done appeared to be unforgivable.

***

Her folly in coming here defied belief; nor could he believe the audacity of her expectations. She could not imagine him ready to ruin himself for her.

There must have been someone else to whom she could have gone; someone whose reputation would not be put at risk by her presence. The presence of Letitia and her step-daughter in the house was, as his mother had said when he had spoken to her through her closed bedroom door, scandalous. Surely Letitia could see that? Surely she would not put him to the embarrassment of demanding her departure? Surely she would leave of her own accord?

Throughout the day, the only thing seen with any clarity by Danno was his own impending ruin. Only the expulsion of Letitia from his house could save him. Once she was gone, then Pansy and her mother might yet be persuaded that they had misinterpreted what they had seen that morning; that their departure had been premature.

He himself had an aunt who might (out of affection for her nephew) be persuaded to take Letitia; but she would never take the girl. The legal consequences were too dangerous. Who was going to believe the story of an adulterous wife and a flighty young girl above the word of a well-respected, Protestant attorney of note?

Who, he had asked Letitia, would believe Marvin Sweetman corrupt enough to undo his own daughter? And she had replied (with a look of contempt which had made him feel momentarily ashamed of his own doubts) no one, if not Danno.

She was right. He was the only person to whom she could have turned. He did believe her. But she had been wrong to expect that because believed, she would therefore be welcome.

***

She had finally taken refuge in her room.

Throughout the day he had refused to see her. He had looked at her, but would not allow his eyes to see.

Now that she was out of sight, she appeared vividly in his mind.

She had done, he realised, exactly what he would have expected of her. He could wish that she had never discovered her husband's betrayal of his daughter; but had she discovered and then accommodated the discovery, he would have been dismayed.

He loved her.

Yesterday he had admitted that he could not live without her. It was true. He could ask her to leave and she would not refuse; but what good would her departure do him? Not only could he not live without her, but without her, he could not live with Pansy. How could he live with Pansy, knowing Letitia lost? He saw, reluctantly, that she would have to stay.

He, Danno McKenna, had been snared by a passion as frivolous as love.

During the night, Danno's sight grew clearer still. Before dawn had broken, he saw quite clearly in his mind a seven year old child, no taller than the distance between a man's nipples and his knees, trapped beneath the convulsed, heavy body of Marvin Sweetman. He heard the sounds of a man sobbing to a climax; saw the child's eyes squeezed shut with terror; imagined a hand clasped across the child's mouth to muffle the cries of pain. Danno's own innocence was violated by this unwanted articulation of Marvin's guilt; and he had never been held in Marvin's arms; he had never trusted that embrace. Letitia had said she felt contaminated. He understood her meaning now. He felt a desire to kill Sweetman; to choke him with his own engorged penis.

He thought that he must go to Letitia's room and offer her the comfort she had previously been denied. He was ashamed of his earlier coldness and hoped she would forgive him. He could not wait for morning.

It occurred to him as he crept along the corridor, that with Sweetman dead, Letitia would be a widow. Once the thought surfaced, he could not understand how it could have failed to do so before. He supposed that until today, the marriage to Pansy had been immovably certain; it had left no room for speculation. This new realisation lay uncomfortably in his mind. It confused him that a death required for military purposes should be so greatly to his personal benefit. Perhaps he would not have considered Marvin's death a benefit before this night. Did he do so, even now? His love for Letitia was, after all, a liability, not an asset. She was penniless; she was socially ruined. Society would forgive him most sins (including those condemned in Letitia), but not the sin of sentiment indulged. Marriage to her could only complete his own ruin; it would make of him an object of ridicule. He might lose his entire business to a love which would probably prove as ephemeral as watercolours in a shower of rain. He would certainly be forced to abandon his weavers. He might have to eschew all trade in silk. No one could cause such deprivation and survive unscathed. He would always be aware of the exchange made, the sacrifice incurred.

He could see, as he knocked gently on her bedroom door, how closely love and hate were allied.

He heard no sound from within the room. Imagining her asleep, he opened the door and went inside. The curtains were pulled back and light was sufficient for shapes to be darkly visible. He could see, in this light-stained darkness, that she was sitting on the edge of her bed. She was dressed and waiting for the arrival of morning. Her head was turned in his direction.

She had heard his knock. She had remained silent because she had not possessed the strength to dismiss him.

Danno crossed the room and dropped to his knees beside her. He laid his head down on her thighs. She accepted its weight impassively.

Caroline slept in the adjoining room; his mother's room lay across the landing.

"Forgive me," he whispered, his face flushed (unseen) with excitement at the enormity of his own words; at the catastrophe they invited.

His breath blew into the limp muslin of her dress. She felt it damp on the skin she had washed so obsessively and so vainly at the beginning of the night. She found the sensation distasteful and a muscle twitched with convulsive animosity in her leg.

He felt the movement and was encouraged.

He turned his head to one side, looked up and saw that she held her hands stiffly, well above his head. He realised, to his dismay, that she was suffering his touch: no more. He lifted his head from her legs.

"Letitia?" he said.

She began to brush agitatedly at the spot on her skirt where his head had lain.

"Do not mistake me for your husband."

She forced her hands to lie still.

"Perhaps you're something worse. I thought I knew my husband well. I know you less than ever I knew my husband."

Danno shook his head.

"Don't deceive yourself," he said sharply. "You knew your husband well enough to refrain from knowing him better. You were afraid of what you might discover."

"I never thought to discover such a secret. Are you saying I failed Caroline? That had I probed I would have discovered what was, until yesterday, beyond the capabilities of my imagination?"

Her voice was staccato-sharp with distress, and she put her hand nervously up to her lips, startled by its sound.

"No. Certainly not. But do not pretend to believe that you knew him and do not know me."

"Do I know you?"

She had lowered her voice, and the question was asked with an air of distant formality.

"Yes."

"I expected your support," she told him, as though no answer had been made, "and was mistaken. Was that not misjudgment enough to allow me doubt the depth of my knowledge?" She yawned and tears filled her eyes. She had lain awake throughout the night. "I shall leave as soon as it is light enough to wake Caroline. I cannot bear the pain of knowing that my presence causes you embarrassment. You asked me to forgive you and I shall try my best to do so. But don't expect me to believe I knew you."

She yawned again. She could see Danno's face quite clearly now. Perhaps it was already bright enough to call Caroline. She was too tired to think. She was tempted to lie back against the pillows, though quite aware that she should stand up.

As though to forestall her, Danno reached his hand up and began to stroke her face.

She closed her eyes briefly; she was so immensely tired. It was morning and she knew that she must leave; but how could she leave without a journey's end in mind? She knew of nowhere else to go. Her head kept falling against his hand. It would not remain upright. Her body swayed as though the bed were afloat on a lilting sea.

"You do know me," she heard him say, his voice as insubstantial as an echo.

***

It was surprising what indignities could be accommodated.

Within the fastness of her bedroom, Danno's mother had contemplated the issuing of an ultimatum to her son: either she goes or I go. But that had been while she had still imagined Danno open to reason. When she realised that Letitia was most certainly not going to be the one to leave, she reluctantly changed her mind, knowing they would be happy to hold her to her word. It was not the moment for rash statements.

It was, on reflection, preferable to stay, mortified (but treated with all the delicacy normally accorded to a flagging invalid), under the same roof as her son's scarlet whore (her own description) than to take up injured residence in the house of her deceptively jocund deceased husband's sister. In her sister-in-law's house, she would be treated with the scant civility of one known to have married above her highest expectations. Besides, she adored her son. She gave loyalty as her reason for staying on.

It was better, she said to Letitia, when she emerged majestically from her room on the second day (Letitia met her on the landing and wondered should she bow), to remain with the sinking ship (as sink it undoubtedly would) than to be accused of desertion while any hope remained.

"Of what?" Letitia asked.

Danno's mother looked at her in puzzlement. Her sentiments had been grand, but not intended to be regarded as specific in any way.

"Hope of what?" Letitia persisted. "Do you hope for a revival of Danno's wedding plans?"

Mrs. McKenna passed wordlessly by. The sound of Letitia's laughter followed her down the stairs. When she had reached the floor below, Letitia called out, "Mrs. McKenna!"

Danno's mother looked up. Letitia was leaning over the banisters. Her face was still affected by laughter.

"This might be God's will."

Her voice was so shockingly sincere.

Who could say what sort of blasphemy was intended by such a girl? According to Danno, the two girls were in flight from some unendurable beastliness perpetrated by the father upon the daughter. Such a story might be true (Mrs. McKenna knew better than her son how deceptive were the outward appearances of

198

others); but this was no chaste flight. It was a flight embraced. Mrs McKenna knew well what she had heard in the course of the second night. Surely not even a woman so outrageous as Letitia (well, she could hardly be thought of as Mrs. Sweetman now) could be persuaded that God would will such sin?

She disappeared from Letitia's view.

Letitia was afraid of God. She did not want to be deserted by God, and yet she had no wish to do what she suspected was His will. His ways grew devious in her imagination. She wondered if perhaps she and Danno had to sin, in order to punish Marvin for his much greater sin; and if so, must they still be punished themselves? And if punishment was due to the guilty, then what was due to the innocent? In what way would God make amends to Caroline?

FOURTEEN

Dear Sir, I must first of all thank you for your kind representations on my behalf. The debts due to me were paid in full just three days ago, and I know you will be gratified to learn that my dear wife (at whose suppurating face one can no longer look with any pretence of calm) has already been dispatched to the country where it is to be hoped that her flow of ill-health will be rapidly stemmed.

I am proud to be able to give you what may well turn out to be an invaluable token of my gratitude in return for your indefatigable efforts to secure justice for a loyal servant of the Crown. You will remember that when last I wrote to you, I was in some despair over the unexpected revival of tribal loyalty in the man whom I had at the point of turning Crown witness. I confess to you now, that for all my air of confidence, I thought him lost. Well, Good Sir, the ways of the Lord are manifold. Two nights ago, I was carried to his house in a sedan, expecting little progress, but aware that I must give no indication of defeat through any slackening of my attentions towards him. At first the servant's most adamant word was that the master was not at home. I took no notice of the denial, but had my sedan carried right into the hall. Even before the servant could be cajoled into an admission of the truth (and his servants are cheaply cajoled), the master himself appeared, distraught, unshaven and in his cups, and pulled me with so much violence from the chair that I almost fell to the ground. There was no man, he kept telling me, that he would rather see than myself.

At first I thought, by his rheumy eyes and his uncontrollable snivelling, that I must have caught him fresh from a death bed and felt myself lucky enough. A man can be easily influenced when in the high emotion of grief and is afterwards reluctant to go back on promises extracted at such sacred moments. Such expressions of concern as rolled forth from my tongue! I could scarcely believe my own suavity: and courage, indeed! Why, I even took him in my arms, and, holding my breath

200

against the fumes, hugged his face against my cheeks, first to one and then to the other.

However, he turned out to be suffering from something even more advantageous to my cause. The man had been cuckolded. His wife had run away three days before and had (I confess this surprised me) taken her step-daughter with her. Should you be wondering, Dear Sir, what particular advantage was given to me by this common-place domestic mishap, you will wonder no more when I tell you that the name of his wife's seducer is Danno McKenna. At first I thought that our Mr. McKenna had revealed an unexpected Achilles' heel. I thought that only a man with an inordinate weakness for women would be so rash as to seduce the wife of a suspect associate . . . until it dawned upon me that the purpose of the seduction had been political and not for love at all. Women are easily used once their affections are engaged. He had wished to keep himself informed of Sweetman's intentions through his wife. My suspicion is that Mr. McKenna fell victim to his own scheme. She developed too great a passion for him. I cannot believe that she was ever meant to desert her husband. I have no doubt but that her flight was to the most reluctantly welcoming of arms.

My friend is as anxious for revenge as a cuckold could be (though I don't think he sufficiently appreciates his good fortune in having such exquisite revenge to hand). It is not, after all, the lot of most cuckolds to have within their power the legitimate hanging of their rival! Nevertheless, I doubt that we could find a more dedicated Crown witness throughout the four provinces of Ireland.

While I doubt that there is now anything on earth which would dissuade him from giving evidence against McKenna, there are reasons other than assuring the services of our Crown witness which would make the early arrest of Mr. McKenna a desirable thing.

Delaney (the weaver) is most anxious to prove himself essential to my ear. So anxious indeed, that I find myself doubting the verity of his information. Some, however, I cannot but give credence to. Rather than allow myself to be the sole judge of what is or is not true (or of importance irrespective of its truth), I have decided to convey the information, unfiltered, to you for your respected consideration.

Word has purportedly come from Paradis (living under an assumed name somewhere in France), doubting French intentions, and urging the cell to action before the present mood of unrest dissipates. A letter to this effect was produced by McKenna at last night's meeting. Its effect was most impressive, according to Delaney (you will bear in mind his concealed interest in presenting Paradis as a dissident of importance); as though the word of God had been received. In such an atmosphere, Delaney insists that no doubts would have been countenanced. McKenna, whose standing has recently been low within the group, made the most of his new-found popularity by calling for wine (paid for from his own pocket) and proposing (amid much hilarity) a series of toasts, which grew increasingly seditious with each bumper consumed. (Delaney claims that the wine, drunk in such circumstances, tasted like gall in his mouth. Such is the power of a loyal heart!)

As if this information was not sufficiently interesting in itself, it comes gilded (if Delaney is to be believed) with an additional layer of intrigue. According to Delaney, the letter is a fake. He is adamant on the point (but would be, since he goes to the trouble of making it). He is familiar with Paradis' hand-writing (from notes written upon silk patterns and suchlike), and the script of the letter bore no resemblance to it. He believes the fabrication to be of McKenna's own making and to be motivated by McKenna's desire to regain the trust of the group; so successful was the attempt that Delaney says he did not dare to question the veracity of the document.

His other claim, which bears the mark of unfounded rumour, and which I would not bother to mention were it not for my determination that all should be placed before you, is that Paradis has, in fact, returned to Dublin. Such rumour is only to be expected and I give no credence to it. Delaney is, of course, an easy prey to such rumour, since Charlotte Paradis is reported to be in great fear of her husband's return. He has, I understand, some claim in equity upon the house; though how she imagines he could enforce it from his position as outlaw, I cannot imagine. It may be that a guilty conscience plays havoc with her reason. Unless, of course, she fears for the safety of her lumbering paramour should Paradis have guessed his perfidy in the matter of the arrest. (I am apt to forget the attachment between Mrs. Paradis and her journeyman.)

As to the Paradis letter: that a letter, purporting to be from Paradis, exists and was read to the meeting, I believe. Whether or not the letter is a fake is immaterial, so long as any fraudulence lies undiscovered.

As McKenna is doubtless aware, it is the letter's effect on those to whom it is read which matters. Whether or not the letter had the effect claimed by Delaney is the material question. Despite his known desire to demonize Paradis, I lean towards believing his report. The raising of Paradis to the status of an outlaw has empowered him to the extent that his presence is no longer an essential prerequisite to rebellion. His word is enough. As the recipient of the word, McKenna inherits the Paradis mantle. This makes it imperative that McKenna should be removed from circulation forthwith and I urge you, Dear Sir, to take immediate steps, for rebellion is surely imminent.

I am, as ever, your obedient servant . . .

***

His agreement to give sworn evidence against McKenna did even less to comfort Marvin Sweetman than the government agent had imagined. He could sleep (and that fitfully) only under the influence of laudanum (two teaspoonsful). He vomited up what little food he ate. He could no longer even bring himself to pray for his own deliverance.

He was in a predicament from which there was no real escape.

If he had not been in fear of his life from McKenna, he would have done nothing. For the abduction of his daughter, McKenna could be hanged. But Marvin Sweetman would not even have risked a civil action for damages as an aggrieved husband. He could rid himself of McKenna; but what of the danger his wife and his daughter posed for his reputation should either one be called upon to give evidence? He could not rely on their silence. Were he to take no action against McKenna, Letitia might say nothing for the sake of Caroline's honour. But what good was his reputation to him if he was dead?

McKenna had to go.

The problem was that as soon as she knew the identity of the Crown witness, Letitia would attempt to save McKenna no matter what the cost to Caroline. His would be the greater need. What better way to save McKenna than by discrediting the Crown witness? And what better way to discredit a witness than by exposing him as the abuser of his own daughter? And with his character thus assassinated, might Marvin Sweetman not as well be dead?

The pity of it was, he loved them still. He could not cure himself of love. He could not banish from his mind the image of his two sweet girls descending the stairs with all the poise of stricken angels; nor could he forget how prettily they had lain together in the same bed only the night before. He had been tempted on both occasions by thoughts of an unpardonably sinful nature; thoughts which he believed could not long have been denied. He was free to admit as much now that they were irretrievably gone.

They were so beautiful and he feared them both so much.

***

There was already talk concerning Marvin Sweetman and his daughter.

It seemed strange to those who considered such matters (and who did not, from the jilted Pansy to the weavers in the McKenna workshop?) that a young woman in the throes of passion should encumber herself with the daughter of her discarded husband; unless the girl had, for some compelling reason, begged to be taken away. Such a reason would have had to appear irresistible, not only in the daughter's eyes (dislike of her father, for instance, would not have been sufficient), but also in the eyes of Sweetman's fleeing wife.

There could be few such reasons.

And when those who considered such matters went on to examine the position of Danno McKenna, it was agreed that the circumstances under which McKenna would allow himself to appear in the guise of the abductor of his rival's daughter were more limited still. It was therefore acknowledged that the presence of Sweetman's daughter in McKenna's house was serious enough to render Sweetman himself suspect. He became a man who, for social reasons, it was safer to avoid, while the flight of his wife began to look less scandalous than it might otherwise have done. Given the possibility that Sweetman might have been a closet dragon, then could McKenna not be cast as St. George, with the two young women as the damsels in distress and therefore legitimate targets for rescue? Society liked an occasional piquant exception to the rules; it was inclined thus to view this affair.

***

Anton Paradis knew that he had endangered himself by revealing his presence to the drawboy; but in truth, he had only speeded up a process already begun. Had he really thought that he could walk unrecognised about the city for three days? Had he really thought that a beard, a wig and a limp would be sufficient to disguise him from his friends and, more particularly, from his enemies? His drawboy had known him; Caitlín had known him. Admittedly he had presented himself to them; but he must have suspected there would be others from whom he could not conceal himself entirely. He had been fortunate enough. His presence in the city was regarded as so unlikely that those who recognised him did not immediately admit the recognition to themselves. To those who saw him, he appeared as nothing more substantial than a memory of himself; the face which might have been that of Paradis had Paradis been in town.

But by the end of three days, too many of such sightings had taken place; rumours of his return to the city grew insistent.

Malachi found himself infected by Charlotte Paradis' agitation when these rumours finally reached the Paradis workshop.

At first he had dismissed her anxiety as unfounded.

It was his opinion that an uneasy conscience made her prone to unnecessary fears. She feared the most harmless of creatures: the girl, Caitlín; Danno McKenna. It did not surprise him that Charlotte should fear her husband's rumoured return.

At first, she lied: it was not, she insisted, that she regretted Malachi's betrayal of her husband; it was simply that she feared the repercussions of that betrayal. But she did regret his betrayal. She regretted it bitterly, for she knew in retrospect, quite plainly, that the betrayal had been unnecessary. Anton had been no real threat; now he was. But they had never thought that Anton would come back. He should have died; if not in gaol, then certainly at sea. The unexpectedness of his survival was sufficient to cast fear. These days, Charlotte did not even rule out God as a possible avenger.

"Anton's reappearance will have consequences."

Malachi was slow to see the wider implications.

"What consequences?" he asked dismissively.

So far as Malachi could see, Anton Paradis could do nothing without drawing attention to himself; therefore they were safe. And what would he have done if free to act? He was not a vengeful man.

"The only consequence of his return that I can see is re-arrest and hanging."

But it was Anton's very inability to avenge himself that disturbed his wife.

"There could be no worse outcome," she told Malachi. "He would be a slain hero. Think of the anger of his admirers towards his enemies. And what greater enemy than the man who originally betrayed him?"

Malachi was not a reflective man. (It showed in the quality of his weaving. He did not foresee problems.) Not until then had he realised that he was the object of Charlotte's concern. Malachi had seen her point. Paradis did have admirers.

Malachi had long been aggrieved by the adulation accorded to the weaver for his refusal to betray his colleagues while held in gaol by His Majesty's servants. (Who would have suspected Anton Paradis of bravery?) He had been astonished then by the power of chance circumstances (in this case, created inadvertently by himself) to transform the seemingly insignificant to a position of high standing. Most gallingly, he had even had to pretend adulation of Paradis himself. He had been glad that Anton had not been able to avail of his own popularity. And that had been before the appearance of the posters with their implication of silence maintained under duress. Now the man was akin to a Messiah in certain quarters. The fact that Anton could not have become a hero had he not been betrayed would not save the betrayer, Malachi knew. Judas was given no credit for being an instrument necessary for the fulfilment of the scriptures. But the betrayer was not known. Not even Anton knew the identity of his betrayer.

Being such a phlegmatic man, a man untroubled either by his imagination or by his conscience, Malachi had (even when he knew its object) thought little of Charlotte's fear until the night on which a letter, falsely purporting to be from Paradis, was accepted as authentic by a group of people so dangerously ecstatic that Malachi had felt himself unable to expose its fraudulence.

It was not until afterwards that he saw the possible consequences of his silence.

Until then, Malachi had felt certain of his own safety. He knew that McKenna must suspect (though could not prove) who had betrayed Anton Paradis; but because of the antagonism so carefully nurtured between the two men by Malachi, he had been confident that any accusation made against Malachi by McKenna would not have been believed by others in the cell. Such an accusation would have been dismissed as an attempt to free McKenna from suspicion of the same crime.

But what if the accusation was to appear as though from Anton himself? What, he asked Charlotte fearfully, if the next letter purporting to be from Anton Paradis was to name Malachi as his betrayer? By then it would be too late for Malachi to condemn the letters as false.

Once Malachi recognised his peril, fear embraced him with all the fervour of a new lover. He was constantly in its arms. Charlotte had been worried by the rumours of Anton's return. Now he saw that danger was not even dependent on the weaver's presence.

He saw that Charlotte's earlier apprehensions were justified. Danno and Caitlín were worthy of fear. They threatened his very existence. He couldn't kill. He had no stomach for killing: not directly. The most he might do would be to set a trap. But it was a poor reward for his loyalty (it took courage to be loyal in such times as these) that he should now be in fear for his life. He had been paid for his efforts on behalf of the government, but what good was money to him in the face of death? When he was being recruited, the agent (his erstwhile landlord) had assured him that the government looked after those who proved themselves as loyal as he, Malachi Delaney, had shown himself to be. But what had happened? He had delivered into their hands a potentially dangerous man (how well, in retrospect, he had estimated the Paradis potential), on the understanding that Paradis would not be seen again; the Castle, through mismanagement, had allowed him to slip through their hands. As if that wasn't enough, they had taken a man made popular only by their own incompetence and, by exaggerating his danger, had turned him into a hero. Now all the agent would say was that the times were dangerous for them all and that it was impossible to protect everyone against all eventualities; and what, after all, had Delaney done for the government? Paradis had been of no assistance while in captivity. Delaney refused to divulge the names of his other cell companions (the agent didn't consider McKenna to be a true companion). The agent had gone so far as to threaten him. He had asked did Delaney think he would be best protected inside gaol? Malachi Delaney was a severely frightened man.

It was Charlotte who first wondered why, if Anton was back, he had not immediately sought the protection of his cell. It was the cell, after all, which most owed him protection.

"He's afraid," she decided finally. "I know Anton. He's no hero. He didn't come back here to lead some insignificant skirmish for freedom; he came back for Caitlín. He's being hidden by McKenna in return for the use of his name."

"Why didn't he write the letter himself?" Malachi asked in puzzlement.

Charlotte nodded her head slowly. "Why not indeed? Anton may not know he's being used. The cost of his concealment may be hidden from him."

But if Anton knew, would he care? Then Malachi saw the real significance. It was not Anton's views that were important; it was the views of others.

"Imagine the anger of the cell," he said, "were it to be discovered that instead of the mere word, they could have had the man himself."

There had been a breeze blowing through the workshop that day and his voice was hoarse from silk dust. He stopped to clear his throat, but held a finger up to show that he was not finished speaking yet.

He had Charlotte's attention.

"What if the cell," he continued, "should be persuaded that Paradis had been forcibly kept from them, so that McKenna, by standing proxy, might take upon himself the glory due to Paradis?"

She was smiling now.

"McKenna would be out of favour," she said, and added drily, "His life would be a more uncertain thing than it had been before the discovery was made."

"And should I be the man to confound McKenna's dastardly ambitions, wouldn't my star be as high as McKenna's was low?"

He coughed and spat some dust-laden phlegm over the side of the bed. Charlotte shook her head, but said nothing. He had grown more slovenly since moving in.

"Anton might speak for McKenna," she said. "He was close to loving him once."

"And what if he did? Wouldn't he only be damning the pair of them?"

Malachi lay back on the bed with his arms behind his head. He was opening and closing his elbows, as though his face was the central panel of a triptych, his elbows the folding wings. The movement stretched the muscles across his upper back.

He laughed suddenly and Charlotte looked across at him, startled.

"But of course Paradis didn't write the letter himself," Malachi said. "His hands! We had forgotten his hands!"

It made no difference. The circumstances under which the letter had been written no longer mattered. Malachi closed his eyes. He hadn't slept last night for fear. Tonight he might not sleep for lack of it. His brain was uncommonly excited. He put himself in Anton's place, forgetting that he was not Anton, but Malachi.

"I warrant you, Charlotte," he said, opening his eyes again and peering at her through the triangle of his bent arm, "that if Anton is delivered to the cell, he'll say nothing at all in defence of McKenna. He'll be too worried about his own safety. He would hardly want them to know of his reluctance to come amongst them, would he? Followers are such fickle creatures."

He underestimated Anton, Charlotte knew. But Malachi had already put his finger on the point that mattered. Any admission by Anton was to their advantage. A confession for McKenna's benefit would damn the pair of them; and Malachi would survive.

"Assuming he's here . . ." Charlotte began; and then she stopped. The basis of her fears kept changing. At first she had hoped that the rumours of Anton's return were false. Now it appeared to be imperative that they should be true. He must be here. Only if he was where they imagined him to be could he be rendered harmless. Or so it seemed for now.

"Have you fallen asleep?"

She shook her head.

"Assuming he's here," she repeated, "he must be found," and then she frightened Malachi afresh by adding, "before the Castle finds him and turns him from hero to martyr."

FIFTEEN

Already Letitia was regretful. Her arrival had not been by choice. It was so clearly not the way to progress in such an affair. Had it not been for Caroline, she never would have come; and Caroline showed little sense of gratitude.

Now there was a frenzied lushness to the atmosphere; a passion already tainted by the knowledge of the resentment that lay beyond its passing. She knew that he would grow accustomed to her, and that, once accustomed, he would wonder what had moved him to such folly in the first place. Even now, when love was so intense, resentment lay in wait behind each failure of perfection.

She said this to him one night (she was incapable of withholding her thoughts from him), and he began to laugh.

Since her arrival, it had occurred to Danno that he might be worrying unnecessarily about his ruined prospects. He proposed to engage in rebellion and he had realised, for the first time, that, should he escape arrest at Marvin's suit, he was more likely to be killed than to marry. In either event, he would not have sufficient time to regret his folly. It was a conclusion he was glad to have reached before Letitia made her comment. It made the comment easier to dismiss. What she described would, in normal times, have happened. Already, it was only a belief in the brevity of his own life which kept his sense of dismay at bay.

"Your imagination," he told her, "is too vivid."

Then, assailed by a sense of imminent death, he seized her face between his hands and looked into her eyes of unflawed green (could he ever grow accustomed to such eyes?). "Don't waste this perfection," he said urgently, "by anticipating its loss."

He had not denied that loss would occur. They were agreed upon their future prospects. In which case, she could do no more than to act as he suggested. At best she could prolong perfection.

211

Letitia ignored the thin-bladed knife. She picked up a peach (brilliant as a bursting evening sun) and rubbed it against her lips; then she bit through its skin. Juice ran uncontrollably from the fruit and trickled from her lips down to her throat.

***

Father was being ill-used. Mama had not come to the house of Mr. McKenna to escape from Father. She had not left Father for Caroline's sake. She had come because she loved Mr. McKenna. Caroline knew that they should return to Father, but she did not have the courage to return alone. Also, though Mama was wicked, Caroline loved her as she could remember loving no one else. Caroline wondered had she, by loving Mama the way she did, embraced the Devil.

Mama and Mr. McKenna were shameless. They kissed in front of the servants, in front of Caroline, in front of Mrs. McKenna herself. They held hands, they chased one another round the house with shrieking laughter. Caroline had seen Mama's legs bare to the thighs while she and Mr. McKenna had lain wrestling like puppies on the drawing room floor. Mrs. McKenna had said to Caroline that she thought them quite diseased by love. She had declared herself, with uneasy laughter, to be in awe of such excess. That Mama should be diseased would explain her sometimes feverish look; the flushed face, the heavy eyelids, the languorous movements which accompanied such a look. Caroline was terrified that Mama might die of love and that she, Caroline, would be sent back to Father, alone.

Mrs. McKenna had already suggested to Caroline that she should go home. "Should you go home, she would be forced, by conscience, to follow." But those diseased by love could not be relied upon to follow the voice of conscience.

Caroline pitied Mama. She had no right to despise her, but she saw Mama to be as filled with sin as Caroline herself and she feared for the safety of her soul. What was so frightening for Caroline was that her darling Mama would not (or could not) see her sins.

Mama had said that what Father had called a punishment was intended as a pleasure between a man and a woman.

Now Caroline could believe that poor Father had been unable to help himself. There was a substance within men, so Mrs. McKenna had told her, which must be expelled if ill-health were not to ensue. What had happened between Caroline and her father had, according to Mrs. McKenna, been akin to the leeching of blood: unpleasant but necessary. Such leeching was not a daughter's duty under any circumstances, and Mr. Sweetman's behaviour could not be condoned; but it should, Mrs. McKenna insisted, be forgiven. It was the duty of a daughter to forgive a father. Caroline, who never would have dared to censure the conduct of her father, found nothing to forgive. Besides, Mrs. McKenna had added in a later conversation (they were thrown upon each other's company a great deal, these two), could Caroline be sure that she had not encouraged her father to vice? Some girls were born coquettes. Caroline was sure of little. She knew that she was full of sin. She also knew that what he had done had been a source of pleasure to neither of them; nor could it be.

Mama had said other preposterous things (some too preposterous to mention to Mrs. McKenna) which, on examination, could not be sustained. She had said, for instance, that babies sometimes grew inside the body of the woman as a result of activity such as had taken place between Caroline and her father. When Caroline had enquired, with scepticism, how babies escaped, when grown too big, from such unlikely containers, Mama had been forced to confess (with a shudder) that she did not know.

There were other sources of distress.

Mama now said that Father was a traitor. But it seemed to Caroline that she was living amongst traitors. She did not believe that Mr. McKenna was a loyal Catholic, and she found it frightening to be in the house of a renegade. Father had talked much of the injustices done to Catholics and how they must be rectified; but he had always said (she noticed how she thought of him as though he were deceased) that the more they were given, the more they would demand, until, finally, they would make demands which would be impossible to concede. Then the Catholics would shout injustice once again and, because of earlier concessions, would be powerful enough to force the granting of all they asked. Mr. McKenna talked of the complete separation of Ireland from England . . . and Mama nodded her head as though in perfect agreement. Were she to be seen agreeing to such sentiments, she would be liable to arrest for treason, like that peaky-faced Protestant Mr. Tone who used, before his exile, to visit Father.

But, as Mrs. McKenna had remarked, had Mr. McKenna advocated the massacre of the King and all his family, Mama would have nodded her head no less eagerly. Such lack of principle surely made Mama the greatest traitor of all.

Mrs. McKenna said that Mama was in thrall to her own passions and that no good could come from such subjection. Reason, Mrs. McKenna had said to Mama, should always rule supreme. Without the supremacy of reason, she had said, we were no better than the animals we presume to control.

Mama had been so cruel in reply.

Only a woman who had never known love could speak so confidently upon the triumph of reason over emotion. God had surely not given us our bodily desires as a torment to suppress for the virtue of our souls?

Mama had deliberately caricatured Mrs. McKenna's advice, but Mrs. McKenna had not been deterred. Passion, she had told Mama, should never be allowed off the leading rein; it could too easily toss the rider.

Mama had laughed, and had said (Caroline had not known why) that Mrs. McKenna's clichés were incontestably appropriate. At which remark, Mrs. McKenna herself had laughed, reluctantly, and with a shaking of her head at Mama. "You are beyond redemption, I do believe," she had told Mama, and had then called hastily upon Caroline to play an air on the piano, as though afraid of what Mama might say next.

It was the loss of Mama's company that was so hard to bear. Caroline saw less of Mama than she had when they were still at home; and when they were together, Mama was too exhilarated by passion to be a fit companion. Mama accepted Caroline's love too lightly. What was for Caroline a rarity to give was, for Mama, a commonplace to receive. The moment of escape had been idyllic. They had been conspirators in flight. She had never been so close to Mama before. Caroline wished she could have remained suspended in that moment forever, like a pansy, pressed at its point of perfection between the pages of a book.

***

The night was close and Caroline was woken quickly from a fitful sleep by an aching head and by the heat of her own body trapped within the heavy covers of the bed. Reluctantly, she threw back the bedclothes to cool her perspiring skin. The air, she knew, would rouse her further still, and she wished only to sink back into sleep. Then she remembered that the window had been tightly shut that evening by Mrs. McKenna, who thought that unhealthy humours circulated in the night air. Caroline lay on her back with her eyes shut and imagined she was beginning to smother in her own used breath. Behind her eyes, her head throbbed ominously. She would have to open the window.

It was while she was leaning on the windowsill, allowing the faint, warm breeze to blow around her face and neck, that she heard Mama moan like a dying animal in Mr. McKenna's bedroom next door. Caroline froze. It was a pitiful sound; a sound which could not be ignored. Caroline tiptoed from her room and stood hesitantly on the landing. Her body, previously so overheated, was chilled now by terror and she shivered (her arms clutched across her small breasts) with the violence of an Eve expelled from paradise to the inhospitable void beyond. Within Mr. McKenna's room, the moans grew louder; they grew faster; they rose higher in tone. Mr. McKenna was killing Mama. Nothing that her father had done to either of them had ever caused such sounds of agony as this. Where was Mrs. McKenna? Where were the servants? Why was no one coming to Mama's assistance?

Caroline could hesitate no longer. She entered Mr. McKenna's bedroom.

Mama was seated naked on a chair, her legs apart. Her face was raised upwards to the ceiling, the sinews tight upon her neck and a look of tortured suffering on her face. Mr. McKenna, also naked, knelt between her legs and was biting Mama there, where Father used to . . . it was insupportable! Such cruelty could not be tolerated! Caroline flew across the room and seized Mr. McKenna's hair in her hands and wrenched his head upwards. She screamed at him in great fury, while Mama beat at them both with her hands.

"It's love! It's love! It's love!" Letitia screamed incomprehensibly at the terrified Caroline, her face suffused with rage.

***

The shutters had been closed across the warehouse windows, the windows in which Caroline had once admired her own alluring reflection, seeing in the glass an unrecognisable and quite enchanting image of sophistication.

Anton sat weaving at the loom.

The silk had been there, waiting.

It had been Danno's gesture of confidence in the weaver's return (a false gesture, made for Caitlín's sake) that silk thread had been purchased to replace the silk destroyed on Anton's loom.

For two weeks Anton had fought his hands in the service of that silk. The fight had been bitter, but Anton had emerged the victor. He had not, on any single occasion, permitted his fingers to refuse the bidding of his brain. Four thousand threads had been drawn painstakingly through the eyes of the mails and on through the teeth of the reed. The tips of the lingo-weighted, mail-eyed leashes had been threaded through the holes of the comberboard. The neck cords had been connected to the pulleys. The tail cords had been stretched from the pulleys to the far wall. From each tail cord had been hung a further cord to create the simple. The cords of the simple had been tied to correspond with the pattern. His fingers had performed none of these operations willingly. They had responded to each command with no more finesse or speed than was to be expected from the rawest of apprentices.

Not once had Caitlín offered him assistance.

Anton was astonished by the maturity of her restraint. He did not believe that another person alive could have watched him on that first, humiliating day and have remained so adamantly silent. Had he not already loved her, he would have had to love her then.

She had not given him a single word of encouragement. She had known that to have done so would have been to concede the possibility of failure. Her only acknowledgement of his difficulty had been the offering to him of a bowl of thick, sour milk in which to soak his swollen hands at the end of that initial day's work.

McKenna came at night. He could not risk a visit by day. His movements were too well-watched. He knew that there were, amongst his weavers, those who would willingly betray Anton Paradis. The reward was high, and the opinion of Anton was low. The McKenna weavers had not succumbed to the Paradis metamorphosis. He remained, for them all, the weaver whose loyalty had lain with the wrong man. He had been too close to the silk merchant and some suspected him still of betrayal. So Danno paid no calls upon the Frenchman and his girl until his weavers had left the premises.

Anton would not work in Danno's presence. Had he not spoken a word, Danno could still not have concealed his thoughts. His admiration, his pity and his doubts could not have been contained by silence alone. Danno could never have controlled the expressions of his face, the tension of his body had he been permitted to watch the weaver's struggle. What, Anton had wondered as he had forced delicacy upon his reluctant fingers, if he had ceased to be a weaver? Would McKenna have loved him still? Why would he? Without his hands, Anton had barely recognised himself. Then he realised that McKenna would certainly have loved him equally had he accepted his role as the leader of a rebellion.

Before the two weeks were up, Anton knew that he was still a silk weaver. He was not as good as he had been. The quality of his finished work had not deteriorated in any way and he remained, without doubt, the best silk weaver in Dublin; but what had been previously been achieved so simply now required great effort. Nevertheless, McKenna could rest easy. He had in his employ a weaver without parallel.

But McKenna had wanted everything. He had thought that he could have both the weaver and the hero at no extra cost to Paradis.

He had come one evening and had described his plan to Anton. His arguments had been persuasive. "The appearance of letters," he had told them, "would be to our advantage. What better way to conceal your presence than to have you urging revolution from France?"

Anton had, reluctantly, seen the logic. He wanted no truck with revolution; but he could not fail to see that any rumour which placed him in France would help to counteract the inevitable betrayal of the drawboy. For Anton, there had been a further, undisclosed attraction. To allow McKenna to put his name to such seditious letters would, to some extent, assuage his conscience concerning his own betrayal of McKenna to the husband of McKenna's lover. That letter had been frighteningly effective. Not twenty-four hours after its dispatch, the young Mrs. Sweetman had arrived at McKenna's doorstep; with her step-daughter at her heels. Anton Paradis had not slept easily since. By then, too much had occurred for him to confess his betrayal. He had accepted silk from McKenna. The offering and the acceptance had been a pledge of love. He could not bear to lose McKenna's love a second time; and what if Caitlín should look at him with contempt? How could he then live? No: he could not confess. He could only make reparation by whatever means came to hand.

"I'll do nothing without your permission," Danno had assured the weaver, but only when he had already sensed Anton's acquiescence. Had he not sensed acquiescence, he might have made no promise. The first letter had been already drafted when he approached Anton. It had lain beneath his hand in his pocket while he spoke. Danno doubted he could have brought himself to tear it up should Anton have rejected the idea.

It had been Caitlín who had shown the greatest aversion to Danno's scheme. What she had previously seen as friendship on Danno's part, she now saw as subtle manipulation. They should have escaped to France. They should have joined that waiting boat. Instead they had dallied (with the merchant's connivance), and the will to leave had disappeared. The waiting silk had been no more than a luxurious snare. The weaver could not resist the lure of silk and now he was imprisoned by it, as Danno McKenna had known he would be. McKenna had hoped to change the weaver's mind. He had hoped that Anton might be persuaded to act the great, heroic saviour of all the poor fools of Ireland. Anton had refused the request. Now McKenna was saying that Anton could be a 'saviour in absentia'; deluding Anton into thinking that he could remain untouched by subsequent events.

"He's not doing this for you," she had said furiously to Anton.

She had not waited for Danno to leave the room, but had spoken disparagingly of the merchant in his presence, as though he were already gone. "He's doing it for himself and his lost cause. Saviour in absentia my eye. We'll all perish in a revolution and Mr. McKenna knows it."

She had turned to Danno then, and had added, "Why you should desire a revolution, Mr. McKenna, I can't imagine. Is it not enough for you to be a silk merchant?"

"We're on the same side, Caitlín," Danno had attempted, but Caitlín had shaken her head vehemently.

"It was my mistake to believe so briefly, Mr. McKenna," she had said, contemptuous of her own error, "but that has never been the case."

Anton had put his hand around her neck. He had felt her skin hot beneath his fingers; he had felt her tremble with the force of her own feelings.

"She is a proper weaver's daughter," he had said, laughing slightly. She had been so flatteringly ardent in his defence. The excess of her passion had amused him.

His voice, when he next had spoken, had been tinged with affectionate mockery. "She knows better than to trust a merchant," he had told Danno, while his fingers had teased her ear. "She also knows that real revolutions arise from hunger. You have never been hungry, McKenna." (They touched one another with the familiarity of brothers, but Anton could not have addressed the merchant by his Christian name. It was not a sense of formality which deterred him; it was simply that he had used the name McKenna for too long. McKenna was, for him, the merchant's most familiar name.) "Caitlín considers your desire for revolution to be the result of an over-indulged imagination. You have, she thinks, too much time on your hands. She believes that boredom has made you mischievous."

Caitlín had brushed away his hand impatiently.

"You've patronised me before, Anton Paradis, and you lived (against the odds) to regret it. My difference with Mr. McKenna is deep, and it concerns the nature of love. We do not mean the same thing by love. I thought we both loved you. He has said he loves you. Now I find that, by my standards, it is not you that Mr. McKenna loves, but revolution. Please God you continue to live, despite Mr. McKenna's love."

Caitlín had turned away from both men, knowing that, in her agitation, tears had risen in her eyes. Anton, staring at her back, had nodded his head slowly. There had been no doubt in his mind but that she was right. He was fully aware that he would regret ignoring her advice.

Yet he had agreed to be used.

He had even offered to write the letter himself, but Caitlín had grown so upset that Danno had been forced to refuse the offer, tempting though it was.

Danno had been upset by Caitlín's animosity. He had considered it unwarranted. He loved Paradis more than he loved any man. It would break his heart were Paradis to die through any fault of his. Danno certainly did not love revolution. One did not love revolution. One embraced it with horror for the sake of the deliverance to follow. Paradis had seen his duty and had embraced it with proper stoicism; Danno had loved the weaver the more for that difficult embrace.

***

It had been put about by Danno that Caitlín had run away. Should the drawboy talk, it would be assumed, with luck, that Anton Paradis had come and then had gone again, taking his lover with him. It was hoped that those in pursuit of the weaver would then, imagining him fled with his lover to France, cease their pursuit. To remain free required, paradoxically, that they should confine themselves with unforgiving closeness.

Such confinement did not bother Anton. Working at his loom, Anton felt safe. The knowledge that this sense of safety was illusory did nothing to dislodge the feeling. He had learnt more of his attachment to silk through separation from the loom than he ever could have learned had the separation not occurred. He had craved the caress of silk. Silk weaving had been his work; he had not realised that it had been his addiction. Now he was no longer merely a weaver of silk; he was its helpless devotee.

It should have been difficult for a girl as active as Caitlín to bear confinement so lightly: but it was not. Unaccustomed to reverie, she found it forced upon her by this period of unavoidable idleness. While Anton worked, he was impervious to all considerations but the implacable needs of the silk itself. It seemed, to the watching girl, that the silk, the loom, and the weaver himself, became the inseparable parts of a single body.

She became infected by Anton's indifference to the peril which encircled them. With or without revolution, their future was hazardous, and it was she who had taught him not to rely on the future, wasn't it? The sense grew upon her that Anton had been no more than lent to her by God; that this was a transient moment of joy to be seized without question. In his absence, she had carried only a partial memory of his features. She had thought she knew the face of Anton Paradis by heart, but had found her recollection treacherously unsure; and then, there had been the aspects which could not be recalled for lack of knowledge. She had not, for instance, known his naked body. Now she grew obsessed by a desire to memorise the details of this fragment of time together: the hairs on his arms, thicker than strands of silk; the shadows cast by his eyelashes upon the skin below his lowered eyelids; a song lingering unfinished in the air while he worked on a complicated action; the heightened sheen of the wood on that part of the bench where he sat while weaving.

She was used to silk. She could share a man with silk. At night, he belonged to her with equal intensity. At night, the silk behaved with perfect reticence; at night it made no demands on the weaver. By day, she remembered the nights.

SIXTEEN

Rumours of Anton's reappearance in the city reached the soldiers who tended the drawboy.

They came calling.

At first they appeared to believe the drawboy when he insisted, with nervous belligerence, that Anton Paradis had not been near him. Indeed, they apparently took his denial to mean that the rumours themselves were false. Paradis could not be in Dublin if the drawboy hadn't seen him.

"How could I have seen him when I know for a fact that he's in France?" the drawboy asked with desperate earnestness, wringing his clammy hands together as he looked from face to face.

"He'd hardly lie to us, now would he?" one of the soldiers asked of another, gesturing with his head towards the tremulous drawboy. The soldier was holding a hot meat pie in his hands. He bit into it and juice spurted out from the steaming centre, dripping down from his hands onto the floor.

One or other of them always seemed to be eating when they came to pester him. The drawboy watched the soldier lick his greasy fingers with slow, voluptuous pleasure. The drawboy hadn't eaten for two days. The smell of the beef and onion filling tormented him to such excess that saliva began to dribble unheeded down his chin. The soldier ate so carelessly. Flakes of pastry, shreds of glistening beef, fell unnoticed from his mouth. The drawboy yearned to cup his hands beneath the young man's profligate lips.

The young men watched their quarry salivate like a dog.

"Who but a fool would lie to a soldier?" a second soldier asked.

The drawboy shook his head agitatedly from side to side. There were other reasons for lying to soldiers. Did they not know that the consequences of truth could be more dangerous still?

"I'm no fool," he assured them nervously.

A third soldier, who was pricking out his initials on the drawboy's wooden table with the point of his bayonet, shook his head wordlessly while he worked.

"But who more foolish than a friend?" the first soldier asked the second soldier, ignoring the assurances of the drawboy. The pie was finished but for some crumbs which still stuck to his damp lips. "If he hadn't told us otherwise, I would have sworn that Paradis had been here. I could have sworn I caught the smell of him."

Only a dog could catch a scent that old, surely be to God. It was more than twenty-four hours since Paradis' visit. Besides, Paradis was not a strong-smelling man . . . and how would the soldier be able to identify any smell as that of Anton Paradis? The soldiers didn't know him. He was being teased. The drawboy tried to breathe more slowly.

"I was not his friend. I was only ever the drawboy." The spittle trembled on the drawboy's chin while he spoke. "I'm not the man he'd turn to."

"A friend would say the same."

"I'll warrant that our drawboy is not a fool," the second soldier said, and he opened up the drawboy's door and began to swing it to and fro from hand to hand. "Fools don't grow so old. Now why should we be tormenting an old man who knows nothing?"

They were playing with him.

"I never know which is the more frightening for a victim: innocence or guilt."

The drawboy realised that not one of the soldiers believed his denials. He felt, as well as frightened, perversely aggrieved by their disbelief. Why should his word not be good enough for them?

On the surface of the table, the upper semi-circle of the initial R swelled misshapenly above its two legs; the second initial, an E, dwarfed the first. R.E. spoke for the first time. "The false confessions of an innocent man are hard to bear."

"But I hate to be fooled by an old man."

"Do you think he'd lie?"

"He might. But he might have a genuinely faulty memory; a bad memory is a hazard of old age. One day an old fellow has a thing fixed in his mind; the next day it's gone; the day after, it's back again."

"Why don't we leave him so? Come back another time and see what has risen to the surface."

When they had gone, the drawboy could not relax. He knew they would be back again and again. In the late evening, he heard footsteps on the stairs. Maybe, he thought desperately, as the sounds grew closer, he was wanted for work in the morning. Someone came as far as the door, paused awhile, then retreated. Inside the room, the drawboy's heart pounded as though he had climbed the stairs himself. He assumed at first that the soldiers were tormenting him; then he wondered, more fearfully still, had the person beyond the door been Paradis.

He decided to go out; to sit in the company of others in a public house might ease his fears.

As soon as he opened the door, he could see that his first assumption had been correct. It was a soldier who had come up the stairs. On the floor outside his door was a dead cat, run through by a sword. Beside the dead and pinioned cat lay a meat pie. The drawboy covered his mouth with his hands and stepped back into his room; he pushed the door closed with a shaking knee. Mother of God, but had they no pity for an old man, that they should mock his lies so barbarously? Then he saw they pitied nothing. For the soldiers, it was as easy to quarter a man as to halve a cat.

What most humiliated the drawboy was the realisation that the soldiers had known, before he knew himself, that he would eventually come crawling out of his room, and, averting his eyes from the cat, would pick up the pie, still warm (unlike the cat) to the touch, and would hurry back inside with it cradled between his palms.

Distraught with self-contempt, the old man ate the pie, crouched over his initialled table, stuffing the pieces into his mouth with the fingers of both hands. Afterwards, sobbing convulsively, he trapped and ate each fallen crumb.

Then he lay on his bed and waited for the soldiers to come.

***

Dear Sir, I urge you to arrest Mr. McKenna without further delay. It has apparently been decided that the Castle is to be attacked; and I regret to say it has been proposed that you, Good Sir, should be assassinated. However impractical their larger designs may be (they are less well-equipped with weapons than I had previously understood them to be, and they rely too much on a natural eruption of violence on foot of their own example), I fear that given sufficient determination, they can hardly fail to succeed in their dastardly plot upon your own precious life. Your figure is so well-known and you move around the city with so little thought for your safety. Do not, I beg of you, dismiss this threat as insignificant.

I am, however, bound to advise you that the arrest of McKenna may not, unless certain steps are taken, lead to his conviction. Our chief witness has, I regret to say, attempted to impose a further condition upon his co-operation with the Castle.

I told you, I believe, that he did not seem as elated by his chance for revenge against his wife's seducer as he should. I have now discovered why; he is in dread of his wife's intrigues. He confessed to me last night, in most maudlin terms, that he desires his daughter's return; but should he attempt her retrieval, he fears that his wife, who is, according to himself, an uncommonly vindictive and inventive young woman, will make false and base accusations against him concerning his relationship with the daughter. He claims that his wife took the girl with her in order to lay the foundation for just such a claim. His daughter is, he says, very much under the influence of this young woman whom he now (in contrast to his earlier love-sick indulgence) describes as a moral degenerate. Having thus described to me his dilemma, he then wondered, in a voice of wheedling coercion, if there might be some way in which we could assist him in the silencing of this allegedly unprincipled creature? Could we perhaps arrest her as an associate of McKenna? I said that the Castle was not in the business of corrupting the due process of law to settle private disputes . . . whereupon he then displayed a very cunning reluctance to give evidence in a case where his private misfortunes were open to such risk of exposure. He whined into his hands that were his wife to spread lies about him, they would be the more readily believed because of the low regard in which Crown witnesses were so unfairly held. I made him no promises. Indeed, I pointed out to him the much greater risk *which pertained to his life, should McKenna be left at large; but I did say that I would give the matter my fullest consideration. I am afraid to say I believe his fears may prove to be a genuine obstacle to his cooperation with the Crown.*

I hope that this information will not deter you from arresting McKenna forthwith. That you cannot hold him long is of no account. He has conjured up a frail beast whose head will fall at the gentlest of blows. But until McKenna has been seized, you are in very certain danger and you should have a care for your own head.

I am, as ever, your obedient servant . . .

***

There was scarcely any sport to be had from the drawboy when the soldiers returned. They had frightened him beyond necessity. They stretched him face down on his own table, with his trousers lowered to his ankles. But before they had so much as touched him with the point of a sword the old man was screaming out all he knew (and that was precious little) of Anton Paradis. Paradis was, or certainly had been, back in town. He had called on the drawboy and had enquired for a young woman who had, up to the time of Paradis' arrest, been living under his protection (and he a married man, the dirty French bastard). He had been told by the drawboy that she was now living under the protection of Danno McKenna (a dirty Irish bastard, by all accounts), formerly the friend of Paradis, now his enemy. Paradis had been, the drawboy swore, on his way back to France. R.E., dissatisfied with his earlier attempt, pricked out his initials once again, this time on the drawboy's buttocks. The R was probably better (though with blood obscuring the outline, it was difficult to tell); the E was definitely worse. But they could get nothing more of substance from the drawboy. They left, with promises to return in the near future.

After they had gone, the drawboy remained, soiled and crying, on his table. He was filled with self-hatred. Could his soul have crawled away from his perfidious body, it would have done so. The drawboy knew that if the soldiers had not come back, he would have gone looking for them. He could not have borne much longer the terror of waiting for their reappearance. Shame caused him to exaggerate his feelings towards the man he had betrayed. Anton was recreated briefly in the drawboy's mind as the man he had loved like a son. His sin grew greater, the greater he imagined his love to have been.

Then a fresh fear began to fester and swell inside his head.

What if the soldiers should fail to find Anton? What if Anton should hear of his betrayal while still at large? The image of a man reproachful, betrayed, but essentially impotent was replaced by a new Anton, vast and vengeful. What was it that Paradis had whispered to him that night? That Judas had escaped murder only by doing the job himself? Holy God, but Anton was no Jesus. Who would expect one man to save the skin of another at the expense of his own? Anton used to be a reasonable man. To expect such sacrifice from a man who did no more than work for him would be perverse.

But what if Anton had turned perverse?

***

Dear Sir, I write this note to you only an hour after dispatching my last to your office, to warn you that the frailty of the beast, referred to in the final paragraph of my last letter, may be deceptive; it may have more than a single head. In the interim, I have been visited by the weaver, Delaney, who grows increasingly unreliable as he grows more fearful for his own skin and will soon, I think, be of more use to us under arrest than at large.

I must, as a result of his visit, urgently revise my advice to you concerning the whereabouts of the Frenchman. I now believe him to be in town. You will recall that Delaney, during an earlier visit, swore to me that Paradis had returned. You will also recall that I was (to his undisguised chagrin) inclined to dismiss his claim as ill-founded rumour.

My suspicions were aroused by Delaney appearing at my house not half-an-hour ago, during his own working hours (an unprecedented innovation), most fawningly anxious to applaud my earlier astuteness. He began the conversation by apologising to me for having insisted so adamantly on that occasion that Paradis was in the country. He had since discovered, he said, that the rumour was, as I myself had suggested at the time, unfounded. He hoped, he said, that I had seen fit to follow my own wise instincts in the matter and that I had not set the Castle to chasing a chimerical man. He had so much the air of the liar: the over-earnestness of delivery, the shifting feet, the evasive eyes; he could not have done more to convince me of Paradis' presence in the city.

When I told him that his change of opinion came too late, and that the Castle had already been informed of his former opinion on the whereabouts of the outlawed Paradis, he grew instantly pale (a fascinating phenomenon, which happens far more rarely than is claimed) and immediately surmised (in the expectation of confirmation from me) that the Castle would, in all probability, have dismissed the rumour as swiftly as myself; and when I said (unfoundedly, you will admit, Good Sir) that in my experience, the Castle allowed no lead to lie unexplored, I thought that he might swoon.

I then informed him bluntly that I thought him a liar, and his face confessed it for him on the spot. His subsequent tears became him no more than would have done the carrying of a twirling parasol above his head to ward off sunstroke. He found himself compelled to take me into his confidence, begging me, with overwrought praise of my past kindnesses to him, to justify his trust in my discretion. He believes himself (justly) in danger of being discovered as the cause of Paradis' arrest and fears that if Paradis dies as a martyr at the hands of the Government, then he will be the object of popular revenge. Were he, on the other hand, to produce Paradis before the cell, thus exposing him as someone who had been kept in hiding, either against his will, for the aggrandisement of McKenna, or at his own request, for reasons of personal cowardice, then he, Delaney, would be the hero of the hour. I did not quite follow his logic here. How he hopes to become a hero by exposing the flaws of others, I cannot imagine.

I dismissed him, telling him there was nothing I could do for him. Did he expect me to lie to the Castle on his behalf? He should consider himself lucky, I told him, that I was prepared to keep this conversation to myself. If he found Paradis first, well and good; if he didn't, well . . . he had, after all, freely chosen to inform. He could not expect adulation. No sooner had he left the premises than I assigned a servant to follow him as closely (and as unobtrusively) as his own shadow.

I remain, Dear Sir, your obedient servant . . .

***

The soldiers had not bothered to close the drawboy's door on their departure. A smell, heavy as damask, hung in the stairway. Malachi, climbing upwards, pulled his sleeve uneasily across his face. It was almost beyond his strength to enter the room itself. The window had already been opened wide by the soldiers. He went and stood beside it. He gathered extra folds of material up to his nostrils and spoke through a veiled mouth to the soiled old man on the table.

"I'm looking for Anton Paradis."

He had come as soon as he had heard that the drawboy had been hard-pressed by soldiers looking for Paradis. The drawboy was said to have succumbed. While he had been talking with the government agent, the soldiers had been extracting information from the drawboy. And the agent had pretended such ignorance of Castle movements. The bastard had known precisely what was happening, and to whom, while they talked. Malachi was (incorrectly) sure of it. How much had he said? Had he exposed himself to any more danger than was necessary? The man terrified him so. Jesus, but he couldn't think straight for the panic to which he had surrendered upon hearing of the soldiers' success. He was sweating and his heart felt like a cat caught in a bird-cage. He shouldn't have run up the stairs at such a speed. People died from such unfamiliar exertions.

Looking at the man face down on the filthy table, Malachi cursed himself afresh for a fool. How could he have forgotten the drawboy? Who closer to a weaver than his drawboy?

The drawboy lifted his head from the table to look at Malachi. His face, but for the bulb of his nose and the swollen rims to his eyes, was pale as bleached silk.

"Who isn't?" He remarked, in answer to Malachi's explanation of his presence.

He was so relieved to see Malachi. He had been afraid, on hearing the footsteps, that the soldiers were returning; or that Anton had already been informed of the drawboy's treachery and was come to seek revenge.

"As a friend," Malachi added with a perfunctory smile. He was probably too late. It was obvious, from his state, that whatever the drawboy knew, the soldiers were also privy to by now. If the drawboy knew where Paradis was, then so did the soldiers. Malachi's chance to reach Anton first depended upon what the soldiers did with that knowledge. Were the soldiers authorised to make an arrest without further instructions? If so, Paradis was already gone.

He should have been here first.

The drawboy shook his head and tears slipped out of his bloodshot eyes. He knew Delaney. Delaney was no friend of Anton Paradis.

"Paradis has no friends in this room," he said. "Don't try to pretend otherwise."

Paradis deserved that much honesty from him at least. He would not pretend to be what he no longer was; nor would he allow others to pretend to what they had never been.

Delaney shrugged his shoulders.

"As you wish," he said.

Then he saw how the old man might be seduced into revealing the whereabouts of Paradis, and his voice grew placatory.

"Though I think you underestimate yourself. There are few brave enough to resist the persuasions of soldiers."

The drawboy's head continued to shake.

"Well," said Malachi, his voice still soft and doubtful, "even if he has no friends in this room, he has plenty beyond. Friends powerful enough to make me prefer to act the friend than to show myself for the enemy I might rather be. I would certainly not have dared to do what you've just done, no matter how persuasive my visitors. There are many who would take it amiss were Paradis to be hanged. They'd be looking for a scapegoat and who more convenient than yourself?"

Malachi stopped short.

Maybe one victim would satisfy them.

But he could see almost at once that this would not be so. The drawboy would have betrayed Anton under duress. Malachi had betrayed him voluntarily. There was to be a third cell meeting tomorrow night. Should Anton be arrested before that meeting, McKenna would certainly produce a second letter in which Malachi would be named as the original traitor.

On the table, the drawboy was crying and whispering prayers to God for deliverance.

Malachi now showed himself in the guise of a possible deliverer.

"Were you and I, on the other hand, to reach Paradis before the soldiers do, and deliver him into the hands of his friends, then would we not both be lauded as heroes? We would, in effect, have double-crossed the soldiers."

The drawboy rolled onto his side.

"But the soldiers?" he whispered fearfully. "What of the anger of the soldiers? When they realise they've been duped?"

Malachi waved his free hand dismissively.

"You told the soldiers all you knew. You're not your brother's keeper. Should you be blamed for Anton's further flight?"

Son, the drawboy thought. He had thought of Anton as a son: not as a brother.

There was no further time for cajolery. Malachi asked the drawboy coldly what choice he thought he had. "You're caught between Anton's enemies and his friends. Which do you fear the most?"

When the drawboy finally told Malachi where he thought that Anton was hiding, Malachi dismissed it as impossible.

"You're lying. He might as well play at the hole of the asp."

"Then why are they still looking for him?"

The drawboy had a point. It was not a place which had occurred to Malachi. Why should others have found it any more likely? Who would expect a fleeing weaver to seek sanctuary at his own loom, in the house of a known agitator, former employer and former friend?

***

Dear Sir, I write in great agitation, having just received a report on Delaney's movements from my servant. He tells me that Paradis' drawboy has revealed to your soldiers that Paradis may be hiding in the McKenna premises. That McKenna should act so audaciously defies belief (which was, no doubt, the reaction he relied upon). While never doubting that help would be forthcoming (though not in such a cheeky guise), I had not expected the Frenchman to look to McKenna for help. I had thought he would be too fearful of his welcome. While it has long been known to us (from his indiscreet efforts to have the Frenchman released from gaol) that McKenna had forgiven the Frenchman his part in the destruction of his silk stock, Paradis would have been the last to be privy to such information; he would not have known himself forgiven. Then there was the alleged perfidy of McKenna in which, you assured me at the time of the interrogation, the Frenchman had a very perfect belief. It seems that this belief did not long survive his release from gaol, for with such a belief he surely could not have dared an approach to the silk merchant.

I urge you (and hope that my urging does not come too late) to refrain from taking any precipitate action against the Frenchman. I am glad that my misguided dismissal of Paradis' presence in the city was disregarded; but I believe that his arrest would be disastrous at this juncture. For reasons other than those which motivate the unhappy Delaney I believe that Paradis should be left at large. My suggestion is this: arrest McKenna and at once cause it to be rumoured that the arrest is the result of a deal struck between Paradis and the government; then allow the whereabouts of Paradis to be revealed to his devotees by Delaney. Should such a course be followed, I guarantee that the outrage of the deluded devotees will be such as to ensure the swift demise of our unwanted hero, and of the threatened rebellion itself. Such a scheme, Good Sir, cannot fail of its intention.

I remain, Dear Sir, your Devoted Servant and Friend . . .

***

He was too late. As soon as Malachi saw the swarm of red-chested soldiers outside the McKenna premises, he regretted having come so far. A crowd had gathered to watch events. Malachi was afraid of being recognised. What if, when McKenna should reveal him as the cause of Anton's initial arrest, his appearance at the scene of the weaver's second arrest should be recalled by some observant passer-by? He was still some distance from the soldiers. He hesitated, his head bent down, as though reflecting on a thing forgotten, then turned and went quietly back the way he had come.

***

The briefest of notes, Dear Sir, to thank you for your gracious letter, and to tell you that Delaney who arrived (uninvited) in a mood of rash aggression, accusing me of treachery and base cruelty, has just left well-soothed and with hope revived. Apparently he saw the soldiers at McKenna's house and assumed that Paradis was being arrested. Great was the self-abasement and the fawning gratitude when it was discovered that McKenna had been the man about to be arrested, and not Paradis at all. He believes, incredibly, that his wishes have been considered and accommodated and his opinion of myself is shockingly high; but still not so high as his opinion of his own importance. He even went so far as to suggest that, as a person of such obvious value to the Crown, he was perhaps worthy of greater reward than he had heretofore received. It will be a pleasure to see such a man undone; so much so that I almost regret his continued usefulness to us.

I told him (as you suggested I should) that a rumour was already circulating to the effect that Paradis had bought his freedom with the arrest of McKenna and that he was prepared, in due course, to give evidence in court against his former friend and employer. All that he, Delaney, had to do, was apprise the cell of Paradis' whereabouts. I believed, I told him, that he need do no more than that to be rid of Paradis for good. I permitted myself to say that he and his mistress would then be able to sleep easy in bed. So sure is he of my ignorance in the matter that he saw no irony. Indeed, he corrected my mistake, telling me that Mistress Paradis is more properly called a master, though a woman. It is, he said, the custom. I evinced surprise.

I trust that this plague of letters has succeeded in stifling our threatened rebellion and that we can both return to the more peaceful occupation of waiting for the French to appear.

Your devoted servant . . .

SEVENTEEN

The arrest could hardly have been more ill-timed.

Caroline could not be reached. She would neither eat nor speak. She lay in bed with her eyes open and screamed if anyone attempted to touch her. She screamed if Danno came into view, and she screamed if Letitia left her sight. So Letitia was forced to sit by her step-daughter's bed, separated from Danno by the tyranny of her step-daughter's terror, her attempts at explanation defeated by Caroline's silence. She was at fault, she knew. Even if one should be spared blame for what one could not cease to do, blame still attached; for there had been precautions she could have taken. Intoxicated by love, she had found Caroline's frail sensibilities insufferable. She had therefore feigned to believe the display of genuine love to be incapable of causing any damage. Last night, for instance, she had not even thought to turn the key in the lock. It was clear to Letitia that she had behaved with inexcusable abandon and she was bitterly ashamed. But even while she acknowledged her fault, she longed for Danno. Acknowledging her fault, she still found her step-daughter abhorrent. Could she have, she would have fled Caroline's presence. It was a loathsome devotion that would drive a young girl to intrude as Caroline had intruded. Letitia believed that Caroline had been stirred by the desire to save her step-mother's soul. Letitia did not fully understand. She had no idea how close to death the cries of love could sound.

They had no chance to say goodbye.

Caroline's bedroom faced the courtyard, and Letitia, trapped within it, unable so much as to rise to her feet without provoking her step-daughter to further screams, was not aware of the gathering soldiers, the gathering crowds in Dame Street. Letitia's lover was arrested quite without her knowledge. When she heard a knocking on the door below, she imagined the raised voices, subsequently heard inside the hall, to be those of the McKenna weavers. It was the day, she knew, on which their wages were paid.

Not until Mrs. McKenna came wailing up the stairs did Letitia discover the truth.

When Caroline heard that Danno had been arrested, she recovered her power of speech; but before she ever spoke, she smiled. "I'm glad," was what she first said to her distraught step-mother. Then she added, more as a statement than as a question: "You can't leave me now, Mama."
When she had spoken, she laid a hand possessively on Letitia's face and began to stroke the skin with her fingers as she had seen Mr. McKenna do so many times.

Letitia, her skin shrinking beneath her step-daughter's disturbingly lascivious caress, had, nevertheless, not dared to move her head.

"I am your protector now, Mama," Caroline whispered joyously, "as you have been mine."

God had finally come to Caroline's aid and she felt strengthened by his support. A fine judgement had been wrought upon the silk merchant. Her Mama should never be forced to cry out in such a fashion again.

***

Anton would not have known of the arrest had Caitlín not seen, glancing cautiously around the edge of the window in the late afternoon, soldiers stationed in the courtyard below.

She thought that they had come for Anton.

"Jesus Christ," she breathed as she sank in terror back against the wall.

Anton was lying on the makeshift bed of silks. He slept soundlessly. This was his second day of weaving. It was not his habit to rest thus while he worked, but for this job he had a drawboy far more fragile than himself. He had been unable to resist Caitlín's offer of help. He could not have left the warp to lie unwoven. Caitlín was not ignorant of the drawboy's work. She had watched her father's drawboy often enough; but she lacked the strength required for the job. She tried to conceal her exhaustion from Anton as she pulled, held and released the lashes on his instructions: she failed. It was quite possible that the whiteness of her face might have gone unobserved by the weaver, had it not been that each time her strength began to flag, the dance of the warp grew sluggish and upset the weaver's rhythm. On such occasions he insisted that they rest awhile.

Even now, the soldiers could be on the stairs.

Caitlín crept across the room to where the weaver lay sleeping. It seemed a journey of immense distance. She knelt down beside him, and, laying her hand over his mouth, whispered directly into his ear that he should not make a sound.

"We're surrounded," she told him in low words that curled like worms of death into the defenceless cavity of his ear, "by soldiers."

They stared unblinkingly at one another for a few seconds.

"I was dreaming of you," he whispered finally, and his moving lips nibbled the palm of her hand, while his breath blew warm and moist on the skin.

She had said that they must live on the assumption that no future existed. Could they manage, even now, to live thus? It was a matter of concentration. He laid his hand low upon her stomach and his fingers crushed her dress around the curve of her pubic bone. Material from her dress caught in the cavity between her kneeling legs.

She looked at him, astonished.

"You could not, surely, now, be thinking . . ?"

Sweat was running down his face as he willed himself to remain erect. He prayed for her to join him in his mind. He could not maintain such fantasy alone.

"Until they are within the door, the soldiers don't exist," he whispered urgently. "Let us leave nothing to regret."

She understood him perfectly.

Tears were running down her cheeks, but she raised her skirts audaciously above her hips and laid herself over him (without so much as a glance towards the door), hip to hip, her thighs clasping his between. The tears fell onto his face as she lowered her mouth to his; but the mouth itself was smiling.

236

If she could only grow about him, like a pearl about a piece of sand. Could she have swallowed him intact, she would. She would even have killed him, had he so desired, in order to protect him from the soldiers.

When they next looked out the window, the soldiers had disappeared from the courtyard. It was impossible to guess where they might now be.

"You invented them," Anton said teasingly (though his face was pale), "to test my abilities."

"Perhaps we should have watched more closely," Caitlín said uneasily, but Anton shook his head with sudden vehemence.

"What difference would watching have made? I believe the soldiers know I'm here. It's more than time for the drawboy to have broken. They know I'm trapped and it amuses them to delay my arrest. They would like us to have watched them without let. We were to be terrorised to stillness by their presence, and tormented with hope by their absence. Instead we defied them. Ours was the response of which legends are made."

Caitlín laughed briefly.

"Had anyone been present to observe it," she remarked drily. But then she began to laugh again. "We should have called the soldiers in to see our bravery."

He put his arms around her waist and held her closely to him. "I need never again lie grieving in a cell for love wasted," he murmured as he kissed her forehead.

By midnight, Danno still had not arrived with their food.

"He might have had a sudden engagement," Caitlín ventured. "And could not bring us word."

Had it not been for that earlier presence of the soldiers, such an explanation would have been reasonable enough. Such unpredicted engagements did occur.

But by morning he still had not arrived and they knew that he had been taken by the soldiers.

Anton was no longer sure how great had been the impact on subsequent events of his letter to Marvin Sweetman. Whether or not the letter had been of any consequence was immaterial. Damage had been intended, and damage, far greater than had been intended, had occurred. His conscience demanded that he should make amends.

"You're a weaver," Caitlín reminded Anton desperately when she saw that he was going to leave.

"And a hero," he said as lightly as he could.

***

The star of Anton Paradis fell rapidly through the day as the rumour circulated that he was in the city and had struck a deal with the government. It was said, with ominous assurance, that he had agreed, in return for his own freedom, to present himself as chief witness for the Crown in the prosecution of Danno McKenna, silk merchant and alleged United Irishman. The fact that McKenna had already been arrested gave a further air of authenticity to the rumour.

"He was ever a coward," Malachi Delaney remarked quietly that evening.

Cell members, shocked by the arrest of Paradis' emissary, were reluctant to give credence to the rumour. Its confirmation would mean an end to their plan to lead a rebellion. Already it was in jeopardy. The leader had said that they would meet tonight, but must not meet again. They were, the leader said, in danger from McKenna's tongue. And when a murmur of condemnation had risen (as though they had already been betrayed), he had warned that no one could guarantee his own silence under torture. They had grown silent, but each had known in their hearts that Danno McKenna had never been their brother. So why should he protect them like a brother?

Besides, the rumour of Paradis' treachery, if true, would make them seem such fools.

Why, they wondered defensively amongst themselves, would Paradis turn now, having kept silence under the wickedest of conditions? He was their hero. Besides, he was in France. Why would a free man make deals? Several members, hearing Malachi's remark, eyed him with nervous dislike. Surely they had not been adoring a coward?

"He was ever a coward," Malachi said a second time, more gently still, looking down at his hands before him on the table. He was afraid that if he saw their eyes, he might lose his nerve. "And greedy too."

It was essential that he should convince them of Paradis' perfidy. He was glad that the rumour had arrived well before him.

A silence followed these comments, which Malachi was eventually forced to break himself. His hands were sweating. He tucked them beneath the table for fear they might be seen to shake.

"I heard tell that it wasn't in prison his hands and feet were broken at all," he remarked, "but at sea. He fell, it is said, struck by sea-sickness, from the main mast in a bucking sea. It was said that his time in prison was soft enough. The authorities, it seems, forgot they had him there, and he was never interrogated at all. I also heard," Malachi added, "that the Frenchman has been in Dublin several days."

A week ago, he would have been thrown out for such remarks. Tonight the atmosphere had changed. No one had the courage to call him a liar.

"Who is your source?" the leader asked wearily. He did not care for Malachi Delaney, though he had, as yet, nothing specific on which to base his dislike.

Malachi hesitated.

"No source is privileged within the cell," the leader warned.

Malachi had hesitated only for effect.

"Well," he said slowly, raising his eyes at last, and looking round the room. "Paradis visited his drawboy. So did I."

He had their attention now.

"You did, did you? And what else did the drawboy have to say?"

Malachi sighed. The strategy, suggested to him by the agent, was working well. "I am reluctant to break a confidence, but . . ." he caught the leader's eye and sighed again.

"Well then," he said reluctantly, "the drawboy told me Paradis expected McKenna to hide him. It was no more than I anticipated hearing. McKenna, as the drawboy said, was ever under the influence of Paradis."

"Why?"

"His weaving," Malachi said in genuine surprise. That his world might be unknown to others did not occur to Malachi. How could Paradis' skill not be known? Malachi nursed no jealousy towards Paradis' professional ability. "The Frenchman's weaving was unrivalled," he said, without hesitation. "And McKenna is a connoisseur of silks."

The leader, a cooper, shrugged without real comprehension. He could turn out a fine barrel himself, but no one had ever fallen under the thrall of a cooper for admiration of a cooper's skills.

"So you're saying that McKenna would have done what was required of him? He would have concealed the weaver?"

Malachi nodded.

"Without a doubt," he said.

"From his own cell, if needs be?"

Malachi nodded again.

The leader shook his head, amazed. He had misjudged the silk merchant. He had not expected such perversity of behaviour.

"And the letter, purporting to come from France?"

"The writing was not in Paradis' script."

"Why did you not say so at the time?"

"Who would have believed me?"

They believed him now, though. Their faces showed it clearly. But believing him did not, he could tell, increase their liking for him. No matter. There would be time enough for liking once Paradis was gone.

"I imagine poor McKenna thought to protect the Frenchman further," said the leader kindly, as though speaking of one fatally diseased. If the leader had a weakness, it lay in his tendency to think well of those better-placed in society than himself. He had been proud to have a silk merchant in his cell. "By locating him firmly in France."

"And Paradis, while agreeing to the letter, as being in his interests, would not have agreed to the writing of such damning sentiments himself."

"A cunning man," the leader remarked bleakly.

"According to the drawboy," Malachi put in maliciously, "Paradis, while flattered by the high regard in which he was so unjustly held, was terrified by the prospect of having to live up to such expectations. By appearing to lend support from France, he hoped to retain the admiration without being called upon to fight."

"At some point he must have decided that the Crown's protection was more reliable than the protection of a suspected rebel."

"But at the cost of losing a reputation so easily won?" questioned one of the others doubtfully.

"The Crown rewards its witnesses well. Paradis may have wearied of the weaving trade. He may be looking to rise in the world."

"He should not be allowed to rise," Malachi dared to say, and around him, the other men nodded in agreement. If they were not to have a revolution, they were not prepared to deprive themselves of revenge on the man who had deceived them into thinking revolution possible.

**

Letitia had heard the rumour too, but gave no credence to it. It came to her from Danno's other weavers. The drawboy had made certain, on Malachi's instructions, that they knew the rumour, though he could not bring himself to disclose the Frenchman's probable sanctuary.

They came to visit the house.

"Where is he, Ma'am?" they asked Letitia, their voices violent with longing. What if others were to find Paradis first? He had disappointed so many.

She said she did not know.

"You wouldn't protect McKenna's betrayer, would you, Ma'am?" She had, in their eyes, seduced the merchant. Who knew why? They had no reason to trust her.

She shook her head.

"No. I would not. But Paradis is not McKenna's betrayer. Notwithstanding which," she added quickly, "I do not know where the weaver is."

The weavers left, dissatisfied.

She knew who had betrayed Danno McKenna, but she would not divulge his name to the men before her. They were not the men to avenge McKenna. Without the silk merchant, the weavers had no work. This was the central cause of their grief concerning McKenna. Only one weaver loved the merchant enough to avenge him. To that man she would give her husband's name.

She was forced to name her husband to another.

On the day which followed Danno's arrest, Mrs. McKenna asked Letitia to leave and to bring her step-daughter with her.

"Your reason for being here is gone," she announced shrilly. Her eyelids were puffed with weeping. Lashes were stuck together by salt.

Letitia sat immovably with the appallingly solicitous Caroline in Mrs. McKenna's sitting room and refused to go.

"We must stay," she said, her voice dull and unyielding.

Caroline nodded in agreement, though neither woman saw. Without Mr. McKenna the house contained no man of consequence.

Mrs. McKenna was astounded by Letitia's affrontery. She sensed, from the very juxtaposition of the two events, that Letitia's shattering arrival had been the catalyst for her son's arrest, though she could not see how.

"You have no right to stay," she said in a voice heavy with authority. "Your presence was an embarrassment before; it is intolerable now."

But Letitia remained impervious to Mrs. McKenna's demands.

When Letitia suggested that as they both loved Danno they should, perhaps, treat one another with the dignity that such shared love deserved, Mrs. McKenna was outraged. She spoke to Letitia (in a voice which shook with anger) as though Caroline had not been present in the room. That the unfortunate and misguided passion which Mrs Sweetman felt for her son could be mentioned in the same breath as the love quite properly felt for him by his mother was inexcusable. She, Mrs. McKenna, felt contaminated by the very idea.

"Had you really loved him, you would have encouraged him to marry Pansy."

Letitia laughed, but remembered uneasily that such had once been her intention; at least, it had not been her intention to prevent the marriage. But still . . .

"Marriage would not have saved your son from arrest," she said gently.

Letitia felt for Mrs. McKenna. She could see that hers was as humiliating a position as Letitia's own. But there it was. What else could Letitia do?

"You could," Mrs. McKenna informed her icily, "return to your husband. Were you to perform your duties as a wife in full, then his daughter would have no cause to fear her father's advances."

Her pragmatism was chilling.

Letitia heard a small moan and, glancing at Caroline, saw that the girl had crossed her arms over her breasts and was rocking to and fro with her eyes closed.

She sighed.

"Caroline," she called gently. "Go to your room. I will let you know when you may return."

Mrs. McKenna looked ashamed.

"I had forgotten her presence," she lied.

Letitia attempted (from a sluggish sense of duty) to touch Caroline's hand as Caroline passed her stiffly by, but the girl (to Letitia's relief) shrank away. (Caroline could not allow her conscience to be influenced by the longed-for, rarely given, touches of Mama.)

The two women sat in silence for a short while after Caroline's departure.

"It was," Letitia finally said, "my husband who betrayed your son."

On the far side of the door, Caroline whispered "Mama!" inaudibly to the painted wood.

Mrs. McKenna was also shocked by Letitia's accusation.

"Has my son been arrested at the suit of a piqued cuckold?" she demanded. "And you hesitate! Go back to your husband, Mrs. Sweetman and the dispute will be at an end forthwith. My son will not long lie in the gaol if you console your husband well."

"You misunderstand," Letitia said.

Outside the door, Caroline's thumb was in her mouth and she rocked inconsolably upon her feet. She had been lulled by Mama's distress into imagining her grown virtuous. Her conscience had fallen asleep and had allowed the Devil to take its place. The Devil had tempted her to see herself as this new and virtuous Mama's protector. Mama was beyond protection. Just to listen to Mama speak thus of Father without protest was surely to participate in wickedness. It was impossible to betray a rebel, and Mr. McKenna, as Mama well knew, was a rebel. She should leave Mama. Caroline believed that she loved Letitia no more than any daughter might love a mother, but still she knew it was wrong to stay. Her primary duty was to her father. Her father might have failed in his duty to his daughter; but that was no reason for his daughter to do likewise. She should return to her father alone, for Mama's sins were multiplying.

To stay with Mama was to be damned, but she loved Mama too much to leave her.

Caroline began to cry. God still guided her conscience, but the Devil controlled her will-power. She could not do her duty.

Beyond the door, Mama continued to speak.

"Their quarrel preceded our affair, Ma'am. The betrayal would have taken place had I been the most steadfast of wives. Its cause is rooted in politics, not love. Your son grew too radical for my husband's weak stomach."

She then described to Mrs. McKenna the conversations she had overheard between her husband and the government agent.

Caroline knew that her father had been doing no more than his duty.

"Your leaving precipitated his betrayal," Caroline heard Mrs. McKenna say forbiddingly.

"Betrayal was overdue."

Another silence fell, and in the silence, accommodation was made. Finally Mrs. McKenna, while sighing, remarked that it was a pity Mrs. Sweetman had ever seen fit to impose herself upon the McKenna household; but she made no more mention of departure.

When Letitia opened the door, she found Caroline shivering on the far side.

"Did you hear everything?" she asked despairingly (though what further damage could be inflicted on the girl's already damaged sensibilities was difficult to imagine), and Caroline nodded mutely. "I'm sorry."

Caroline shook her head.

"It reminded me of what I am," she said, through the fingers stuffed into her mouth. "The Devil's creature."

"Oh God!"

Caroline shook her head a second time.

"He will not hear you, Mama," she told Letitia painfully.

She was her father's creature. Her father's mutilated creature. Letitia found within herself an unexpected seam of tenderness for this girl, this ghastly girl (no more than four years younger than herself), who so absurdly called her Mama.

"Caroline: you are good; it is within your father that all fault lies."

Caroline began to cry. Mama was so cajoling when she sought to entice one to further sin.

"Not the fault of treachery, Mama. He is no traitor. It has ever been Mr. McKenna who has spoken treasonably. He spoke warmly of separation. Surely one cannot betray a traitor, Mama?"

"They were friends."

"And is friendship to be put higher than duty?"

"Yes, where both perceive their conflicting causes to be honourable."

Caroline laid her head on Letitia's shoulder. She could no longer bear to see her face. Mama's lies were pronounced from a face which shone so plausibly with truth. Why was it not possible to entice Mama to virtue?

"I love you," she whispered helplessly.

***

Letitia had lied to the weavers. She knew exactly where Anton Paradis and the girl lay hidden.

Danno had not told Letitia of the weaver's return.

Like the leader, he trusted no one's silence under torture. Were Letitia (God forbid) to be interrogated by soldiers, she would not be able to confess what she did not know.

But Letitia, seeing him one night, from her window, walk cautiously round the edge of the courtyard with a tray in his hand, directly after he had made an elaborate play of tiredness for her benefit, had been curious enough to follow him. She had, after all, heard him close his bedroom door with unmistakable finality. Why, therefore, had she not heard him open it again? She had been, in honesty, besieged by jealousy and could not have restrained herself from pursuit, had broken glass strewn the path before her.

It had seemed to the shaken Letitia, as she had listened outside the warehouse door, that the warehouse was the centre of all her lover's intrigues.

She had heard the girl's voice first and her heart had seemed to shrink within her. Her lover was no better than a cock in a yard of hens. She herself could tell no difference between one hen and the next. Was that how women appeared to Danno McKenna? She had known the voice, but had been at a loss to place it. Then she had heard the weaver's unmistakable accent, and the reason for her lover's secrecy had become clear. She had crept away, ashamed for her own suspicions.

Afterwards, she had been disturbed to realise that, had the voice of the Frenchman not been heard, she would still have crept away. She could not have borne to confront McKenna with his own infidelity. To confront him would have been to lose him and she could no longer contemplate such loss. She had been weakened by love.

***

When she heard the frail tapping upon the door, Caitlín's heart soared. She thought it must be Anton returned. She opened the door with no thought of caution.

Letitia Sweetman stood there, her face salt-stained with old tears.

"Who told you we . . ." Caitlín began.

Letitia, searching for Anton, peered beyond the shoulder of the girl. She saw the bed of crumpled silks and began, despite herself, to laugh. That she should have a common bed with servants! She would always be prey to her own sense of the ludicrous.

"We have a closer connection than I knew, I see."

She had no sense of what was fitting.

"We have little time for pleasantries, Ma'am," Caitlín whispered sharply, pulling Letitia quickly inside. "You put us in jeopardy by your presence." She thought Letitia quite detestable.

"He's been arrested," Letitia said abruptly, once the door was closed. She spoke in a flat voice and her eyes remained quite dry. She had business to do with the weaver. Tears would not serve her.

She was immediately misunderstood. Caitlín, believing Anton to be the one arrested, gripped her by the arm and began to shake it, as though Letitia herself was responsible.

"How can you say so?" Caitlín cried desperately.

It was only when Letitia began to describe the arrival of the soldiers on the previous afternoon that Caitlín realised her mistake.

"You are speaking of Mr. McKenna?" she ventured with apprehensive hope.

"Of course."

"Oh, thank God!"

Observing Anton's absence, Letitia understood the error. She put her hands up to her face and began to laugh hysterically. She might have said the same had their positions been reversed. When she looked up, Caitlín still smiled with her own relief. She had, Letitia thought, no cause for such relief. If the weaver was at large, he was safe from no one. Had the girl not heard the rumours?

"Where is the weaver now?" she asked.

Caitlín's eyes filled with tears. The morning had been long. "He would not be restrained. Once it was clear that Mr. McKenna had been arrested, he could not remain within, but must offer his services to their mutual associates. He is seen," she added, attempting a show of pride, "as a hero now."

"You have heard nothing?"

The girl (What was her name? Colleen? Katie?) looked at her, answering neither yes nor no. She did not understand the question. Letitia sighed and rubbed her eyes.

"There are rumours," she began.

"I beg your pardon," Caitlín said, frowning.

Letitia shrugged.

"It is widely rumoured in the city that the weaver offered himself as a Crown witness for the prosecution of Mr. McKenna, in return for his own immunity."

Caitlín's face reddened with anger.

"Is that your own belief?"

Letitia gave her no immediate reply. Instead she walked over to the loom and looked down in silence at the silk.

"It was a pattern best forgotten," she said coldly. "It seems to bring bad luck." Then she turned round to face the weaver's girl.

"My husband betrayed Danno McKenna," she said.

***

When Mrs. McKenna did persuade Letitia to leave the house, it was for Letitia's own protection that she did so.

"Your husband must fear your tongue," she said thoughtfully to Letitia two days after her son's arrest. "He may baulk at appearing in the witness stand for fear of it; and if the government finds you to be the curb upon your husband's tongue, then we should fear the government. Indeed, dreading your tongue as he must, I should not be surprised if your husband made sure that the government knew you to be threatening his position as witness. Your unfortunate step-daughter, too, is little safer than yourself." Letitia had not considered herself and Caroline to be in danger until then. "But Marvin loves us," she protested, then added, more cautiously, "Well, most certainly, he loves Caroline."

"I imagine he loves his reputation more. Women are so much more easily replaced than a reputation."

It was Mrs. McKenna who suggested the empty warehouse as a hiding place.

"It has not been used since poor Anton's arrest. It will suffice until a better arrangement can be made. Should they come looking for you, I shall tell them that I threw you out. I shall ask them did they seriously expect me to keep my son's mistress under my roof in the absence of my son himself. I shall not find the performance difficult."

"I do not doubt it, Ma'am," Letitia said drily, but then she added, "I thank you, nonetheless."

But Mrs. McKenna would acknowledge no kindness in her actions.

"It is in my son's interests that you should remain at large," she insisted coldly. "For his sake alone I have a care for your well-being. Should your husband be deterred from giving evidence for fear of your revelations, then my son can scarcely be tried."

***

So Letitia returned to the warehouse. Caroline, seized by an inexplicable spell of unnerving happiness (like birdsong heard at dead of night), came humming at her side.

Letitia explained their need to hide while Caitlín, her eyes swollen with crying, looked at her with distrust. She saw Letitia as being, in some obscure way, the cause of Anton's departure.

"You can stay or go as you please," Letitia told her graciously. She hoped the weaver's girl would stay. The prospect of being left alone with her increasingly demented step-daughter was almost unbearable.

"You're very kind, Ma'am," Caitlín murmured derisively.

Letitia's wishes were immaterial. Who, after all, was Mrs. Sweetman now? The adulterous wife of an informer; the mistress of a traitor; the custodian of a poor, mad step-daughter. (Caitlín knew of Caroline's torments. McKenna had spoken of them compulsively on his nightly visits to the warehouse. But he had not said the girl was turned mad by her suffering.) Caitlín could not leave. She was in the only place where Anton could be sure of finding her, should he happen to survive.

She was unfair, she knew, to see Mr. McKenna's mistress as the cause of everything.

"Well," she said finally. "We have this much in common: the men we love both love one another."

So they sat together on the ragged silks throughout the day, uneasily allied in love.

EIGHTEEN

Hatred of the Frenchman was spreading like dye through wet silk.

The McKenna weavers were feverish with it. Not even Peadar Howlin's trust in the Frenchman could survive this final rumour. Paradis had sacrificed them all (Howlin included) to revenge himself upon McKenna for the wrong McKenna had done him; as though McKenna were a false friend. But what more had McKenna ever been, other than a silk merchant? The trouble was that Paradis had always had ideas above his station. He had never accepted the boundaries. The fool had thought that friendship knew no bounds. And now, by way of revenge, he was committing an act beyond forgiveness.

They did not love the silk merchant, and would not have attempted to save him for his own sake; but they were all agreed that Paradis could not be allowed to profit from his own evil while the rest of them starved by it.

Paradis had flown too close to the merchant and had been burnt. What else could he have expected? Had he really imagined that the so-called friendship could survive his own disloyalty? He had behaved as treacherously as the rest of them and had paid a just price. It had been inevitable that the most trusted weaver (the merchant's friend, as Paradis would have it) would receive the greatest punishment. The fury of a merchant scorned. They had been given back their jobs; Paradis had been sent to prison. "A scapegoat for you all," the foreman had said at the time by way of explanation. By that singling out of one for punishment, the rest had been saved; but naturally Paradis could not accept such obvious justice.

The weavers' memories were stagnant with falsehoods. They believed now that they would have pleaded for Paradis had they known, in time, of McKenna's intentions. They were sure, now that they had just cause to revile him, that they had always reviled him justly; but that their magnanimity would have forgiven the Paradis failings was beyond question. Had he come to them in suitable humility to beg for their aid, it would have been forthcoming. Yet Paradis had betrayed them all without compunction.

Only McKenna's release could save their jobs. Paradis had been sacrificed before for the good of the greatest number. He could be sacrificed again, this second time with justice. But for a sacrifice to take place, a body was required. It was decided that the drawboy should be recalled.

But before he could be sent for, the drawboy appeared of his own accord and told them, with babbling anxiety, where the weaver lay hidden.

There had been no need to press the drawboy; he had been already pressed.

Malachi had returned to the drawboy's lodgings (on the orders of the government agent) that afternoon, and had presented the drawboy (in a voice hysterical with his own increasing fears) with his options; they were limited. Were the drawboy to reveal the whereabouts of the silk weaver to his fellow weavers, he would get nothing by way of reward; were the drawboy to persist in concealing Paradis, well . . .

"A quick thrust of the pike, your body dropped in the river and no one the wiser." Malachi was repeating what he had been told to say.

"Why me?" the drawboy had inquired, with brave animosity. The question was rash, but who was Malachi Delaney to be making threats? There was sweat, he had noted, on the weaver's forehead and cheeks, though the afternoon was cold. "You know where Paradis is. You tell them."

But Malachi had shaken his head emphatically. "They know the differences which exist between Paradis and myself. You would be the more readily believed," he told the drawboy urgently.

Malachi was a permanently frightened man. The choice that he had been told to offer to the drawboy did not, in fact, exist. The drawboy was, according to the agent (who had kept a letter, half-written, on the table before him while they spoke), a mouth too many in the chain. A small bauble of ink had dangled like a drop of blood from the point of the agent's resting quill. Once the drawboy's message was delivered, the pike thrust would be his.

251

Dear Sir, I cannot begin to express my gratitude for your kindness in entrusting to me this present, delicate, task. I take it as an expression of the highest confidence in my capabilities and am, accordingly, flattered (though apprehensive of my own safety should my participation become known). I allow myself the liberty of hoping that my courage will be well-rewarded.

You must pardon me, but the weaver has just arrived . . .

The agent had smiled while confiding the truth to the terrified Malachi.

"We (and I speak on behalf of the government) want no connection between Paradis' death and ourselves," he had explained, while scraping his quill dry on the edge of the ink horn. "There must be no way in which the weaver's reputation can be revived, even posthumously. Suppose the drawboy were to suspect, for example, that you are working, not as an independent man, but as an informer . . . might he not blab of his suspicions?"

But the same risk attached to Malachi. He too was capable of linking Paradis to government machinations. Jesus Christ. "You were right to pick a man you could trust," he had whispered, dry-mouthed with fear, to the agent.

"I have never trusted any man," the agent had said slowly in reply. "Suspicion has always served me well."

Malachi was the agent's pawn. He could see that clearly now. He was compelled to do the agent's bidding, because he could not live entirely without hope; but his future was as bleak as the drawboy's own. There was to be no reward for Malachi Delaney either. Once he ceased to be of use, he would be destroyed.

So numbed was he by fear, that Malachi had doubted (unjustly it transpired) his own ability to walk unaided to the door of the agent's office.

A dead man could not bear witness.

. . . he has left a chastened man. He realises, for the first time, his own dispensability and how imperative it is that he should continue to be of use to me. He now regards the mere retention of his own skin as the most precious prize he could receive for his much-vaunted loyalty.

I have, my Friend, set so many people to catch the unfortunate Paradis that I almost fear his escape in the melée! I have set a pair of my best young men to watch (unseen) the McKenna establishment and I anticipate good news before the night is out.

As for McKenna's treasonous associates: when I hear how readily their revolutionary spirit has collapsed, I begin to doubt that their threat was ever of any great magnitude. They lack the necessary fire. A plan to storm the prison where McKenna lies (they fear his tongue while he remains in custody) was, for instance, abandoned, when it was realised that they did not know which one to storm and did not dare to make inquiries for fear of drawing attention to themselves. Their dread of publicity divides them in their solution to the problem of Paradis. They fear they will be casualties of Paradis' apparent decision to take the witness stand against their colleague; but they fear their own detection should they make any move against Paradis now. They presume, logically enough, that a Crown witness of such importance as Paradis would be were he such an animal, must be protected to the highest degree. I had not, I confess, expected such caution from those so lately proposing rebellion. I have told Delaney that should the weavers fail to deal with Paradis, then he, Delaney, must bring Paradis before the cell. They must not be allowed to evade their responsibilities. I do not, however, expect the weavers to fail. To have Paradis both dead and discredited will be a coup worthy of reward. I must allow myself to hope that any such reward will be mine.

I must thank you, incidentally, for your inquiries as to my wife's health. I regret to report that her visit to the country has not been as beneficial as had been hoped for. The pustules upon her face seem but the outward expression of some rapacious inner condition which quite consumes her. It seems a pity that such an expensive sojourn should have been in vain. (Not that I regret the attempt, you understand!) So debilitated is she that she can no longer rise from her bed, but must be carried, even the short distance to the chamber pot. I fear the Good Lord intends her departure from me and can but pray for courage to bear the loss.

I remain, Good Sir, your obedient servant . . .

There was a wind blowing strongly from the north-west that night to fan the hatred of the weavers. They too had reached the conclusion that a dead man could not bear witness.

They stood, their faces flushed with agitation, their hearts pounding like palm-struck skin drums, chanting Paradis' name menacingly at the dark base of the stairs leading to the upper warehouse. The agent's two young men, with one of whom the agent (unbeknownst to the young man) was enamoured (and the young man would not know, for the mere existence of an object of desire sufficed for the agent's modest needs), watched as well as they could from another doorway within the courtyard. They had entered the courtyard that morning without hindrance. The new wrought-iron gates had not been closed since Danno's arrest. At noon, they had observed two young women walk hand in hand through the entrance where the weavers now gathered. Neither woman had come out again. Other than by noting down the time of the arrival, they had paid no mind. The passage to and fro of women was not of any consequence. Their duty was to watch for the Frenchman.

Paradis did not appear.

The weavers grew hesitant. What if they were gathered at the wrong place? What guarantee did they have that he was there? The word of Paradis' own devoted (if cowardly) drawboy was scarcely to be relied upon. If Paradis was of such importance to the Crown, why would they leave him at large? So many people must wish him ill. But then again, who was to say that Paradis was not inside? Why would he come out before his time?

"We could smoke him out."

It would, of course, have been possible for the weavers to mount the stairs and break into the warehouse. It was not a task beyond the strength of seven men. But such a course was quite without finesse. They needed some recompense for their debilitating sense of uncertainty. They preferred (if he was there) to tease him out with smoke. If Paradis did not emerge, they would still have the fire with which to assuage their passions.

***

In the light of her inability to erase certain events from her step-daughter's mind, Letitia could only resolve not to fail Caroline a second time; it was a resolution she found herself unable to keep once Caroline found herself courted by fire.

All three women heard the low, incessant chanting of Paradis' name by the weavers down below. Letitia and Caitlín wondered who was calling and how they should respond.

Caitlín, from grieving for him, turned to thanking God that he was gone.

As they stood, irresolute, inside the room, smoke began to percolate through the cracks and orifices of the closed door. All remaining traces of Caroline's sanity evaporated. Flames, she knew then, were what she most desired. She crawled around the door, trying to feed the tentative wisps of smoke into her own mouth.

"Purged by fire," she crooned. "We shall be purged by fire, Mama."

Letitia stared, horrified, at her kneeling step-daughter, and at the lazily encroaching smoke.

"She's mad!" Caitlín whispered, clinging to Letitia's arm, as she too stared at the ecstatic girl, who now sucked tendrils of smoke up through her funnelled, pink tongue. "Her father has turned her mad."

(Marvin Sweetman had been right to fear his daughter. In her shame for her own much greater wickedness in abandoning her father, Caroline had, throughout the afternoon, compared it unfavourably with his own small wickedness to her. Whereas before, Caitlín had known merely that there had been a crime committed upon the girl by her father, now she knew precisely the nature of that crime.)

"Yes," Letitia said, and she began to cry. Letitia was not like Caroline; she was realistic. She knew where responsibility principally lay; but she also knew that she could not be completely absolved from blame for this metamorphosis. She had plucked the bird from the cat's mouth, but had not thought to heal the wounds. By removing the girl from her father's house, Letitia had taken upon herself the burden of Caroline; and had failed to do her duty by it.

Caroline, gorging herself on smoke, began to cough.

Letitia and Caitlín ran together to drag her back from the door. She writhed within their grip.

"The fire is not meant for us," Letitia told her struggling stepdaughter. "It was meant for Paradis."

"But Paradis is not here. Those outside intend the fire for Paradis. God intends the fire for you and me. The refiner's fire."

She was beyond restraint.

"We must not hide from the flames, Mama!" she cried eagerly, breaking away from the two young women. She ran back to the door and wrenched it wide open.

Smoke gushed in. Caroline staggered backwards, coughing. She allowed herself to be caught in Letitia's arms; but then, she closed her own arm tight around Letitia's neck and, relentless as the figure of death itself, began to draw Letitia forward with her through the smoke-fogged doorway. Letitia, struggling to free herself from her step-daughter's choking grip, felt her feet slipping on the floorboards. Surely she could not be about to die for sins she was falsely seen by someone else to possess? A ball of flame exploded through the smoke and set the young girl's hair alight. Beneath her hair the skin began to fry, as pungent to the nostrils as roasting pork. Caroline, raising her hands to beat at her burning hair, released Letitia. Unsupported, dazed by smoke, Letitia fell to the ground. Scorched pieces of her own hair crumbled and dropped like powdered leaves from her head. The air was clearer close to the floor. Letitia crept blindly on her hands and knees towards Caitlín's calling voice.

Caitlín had opened the window. It gave more air, but drew the fire further into the room.

"Mama!" screamed Caroline through hoops of flame.

Letitia had reached Caitlín's legs. She clung to them and pulled herself to her knees. The smoke was dense and the flames surrounding Caroline shone mutedly like a sun seen through fog.

"Mama!" screamed Caroline again.

Letitia buried her ears between Caitlín's thighs.

"Go to God," Caitlín called out suddenly in a loud voice. She could think of nothing kinder. She thought the young girl, like an irrevocably injured animal, better dead.

The first floor was not high above the ground. Letitia and Caitlín in turn hung themselves by their hands from the windowsill and dropped heavily to the cobbles below. They lay coughing on the ground. Smoke had stained their faces and had caused their eyes to run with tears. And then, above Letitia's blinking eyes there appeared the blackened silhouette of Caroline, framed by the window from which the two women had so recently lowered themselves. Her mouth seemed open but no sounds came forth. She stood for a moment on the window sill, her smouldering arms reaching convulsively out to the watching women; then, overbalanced by the twitching of her own agonised body, she fell. Small flames broke out afresh, fanned by the passing air. Her body, by the time it reached the ground, had died, its heart failing it in flight.

The weavers were horrified by what had come forth from their fire. The fire itself had grown far bigger than intended. The treads of the stairs themselves had caught fire with such unexpected ease. The charred, yet living, body which had wavered on the windowsill would haunt each one of them for as long as their minds survived the decays of age. It had been unrecognisable. It could have been Paradis, though it seemed too small (but who could tell what way a body shrank in fire); it might have been a woman. They could only be sure that it had been a human being. While Caitlín and McKenna's woman crouched weeping over the ruined body, and flames blew out through the open window, the weavers crept away. They feared the consequences, unaware that they had done (it seemed to those sent to watch), just what had been hoped of them. In any case, the consequences they feared might well arise; that they had (unknowingly) satisfied the expectations of others would give them no immunity. It had been hoped that the weavers would act against the Frenchman with unlawful violence. They had apparently done so. The destruction of Paradis' reputation would be complete were his justifiably inflamed fellow weavers to be punished for the murder of a man so lately described as being beyond the protection of the law.

The agent's men had seen two women go in. They saw two women come out. They assumed that the third, burnt body, was that of Paradis, the man they had been sent to observe. They saw the body doused with water and heard the water hiss on the hot flesh. They watched as the two women concocted a sling of silk in which to catch the skinless body; they saw the women's hands grow dark with flecks of sticky, shifting, sodden flesh as they lifted the body onto the knotted strip of silk; saw them blowing afterwards on their fingers to cool them, wiping their hands clean on their dirty dresses.

Then, each shouldering an end of the sling, the women filed silently out with it through the archway.

***

Their passage through the streets was formidable. Letitia, who knew their destination, walked at the front with the unswerving doggedness of a sleepwalker. She held her head immobile and her eyes stared straight ahead, like vast, glass beads fixed into porcelain. Her face, emptied of all expression, was singularly chilling. People moved silently from her path when she approached. She was profoundly shocked; she seemed possessed. People dared not imagine what the sling contained. So mesmerised were they by the awesome sight of Letitia that Caitlín, walking solidly behind, was scarcely seen, or seen, at best, too late. Questions which might have been asked of her were not asked. Not that such loss of opportunity made a difference. Had questions been asked, Caitlín would not have replied.

Marvin Sweetman saw his wife's approach from his study window, before which he spent a large part of each day. Recognising her, he imagined the second figure to be that of his daughter. His heart grew turbulent within his chest. He knew of McKenna's arrest (how could he not have known, given the pressure put upon his conscience by the agent ever since?). Could it be that his wife and daughter were come to purchase his silence for the silk merchant? The notion enchanted while it terrified. From what insanity could he be trusted to withhold himself in such circumstances? Marvin withdrew to the interior of his study lest his face, being seen, might frighten his two girls to flight. What possessions had they, he wondered, which needed to be carried with such touching solemnity between them? There had been a poignancy about the procession which flooded his heart with sentiment.

He understood with overwhelming clarity as he waited, in the aftermath of that anticipated knock upon the door, the father's forgiveness of the prodigal son.

When the servant came, with terrified face (what was it he had seen when the sling was being lowered to the floor?), to announce the arrival of Mrs. Sweetman, Marvin Sweetman walked out, fortified with emotion, from his study.

"I've brought your daughter home," Letitia said, nodding at the floor.

Marvin could not bring himself to understand his wife's gesture. He looked hesitantly at the second woman who stood implacably beside his wife. He had been easily mistaken. She bore no resemblance to his daughter; why, she was dark, where Caroline was fair. He turned back to his wife. He could not look elsewhere; but her finger was before him and it pointed to the floor. The eyes of the servant, who leaned, white-faced against the wall, with his hand clasped across his mouth, were transfixed by what lay at Marvin's feet. He was compelled at last to look down. Fluid had leaked from the partially covered bundle. It welled against his shoes. The hall, he realised now, was dense with the smell of woodsmoke and charred meat. His wife's hair was scorched.

"What happened?" he whispered.

No one bothered to reply.

Then he saw that from the bundle a burnt arm protruded.

Marvin Sweetman screamed, his voice high-pitched as that of a woman, and he sank to his knees beside the shrouded body of his daughter. At the sound of that scream, the servant ran, terrified, from the hall.

It did not occur to Marvin to question the identity of the body, but Letitia knelt beside him and pointed to the remains of a ring, melted into the remains of flesh which still adhered to the exposed bones of the middle finger on his daughter's blackened right hand.

"Her mother's eternity ring."

He nodded speechlessly. It too was unrecognisable. A shapeless meandering of metal through flesh. But he knew his daughter. She was the flesh of his flesh.

"She had no need to die. She walked deliberately into the fire."

Letitia rose again to her feet. On her knees, she felt herself too close to her husband.

She was flesh of his flesh.

"But I am still alive."

For a moment, Marvin thought his newly-risen wife was offering him comfort and he shook his head without comment. He had no further use for her. He knew now that she had never been more than a substitute for Caroline. She would never have been desirable in the absence of Caroline.

Then he realised that he was being, not comforted, but threatened and he bowed his head submissively. She was in his house; she could quite easily be detained, but he no longer had cause to do so.

Letitia stood above him, looking down. He had lifted the shrouded, blackened corpse into his arms and was rocking it to and fro. She heard him whisper sensuous words of love to his daughter's charred, dead ears. She herself might never have existed for all that Marvin cared. The top of his bent head was bald, but for two long, coarse, black hairs which sprouted from the centre of a stranded mole. The sight of the mole disgusted her; it was as though the mole represented the centre from which all corruption spread. It seemed that, even as she watched, the mole grew bigger; it began to weave in malevolent circles on her husband's head. She started to shudder violently. Then she felt Caitlín's arm around her waist and she draped her own trembling arm thankfully around the younger girl's shoulder.

"We've done our duty, Miss Letitia," Caitlín whispered (how could she call the poor creature ma'am in the light of what she had just seen?).

"Almost."

Letitia poked at her husband with her foot. "Marvin," she said sharply. "Look at me."

Her husband obediently looked up. His face was smeared with traces of his daughter's burnt substance.

"Yes?" he asked politely.

"Your daughter died because she believed herself sinful. She thought her failure to return to you a dereliction of her duty. She thought her fear of you a sin; she thought her love of me a greater sin."

"But she loved me too."

Letitia shook her head contemptuously.

"She hated you . . ."

Her husband shook his head as though to clear his ears of water. "No," he said.

Letitia was crying again when she added, ". . . and thought herself the sinner for her hatred."

Marvin turned his face back to his corpse. He began to speak to it once more.

"Miss Letitia?" Caitlín said questioningly, and tugged gently at Letitia's waist.

Letitia nodded.

"Yes," she said. "I'm ready now."

Arm in arm, the two girls left the house, closing the door behind them.

He told himself that he had only asked what could be done; he had never meant that it should go so far as death. But death, he knew, was just what he had hoped for at the time of asking. Marvin Sweetman believed the fire to have been the deliberate attempt, by agents of the Government, to rid their Crown witness of those who might cause his evidence to falter. And now his wife was still at large, while his daughter, his much-loved daughter was dead. She had been his own creation; of his own flesh. To enter her had been the closest fleshly communion a man could have.

Remorse (of an unusual kind) came finally to Marvin Sweetman.

Caroline Sweetman had been monstrously loved. Her father had loved her body; but he had also loved her soul. Now it seemed that she had betrayed her soul by deliberately seeking death. Remorse did not arise from knowing himself to be the cause of his daughter's desire for death; for he did not so know himself. But he, by his hintings to the agent, had provided the means of destruction, and this was the cause of Marvin's remorse.

He had loved his daughter with extreme devotion; a devotion selfless enough to allow him to see with perfect calmness what it was that he must do for her protection.

Standing up, Marvin Sweetman carried his brittle, shrouded daughter into his study. He was an orderly man. Before settling himself securely with his daughter in a chair, he removed his pistol from the inner pocket of his morning coat. He had allowed Letitia to leave, because he knew that she could do him no more harm. To Marvin Sweetman, it had been clear, from the moment that his daughter's suicide was revealed to him, that he could only protect his daughter Caroline by joining her in hell. Putting the pistol in his mouth, he bit firmly on its barrel. Then he pulled the trigger without thought of God.

NINETEEN

❦

It gives me great pleasure, Dear Sir, to inform you without delay of the demise this very evening of the pestiferous Frenchman at the hands of his fellow weavers. The unfortunate Paradis was seen by my agents to jump, flaming, from the window of his own infernally burning workshop. One agent heard him shout quite clearly (in a strongly-accented voice) as he fell, that Liberty would finally be King throughout the land; the other agent was doubtful as to the words. Two unidentified women were seen to emerge, unscathed, from the same window. The same women were subsequently observed removing the body for burial. Should you wish to make any arrests, my agents, on whose reliability you can depend entirely, will have no difficulty in identifying the perpetrators of this 'dastardly' crime against our recently-unveiled Friend of the Crown.

I am puzzled by the emergence of two women. One I can readily understand as being the weaver's paramour. Three I could have understood with equal facility, for why should the Sweetman ladies not have gone into hiding along with the weaver? Would they not be wise to fear for their safety in such treacherous times? But two? Were it not for the certainty of my agents in their identification of the burning body as that of Paradis (and the voice is conclusive evidence), I would have wondered whether the body seen might not have been that of a woman. Indeed it occurs to me as I write that it might be worth searching the burnt out workshop for a second, female body. I must apologise for the disappearance of Paradis' body. When I reprimanded my men for their failure to follow the corpse, they said, in their defence, that they were reluctant to stray from their orders. They lack the necessary imagination, I am afraid, to improvise when events take an unexpected turn.

Should the second woman turn out to have been Sweetman's wife, then we were close to killing three birds with one stone. With such a coup, I would surely have been able to retire on the strength of my reward. Unfortunately, Sweetman still refuses to give evidence against

McKenna for as long as his wife remains at large.
I hope, Dear Sir, that the news of Paradis' death rejoices your heart
as it rejoices mine, and I remain, as ever, your obedient servant . . .

***

Under instructions from the agent, Malachi, his powers of
persuasion whetted by fear, had induced the cell (against the better
judgement of its leader) to meet again. It was imperative, the agent
had said, that should the weavers fail to deal with Paradis, others
would be prepared to take on the task.

"They are reluctant," Malachi had said.

"Convince them," the agent had replied icily. "Your own most vital
interests are engaged."

But before the meeting could take place, Malachi was summoned
to the agent's house.

No sooner had he arrived than he told the agent nervously that
he was short of time. "The cell meets less than an hour from now."

"The meeting is no longer of any importance."

"Sir?"

"Paradis is dead."

"Praise be!" said Malachi. Then he began to sweat with familiar
fear. If Paradis was dead, then so was he.

"His former admirers will be relieved."

Malachi nodded eagerly. He had, from nerves, a pressing need
to urinate.

"I may tell them the news?" he asked, squeezing his hands between
his legs. He would welcome any task which called upon his services.
For as long as he continued to be of recognisable service he might
hope to survive.

But the agent shrugged.

"It is of little consequence."

Malachi remembered Charlotte's advice: "You will remember,
good sir, my devotion to the Crown?" he begged. The words were
hers. The tone of shaking uncertainty was all his own. "A loyal
subject is worthy of cultivation irrespective of his immediate use
to Government; for the assurance of his future usefulness."

"My own sentiments entirely, Delaney."

Malachi smiled gratefully. Such was his sense of relief, he lost control of his own muscles. Urine flowed (unseen by the agent) down his leg. Humiliated, he made hurriedly for the door.

As Malachi was leaving, the agent added conversationally, "A pity that such creatures are so rare. More rare than bearded women."

"I am such a creature," gasped Malachi. He could feel his own warm piss trapped (mercifully) in his boot.

"A bearded woman?"

"A loyal subject," Malachi screamed.

Who could judge an event's importance in advance of its happening?

Malachi did not put the question to himself so succinctly as he stopped to tip the contents of his boot into a gutter. He merely thought, his mind abject with fear, why go elsewhere? In the course of an hour or two, some remark, sufficient to engage the agent's interest, might be passed. To benefit from such a chance, he must be there.

By the time he reached the meeting place, his trouser leg, though stained, had dried completely. He wondered uneasily how noticeable was the smell. He had no wish to be the butt of laughter.

Anton, watching from a grocery storehouse on the far side of the street, saw Malachi Delaney inexplicably (unless the Defenders had invented a new form of recognition) bend to kiss his own thigh before entering the public house.

Anton had been waiting there with reluctant persistence throughout the day. He knew his duty to the silk merchant. He did not know the cause of McKenna's arrest; he was not so naive as to imagine that McKenna could be rescued; but he did know that he could best demonstrate his love for the merchant by taking upon himself his allotted role as hero. No other gesture could alleviate his guilt. It might be a gesture disproportionate in its size to the insignificance of the actual crime committed (an anonymous letter, the contents of which were probably already known to the recipient). But nothing smaller was sufficient to repair the loss of faith in friendship which had led to the writing of such a letter.

But he had not been able to prevent himself from hoping, while he waited, that no one would turn up that night. What if the entire cell had been arrested? To whom could he then declare himself willing? He knew no other revolutionaries. Such people could undoubtedly be found, and Anton knew that he would not evade the necessary search. But the search would not have begun that night; that night, he could have returned to sleep with Caitlín. Even one more night with Caitlín had seemed, as he waited, an indescribably precious prospect.

By the time Malachi arrived, Anton was accustomed to the loss of such a prospect. Malachi, delayed by the agent, was the last to make his appearance. By then, Anton already knew that his career as a hero was about to recommence. Already he was dreading the intensity of their welcome.

He knew the cause was hopeless; even had all those disaffected subjects of the Crown been agreed on what the cause was, ultimate victory was unattainable other than by the consent of those who governed. As for reliance on the French! The French were never going to come in sufficient force, unless to replace the British as oppressors.

Malachi was not looking well. Anton was pleased to note the deterioration. Such men, Anton thought, should not thrive. Malachi's face was drawn and grey, like the overworked sampler of a maladroit child. He looked like a man who had suffered sleepless nights and anxious, pin-pricked days. His plans, of course, had gone awry. He had arranged for an arrest to be made (had Malachi rendered the same base service for Danno?), on the assumption that the undoubted consequence of such an arrest would be the death of the man arrested. Instead of which, his lover's husband had not only survived prison, but had returned to the country a mutineer and a hero. An outcome both unfair and unexpected; a sparrow invested with the properties of a hawk. Malachi quite probably feared (while despising his own timidity) for his life at the hands of a man he had been formerly accustomed to ridicule. He looked unkempt with fear. The thought gave Anton satisfaction as, slipping cautiously out from his hiding place, he crossed the road and followed the curiously plump-backed Malachi up the stairs to the meeting room. He longed for Malachi's reaction to the sight of the much-feared Paradis face. He wore upon his face a false and disquieting air of tender solicitude, and he made no effort to conceal the sounds of his footsteps. But Malachi, perversely, would not look round.

"I am the resurrection," Anton whispered cruelly to Malachi's back. He could no longer bear the weaver's lack of attention.

Anton's desire to shock was fully satisfied.

At the sound of the familiar voice, Malachi turned slowly, as if glazed stiff by ice. Upon seeing Anton's face no more than a step below his own, he looked ripe to swoon. Pressing his back to the wall, he sidled up the final steps, the cloth of his shirt scratching audibly against the rough bricks, his arms locked across his chest. Beads of sweat gathered on his discoloured face; his tongue protruded through his parted lips; his eyes stared. He attempted to speak, but no sound came forth. He swallowed, dredging for spittle sufficient to dampen his throat.

"You doubt my reality, Delaney?"

Malachi had reached the top of the stairs, and was trapped by the closed door behind him. Anton moved closer. His wife's lover cowered against the door, terrified.

"Touch me," Anton urged mockingly, and held a hand up to Malachi's paralysed eyes.

Malachi whimpered and turned his head aside.

Anton scoured the exposed cheek with a sharp fingernail. Blood welled along the line. Malachi winced and his shoulders drew closer to his ears. He made no sound.

"Proof enough?"

The door was opened suddenly from the far side, and Malachi stumbled backwards into the dim room, with blood running down his face, his arms still crossed like a seal over his heart. The leader caught him and steadied him before he could fall to the ground.

Anton stood exposed in the doorway.

The men inside the room stared at him in silence. Meagre evening light was retreating from their faces. They were all disturbed by the Frenchman's appearance; no one, not even the leader himself, knew how to react. If he was the traitor rumour described him to be, he should not have dared to show his face in public.

Unless, the leader thought suddenly, he did not know himself uncovered. What if Paradis, imagining himself safe, had come in the guise of a hero to lead his followers into a trap? Before anyone could speak, the leader set Malachi aside, stepped forward and embraced Anton Paradis with all the warmth he could invent.

Anton laid his head down on the older man's shoulder.

A submissive hero indeed, the leader thought contemptuously. Nevertheless, he remembered, unwillingly, how much he had liked Anton Paradis; how little he had ever trusted Delaney. His heart still thus directed him. It was as well, he realised, that his mind could work independently of his heart. Those who most successfully betrayed were those best trusted by their victims. And on reflection, it had not been Anton Paradis that he had liked; he had scarcely known the man. How many meetings had he attended? Two? Three? No. It was the subsequently imagined Paradis who had really captured his heart; a creature who had, in all probability, never existed.

"McKenna has been arrested," Anton whispered bleakly, without raising his head from the leader's shoulder. He had not expected to be affected by grief; but the warmth of the leader's false embrace had touched him to tears.

So the Frenchman's treachery had not been without cost; but perhaps his tears were too easily summoned. Perhaps they originated in self-pity. One could regret one's own weakness in the face of temptation. Or were the tears quite meaningless? A performance to mislead.

"We had heard," the leader said without emotion.

Paradis raised his head to look beyond the leader's shoulder.

"I thought they were come for me."

Within the room, the figures had begun to merge one with another and with their own surroundings as the light withdrew defeated. Anton could not see with any clarity the men whom he was addressing.

He had neither been what they had formerly imagined him to be; nor was he what they now thought him to be. But what Anton Paradis actually was had never mattered in the least. The men inside the room had seen the submissive droop of Paradis' head. From that moment, they knew him to be their prey.

Apart from Anton himself, the only other person in the room to be deceived by the leader's embrace was Malachi. Why not? Why should he not be deceived by the leader? He could accommodate no further layers of intrigue. He had been deceived by everyone else. He wanted one man whom he could take at face value. Who better than the leader? Malachi, who was feverish with terror, now sat shivering on a bench, knowing himself to be beyond all possible assistance. The leader believed Paradis and Malachi no longer knew whether this was good or bad. He did not dare to intervene.

But the leader was speaking to him and his voice was cruelly sharp.

"You were late, Delaney. We have been gathered here close on half an hour at your urging; yet you failed yourself to arrive. I doubt that Paradis was the cause. By your demeanour, I would guess that Paradis did not come here at your persuasion."

Why should the appearance of Paradis have so malignly affected Delaney?

"I had heard a rumour that Paradis was dead," Malachi confessed, and hoped that with such a confession he had not already said too much. "His appearance from behind me on the stairs did palpitate me close to death."

He had never thought Anton a hero. Why should he now be the one to fear him most? Like Charlotte Paradis, he had begun to fear Anton for his powers of reappearance. He did not know their meaning. He did not know what cause lay behind Paradis' continued survival. Unlike Charlotte, he was more inclined to blame the machinations of the Crown, than to blame God himself. The agent had called Malachi to his house particularly to inform him that Paradis was dead; that his body had been observed to fall, burning, from the first floor window of the warehouse in which he had been concealed. Had the account been a deliberate deception on the part of the agent? Or had he imagined himself to be telling the truth? Malachi had no idea.

And now he had further cause to fear Paradis. If Paradis was to accuse Malachi now of betrayal, might not the leader (whose arms still enclosed the Frenchman) believe him? In this room he would be defenceless against such an accusation. Were it to be believed, he would not leave the room alive.

"I came late," he suddenly stuttered. "And I regret that I must leave early."

"Why Malachi! I have not yet had the opportunity to enquire for news of my wife! I would have called, but circumstances . . ."

Anton dared a small provocation from the shelter of the leader's arms.

"She understands."

"I'm sure."

"You can't leave before our business is finished," the leader told Malachi sharply. It was Malachi who had called the damned meeting, wasn't it?

Malachi dampened his dried lips with his tongue. He nodded at the leader. He couldn't summon up the strength to speak. Malachi had been assailed by a fresh fear. He was to be trapped here. That was the agent's plan. He, Malachi, was a government informer; who was to say that others in the room were not informers too?

But Malachi had explained his own shaking condition to the leader's satisfaction, and had ceased to be an object of suspicion.

"You must have joined us for an overwhelming purpose, Paradis. We know the risk you run through coming out of hiding. It is in itself an act of commendable bravery to which many of us would not dare aspire."

Sporadic murmurs of agreement drifted across the room from the previously silent men. They were slowly finding their own parts to play in the leader's strategy. Silence, they had all now realised, would not be sufficient. They must display admiration for the man come so deceptively amongst them. He must be completely gulled by their enthusiasm. One of them stepped suddenly across the room to shake Anton's hand.

"You didn't let us down, Paradis."

Others followed with words of praise and welcome. Even Malachi was forced to join the queue.

"How am I reported to have died this time, Malachi?"

"I wasn't told."

Malachi could not meet Anton's eyes, but thought that the fires of hell would not have been hot enough to burn Anton Paradis as he deserved.

Malachi need not have feared Anton's tongue. Anton was not about to reveal the identity of his original betrayer here.

Anton had undergone sufficient, unwelcome adulation to recognise its absence. It was clear that in this room, he was not a hero. He was not surprised. They had known him before his transformation. In his absence, fantasy was possible; faced with his physical presence, all notion of heroism vanished. He could only be a disappointment. He was, after all, no more than the person he had been before he left. In any other circumstances, such a discovery would have relieved him. Now he feared that without adulation, heroism might falter. He had as yet sensed no duplicity. They might have known him before his rise to heroism. But they had not known him well. He had known them no better. He certainly did not know them well enough to detect insincerity. But a hero could not operate without a ferment of disciples. The hero could be false; but the disciples had to be genuine.

"I understand that an assassination was planned; with the Chief Secretary as the victim. I offer myself as assassin."

So Delaney had been right. McKenna had known all along that Paradis was in the country. The letter purporting to be from France had been a hoax. Who but McKenna could have told Paradis of the intended assassination?

To whom, the leader wondered, had Paradis subsequently passed on the information?

"I thought you might wish to attempt a rescue of McKenna. They say he was your friend."

Anton shook his head. "A waste of resources. McKenna would be the first to agree."

"You should know."

A pair of cowards. They well-deserved one another.

"Perhaps the Crown has a willing witness. If so, far better that we should eliminate the witness."

One had to admire the Frenchman's insouciance; casually advocating his own murder. He must be very confident of his protectors. Unless, of course, he was innocent.

"Of course," Paradis added with sudden embarrassment. "If there is already a candidate, I wouldn't dream of . . ." There were those, he had recalled, who enjoyed such risks. He must not assume otherwise. "I probably make my offer too late in company such as this."

The Frenchman had subtlety.

But none of them was fool enough to take the bait. He would be given no name by them. Someone (whose identity was so far known only to the person chosen and the leader himself) had indeed been chosen to act as assassin; and a night (known to all) had (since Danno's arrest) been chosen on which the assassination might yet take place (though spirits had sunk sorely since the arrest of McKenna and the revelations which had come out in its wake). Paradis, if all went well, would never know.

He could be innocent.

But such a possibility could not be allowed to hold sway. They could act only on the assumption that he was as rumour depicted him to be. Better to eliminate an innocent man than that they themselves should be eliminated for an excess of trust in one who subsequently showed himself to be a deceiver.

The leader drew Paradis to a corner of the room. He and the other cell members would discuss Paradis' offer, the leader whispered, alone; if Paradis had no objection. Paradis should return the following evening and he would be notified of their decision (which, as leader, he could guarantee would be in Paradis' favour). He had no right, the leader confessed with engaging intimacy, to exclude Paradis from discussions, since Paradis himself was an honoured member of the cell; but as a member of such prolonged absence, the leader had no doubt but that Paradis would understand that there were sensitivities which might have to be addressed. While Paradis was the obvious man for the job, there were others who might (erroneously) see themselves as equally suitable. They must be pacified.

"I wish only to achieve what McKenna desired," Anton whispered in reply. "I have little taste for such work myself; my courage is frail. I would not put myself forward but for the fact that he gave me to understand that my name was now such as to provide a rallying point for all rebels in the city. Can any other man provide the same, by all means let him do so. And of course, McKenna may have been deceived by his own fondness for me into thinking me a more important figurehead than I actually am. You must understand that I am relying, not on my opinion, which sees my own importance as negligible, but on his."

If Paradis was not innocent, then his acting was to perfection.

Listening to Paradis, the leader found his mind still troubled by his heart. He was ashamed of his own ability to deceive. But if he could deceive so easily, then why should Paradis not have an equal facility for guile?

"Come back tomorrow night," he repeated.

If Anton hadn't come looking for them, they would most likely have let him be.

***

"Paradis!"

Anton, who had (in obedience to the leader's wishes) left the meeting, heard the call but hurried on, fearfully. He was terrified of discovery. Surely he was not so easily recognised in this light? If he failed to react to the sound of his own name, whoever was in pursuit might think himself mistaken in his identification.

"Paradis!"

He looked around, reluctantly. He could not allow his name be broadcast through the streets. The man in pursuit was Malachi. Anton slowed his pace. Malachi caught up with him. He was out of breath.

Malachi too had left the meeting. He could hardly have stayed after the leader had reminded him, shortly after the departure of Paradis, of his expressed desire to leave early. "Remember," the leader had warned him, "that Paradis is our friend. Do nothing that would have him believe otherwise." Relieved as he was to have escaped the meeting house, his relief was tempered by the fear that he had been forced to leave because they no longer trusted him.

He had seen Paradis ahead of him and had decided, despite his own tormented state of mind, that he was due some sport. Anything to subdue his churning apprehensions for a few minutes.

"A warm body waiting for you, Paradis?"

He would heed the warning of the leader to this extent; Anton would be given no cause to doubt the friendship of the cell. Malachi's personal friendship for the Frenchman was another matter. To have pretended one would have been the greatest cause for suspicion that Malachi could have devised.

Anton said nothing.

"It may be warmer than you think."

Still Anton said nothing.

"You asked me how you were rumoured to have died."

"It is of no importance."

"Perhaps not." Malachi laughed maliciously as Anton quickened his footsteps. "But still, I think I should tell you."

Anton heard the malice. Malachi was not an inventive man. The malice was real. Anton stopped and turned to face the other man in silence.

"Your body was seen to fall burning from the window of McKenna's warehouse," Malachi told him, smiling. "Yet you are here. Whose could the body have been, Paradis?"

There was only one other person whose body it could have been. Caitlín. He had told her to wait for his return. (Anton knew nothing of Letitia and Caroline's arrival at the warehouse.) It was clear, from his demeanour, that Malachi was telling him the truth as he knew it. Anton's only hope was that the rumour itself might be false.

He was, he realised, already running towards the warehouse. Malachi had disappeared. All thought of his own concealment had vanished from Anton's mind. If Caitlín was dead, what need was there for concealment? They could do what they would. His imagined obligation to Danno was equally obliterated.

There had been a fire. He could smell it long before he reached the McKenna premises. He was calling out to God as he ran, but was not aware of doing so. Those few who saw him, stared with curiosity; but his behaviour was not sufficiently exceptional to provoke a following.

It was almost dark. He stood inside the door where the staircase had once been. The shell of the room remained suspended on the remnants of its sodden floor beams, like a stage set high above the ground. Some unburnt fragments of his loom had fallen through the beams and lay now, mixed with other debris in pools of thick, discoloured water, at his feet. A blizzard of ash flew overhead in a sudden gust of wind through the upstairs window. As the wind died, the ash began to fall around him like flakes of dead skin. He wished it could have buried him.

Standing in the empty well below the skeletal room, Anton began to cry.

TWENTY

❧

Dear Sir, I must confess myself embarrassed. Delaney called to the house this evening, most inconveniently. My wife, who is sinking fast, had begged for my company by her bed (she fears death greatly) and, out of pity for her (and from long-standing affection), I had agreed to sit with her. I had given instructions to the servants that I should not be disturbed for anything but the most urgent of business. Nonetheless, so hysterically insistent was Delaney that he should be seen, that though I twice refused (through the offices of a servant) to see him, the commotion in the hall below grew so great that I was forced, upon the servant coming to the bedroom door for a third time, to yield to his request for my presence. I do not mind admitting that what he had to say astounded me. According to Delaney, Paradis is still alive. I charged him with lying for his own aggrandisement. What, I asked him, of the categorical evidence of Paradis' death, given to me by my own well-trusted agents? He actually began to cry. He said (blubbering all the while) that he, personally, no longer knew whose word he might safely trust, but that he had touched the man known to him for several years as Anton Paradis with his own hands; he then added, with melodramatic insistence, that his hands had been stayed in their passage by the intervention of real flesh and bone.

I dismissed him, without any indication that I believed his tale; but then sent, without delay, for the two agents. Upon demanding an explanation of the contradiction in evidence which had transpired, one confessed to having contracted heavy gambling debts. Being afraid that my promised fee would not be forthcoming in the absence of a definite identification, he therefore invented the speech claimed to have been made by the falling body (which may already have been a corpse at the time of its alleged rallying cry). He would not have taken such a liberty, he said, had he not known in his heart that the body was that of Paradis (a man never seen by my agent in the flesh). So I am afraid to say, Dear Sir, that, on the more certain evidence of Delaney, Paradis would *appear to be still at large, while an unidentified corpse has gone missing. Thankfully, my wife has not yet passed on (though she breathes only with the greatest of effort), and I write this note to you while seated back at her bedside.*

You will, I am sure, accept my apologies for having rejoiced your heart prematurely in the matter of Paradis, and I remain, as ever, your obedient servant . . .

***

Danno McKenna was not used to being alone. He knew of men who, while in prison, called upon their memories for entertainment. Verses of poetry, plots of stories and of plays were aroused from a small part of the mind for the amusement of the whole. *Wheneas in silks my Julia goes, then, then methinks how sweetly flows that something something of her clothes. Next . . .* These were the only words of poetry that came to Danno's mind; and they did not so much come to his mind, as lodge there obsessively until he thought he would go mad with the interminable sounds of them revolving round and round in his head.

He had not been ill-treated, unless to be kept in isolation was ill-treatment. He found the food inedible, but that was the fault of his own querulous stomach which rejected everything that reached it. He was frightened. He knew so much about so many and who could gauge his own courage in advance of trial? He considered his own suicide, not as an act of cowardice, but as an act of bravery. Suicide was a sure means of protecting information.

They had told him nothing.

But from their very failure to abuse him, he guessed that they must have a witness willing to give evidence against him in court. The witness was surely Marvin Sweetman. He could not ask, for fear that he was wrong. It would not do to give them Marvin's name by accident. If he was correct and Sweetman had agreed to appear in court as a witness for the Crown, then he could remain silent without fear of duress. Yet suicide was still a valid act. Without a defendant, there could be no trial. Sweetman could not be called upon to give sworn information against a corpse.

Marvin's wife: Marvin's daughter.

He could not think of one without the other appearing by the side of the first. There were girls of such an age as Caroline, already married; there were whores of much more tender years; and there was Caroline, who had been used for a wife since early childhood by Sweetman and who could not conceive of sexual love as other than a punishment. Upon seeing her precious Mama savaged by the dubious Mr. McKenna, how could she not have flown to her Mama's rescue?

Prison lice had bred in Danno's warm, moist armpits. He scratched at his bitten, itching skin.

Deeds of love which had taken place in the bedroom that night were contaminated by exposure to the child which Caroline, despite her age, undoubtedly was. The passionate became, in retrospect, the lascivious. Invention became titillation. In retrospect, Letitia had disported herself, while in his house, in the manner of a courtesan. It seemed to Danno's unhappily imprisoned mind, that Letitia had lost, since coming to his house, her spontaneity; her love had grown calculating. She had seen the future failure of love too vividly. He had done nothing to reassure her, he knew; but what could he have said that she would have believed? He had never ceased to resent loving her as he did. Love had been magnified beyond its value and he had (though this was immaterial now) suffered ruin for it.

Had Letitia not turned from spontaneity to effort, perhaps he would not have this distaste for his own memories. He could not remember Letitia with passion (for the intervention of her step-daughter's terrified face); nor could he remember her with love.

Danno's thoughts affected him like lice. They were prison thoughts. Small-spirited, mean and biting; inescapable and requiring his constant, resentful attention.

***

a.m. . . . since receiving the regrettable information concerning the suicide of our chief witness, a man so carefully nursed to the point of revelation by myself, I have been in the lowest of spirits. It is indeed a pity, as you say yourself in your kind note to me, that the agents did not see fit to follow the two women and the corpse. However, their doing so would not have prevented the suicide of Marvin Sweetman from taking place. Who could have imagined a man's devotion to a child so deep? I hope, Dear Sir, that you attach no blame to me for the unsatisfactory performance of my two agents (it is hard to be blamed for the faults of others) in this matter, and that a certain stiffness I detected in your note was occasioned only by the urgency of the matter to be communicated. I have, you must acknowledge, served the government faithfully, and for little reward, for many years now.

I have a further suggestion, but am reluctant to put it to you for fear of being considered unworthily forward. I have ever been sensitive to the opinion of others. My poor wife describes me as a very pincushion of sensitivities. I shall, therefore, withhold my suggestion (concerning the detention of McKenna) until such time as its airing is requested.

I am, as ever, your very humble servant . . .

p.m. . . . I was very grateful to receive your reply so soon, as any unhappily-imagined trifle, when one is in thrall to what my wife refers to as the blue devils, can seem well-nigh unbearable. It is, as you say so aptly, easier to be praised for the success of others than to take the blame for their mistakes. I accept your gentle reproof without resentment, glad only that you acknowledge the existence of a difficulty. As you so graciously suggest, I shall put the episode behind me without further ado.

As to my suggestion: it undoubtedly comes late to a mind so incisive as your own. But since you have so kindly invited me to make it, I shall do so, despite its probable redundancy. You remarked, in your first communication of the day, that McKenna would now have to be released. The Government, you stated, had no further cause to hold him. It occurred to me that, at all times, we have been thinking of Mr. McKenna purely as the prey of a Crown witness. We have thereby completely overlooked his significance as a witness of some importance himself. It may be that you have dismissed his value as a witness. There is, perhaps, a reluctance to bring unseemly pressure to bear on well-connected United Irishmen, for fear of provoking a backlash of proportions incommensurate with the information gathered. Such fear is most likely justified. But it struck me that the comely Mrs. Sweetman might still prove an Achilles' heel to the chivalrous McKenna. What, I thought, if McKenna should be given to understand that Mrs. Sweetman was being tortured for his silence? Suppose that McKenna was to glimpse the good lady being hurried by his cell? Suppose that he was then to hear the screams of his beloved Mrs. Sweetman arising from an adjacent room? There are doubtless many amongst those women who wait so interminably for news at the prison gates, willing to scream with the greatest of conviction for small reward. Mrs. Sweetman herself need not be touched; indeed, must not be touched. For to do so would give him excuse for having disgorged himself of information best kept private. She must think herself brought in for the best of reasons; while within the prison, she must hear no screams. As soon as McKenna has disgorged himself, she must be brought to his cell. She will be smiling, for she will imagine herself to have negotiated his release . . . he will be dumbfounded by her good health and unblemished features. She will deny ill-use; she will deny having screamed; she will deny having heard screams. She will doubt (privately) his courage. He will, in the face of her bemused denials, doubt his own sanity; and will not dare to confess to anyone, ever after, the truth of his interrogation, no longer trusting to its truth himself. For if she cannot believe him, who will? He will be a broken man. How you use him after that is your affair.

My two agents, anxious to restore themselves to favour (an impossible task, I fear), took it upon themselves to find out the present whereabouts of Mrs. Sweetman and Paradis' girl. They say both girls are residing with McKenna's mother. I gave them to understand that a) I could place no trust in the information and b) the information, if true, was unimportant. They departed disconsolate and quarrelling between themselves. I believe, privately, that their information may be correct; I pass it on to you, but cannot guarantee its verity.

I must further say to you that I believe Delaney should be arrested without further delay. His behaviour is growing so erratic that he is in danger of exposing himself as an informer, and doing, in the process, great damage to the anonymity of our own fruitful connection. Should he so expose himself, he will not survive. Arrested, he can be milked of what information yet lies undiscovered, and then . . . it is a shame that Delaney cannot be used as a substitute for Sweetman. But he does not have enough of substance on McKenna. He has nothing on the United Irishmen connection. I remain, as ever, your very obedient servant . . .

***

Letitia could no longer view her own soul with composure. Up to now, she had regarded herself as high-spirited, but unblemished. Up to now, she had not harmed the innocent by her behaviour. Pansy, though innocent, and quite probably regarding herself as injured by Letitia had, though she might never know it, been rescued from a loveless match with McKenna by Letitia's behaviour. Miss Wollstonecraft would surely have rejoiced for Pansy. But for her failure to Caroline, Letitia was condemned by her own conscience. She desired to make amends, but did not know how.

"But do you not feel some relief, Miss Letitia?" Caitlín had asked in callous innocence, unaware of there being hidden circumstances fit to cause her companion unease. "She would ever have been, at best, the butt of people's pity. Her brain was too much harmed to mend."

Letitia did feel relief; which only served to prick her conscience the more.

"It is better that she should be with God; without the burden of a body."

But Letitia thought that she could have healed Caroline. With love.

"You never would have had enough to feed her appetite."

It was Mrs. McKenna who made the remark, and it was the most consoling thing that Letitia, dabbling her fingers desultorily in the strings of an untuned harp, had heard throughout the day. It was not that Mrs. McKenna made the mistake of lying. She did not say that Letitia had done all that she could. She merely said that had Letitia done her best, her best would not have been enough.

"She had within her soul the worms of deprivation. They would have devoured all the love that you could give, and her soul would have remained famished."

It was night time again. The three women occupied the drawing room, besieged by an increasing swarm of fears.

"Why are we waiting?" Letitia demanded with unexpected savagery at one point. "Why should our happiness be at the mercy of men whose happiness depends on things other than ourselves?

Why, I do believe that Anton's devotion to honour is greater than his devotion to you, Caitlín."

"I would despise him were it not."

"But do you have the same definition of what constitutes honour? For love of McKenna, Anton offers himself as the pivot for a cause in which he does not believe. Does honour demand such sacrifice?"

"From Anton it does," Caitlín said firmly, but could not meet Letitia's eyes. The question was distressing; she did not think McKenna worthy of such excess of love, but her own honour demanded loyalty to Anton.

"At your expense?"

Caitlín made no response. It was the worth of Mr. McKenna which was being valued: against her own.

"I'm sorry," Letitia conceded finally.

Each was afraid to be alone, and since Letitia (with all her usual excess of passion) would not be separated from Caitlín, Mrs. McKenna was forced to tolerate her presence for the sake of Letitia's company. That she should find Letitia's presence a necessity was comical enough; the presence of a weaver's paramour (a girl who had, up to the previous week, been measuring dress-lengths of silk in the shop; a girl whom Mrs. McKenna had suspected her own son of having attempted to seduce) was mere icing on the cake of comedy.

Two nights before, near midnight, they had come to the door arm-in-arm and Mrs. McKenna herself had let them in without demur. (Anton Paradis had, by then, left the warehouse and drifted through the streets in mists of grief.) She had seen the fire; she had seen the falling body. She had seen the grave departure of the two young women with the body slung between them, and had actually been seized by an urge to follow. But by the time she had reached her own front doorstep they were too far away and, in any case, the desire to participate had disappeared. She had turned from the door, drained and feeling vaguely ridiculous. But she had stood by the window of her drawing room, with her hands anxiously linked together, watching for their return; for she knew that, if not prevented, they would return. They had nowhere else to go. Mrs. McKenna had wondered, fearfully, were others watching for their return with equal intensity. Her feelings towards Letitia no longer could be described with any accuracy. Letitia was the thing her son most loved. For that reason alone, she must be kept intact.

They did come back. They had walked, unmolested, through the night-time streets, protected by the strangeness of their own bearing.

It was difficult to say where their grief for Caroline ended, and their grief for their young men began. They were united in so much grief. Both were sure that their loves would not be seen again. McKenna was in a gaol from which, should he survive the fevers which abounded, he could only emerge on the end of a rope. Anton had innocently put himself into the hands of people whom he believed to admire him beyond his worth; instead they now knew him (falsely) for a traitor. He would not be permitted to escape their vengeance.

"I should go in search," Caitlín said, rising, in agitation, to her feet. "I should have searched him out yesterday. Tonight may be too late."

But she didn't know where to look. Besides, as Mrs. McKenna pointed out, were she to make inquiries, would she not be drawing attention to the fact that he was at large, thereby endangering him further?

Caitlín sat down again, biting her lip in desperation. Letitia, seeing the gesture, was reminded of Caroline, and began, quite unexpectedly, to cry.

The other two were pleased. Letitia's tears gave them something on which to focus their attention and they fussed about her with excessive zeal: and then there was a knocking on the door. All three women grew quiet as cats gone to die in long grass. They heard the footsteps of Eileen, the pantry maid, pass through the hall. The stout, socially well-risen Mrs. McKenna found herself clasping Caitlín's hand to her trembling face. Letitia rose quietly from her chair. All three were standing now. It seemed more fitting to face whatever was about to befall them upon their feet. Caitlín's free hand had found Letitia's fingers.

They heard Eileen's voice raised in protest. Letitia's fingers closed on Caitlín's hand. There should have been another voice. Such silence was more frightening than noise. Mrs. McKenna swallowed down an upward surge of bile; and shuddered with distaste.

The door opened and Pansy walked in.

She was known to all three women. Caitlín even knew the size of Pansy's waist, and that it was, when quite at ease, two inches smaller than the waist of Letitia Sweetman.

She was not a soldier; but she found herself confronted by a blockade of women.

Mrs. McKenna's laughter sounded uncannily like a scream. Tiny spots of saliva (if not bile) showered from her mouth.

Pansy had not expected derision.

Her appearance in the McKenna household was the result of unprecedented bravery. It was night time; she was alone; she was here unknown to her parents. Her behaviour would be considered, amongst her friends, as wanton. How she might return undiscovered to her parents' house (in the unlikely event that her absence had not already been uncovered), she could not yet imagine. She did not, she knew, deserve laughter.

Nor did she deserve to find the appalling Mrs. Sweetman still in residence. She had not thought her influence would survive the departure of Danno.

She stood there in silence until Mrs. McKenna's laughter finally died away.

Mrs. McKenna began to apologise for her mirth.

"It was relief, you see," she said, her voice still shaking with nerves and the remains of laughter.

But Pansy did not see at all. She had, in the first place, no idea of what had been expected in her stead. In the second place, she had begun to realise, as her confidence evaporated, that a jilted woman might well, in such circumstances as she had so unthinkingly (if bravely) placed herself, be a derisory creature.

Only then did it occur to Mrs. McKenna that the visit was irregular on many fronts.

"Pansy, my dear," she said quietly. "Where is your mother?"

"At home."

By staring, without deviation, at Mrs. McKenna's discomfited face, Pansy found it possible to avoid all sight of Mrs. Sweetman.

"But she knows you are here," Mrs. McKenna stated, without belief.

Pansy, as expected, shook her head.

"I am to forget your son, Mrs. McKenna."

Danno's mother nodded.

"It would be as well," she said without hesitation. Marriage arrangements had been terminated beyond possible revival before Danno's arrest. Even did any hope exist for Danno's release, why encourage a daughter whose parents were past persuasion? Pansy held little attraction without her inheritance. (It was difficult for Mrs. McKenna, even now, to think in other than such terms.)

"I would give much to do so. But the feat is beyond my means."

She had been saved from a loveless marriage, hadn't she? Miss Wollstonecraft, Letitia thought defensively, would surely have approved the rescue (if not the rescuer).

"He didn't love you," she said with incisive brutality. She detested things which lingered beyond their time. Pansy was a dead vine, still coiled about McKenna and herself. "You are better off without him."

Pansy moved her eyes at last from the safety of Mrs. McKenna's face. She allowed herself to see Letitia properly for the first time that evening.

"How dare you presume to know what is good for me?" she asked, and her voice was limpid with hatred.

Was Pansy another harmed innocent? Letitia wondered uncomfortably.

"I would accept such presumption from no one, and yours is tainted advice besides," Pansy added.

It was, Mrs. McKenna reflected, Pansy's finest moment.

Letitia was shaking her head, surprised to be thus engaged by one she had so easily dismissed.

"I may be tainted," she said, and her voice sounded almost plaintive. "But my advice is unaffected."

Pansy looked at her without kindness and without belief. "It is the advice that I would give were our positions reversed."

"But why have you come here now, my dear?" Mrs. McKenna asked gently of her visitor. "You have surely heard of his arrest?"

Pansy nodded

"It is because of his arrest that I am here," she said. "I found that I must be with people who love him."

"And what if I had been the only person available?" Letitia asked spitefully. But then she found herself humiliated by Pansy's response.

"I would have had to come to you."

No one knew what to do with her.

She had, Letitia supposed grudgingly, a right to be there (Mrs. McKenna allowed for no such right). She had been encouraged to love Danno McKenna; but what did she expect of them now when they could hardly bear to speak of Danno amongst themselves? When his absence was too grievous to dwell on?

Pansy herself could see that her arrival had been a grave misjudgement. Her gift of unqualified love was an embarrassment.

"I thought there might be something I could do," she offered wanly.

Perhaps she had hoped by some means to accumulate for herself a debt of gratitude so great that it could only be paid for with love.

"Had any action been possible, it would already have been taken," Letitia said coldly. Her conscience had been most uncomfortably roused; and such arousal was quite probably the girl's intention.

"Indeed, Pansy dear," Mrs. McKenna broke in, "kind though your intentions are," (and Mrs. McKenna, too, wondered as to the actual origin of those intentions) "it might be best if you went home without delay." She paused to yawn. "My troubles are great enough without drawing the wrath of your father unjustly upon my head. Caitlín, ring the bell for Eileen."

Caitlín did so.

Mrs. McKenna longed for her bed. She had an urgent desire to sleep. It was the way sleep always came to her. She lowered herself into a chair and yawned again. Tears of exhaustion rose in her eyes, but no one noticed.

Pansy had crept from her father's house in a state of such exalted excitement, spurred on by the thought that though she could not be with him, she could be with his mother, who loved him as she did herself; his mother, who had assured Pansy repeatedly that her son, Danno, loved her to the very point of excess. From his mother, Pansy had hoped for reassurance. She had hoped to hear that love and infatuation (if he was really, as her own mother had reported, infatuated with the calculating Mrs. Sweetman) could exist side-by-side; until infatuation died defeated by love (as Pansy's own mother had been so foolish as to suggest). Pansy's mother was ambivalent upon the subject of the broken engagement, veering without warning between dismissal and encouragement of her daughter's continued professions of love.

Instead of reassurance, she had found contempt (Pansy sensed none of the admiration which was undoubtedly, if reluctantly, present in the room); a dismissal of her love as an unnecessary whimsy on the part of one to whom real love was unknown.

For this, she had braved a journey alone in a hired carriage, not knowing herself, until the moment of her arrival, safe from abduction.

Eileen came into the room

"You rang, Madam?"

"Miss Pansy is ready to leave."

Decisions continued to be made on her behalf. Tears came to Pansy's eyes. She blinked them away. She would not be reduced to tears in such surroundings.

"My love is no less real for being rejected."

There was a silence.

"No one doubts it, Miss," Caitlín said finally.

What, Letitia wondered as Pansy left the room with the pantry maid, were the pathetic components of such a love as Pansy so earnestly professed? Upon what false sentiments (both Danno's and her own) had poor Pansy created a structure of love? The love might be real, but its object most probably did not exist.

Letitia saw no parallels. She believed herself to have reached the heart of Danno McKenna.

These damned young girls who thought their hearts so irreparably damaged, thought Mrs. McKenna without pity. Then she fell suddenly asleep.

Caitlín looked at Letitia.

"She should not have been dismissed," she murmured.

Mrs. McKenna stirred but did not wake.

Letitia closed her eyes. She did not want to hear what Caitlín was bound to say.

"She's not herself," Caitlín continued unyieldingly. "And she is no more at fault for her condition than Caroline ever was. She only loved obediently, where she was told to love."

Letitia was still standing. She walked slowly towards the door.
"She should go home," she said.

"But cannot."

How could Pansy have gone home?

The images of home grew monstrous in her mind as she stood
terrified on the McKenna doorstep. She was bound to have been
missed by now. But whereas she had earlier imagined a house
formidable in its blaze of lights, its gaping doors, its agitated
servants, now she saw it dark, bleak and impregnable. A place to
which she no longer had any right of access.

Pansy could not think of going home. Darkness magnified her
imagined sins. She believed herself (almost fainting beneath the
magnitude of her plight) to be beyond forgiveness: the house
already barred.

She had come out tonight for the finest of motives. She had been
misunderstood.

And then a soldier came out of the shadows.

"Are you Mrs. Sweetman?"

The question was most courteously asked.

She shook her head.

The question had been a formality. Denial was to be expected.

"Mr. McKenna is to be released, Ma'am," the soldier said, and
paused.

Pansy looked at him. "And what has that to do with Mrs.
Sweetman?" she asked.

A carriage had drawn close while they were talking.

"Mr. McKenna has suffered a bout of prison fever, Ma'am. He
is weak (though recovering) and has particularly requested that Mrs.
Sweetman should be allowed to assist him home."

"I'll come."

As she was climbing into the carriage, Pansy heard the voice of
Letitia Sweetman calling out, "Pansy! Pansy! Where are you going?"

"Tell her," she said to the soldier, and her eyes glowed with mirth,
"that my father has sent for me and I dare not delay."

"How well," Letitia remarked to Caitlín as they closed the front door, "her father knew where to find her."

"It's better for her that he did," Caitlín said, turning the second key. "I believe she would regret more deeply the loss of her parents' affection than ever she would regret the loss of Mr. McKenna."

TWENTY ONE

The appearance of Anton Paradis had been a salutary lesson in disillusion. It was, as one of the men remarked, like discovering that the voice of God was just the sound of your uncle, speaking through a horn of paper from behind a screen.

Had they really imagined that such a man as Paradis, a man so utterly lacking in charisma as Paradis, could incite the City of Dublin to rebellion? They must all have been possessed.

"Misled, perhaps," was all the leader would concede.

But by whom?

"He lay on your shoulder like a friend."

"A Judas touch."

Unless it had been a gesture of trust.

But the others would concede nothing to Paradis. Whether or not he was an informer, they already had good grounds for hatred. They hated him for his exposure of their own gullibility; for his failure to be what they had most desired him to be.

"Paradis is a Protestant. Contact with him was bound to lead to treachery."

Because Paradis had appeared, they could no longer afford to ignore him. But what could they bring themselves to do with him? What was the safest course of action?

He had presented himself with the exact air of a man reluctantly doing his duty by his conscience. Or had it been the air of a man reluctantly failing his conscience? The leader could not decide.

With the arrest of McKenna, the desire for rebellion had died within the group. Paradis had been handicapped before his arrival. It would have taken an uncommonly charismatic man to revive their former ardour. All urge to assassinate the Chief Secretary had vanished, while the idea that such an action should rouse the City to insurrection seemed ludicrous to them now. They were all humiliated by the naivety of their former ill-judged enthusiasm. They were also frightened of the possible repercussions to which that naivety now exposed them. They had grown quarrelsome with fear. Some now saw the leader as, at best, a dangerous fool; but he could be something far more sinister.

"Paradis has been hung out for us like poisoned bait."

The leader nodded. He knew that the others had ceased to trust his leadership. His power to influence was dwindling. But what if Paradis was no wiser than themselves? What if he not only did not know himself named as an informer, but was also not an informer in fact? It was Malachi who had passed on the rumour. Who were Malachi's friends that they kept him so well-fed with rumours? Who, for instance, had told him Paradis was dead? And why, when this was so clearly not the case? What, the leader wondered, if Malachi was the real informer?

The leader stated the problem as he saw it. It was his duty to do so.

"If Paradis is left at large he will, according to rumour, give evidence against McKenna in a court of law. He is also likely to betray us. Why should he not? It is in his interests to do so; for at large we pose a physical threat to him which is removed with our arrest."

"Do you believe the rumour?" someone asked. "Given its source?"

"Can I afford to doubt it? But . . ." the leader paused and looked around. "Perhaps it is not impossible to reach the truth."

"He should be eliminated. Best not take any chances."

"But what if he is, in fact, an innocent?"

A butcher's apprentice from Ormond Quay shrugged his shoulders impatiently. Weavers had been killed by butchers for less in street brawls. A history of enmity lay between the two groups. (Yet even the butcher's apprentice had seen the French weaver as a Messiah. To him, the mistake was a particularly savage humiliation.) "What matter?" he muttered now.

"We hardly want to kill a man who is no threat to us, when by killing him we only draw unwanted attention to ourselves."

The argument was undeniably persuasive.

Uncertainty was their dilemma.

"Do you think Delaney a brave man?" the leader asked thoughtfully.

No one so considered Malachi.

"Then let us question him again with more precision; with greater attention to detail; with greater ruthlessness."

But Malachi was arrested before he could be questioned.

***

. . . I write with a heavy heart. My poor, suffering wife passed away this morning. I believe, most sincerely, that her death is a release and that she has gone to a happier place. Nevertheless, I cannot refrain from grief for my own loss; for she was a treasured companion and leaves me much bereaved in this vale of tears.

In accordance with your suggestion, I summoned Delaney to the house (though the timing was, as you can imagine, most distressingly inconvenient for me). I had been expecting resistance and disbelief, but so frightened is he by those who now surround him, that anything seems preferable to being cast unguarded amongst them. When I told him it had been decided by Castle officials that he should be taken into protective custody, he embraced me tightly and called me a good and generous-hearted man; for he knew, he said, that I was his real protector. I was so relieved by his response, that I returned the embrace as fondly as though I were his own brother. I told him that no man had done more for the Crown than Malachi Delaney, a humble weaver, and that the Crown intended its own reward. He did not ask what that reward might be (though his eyes brightened) and I (understandably) gave him no hint. I then escorted him to the front door, and found your two men in attendance. I introduced them as his escorts and assured him that his troubles were now over. He, poor fool, believed me, and set off between them as eagerly as a bride to a wedding. Your obedient servant . . .

***

A Defender (not the leader himself) had thought of an ingenious way to silence Paradis; a solution to their dilemma which would force none of his colleagues to be unwilling parties to murder. When it was discovered that Delaney had been arrested, it was agreed (reluctantly on the part of the leader) that the suggested solution should be put into effect without delay.

***

Either the turnkey had been given the wrong instructions (as he himself insisted when complaint was lodged), or else (and this was subsequently considered by the Castle to be the more likely explanation) he had misunderstood the instructions actually given.

By the time Pansy's carriage arrived at the gates of the prison, she was already terrified. The behaviour of the soldier escorting her had deteriorated shockingly within the confines of the carriage.

He was a good-looking man, and Pansy had responded to his initial remark, to the effect that the prisoner had a good eye for the ladies, with flustered coquettishness.

She was in a state of feverish agitation brought about by the unexpectedness of her own behaviour. What little good judgement she normally possessed had, by now, deserted her. She had perpetrated a magnificent deception upon Mrs. Sweetman and she was quite giddy with her own triumph as the carriage began to move. She had usurped the brash Letitia Sweetman's place; she felt herself to be deliriously infected by some of Mrs. Sweetman's normally despised bravado. She was not going home and she had ceased, briefly, to care. Pansy was sunk in the comforting embrace of delusion. Danno McKenna was to be released into her hands. He had asked for Mrs. Sweetman, but Mrs. Sweetman had not been there when called upon. Pansy had been there instead. Pansy had stepped into a breach caused by the favourable workings of fate. It would be his responding duty to protect her from the wrath of her parents. Her delusions grew ever more indulgent. He would be so astonished by her bravery that he might be forced to reappraise his former view of her. He might find himself regretting his hasty embrace of the invidious Mrs. Sweetman. He might even beg Pansy's forgiveness, and she, after a decent hesitation, would accept and then . . .

So when the soldier said, as he slammed the carriage door shut behind him, that the prisoner must have a good eye for the ladies, Pansy giggled from behind a protective hand; and then said, most astonishingly, "All his ladies are not so well-chosen as I."

It was a comment rash beyond the furthest bounds of common sense; but she had grown senseless with imagined success. She was, perhaps, also thrown by her unaccustomed proximity to one of the military rank and file. She had never been so recklessly exposed before.

The soldier was not surprised by the young woman's remark. Mrs. Sweetman had been described to him as excessively forward.

But not even the intemperately excited Pansy could mistake for normal the familiarity with which the soldier, standing over her in their slowly moving enclosure, suddenly caught hold of her flushed face in one hand and turned it up to the window to catch light from the street-lamps under which the carriage passed. She realised, with the first flutter of panic, that she was alone in a carriage with an unknown soldier. When she attempted to twist her face out of his hand, his grip tightened and her lips were pushed apart.

"Pretty, indeed: and all your teeth intact, I see," the soldier said, bending forward; then, pushing his face close to hers, he thrust his tongue through his lips and began to pant in a mockery of desire. It was not a sound that Pansy recognised; but she knew that she was threatened. She could smell his breath, yet dared not show disgust. Then she felt his other hand groping at the hem of her dress where it touched the floor.

His fingers closed around her ankle and she screamed in terror. He laughed, gratified by the scream's authenticity.

"You're choosier than they said, Mrs. Sweetman. Your husband reported you for a veritable tart. Yet you scream at the merest threat of a soldier's attentions."

She felt his fingers play upon her calf.

"Surely any prisoner would sing at the sound of such a scream? Do you think, Mrs. Sweetman, that your lover would inform upon his colleagues to prevent the repetition of such a sound?"

"I'm not Mrs. Sweetman," Pansy whispered fearfully as his hand climbed further up her leg and her dress rose upwards on his arm.

She could speak no higher than a whisper, so paralysed was she by apprehension now. She had been misled. For what purpose was she to be used when once they reached the prison? If the prison was their destination. And Jesus, dear God, but what was he doing to her thighs?

The soldier laughed again. He recalled the name by which that other woman had attracted her attention. "You mean, I can call you Pansy?"

That protest was the only effort Pansy made to defend herself; indeed, so ignorant was she that she scarcely knew what it was she should defend. It had never been imagined by those who managed her that Pansy would be required to come to her own defence. She felt cold draughts of air on her exposed legs and they began to shudder as though infected with an ague. She was capable of nothing further. To swoon would have afforded some relief from shame, but swooning was not easily achieved. She thought herself ravished finally, but could not, for ignorance, be sure. Could there, she wondered with terror, be something worse? What had happened had been, before its occurrence, unimaginable. Who was to say that unimagined possibilities did not still exist?

It was so easy to subdue a woman. They had so few defences. This one barely struggled. He had been told to desist rather than that damage should be inflicted. No damage could be seen; yet he had not desisted. His instructions had been vague. He should not have gone so far as rape perhaps. But she had put up no resistance, except to whisper, once or twice, her mother's name. They had said she was not easily intimidated. He had been misinformed. She had not behaved at all as he had been led to expect. She had grown quite still with fear. Rape had been unnecessary, he knew. She had been crushed by terror long before. But she was so small and pretty; all too easy to desire. The soldier was, after all, a member of that army to be described by its own Commander-in-Chief in the February of the following year as being 'in a state of licentiousness which must render it formidable to everyone but the enemy'.

Why was she still shivering? And why did her eyes remain so uncannily immobile? As though fixed into her head by pins. She should have resisted, he thought again, resentfully. Were she to make any protest, he would accuse her of compliance and might well be believed, for there was, as he well knew, no visible damage. Was she not already known for an adulteress? The horses were slowing down. The soldier peered out through the curtain, then turned back and dusted down Pansy's dress with sharp, flicking movements of his hands.

As though he were her Nanny, she thought dreamily, preparing pretty little Pansy for her entrance to a party. She smiled at the memory of her own prettiness. Why not? She had early been taught its value. And Nanny would next dab her tongue upon a handkerchief to rub imaginary smudges from Pansy's face. Pansy did not care for Nanny's spit, but she nevertheless turned her white and tear-stained face obediently for inspection.

"We've arrived," the soldier told her.

She looked, he thought with satisfaction, in a state of abject fright, but not in a state of indecency. He had not even kissed her. Her eyes were swollen with tears, but her mouth was quite untouched. As for her dress, they had knelt (most awkwardly) on the floor of the carriage, and it was hardly crushed at all.

It was as he was lifting her from the carriage (for her legs, she claimed, would not support her) that he noticed the blood, a patch of it, upon her skirt, and hoped that he had not pricked her thigh inadvertently with his bayonet. Such a mark, if evidence were looked for, would point to force.

When he put her on the ground, she would not walk alone.

"I am not Mrs. Sweetman," she whispered yet again as she walked unwillingly towards the formidable door, propelled within the circle of the soldier's arm. "I am Pansy," she insisted urgently. "Mr. McKenna does not wish to see Pansy. He would not inform upon his colleagues for a mere Pansy."

"Honour versus love."

I could not love thee, dear, so much, loved I not honour more. And she was not Lucasta. Her legs were wet; from what cause she could not say. Mama had said that he was just infatuated. That love remained when infatuation had long died away. Mama, Pansy thought suddenly and shockingly, was probably a fool. The most that she could hope for was Danno McKenna's compassion.

***

In accordance with instructions issued by the turnkey himself, Danno had not been forewarned.

Marvin Sweetman's wife was to be shown briefly to the prisoner; she should appear to be in a state of anticipatory terror. To preserve her silence (suppose she were, for instance, to impart news of her husband's suicide), her mouth should be bound. Then she was to be taken to an adjoining room and there be persuaded, by whatever means necessary, to issue forth sounds of terror.

Danno looked at the mouthless, swaying girl, her eyes buried in swollen flesh: like objects ingested by sea anemones. Could she have been beaten around the eyes? She had been announced as Mrs. Sweetman. "This is not Mrs. Sweetman."
But he knew the futility of the denial. Had Letitia been the woman before him, he would have made the same denial.

Where had Pansy been discovered, that they could be so mistaken? He saw tears ooze from her eyes at the sound of his voice.

"Don't cry, Pansy," he said helplessly. "You have no cause for fear. Nothing will happen to you."

He saw her eyes close as she turned her head away. A sound of despair reverberated deeply in her throat.

The soldier who had over-assiduously applied himself to the inducement of fear, now wondered apprehensively, as he urinated in a gutter several streets distant from the prison, had there been some mistake. He had blood, he saw, upon his own person. Could she have been, as she had claimed, someone other than Mrs. Sweetman? A virgin? It would explain that awful stillness. Why then had she deceived him into thinking otherwise? Bloody cow. The soldier wondered was he in trouble. What if a complaint should be lodged? Would the authorities not require a scapegoat? And who better than himself? He would be said (even if she could be proved to have misled him as to her identity) to have exceeded orders. To say that his orders had not been explicit would be no excuse. For what authority would ever openly sanction rape as a weapon of intimidation?

They were already moving her away from his door. Danno pointed desperately to the retreating Pansy's hand and noted, as he did so, the stain which marred her skirt.

"Look! She doesn't even wear a ring!"

The accompanying guard yawned as he led his faltering charge down the dark and noisome passage. It was nearing the end of his shift and he was both tired and hungry. The excuses so earnestly stated were always so familiar. The initial denial of identity; the observation to prove the truth of the denial. He did not so much as glance at the woman's hand. What would the lack of a ring prove? That Mrs. Sweetman possessed an extra layer of cunning? Or that she was brave enough to repudiate her marriage? Or that, knowing her husband to be dead, she felt entitled to remove his ring?

He had an Achilles' heel. He knew that now. His Achilles' heel was called compassion. He should have committed suicide; he was a danger to the safety of others. Danno had contemplated the endurance of his own pain. He had never considered being forced to endure the pain of others; a pain suffered innocently on his account, the arrest of which lay entirely within his gift.

He would have answered any questions put to him at the sound of that first scream. He clung to the bars of his door and begged for an audience; but no one came near him. He thought (but without any certainty) that he could have endured Letitia's pain more easily, knowing her more capable of endurance, and knowing that she would understand the reason for his silence. But Pansy's pain? There was no sense in which it could be justified. She owed him no duty of loyalty, while herself due immeasurable compensation for cruelty already delivered. When he heard her scream a second time, he began to scream himself. He screamed out names, dates, plans, contacts, passwords, the words tumbling nonsensically up and down the passage, like beads inside a drum.

Still no one came.

In a room reserved for their use alone, four Government officials waited, with increasing impatience, for the arrival of Mrs. Sweetman.

The night promised pleasure.

On her arrival, two of the four officials would descend to the cells, ostensibly to collect McKenna. There they would interrogate McKenna while he listened to what he would imagine to be the screams of his beloved (previously glimpsed briefly passing by) in an adjoining cell. Mrs. Sweetman, oblivious to events downstairs, would await McKenna's release in the company of the two remaining officials. As soon as the interrogation of McKenna had been completed (it was not expected to take long), McKenna (believing Mrs. Sweetman to have been severely mistreated) was to be brought into their presence. His inevitable claim to have heard her screams would be undermined by: a) her own denial and obvious good health, and b) the counterclaim of those accompanying him that, upon being offered (in return for information) his release, and having glimpsed Mrs. Sweetman passing by his cell, McKenna had been unable to resist the bargain. The screams, it would be claimed, had existed only in the imagination of Mr. McKenna. It would be allowed, in his defence, that he had not been well.

Finally the turnkey was sent for to explain the delay.

Slowly, a complex series of misunderstandings was revealed.

When it was discovered that a lady of the social rank (adultery notwithstanding) of Mrs. Sweetman had arrived at the prison already in a state of terror, and was even now being subjected, without proper authority, to mishandling of God knew what degree in a downstairs cell, consternation raged. The fact that McKenna had not even been interrogated while this error was taking place only compounded the initial disaster. Accusation and counter-accusation were exchanged with increasing venom as the enormity of the blunder became ever more apparent.

The revelation that the woman interrogated was not even Mrs. Sweetman (though her equal in breeding) at least had the merit of settling the most outstanding matter. McKenna and the woman, whoever she was, must be released immediately and as unobtrusively as possible. Accordingly a night guard of small consequence was instructed to discharge both prisoners. He was warned that he should maintain silence in the face of any questions. Neither explanation nor apology should be attempted (a feat which would, in any case, have been beyond the capabilities of the man, given his complete ignorance of the night's events).

It was now no longer even clear that McKenna and the woman were acquainted.

By the time the night guard reported the two persons to have been dispatched beyond the prison gates and to have been observed walking arm-in-arm (the gentleman supporting the lady who had seemed in some distress) towards the river, the turnkey and the four officials were in agreement only in their individual determinations that one of the others (if not someone extraneous to them all) should take the blame for the fiasco which had occurred.

***

The two girls were restless.

Caitlín sat with one leg crossed uneasily over the other, rotating her cocked foot in circles, the delineation of which she followed listlessly with her eyes.

Letitia stood before the empty fireplace and pressed her forehead against the cool, curved edge of the high marble mantelpiece. From the vantage point of a clock face, gilded cupids pointed blunt arrows at her head.

There must be something they could do. They could not simply wait without end. They were not stones to be shaped by the passing water. Even Pansy had seen fit to struggle, and by appearing in their midst had shown herself less amenable to confinement than themselves.

"She showed courage," Mrs. McKenna admitted, "far beyond my expectations."

It could not be right that men caused events, while women accommodated themselves to the results. Even their delivery of Caroline's body to her father's house had been a form of accommodation. (Neither girl was yet aware of the consequences of that delivery.)

"Marvin must be in desolate mood," Letitia said at last; her voice was leaden with self-pity. She knew what she was going to do: for Danno's sake, and for the sake of Anton. "I believe he may be ripe for consolation."

Caitlín ceased to spin her foot.

"You would go back?"

Letitia rolled her forehead slowly up and down on the edge of the mantelpiece. It seemed it was her duty to go back.

"Yes."

"My son would not ask that of you," Mrs. McKenna said with unexpected vehemence.

"Were your son to ask, I would not think him worth the sacrifice," Letitia said dismissively. But she was taken by the intervention.

"I believe," Mrs. McKenna persisted, "he would rather die than allow you to take such a step on his behalf." She addressed Letitia's curved back.

"I never was within your son's control."

Mrs. McKenna could not deny the truth of that. She had sat forward in her seat to speak. Now she sank back and closed her eyes again. But the desire to sleep had come and had been too easily assuaged; now it was gone. Her eyelids fluttered and would not keep out the light.

It was not a question of obedience to the orders of others. In Letitia's imagination, Marvin still crouched on his own hall floor, whispering vile words of love to the obscenely cradled corpse of his daughter. It was a question of whether or not she could fulfil the demand she was making upon herself. Could she, for the sake of Danno McKenna's life, force herself to return to such a man?

Letitia had not lifted her forehead from the mantelpiece. Caitlín stood up and crossed the room to join her. She put her hand on Letitia's neck.

"I shall accompany you," Caitlín said. She made no attempt to dissuade. She had seen Marvin Sweetman with his daughter. She knew the depths of the sacrifice. It was a sacrifice which could only be offered. No one had the right to demand such heroism. But Caitlín found herself tormented by untimely darts of optimism. Before, there had been no hope for Anton's survival. Now a tantalising fragment existed; a fragment so small that it seemed more like a mockery of hope than hope itself. Should Anton survive until Mr. McKenna's release (should Mr. McKenna be released), then it would be realised that no witness for the Crown existed, and Anton might cease to be in danger from his deceived followers.

Mrs. McKenna was crying. "You shouldn't go," she whispered, scarcely believing her own sense of upset. "You said before that the quarrel preceded your affair; you said that your return would not reprieve my son."

"I could not have returned with Caroline. Without Caroline I was of no importance. Or so I persuaded myself to believe."

Mrs. McKenna recalled, with an unaccustomed flush of guilt, how she had attempted to coax Caroline to return to her father, knowing that Letitia would be obliged to follow.

"You are still of no importance to him," she said now.

"Perhaps," Letitia agreed. She could allow herself that much hope. "But I must allow him the chance to show me otherwise."

A thought (which she could only bruise, but not annihilate) curved treacherously into Mrs. McKenna's mind; it was that Danno's marriage plans might yet be revived.

"But even if I should be wrong," she said, and her voice rose shrill above the thought, "Danno shall know the sacrifice."

The thought sank upon its belly.

"He will not abandon you."

And dust filled all its orifices.

Letitia came over to Mrs. McKenna and kissed her face.

"Thank you," she said.

This time they took a carriage.

"Please wait," Letitia said to the driver as they descended. Marvin might, she thought with cowardly hope, refuse to see his wife.

It had begun to drizzle while they travelled, and the steps up which they ascended were treacherous underfoot.

"The stone could easily be roughened, Miss Letitia," Caitlín said, while Letitia clung in terror to the young girl's arm, "with a chisel."

"You won't leave me with him, Caitlín? Not tonight."

Letitia's mouth could scarcely form the words for the trembling of her lips.

Caitlín shook her head.

"We need not stay, Miss Letitia," she said urgently, recoiling from her own recollection of what had occurred on the far side of the door before which they waited.

The servants were slow to come.

"Perhaps the hour is later than we imagine," Letitia said, and her mind hovered fitfully between regret and elation at the thought. She knew that if she left she would not return.

They heard steps in the hall, and Letitia's fingers pinched more tightly into Caitlín's arm.

It was the same servant who had let them in upon that previous occasion. He looked fearfully beyond them, to the waiting carriage.

"We are alone, Thomas," Letitia assured him and even held her empty (and ringless) hands up to his light.

"We weren't sure Ma'am, whether . . ." the servant's sentence died unfinished. He began again. "You wish to see the Master, perhaps?"

Letitia nodded, not trusting herself to speak. The substance of her legs turned suddenly to water.

"He's in the drawing room, Ma'am. We thought it best."

So they had seen the carriage come and had conferred as to their strategy. It would explain the long delay.

"Will you dismiss the carriage, Caitlín?" Letitia said, releasing the other girl's arm with the greatest of reluctance.

Caitlín hesitated. "It's not too soon?" she asked. She could see the stain on the hall floor where Caroline's body had lain and thought now that Miss Letitia was demanding too much of herself. Allying herself to evil for the sake of virtue.

"No." There was to be no reprieve.

"We'll wait for her return before continuing," Letitia said to Thomas, and thought she saw a muted glance of pity, which frightened her the more. One received unsolicited sympathy from servants only in the most extreme of circumstances. He said nothing, but merely inclined his head with understanding; then stood self-effacingly at her side, his head still bowed, his hands held together before his stomach.

The drizzle had turned to rain. Caitlín's arm was damp beneath Letitia's hand as they passed through the hall. Even Thomas, Letitia noted, avoided walking on the stain.

Thomas stood for a moment with his hand on the drawing room door. "We had to close them both in," he said apologetically, his voice low.

"Both?" Letitia said sharply.

"His daughter is with him, Ma'am." The servant's voice was defensive. "We could hardly part them now."

Marvin must have turned quite mad. Caroline's body was two days old and the weather had been muggy. It must be well-nigh putrid. Letitia drew Caitlín more closely to her.

"We will see my husband, and then we will leave," she said to Caitlín in the whisper demanded by the atmosphere. "Compassion requires that much. But surely," she added, and her voice was strained with apprehension, "not even duty could require more?"

Caitlín nodded reluctantly. She thought that Letitia put the requirements of compassion and duty too high. "We could still halt the carriage if we ran," she suggested beguilingly; but Thomas had already opened up the door.

They saw the coffin laid upon a table, brought for the purpose from another room. Its lid was closed. It was really too large a coffin, Letitia thought inconsequentially, for the thing which they had carried between them through the streets.

Marvin was not to be seen.

"Where is my husband?" she asked, and even as she asked, began to comprehend. She looked again at the coffin.

"I told you, Ma'am," Thomas said patiently. "We put both bodies in the same coffin. By the time the doctor came, the Master's body was so stiffened, and the other body in such poor condition, that they could not with any safety have been prised apart."

Her body might still be trapped in her father's arms; but Caroline's soul would have escaped.

"I was not told."

Letitia gave the information by way of explanation for her slowness. Thomas took it as a criticism and began, immediately, to defend himself. "We did not know where you were, Ma'am."

Letitia did not believe him.

"And the family," he added, referring to Sweetman relatives, "were reluctant to initiate inquiries. They could not bear, they said, the further scandal which disclosure of your absence might give rise to."

"How did my husband die?" Letitia asked, without much curiosity. She felt an airy remoteness from events.

"An accident with his gun, Ma'am."

He was lying again, but Letitia didn't care. She had an unseemly desire to dance around the coffin; not for revenge upon her husband, but for the commemoration of her step-daughter. She and Caroline had danced together in this room; it would be a tribute more fitting than prayer. But she stood quite still beside her servant who had, she discovered, his own apprehensions.

"The rest of the staff, and myself, Ma'am," he said, "are anxious to know our position."

He was terrified. Caitlín well knew the source of his terror; it was that his livelihood depended on a whim. She pitied him.

But Letitia stared at him without comprehension.

"Will we be retained, Ma'am?"

Was the decision hers to make? Letitia had no idea. Thomas appeared to think so.

"It is too soon to say," she remarked cautiously.

"Yes, Ma'am."

She might also dance in celebration of her own release from a cruel obligation. The Crown witness was dead. He need not be consoled.

Letitia turned, with elation, to Caitlín. The other girl's face was in disorder. Hope fought with fear. The Crown witness was dead and Mr. McKenna would undoubtedly be freed; but was Anton still alive?

Caitlín made a small sign of the cross in the air above the coffin. Then she turned and left the room.

"Caitlín!"

She stopped briefly in the hall, by the stain, but did not look around.

"Where are you going?"

"To look for Anton."

Letitia picked up her skirts and ran out to the hall. She was angry. "Alone?" she asked coldly. Caitlín's withdrawal seemed like a betrayal of trust.

"Yes."

"Did you accompany me to this house as my friend?"

What if she had come as a loyal servant? Letitia could scarcely bear to hear the answer.

"Yes."

Letitia closed her eyes. She could not have borne for such a friend to have existed only in her imagination. She realised that she was shivering. Caitlín, she saw, was shivering too.

"Did you think that I would do less for you?" She asked quietly, and again could scarcely bear to hear the answer. She was not, she knew now, a fine person.

"No."

But in truth, Caitlín had not been sure. She was of the class that served others. Letitia was of the class served.

"Why then?"

Caitlín looked at the girl beside her.

"Tell me, Miss Letitia: did you presume that I would come here with you?"

She could easily have so presumed, Caitlín knew.

"No."

"Then how could I presume where you did not?" Caitlín put the question triumphantly.

The front door was still open. Caitlín had left them their escape. Rain fell lightly. It could not be heard; but could be seen where it fell into an illuminated, shallow pool which had collected on the uppermost step.

From his position by the coffin, Thomas saw the two young women embrace one another in the hall before walking with determination from the shelter of the house to where the wet night began.

"The funeral, Ma'am!" he cried out. "We have not discussed arrangements for the funeral!"

Letitia peered back into the house. She could see little. "Have arrangements been made?" she called out.

"Yes."

Thomas was no more than a floating voice.

"Then let them stand."

Thomas heard his master's widow ask where should they start. He saw the other woman shake her head slowly.

"I don't know," Caitlín said despairingly to Letitia.

TWENTY TWO

What had been done with her body? Who had taken charge of it? Anton did not dare to make inquiries at the McKenna house. He had been the target of the fire: not Caitlín. They (whoever they were) could be waiting for him yet. By the time Letitia and Caitlín had returned from delivering Caroline's body to her father on the night of the fire, Anton had already left the warehouse. He had thought death would be welcome, yet he left for fear of being discovered; believing that were he to be discovered he would be killed. He would not allow his death to happen so trivially.

For two days, Anton Paradis hid in the city. In all that time, he neither ate nor drank. He was not aware of hunger, but his tongue grew fat and sticky in his mouth; his saliva was not fit to wet his lips. The salt from his tears, which flowed sporadically and without warning from his eyes, lodged in the cracks of his lips and caused great pain. He paid the pain no heed.

He could make no sense of what he had become, nor how such change had come about. He told himself repeatedly that he was a weaver. Caitlín had known him to be nothing else; Danno too, when forced to face reality. But Anton could no longer recall the smell of silk; in his nostrils there existed only a smell of burning flesh. He could not feel cloth flowing through his hands; in his hands there existed only ash and flakes of blackened skin. He saw no lengths of glowing, woven silk held against women's warm faces; in his mind, all silk had turned to shrouds.

He could no longer be a weaver. Instead he was to follow the path of heroism.

He did not believe in the viability of the cause for which his heroism had been originally invoked; he did not believe himself to be heroic; but his death, he had finally decided, would be in the cause of heroism attempted. He had abandoned Caitlín to do penance for a small treachery unadmitted. Had he confessed the treachery to her, she might have understood his need to atone; but she might have said that the size of the betrayal did not warrant the penance proposed. He had remained silent for fear of her dissuasion. I could not love thee, dear, so much, loved I not honour more. But how should honour be defined?

He regretted that silence.

But having abandoned Caitlín to indulge an overheated sense of honour, he could embrace nothing less than heroism now that she was dead.

He could be heroic but would never now be seen as such. Anton had no followers. He knew he had no followers. But he was not aware that his former comrades had become his ardent enemies.

***

It was through Charlotte Paradis that the cell heard of Malachi's arrest.

Soldiers had been to the Paradis workshop. All the looms had been broken. The finished bales of silk had been taken away. One soldier had swathed himself in silk from head to foot and had forced an apprentice to dance with him (in an embrace close enough to hold the silk in place) from one end of the workshop to the other.

Malachi Delaney had been arrested. There was no longer any talk of protective custody.

"Why?"

Charlotte knew the truth, but had wished to hear their lie.

"He is a self-confessed rebel."

He had ceased to be of further use at large. Malachi had lost his nerve; he had become a liability to the Crown. She had guessed that it would come to this. Poor Malachi. She had not thought him so weak; nor so greedy. She loved him still, but with less reason. He had informed, not from conviction, but for reward. He had revealed himself to be a greedy man and had raised for Charlotte a question which could not be ignored. Had he seduced the daughter of Lucien Paradis all those years ago for love, or for reward?

The weavers had crowded protectively around Charlotte. She had not dared deny the accusation of the soldiers in their presence. They had not imagined Delaney a rebel; they were impressed. She could not have then revealed him to be an informer. (And what good would such revelation do, when those who held him already knew the truth?) Charlotte had watched with stony fury the ruin of her business at the hands of those whom she had supported with such ardour for so many years.

Malachi's greed had caused her ruin.

"Why this?" she had asked an officer bitterly, gesturing to the splintered looms, the severed webs. "Is it not enough that a man should be arrested? Must all those within his ambit suffer too?"

"Deterrence, Ma'am," the officer had blandly replied. "Where there is one, we usually find that there are others."

Was her loyalty so insignificant that they should risk losing it thus?

How, the weavers had wondered afterwards, had Delaney been discovered for a rebel? They had not known of his subversion. The betrayal must have come from among his fellow rebels; whoever they might be. No one but Charlotte knew their identity (Malachi could not have kept such information back from Charlotte) and she had disclosed no names. But she had allowed the weavers their speculation. Should he (God willing) be released, Malachi would be more secure if known for a betrayed rebel than for an informer.

She spoke no word of Anton Paradis.

How could it be that Anton Paradis was still alive? He had been transformed brilliantly by the government from hero to informer: a man to be reviled. Yet he survived untouched, while Caitlín (according to Malachi) had perished. Only last night, Malachi had cried with terror in their bed. The leader, he believed, was inclined to think Paradis innocent: and Malachi, therefore, guilty of deception. Malachi had expressed the belief (drawing no distinction between the justice of his own death compared to that of Caitlín) that he would perish too, in Anton's place. Sacrificial lambs, he had said hysterically, the pair of them.

Charlotte was frightened of Anton and had been for some time. His powers of survival were unnatural. The cell, she knew (through Malachi's profligate disclosures), had earlier been reluctant to touch

Anton, for fear of drawing attention to themselves. Would they still be so reluctant to act upon hearing that yet another of their number had been arrested? Especially when that man was the one against whose word that of Paradis had, up to now, been weighed. Charlotte determined that the cell should not be kept in ignorance of Malachi Delaney's arrest. She therefore sent an unsigned note to the leader, informing him of the event.

**

With Malachi's arrest, there was no longer any scope for indulgence. Had the others wished to kill Anton, the leader would not have been able to prevent them from doing so. His own sense of Anton's innocence remained, but, like a sense of God, could not be proved; and the desire to believe was lacking amongst the others. It was caution rather than compassion which dictated the mere maiming of Anton. Knowing the proposed nature of that mutilation, the leader was forced to wonder if Anton would perhaps have preferred death. The mutilation of the Frenchman was unnecessary, other than for purposes of revenge. His fate was immaterial. The cell was already doomed. Malachi's arrest assured them of that. Malachi was not a man to endure torment in the cause of loyalty. He would name them all without compunction.

A lesser man than the leader might have refused to attend that final meeting at *Nelligan's Ale House*. But the leader was there. He was alone. Either his colleagues had determined to spare his sensibilities; or they had feared his ability to undermine, at the crucial moment, their communal resolve.

For whatever reason, Anton had been trapped in advance of the meeting.

He was so compliant.

Such docility stank of guilt.

Or innocence?

It had not been the leader's idea; but his words had brought the idea to the mind of another. For it had been the leader who had remarked so bitterly after receiving word of Malachi's arrest that

many have fallen by the edge of the sword: but not so many as have
fallen by the tongue.

"Even the tongue of the dumb shall sing for sufficient reward,"
someone had added in sour parody.

"Unless," the butcher's apprentice had said in a voice slowed by
pleasure, "the tongue has been removed."

And the hands, the leader had thought immediately. The hands
are as tongues to the dumb. He had been disgusted by the
meticulous workings of his mind; that it should register its
displeasure at the inadequacy of the butcher's proposal before
registering its revulsion.

He had not revealed his mind's objection.

The thought had occurred to no one else. Why should it? They
were all illiterate. They had been so mesmerised by the seeming
perfection of the solution. They had been shown an image of the
weaver silenced: a violin with its strings removed; a bell without
its clapper; a viper without its fang. Unable even to name his
mutilators. It was a remedy which so exactly solved the problem.

"As a tongue fits its groove," the butcher's apprentice remarked
with sly humour, when praised for the aptness of his solution.

The leader's protesting voice had been ignored.

They had worn masks and unfamiliar clothes so that they might
have some chance of escaping unidentified, should they be surprised
by soldiers or by the industrious Major Sirr and his hirelings while
engaged in the punishment of Paradis. They had also agreed a rule
of silence. It had not occurred to them that, because of such
precautions, Paradis himself would fail to recognise his assailants.
For Paradis himself, they would have concealed nothing; they
imagined themselves to be rendering Paradis harmless. Why should
they fear his recognition?

It is easy to be deceived by the treachery of imagined allies. Even
so, Anton might have known his assailants had he not been expecting
attack from another quarter. But Anton was only surprised that he
had been allowed to remain at large for so long. Government agents
knew that he was in the city. He was sure of that. He had never felt

himself free from the pursuit of their shadows. His assailants had seemed, when they gathered mutely about him in the drizzle, dark-clothed and faceless, like those familiarly-felt shadows made flesh. His initial sensation upon capture had been oddly close to relief. The weariness of terror-stricken anticipation had finally been terminated. The government, it seemed, had tired of playing upon the nerves of their well-stalked prey, and had closed.

He thought his assailants government agents and rejoiced that at least he had not led them to the cell.

It was perhaps partially this belief which made Anton so docile in their hands. He was a plover, heroic, feigning injury to draw the enemy from the nest. Mainly, he was too frightened to struggle.

His assailants could hold his head between their hands and cup the truth in their palms; they could squeeze his throat until his tongue protruded almost to its root; they could wag the tongue to and fro with toasting tongs while the butcher silently tantalised their senses by testing the shining blade of a knife on his own forefinger; but the loyalty of Anton's thoughts would lie undiscovered within his mind. Were they to split his skull apart, and plunge their hands into his very brain, his innocence would not be found.

Afterwards, they agreed that he had seemed to take the punishment as his due. He made no plea in his own defence. Almost as though he desired to be rid of his own tongue; as though he knew its treachery.

It was their silence which most terrified Anton. They sought no information from him; they told him nothing. Silence, he remembered, had ever been a government weapon. It had been silence which had so reduced his mind while held in prison. In the presence of such silence he was incapable of speech.

Now he had been rendered silent for good. He had no notion why: unless for entertainment. To show that he was entirely at the disposal of the Crown? A tongue today; a finger tomorrow; an ear, perhaps, next week.

Anton Paradis watched his colleagues play ball with his own severed, slippery tongue while blood flooded from his screaming, denuded mouth, his gargling throat (he could, at least, still scream), and yet believed them to be government agents. The rain grew heavier and the men, gone briefly wild with their own ferocity, came back to their senses. They wished to remain unknown to the authorities; instead they were conducting themselves with a rowdiness certain to arouse interest. They should have left before. They threw the mangled tongue to a passing dog and then they disappeared.

Anton lay propped against the wall of a house. His screaming died away. He thought that he might suffocate in blood: or drown. It seemed that his head was a cup, brimming over with blood. He assumed, as he felt himself grow faint, that he was bleeding to death and was glad. He believed himself sufficiently cleansed of sin to die with equanimity. He might (though Anton doubted an afterlife) be reunited with Caitlín in death. If he did not turn into a nightingale, he thought unexpectedly, and without apparent reason.

He was a nightingale singing pitifully (jug, jug, jug, jug, tereu) in a tree at midnight. His hands were claws which clung to a fragile twig; his legs were sharply feathered wings. He feared to lose his balance, should the slightest breeze begin to shake the branches of the tree. This was the image etched on Anton's mind as he lost consciousness.

A despoiled nightingale, but capable of song and therefore not lacking tongue; yet the image (when unravelled) was appropriate enough.

It began with a silk, hung in the McKenna hall, which showed a red-throated, fork-tailed swallow in flight, a nightingale (not brown, but glorious in golden thread) perched singing in an ash tree, and a crested hoopoe pulling at a scarlet, fleshy satin heart caught in a snare upon the ground. Woven in silver thread below the birds was the following verse:

What bird so sings, yet so does wail?
O 'tis the ravished nightingale.
Jug, jug, jug, jug, tereu, she cries,
And still her woes at midnight rise. (John Lyly c.1554-1606)

The image and the verse on silk were no more than an illustrated note upon a myth. Sufficient to recall the myth to those in whose mind it had been planted; an obtuse irritation to others. Of what significance were the other birds? The heart? Anton had been irritated; Danno had fortunately known the myth and had related it to the weaver. A girl, Philomela, is raped by her sister's husband, Tereus, King of Thrace. To ensure her silence, Tereus has Philomela's tongue cut out. But Philomela cunningly contrives to illustrate the truth upon a tapestry and has the tapestry delivered to her sister. Her sister, to avenge the wrong to Philomela, kills her own son and serves his tender flesh for a delicacy to Tereus, her husband. When Tereus, discovering the horrible deception, attempts to kill the sisters, he is turned into a hoopoe (despised as an unclean eater, a prober of dung-hills); his wife becomes a swallow. Philomela, the tongueless, is turned into a nightingale, to sing incessantly of her own ravishment: jug, jug, jug, jug, tereu.

Anton of the raided mouth dreamed himself a lying nightingale (he had not, after all, been ravished), while blood drooled through his parted lips.

**

It was raining heavily, and cab after cab passed them by.

Mud and water splattered like grapeshot from beneath the punching hooves of the passing horses, from the spinning wheels of the carriages themselves.

Danno's appearance no longer commanded respect. He had no substance; he was no longer seen. His attempts to hail a driver went unobserved. Even had Danno been able to attract the attention of a driver, no driver would have stopped; had he somehow enticed a driver to stop, it is doubtful that Pansy could have been persuaded to climb into its interior. But Danno was not to know that. Pansy (upon whom some of Danno's lice were now beginning to congregate) had not yet spoken.

Pansy had lost her hat, and her hair clung to her head like hanging clumps of wet, raw silk. Her waterlogged dress dragged heavily against her legs. Their shapes grew visible through the material. The bloodstain blurred and ran outwards in tapering fingers. She shivered continually like a stammering heart against his side. Danno had not so much as a jacket to throw about her shoulders. His arm and his side seemed little shelter against such deep-set quaking.

314

She had not shivered so when he had first approached her.

"Pansy!" he had called, when he had seen her walking uncertainly (as though on borrowed legs) ahead of him on the street outside the prison.

He had been so relieved to see her.

The night guard who had ushered him from the prison had refused to tell him whether or not she had been set free. He could not leave, Danno had insisted, as they walked through passages, unless assured of the young woman's safety. But he had received no assurance and yet had not turned back to his cell. What would have been the point of such resistance, even had it been allowed? He was humiliated by his own inability to influence events.

Pansy had not looked round; she had not been walking at any speed, but she did not slow down at the sound of his voice. She had flinched at the touch of his hand on her shoulder, but then had allowed him to draw her close without complaint.

"Are you hurt?" he had whispered.

She had shaken her head in bewilderment. She didn't know. What was it that constituted injury? The question was so inadequate it was scarcely worth considering.

Why was she here? he wondered yet again as they began to walk painstakingly towards the river. Under what circumstances had she been mistaken for Letitia? Letitia would surely not have been so treacherous as to propose Pansy for a substitute? Unless she had taken the deception for a game. An irresistible game. Was Letitia capable of such cruelty? Danno could no longer be sure. He had constructed a new Letitia while in prison.

Pansy was not so tall as Letitia, he noticed and started with guilt at the unseemliness of the observation. Yet it was not unjustified. He could not so easily see Pansy's face. Letitia's lips, when they walked together, were almost level with his own; her eyes were rarely hidden from view. He could not even recollect the colour of Pansy's eyes: red about the rims.

"You can trust me," he added gently, for she hung sharp as an icicle by his side. He had imparted no sense of safety by his presence. This failure surprised him. She had been misused indeed, despite the invisibility of the wounds. But still Danno did not guess the nature of the misuse. He knew her to be timid; he knew how easily terrorised she might be. As for trusting him; not knowing the interior of her mind, his assurance had, he thought in retrospect, been rash. To what outrageous reward might the fanciful Pansy see herself entitled, now that she had suffered for him? What if she had heard his wanton confession? It had been made in an empty room; but had the room been full, confession would have been made more eagerly still. Might she not attempt to bargain marriage in return for silence upon the subject of his weakness?

Pansy said nothing.

She had now discovered the jeopardy in which she had lived unwittingly all her life. Her safety was a matter of chance. It depended on the whims of the men about her. Within the interrogation room, her breasts had been plucked out from her loosened bodice by the interrogator. First one, and then the other. They had hung there, exposed to the man's indifferent gaze. He made no move to touch them. But when he told her to scream, she had screamed; when he ordered her to stop, she had stopped. She had not been further violated. But it was clear that this reprieve did not depend on her ability to scream to order. The integrity of her body was dependent on the whim of her interrogator. Danno McKenna restrained himself now; but who could say that this would always be? Danno's own mother had said, confessing the liaison between her son and Letitia Sweetman, that her son was a prey to his own sudden lusts. A full-blooded man, she had added in his defence. Pansy had not understood her meaning until now. Pansy wished nothing so fervently as to return to the protection of her parents, if they could be brought to accept her, violated as she was. For their protection, however inadequate (for was her mother not as vulnerable as Pansy herself?), she would serve them gratefully for the rest of her days.

But why should Pansy have felt safe by virtue of his presence? Danno thought a little later, to comfort himself for her silence.

There was no reason, he concluded.

Danno had not felt safe himself as he had hurried her away from the prison. Only a fool would have rejoiced so soon. The administration of justice was an arbitrary affair which yielded without protest to expediency. Their release had been so curious. Who was to say what was intended by it? It could have come about by error. Or it could, more chillingly, have been a deceit. What easier, for instance, than to release them from the prison, and then to shoot them both in flight? A foiled escape. (Such an idea occurred, too late, to those still within the gaol.)

Who was to say (in the absence of word from Pansy herself) that she had not reached the same conclusions as Danno? Indeed, she could justifiably have concluded that he was more a liability than a comfort at her side.

They crossed the Liffey by Essex Bridge and began to climb the hill through swathes of rain to the Exchange.

They were like things dredged from the riverbed.

A weave of drunken soldiers and women came swaying down the streaming hill towards the river. Pansy stopped dead when she saw the soldiers. "No," she whispered, "No, no, no." Then she broke violently away from Danno and ran into an unlit side street.

She would have let him pass her by.

She made no reply to his low calling of her name.

He found her only by her breathing. She had taken shelter in a recessed doorway, and was sitting on the doorstep with her arms wrapped round her legs. Her face was turned into the shadow. The sound of her breathing had been heightened by the speed of her flight.

Danno sat down beside her, and took her cold hand in his. Rain fell straight through their sodden clothes and ran in fickle, wandering streams over their chilled bodies. Such cooling rain gave Danno's frantic skin its first relief in days.

They sat together in silence for some minutes. Danno felt himself grow drowsy with cold. Such coldness in September was unseemly. His body, moreover, was not fit for it.

"I am more to be trusted than not," he ventured finally, and his voice was slurred with cold. He did not dare to promise more.

She gave no indication that she had heard him. Her head leaned against the door behind and her eyes were closed. She had even ceased to shiver. Danno was too tired for any further effort. They should move on, he knew, but he could not bring himself to stand up. He closed his own eyes.

"I am no Clarissa."

Danno opened his eyes again. It was the first time Pansy had spoken. She wished to declare herself. She saw him as a necessary audience. "I do not intend to will myself to death for someone else's crime against me."

For the first time, Danno understood the nature of Pansy's misuse. Clarissa had been abducted; she had been ravished by the infamous Lovelace.

"Dishonour was done to me. But I am not myself dishonourable."

Pansy was speaking of her own imagined ravishment.

Danno spoke with the greatest of caution. By whom had she been ravished? The interrogator? He had heard her scream within the cells.

But Pansy shook her head.

"I screamed when I was told to do so."

"And not from pain actually suffered?"

"No."

He had been lured falsely to confess. He could not believe that he had been so duped.

"By whom, then, do you imagine yourself ravished?" he asked, and contempt had crept into his voice.

Pansy stood up and shook herself like a dog. The rain had eased.

"I imagine nothing, Mr. McKenna," she said quite calmly, as he rose to his feet beside her. "I was ravished. By a soldier as we travelled to the prison in a closed carriage. Your belief is immaterial."

"Describe the act," said Danno with great cruelty. But it was cruelty deserved. She had forced him to a betrayal of himself. Without good cause.

She stared at him for a few seconds while belief settled, then said: "You are unkind. I knew always that you were unkind. I had not known how unkind before tonight."

She turned her back on him and walked away. He let her go.

She was quickly invisible and he could tell her whereabouts only by her fading footsteps on the wet pavement. It was the sound of conflicting footsteps which brought him back to a sense of duty, and he hurried reluctantly after her.

"It would not be wise to expose yourself further to the night streets without such protection as I can offer."

"It makes no matter now," she said indifferently.

"Let me see you safely home."

"Not home," she said, and she began to cry. "They will not find me fit to be received."

"They would scarcely turn you away."

Though her appearance, on reflection, was alarmingly abandoned; and she was in the forbidden company of a revealed libertine and rebel.

"Not home," she repeated wearily.

She was close to collapse, Danno realised. He had been too harsh. She was not to be blamed for what she could not help. She had no capacity for bravery; and an untempered imagination buckled easily in the heat of fear. In prison, he believed himself to have been a fool. Pansy had seemed a small price to pay for financial ease; Letitia too high a price for poverty and the condemnation of society. In Pansy's presence, such a belief was difficult to sustain. She was distressed; an undeniable object of pity; and already he longed to be out of her company. His own home was not far from the Exchange. He would bring her there.

***

Letitia and Caitlín had searched vainly for Anton throughout the greater part of the night. How could you find someone whom you dared neither to name, nor to describe? That he had political associates (now likely, on foot of his rumoured treachery, to be his enemies), Caitlín knew. But their identities were quite unknown to her.

She knew nothing of Malachi Delaney's political connection to Anton Paradis. That he had betrayed Anton was clear enough; his desire for Anton's wife (together with her business) had been the cause; his method of betrayal she had never understood. She did not, therefore, contemplate Malachi Delaney as a possible source of information concerning the whereabouts of Anton Paradis.

But towards the end of the night, Caitlín became transfixed by the conviction that Anton might have gone to Charlotte Paradis for succour.

"Why?" Letitia had asked, flat-voiced with weariness.

"Because he would not be expected to do so."

He could no longer turn to Caitlín.

"But that is not sufficient reason," Letitia persisted while she massaged the sides of her aching head with the tips of her fingers (her hair was drying out at last), "to deliver yourself into the hands of your enemies."

But Anton had always been apt to find excuses for his wife, as Caitlín recalled.

"Charlotte is not merely his wife," she said with desperate enthusiasm. "She is also his cousin. There is that tie of blood."

"And Cain was Abel's brother."

But they could think of nothing better to do, so they went to call on Charlotte Paradis.

It was just before dawn.

***

When Charlotte heard their knocking, she was not surprised.

She assumed, at first, that the soldiers had returned.

She hesitated uneasily on the stairs (she was only now, shortly before the time she would normally arise, on her way to bed), while candle flames multiplied before her eyes. She was so tired. The desire for sleep almost outweighed her sense of terror. She hoped that this puzzling blur of light could not be seen through the unshuttered landing window; but she did not dare to blow the flame out for fear of the darkness which would then envelop her. Her spirit was already dark; she could not allow her body to be encircled too.

She had sat in the warehouse throughout the night, waiting for the return of the soldiers. They were said to be rarely satisfied by a single visit. She could not have slept for apprehension; nor could she have slept for the sense of bitterness which assailed her.

She had been betrayed by Malachi. She was sure of it. She had been gulled by false professions of love; professions made to her by a man whose ambition would always be for more, no matter how much he succeeded in possessing. Her thoughts lost all perspective and would concede no possible complexity: either to Malachi's motives, or to her own naivety.

Was it possible to hate the object of your love? For your inability to cease loving it? During the night, Charlotte came to believe such a thing possible.

She had also been betrayed by the Government. She was stunned by its contempt for justice. Loyalty was no guarantee of safety. Punishment was to be distributed without distinction, like the rain which falls equally upon the just and the unjust. This was frightening enough.

But what if the Government was merely the tool of God? Were the events of the afternoon not a fitting punishment for her treachery? Then things became more frightening still. For after such punishment, she had committed further treachery. She had informed the cell of Malachi's arrest, knowing the likely consequences for Anton. Further punishment was therefore due.

It was the recognition that a closed door would present no barrier to soldiers which convinced her that she must open it without delay. Soldiers enraged by resistance were intolerable to imagine.

She hoped that her children would sleep through the visitation.

Then she wondered if it might be Malachi, unexpectedly released; and she stumbled down the stairs with the flame trailing like a dog's tail from the candle.

Neither Caitlín nor Letitia had expected such a quick response to their assault upon the Paradis door. Charlotte (if she was to yield at all) had been expected to yield from weariness. They had been prepared to knock upon her door for the remainder of the night. They had (as they had previously recognised) no better plan.

And then, who could have imagined that the sight of two young women would provoke Charlotte Paradis to scream as though, they agreed afterwards, she thought herself confronted by spirits.

Upon seeing Caitlín, Charlotte tried to close the door again. But who could close the door against a ghost?

She could not have succeeded. The two girls had been expecting the weight of Malachi.

As soon as Caitlín saw Charlotte, her conviction died. Anton would not have come to Charlotte for succour. The visit was without point. But they had come to ask a question, and it would be asked. Then they would leave.

"Is Anton here?"

Charlotte stared at her.

She was not, of course, a ghost. The report of Caitlín's death had been a deceit to terrify poor Malachi.

But if she was not a ghost, then she was alive.

Was she another of God's tools? Sent to persuade Charlotte Paradis away from evil paths?

"Anton can't be here," she said eventually.

Her voice took both girls by surprise. She had been silent for so long that they had ceased to expect an answer.

"Why not?"

Charlotte glanced apprehensively around her. Why not indeed?

She was sweating. He was probably dead by now. But what if Anton had survived once more, in defiance of his odds? Would such uncanny luck not irrefutably show the hand of God reaching out to protect the innocent? And would it not follow, equally undeniably, that her own ill-fortune was also caused by the hand of God?

She would shrive her conscience to the extent necessary: but no further.

"He was expected in *Nelligan's Ale House.*"

So saying, Charlotte began, meagrely, to make reparation for sins committed.

***

At first they thought he was dead.

There was so much external blood; and his face was so devoid of colour. Letitia claimed to feel a pulse; Caitlín could not be sure. When Caitlín blew directly onto them with pursed up lips, his eyelids did not flicker.

"He's dead," she mourned.

But then she saw a pulse, visibly beating on his neck and fell to kissing it rapturously.

They could not make out the nature of his injury. But because the blood appeared to have issued only through his mouth, they supposed him to have suffered some internal rupture. They feared, therefore, to shift his body.

But they could not leave him where he was, a curiosity to the authorities, a temptation to his enemies.

"Better to have him die in our care than in the care of his enemies," Caitlín decided finally.

Dark clots of jellied blood slipped from his mouth when they raised him up. His lips fell open.

"Dear God," whispered Caitlín, staring into the hollow of his mouth. "He has no tongue."

Letitia looked, then looked away.

"We must not look again," she said. "We can afford no pity for him. Pity will not transport him home."

"He has no tongue," Caitlín whispered again, then fell silent for shame of having used her own.

They wound his arms around their own necks. His head lolled between them and his leaking mouth was mercifully hidden from their view. He was heavy. They had not imagined him so heavy. He was not, after all, a tall man. His feet dragged like still-connected brakes along the ground behind. They were almost defeated by his weight. They could not pull him for more than two hundred paces without stopping to rest. Before they reached the McKenna house (no other destination had occurred to either girl), they could scarcely walk fifty uninterrupted paces. They had ceased to look for his pulse. They were afraid that were they to discover him to be dead, their strength might abandon them and they would find themselves unable to carry him further.

They could not pull him up the steps.

They laid him on the pavement. Caitlín sat down on the lowest step and took his head onto her lap.

Letitia climbed the steps and knocked on the door.

Danno opened the door.

Pansy stood behind him in the hall. She had hoped to see her mother.

TWENTY THREE

It had been Mrs. McKenna who had discovered Pansy's story to be no more than the truth.

"Dried blood was lodged between her thighs," she told Danno when she came downstairs. "The only place where rain had failed to penetrate."

"Yes, but . . ."

"She was raped, Danno."

"Yes."

Danno buried his head in his hands. He had ridiculed her claim. Bucks and pinkindindies.

Yet the incident had been so unnecessary.

She had been taken, erroneously, for Letitia.

Pansy had said, on being questioned by Mrs. McKenna, that she had been given no opportunity to prove her own identity; nor, she insisted (with sliding eyes and dark-flushed cheeks), had she been given any opportunity to escape. When Letitia had called to her from the door, she had been prevented by the soldier from replying. It was obvious from her demeanour that she was lying.

"She came here for love of you," Mrs. McKenna said now. "And we showed her no great sympathy. She was presented with an opportunity to prove that love, and she couldn't resist it."

Word had been sent to her parents; there had, as yet, been no reply.

"She came without permission."

"But surely when her circumstances are understood?"

"They are of her own making."

"But . . ."

"Her father is an intractable man. I fear we may be poor Pansy's only friends."

"Oh God."

Letitia would not have allowed herself to be raped in a public carriage. She would have screamed; she would have kicked; she would, if necessary, have jumped from the moving carriage with her clothes in disarray. Nor would she, when in custody, have screamed for anything less than unbearable pain inflicted; and her endurance of pain would have passed all normal bounds.

But Letitia had returned to her husband.

"Impossible," he had said on hearing the news.

But his mother had shaken her head.

"She felt it was her duty."

"But why?"

"His daughter died," was all that his mother (the pragmatic Mrs. McKenna) would vouchsafe. (The circumstances of the fire, in so far as they were understood, had been explained.)

"Her return was not to be dependent on my release?"

Even to have offered herself to her husband in exchange for his release would have been intolerable.

"I am not aware of such an intention," his mother lied. "She doubtless looked at her position and found it indefensible."

Mrs. McKenna had lied, but for what she believed to be the best of motives. She knew better than all these young people where their interests lay. Pansy's father was an intractable man, but he had no other heir. Were Danno McKenna to stand by his ravished daughter, such integrity must eventually find favour with her father. She even had Letitia's own interests in view. For what could Letitia hope for from such a liaison as the one which had existed between Danno and herself? Social devastation now; followed by the failure of love.

"You drove her out!" Danno accused finally. He could think of no better reason.

The accusation wounded Mrs. McKenna deeply.

"I loved Letitia! Indeed, I begged her not to go!"

It scarcely even occurred to Mrs. McKenna that, with such a statement, she contrived to make Letitia's desertion seem baser still.

Pansy called for her clothes at first light. Though they were not yet properly dried, she insisted that they should be brought to her room.

Dressed in her damp clothes, she stood in the hall, waiting for the arrival of her parents. She refused breakfast, for fear of delaying her parents should they arrive while breakfast was still in progress. She was persuaded to accept a cup of tea.

"The wait could be longer than you imagine, Pansy dear."

It was while Pansy was still drinking her tea that Letitia and Caitlín returned with their new burden.

***

Climbing the steps had taken the last of Letitia's strength. Reaching out to touch Danno, she overbalanced, and would have fallen but for the fact that he stepped forward to catch her.

It was then Danno saw that she was not alone. Caitlín was on the bottom step, crying over Anton's body.

He thrust Letitia (hot-skinned and damp with exertion) into Pansy's arms and ran down the steps. He knelt down beside the still weaver and began to stroke his hair. His eyes were transfixed by the blood-crusted mouth.

"Is he dead?"

Caitlín shook her head. She had found his pulse again, and once his eyes had moved behind his eyelids.

"Well then," he asked with gentle cajolery (though he was himself shaking with emotion), "what cause for tears?"

He put his hand on her shoulder, but she shrugged it away and the tears ran faster from her eyes.

"It was for you he sought them out."

He could barely understand her words for the sobs which shook her when she spoke.

"For love of you, he offered to be the figure of their imagination."

He watched her fingers comb the weaver's hair.

"No one told him that the figure had changed."

Tears from her face were falling onto the face of the weaver. She wiped her cheeks, first against one shoulder, then against the other.

"A rumour was circulated that he had done a deal with the Government; to give evidence against you."

"Bastards," Danno breathed.

Caitlín paid him no heed.

"He has been punished fittingly; they cut out his tongue."

"What?"

"Your friends. His tongue. They cut it out to protect you from what it might reveal."

Danno's hand was at his own mouth, rubbing backwards and forwards across his lips. He was shaking his head in horror. (But even while he shook his head, appalled, he noted that the weaver's hands were still intact.)

"No," he was whispering. "No, no, no . . ." Tears fell from his face too, and soaked into Anton's blood-stained shirt.

Caitlín watched them form dark spots.

Mr. McKenna's adventure was over and he was home unharmed. He had stories to tell. Anton, too, had stories to tell: but never would now.

"You told him he was a hero, Mr. McKenna," Caitlín said bitterly. "And he believed you."

Anton's eyes rolled open and saw the two faces above his own. His lips attempted to smile, and then his eyes rolled closed again.

"Anton," Caitlín called out with agitation. "Stay awake, love. Stay awake." She bent down and touched each lid in turn with her lips.

He sighed, but his eyes remained shut.

"And was I not right, Caitlín?"

"He should be inside the house," was all she said.

She had seen Anton's smile and knew that she must, at all times in the future, curb her tongue. She would have reminder enough, God knew. Anton loved Mr. McKenna. Should he survive, Anton must never know that she thought his sacrifice made in an unworthy cause.

Then she added: "Miss Letitia needs you."

"I doubt it," he said.

"She called your name."

***

"She thinks she saved you."

Letitia was standing at the top of the steps, looking down at him. Pansy stood pale and unwilling at her side; Letitia's thumb and fingers were snapped, like mandibles, to her wrist.

For Danno, it was like seeing the sun and its copy side by side.

"Let me assure you," Letitia called down, "lest you think yourself under an obligation to her for her masquerade, that she did not."

She was jealous! Pansy, by her deceit, had denied Letitia the chance to be his deliverer.

"How can you be certain?"

Letitia (who did not know how dearly Pansy had already paid for her folly) dropped Pansy's wrist and came down the steps to kneel between Danno and Caitlín. She put an arm around each neck.

"How is he?" she asked apprehensively, looking at Anton's impassive face.

"Alive."

"No more?"

"He opened his eyes," Caitlín conceded reluctantly. She feared the consequences of rash hope.

"And smiled," Danno insisted.

Letitia's fingers caressed Danno's face with avid love.

"You've grown so thin!"

His mother had said the same. It required no lover's dedication to observe his loss of weight. Letitia had returned to her husband while he was growing thin.

"To whom am I obliged, if not to Pansy?"

Letitia's fingers hesitated, and grew still on his cheekbone. She had already put Pansy from her mind; he, clearly, had not. His question had been stiffly put.

"You were not released on Pansy's account. You were released because they could no longer hope for a successful prosecution."

Was his mother wrong? Had Letitia begun to bargain Danno's liberty with her husband in advance of her departure? Had she returned to Marvin on hearing word of Danno's imminent release? If so, why was she here? To check that the bargain had been kept? Letitia's fingers had resumed their wandering. Danno could scarcely bear in silence their touch on his enthralled neck. He looked at her through half-closed eyes, and smiled. (Why was it that between them desire could erupt at the most impossible of times? Even as the mutilated weaver threatened to die, desire erupted.)

"Their Crown witness is dead. Marvin shot himself."

He was released because of Marvin's death; not because of any bargain made.

"How convenient," he remarked.

"I suppose so."

But she shuddered at the memory of that closed coffin: its unseen contents. She did not understand the import of his remark. She thought it a passing homage to chance. She laid her head on Danno's shoulder.

He let it lie there while he turned his head to look back up the steps to Pansy. She gazed unblinkingly in the direction of College Green. Her father's carriage had not yet appeared: nor would it, despite her mother's pleadings on Pansy's behalf.

He rose, without warning, to his feet.

"Who says that an obligation ceases because a deed done on one's behalf turns out to have been done unnecessarily?"

"It was done on her own behalf, not yours."

Letitia looked up, frightened by the abruptness of his move. His face, looking down, was cold.

How could it be that they were fighting thus, within minutes of reunion? They didn't deserve their tongues (was she always going to think in such terms?). Caitlín's hands closed over Anton's ears to protect him from the sounds of bitterness; but then she opened them up again. He could not see; he could not speak; she must not deprive him of his hearing, for fear that he should dream himself to death.

"And you are not guilty of acting to your own advantage?"

Letitia stared up at him. "Do you have a particular occasion in mind?"

"This occasion serves for as fine an example as any."

"I do not understand. It may be that I am so used to acting to my own advantage that I no longer note the occasions. Enlighten me."

She was as he had imagined her to be while in gaol. All artifice and calculation. He had been deceived by his heart at first sight of her into a dismissal of those thoughts as ill-made.

"You think that your husband's fortuitous death, combined with my release, allows you to fly to my side as though no desertion had taken place. Perhaps you thought I would know nothing of it; that it would remain an undisclosed error of timing on your part. A single day's delay would have been sufficient."

She must be kind. It was too easy to forget that he had been in prison. "Were you isolated from all company?"

"Except yours," he answered her bitterly. "You would not leave me for an instant."

Anton opened his eyes and began to make a moaning cry. They all looked down. He was trying to make words with his lips, while tears poured from his eyes. His head rocked from side to side, most probably with pain, while his hands clutched at the air. His cheeks were flushed, and sweat was gathering on his forehead. Caitlín mopped at Anton's sweating forehead with a corner of her dress.

"He's turning feverish."

"Move the weaver indoors," said Letitia quietly to Danno.

"He was so cold before."

Letitia watched Danno carry his weaver into the house, past the unmoving Pansy. She rose to her feet and began to walk down the street in the direction of the college.

***

Caitlín was alive. He could live without his tongue if Caitlín was alive. Danno was alive and at large. His throat burned with thirst. Could one drink without a tongue? Could one taste without a tongue? Towards the back of his mouth, a stump existed. If you pluck out the tongue, will six grow in its place? Did they even know that his tongue had been cut out of his mouth?

As Danno carried him up the stairs, Anton opened his mouth wide and pointed into it with his finger.

"He wants something," said Danno to Caitlín, who was following behind. "I think he's looking for food."

"He's thirsty," said Caitlín.

They spoke as though he wasn't there. Even Caitlín. Anton closed his eyes. Tears oozed out between his lids.

***

Danno carried the weaver to his own bed, and there they gave him water. Anton drank water; water and blood trickled from his mouth; he was washed with water; water cooled his burning face.

A doctor was summoned, who gave it as his opinion that Anton should be already dead from loss of blood; the fact that he was not dead was, so the doctor assured them, greatly in the weaver's favour. For his opinion, he accepted two guineas. He made no inquiry as to the identity of his patient; nor did he ask how the injury had occurred. It was for this reticence that two guineas were willingly paid.

"If he should recover," and the doctor looked uncertain, "Remember that his tongue is the only organ to have been damaged. Do not treat him as a petted idiot. Can he write? Yes? Then let him have quills and paper by him at all times."

They took his advice.

In one of Anton's periods of consciousness, Danno dipped a quill into ink and handed it to Anton, together with paper and a board.

"Who attacked you?"

Anton stared at the quill in his hand for some time, as though he did not understand its connection to the question asked. The answer, comprising of only six letters, surprised them both. GOV MEN.

"Not members of the cell?"

Anton wrote down the letter N, then stopped and shook his head instead: with vehemence. He was sweating profusely. The effort had exhausted him and he closed his eyes.

Danno looked with triumph at Caitlín, but she refused, by the slightest look, to acknowledge a victory.

***

It took two hours to settle Anton.

Throughout that time, the quarrel lay in wait: a cat poised for attack, so Danno thought.

But when Danno went to look for Letitia, she had disappeared.

"Did you expect her to stay?" Caitlín asked him contemptuously. They were standing outside the room where Anton lay.

"I believed her braver once."

He thought her contempt directed at Letitia; but quickly discovered his mistake.

"You question her bravery?"

"She found it expedient to return to her husband."

"Miss Letitia deserves better than you, Mr. McKenna."

Caitlín spoke dismissively, and turned her back; as though she were his equal with no call to curb her manners. She made to enter Anton's room, but Danno drew her sharply back.

"You would consider her husband my superior, Caitlín? Your opinion of me is so low?"

He had done her great kindness as well as harm. The kindness had ever been from the heart; the harm unintentional. She must bear in mind that he was not a worthless man. She put her hand quite sympathetically on his arm.

"Don't be a fool, Mr. McKenna. She went back to him for you."

"For the preservation of her own good name."

"Prison has warped your judgement."

It would have been possible. Had he been relying on his own judgement alone, he would have had to concede that as a possibility; but he was not.

"My mother . . ."

"Even your mother said that you would not expect such sacrifice."

"What?"

She laughed. "You think your mother holds you too lightly in her affections? She is certainly uncommonly fond of Miss Letitia. She begged her not to go; but knew she would not prevail."

To have believed his mother was, of itself, a failure of judgement.

"I have looked for her throughout the house. Where do you think that she might be?"

"Home?"

"Hardly."

"Is she not the mistress of an empty house?"

A chair had been placed for Pansy on the door step, since she could not be persuaded to wait elsewhere. She was, of course, the reason for his mother's lie. His championship of a ruined young woman would earn, eventually, the gratitude of that young woman's parents.

"Have you seen Letitia, Pansy?"

Pansy smiled politely, but made no reply. She could not look in his direction, for she was intent on watching the traffic.

"Did Letitia pass down the street?" he asked, placing himself firmly in her line of vision.

"Umm," she said, craning her head to see around him.

The answer could have meant anything at all.

Mrs. McKenna hurried out of the sitting room when she heard Danno talking to Pansy. She had been disturbed by Letitia's return. From the sitting room window, she had watched (but could not hear) the gathering around the wounded weaver. She had seen the weaver carried into the house. Finally she had seen (with relief) the departure of Letitia.

"Poor darling," she said now, stroking Pansy's hair. "Why don't you take Danno's arm and come inside?"

An elderly woman was toiling up the hill.

Pansy rose from her chair in some excitement.

"Nanny!" she said. "They've sent Nanny!" She turned to Mrs. McKenna. "Is my face clean?" she asked anxiously.

Mrs. McKenna glanced at Danno.

"Perfectly clean," she said, but Pansy had already sunk back onto her chair.

"False alarm," she remarked as the old woman passed by the house.

"It will take us a day or two to acclimatise to the truth," Mrs. McKenna remarked to the air. "Then we'll be grand."

"And the Prince and the Princess married and lived happily ever after."

"Quite," said his mother, smiling at him. They were at one, it seemed.

Pansy began to cry.

"The Princess went home to her Mama," she whispered.

Danno nodded his agreement.

"Good for you, Pansy. A fine variation on the theme." He laughed at the betrayed look on his mother's face. He patted Pansy on the shoulder. Her shoulder shrank from his touch.

"And the Prince died in battle."

Mrs. McKenna shook her head and clucked her teeth despairingly.

"You lied!"

Mrs. McKenna looked at her son. That he would discover her lie had been one of her fears. But no matter, since Letitia had left.

"And Letitia is gone."

Mrs. McKenna nodded her head.

"Yes."

"You saw her leave?"

"It was for the best that she should go." Mrs. McKenna could see no connection between Letitia's return to her husband and Danno's release. The two events were far too close in time. But Sweetman's contentment was of importance, she was sure. "You were released; she is therefore tied to Sweetman."

"Sweetman is dead," said Danno over his shoulder as he walked down the steps. He would find Letitia and he would apologise. She would have to forgive him, for he loved her so much.

His mother stared after him.

"Letitia surely . . ?" she called out.

"He shot himself."

"Good heavens!"

Mrs. McKenna crossed herself, then looked aggrievedly up and down the street for witnesses. Such demonstrations of religious fervour were disparaged in the circles Mrs. McKenna desired to enter.

She watched Danno hail a carriage.

The death of Sweetman put such a different complexion on affairs. Mrs. McKenna's mind was, as ever, active on her son's behalf. Letitia Sweetman had turned from liability to asset overnight.

In the same period of time, Pansy's prospects had also changed.

She turned to the waiting girl.

"Well, Miss Pansy," she said brusquely, "If Mohammed won't come to the mountain, then . . ."

The tiresome creature did not stir.

She was making a show of them all. It really was not to be tolerated that she should sit like an idle housemaid on the side of the street for all their friends to see.

Mrs. McKenna pulled her so sharply to her feet that the chair tottered on the step. "Time to put a stop to this nonsense, Pansy," she said. "I'm bringing you home. Your father must take charge of his own responsibilities. Come inside while I arrange the carriage."

***

The fact that Letitia Sweetman arrived home while her husband and step-daughter were being buried caused her servants no visible surprise.

But Thomas took it upon himself to remind her of the occasion.

"I know," she said indifferently. "I passed by the funeral procession on my way home."

Probably he loved her.

She certainly still loved him.

When he found himself to have been mistaken in his accusation, he would apologise and beg forgiveness; but contrition would not cure the underlying flaw. Danno McKenna would always be inclined to attribute the basest of motives to women. He saw them as inherently dishonourable. Lesser creatures than the men they beguiled.

When she called for a bath to be drawn, no one demurred.

"And then I'm going to bed," she added. "I must not be disturbed."

"But the mourners, Madam? What should I tell the mourners?"

In the dining room, baked meats were laid out on the table where the coffin had so recently rested. Glazed ham, jellied chicken, mutton, dishes of glossy leaved salads, venison pie. The chief mourners were expected back to mark the passing of Marvin and Caroline Sweetman.

"Nothing, Thomas. Tell them nothing. They will mourn more comfortably in ignorance of my presence in the house."

It was agreed, among the servants, that the mistress looked like a thing escaped from Bedlam; a thing best not seen by the late master's relatives.

***

By the time Danno arrived, the mourners were all congregated in the dining room, heroically bracing themselves against undue grief with Marvin Sweetman's claret. The funeral party was beginning to take shape.

"Is Mrs. Sweetman amongst the mourners?" Danno asked Thomas.

His voice expressed doubt.

Thomas shook his head. He recognised Danno McKenna. The man had been to dinner. His attentions to the mistress had been observed on that occasion. The servants had foreseen the affair before it took place. "Mrs. Sweetman," he said, "is too distraught to attend."

"But she is here?"

Thomas did not rightly know where his best interests lay. He sighed and maintained silence.

"She was in my house an hour ago."

Thomas sighed again and shrugged his shoulders in desperation.

"Upstairs, perhaps," Danno pressed.

Thomas capitulated. "If you say so, sir," he said. Then added: "Though she did ask not to be disturbed. I would be grateful, sir, if you were to pretend your discovery of Madam's whereabouts to be a lucky chance."

"Certainly."

"It is the third door on the left."

She was not asleep. She lay on top of the bedclothes, fully dressed, staring, without direction, at the space above her eyes. At the sound of Danno's entrance, she turned her gaze towards him.

"I was waiting for you," she said unsmilingly. "I knew that you would come . . ."

Actually, she had thought that he would never come. It had been with great difficulty that she had forced herself to lie in such a room as this, and wait. But it was her house now; her revulsion for it must be conquered. The house was inanimate. It knew no memories. They were all hers, to remember or forget as she chose.

Was that the bed in which Sweetman had . . ? How could she lie there so indifferently now, in his presence? Did she lack all sense of fitness? Danno was astonished by her composure. Perhaps, he thought forgivingly, she was too tired to care.

"I'm sorry."

" . . . to apologise."

"My mother . . ."

"Of course. Who else? But why did you believe her, Danno?"

Letitia looked at him with longing. She wanted Danno to give her a reason so compelling as to exonerate him in her eyes.

He shook his head helplessly. It seemed so foolish now.

"It is in your mother's character to lie for your advancement; it is not in mine to act as she described." Letitia spoke slowly, as though to a child. "That you should have believed her lie demeans me."

Downstairs, a swell of voices rose and fell.

"My judgement went awry in gaol."

Letitia wished she could believe him; but her judgement, she was sure, was not amiss. He would always underrate the capacity of women for honour.

Danno shook his head again. His mind was silting up with weariness. He could see, by her face, that she was not persuaded. He wanted most desperately to persuade her, but he could think of nothing fine to say. He sat down abruptly on the bed.

"I'm not a worthy man," he said hopelessly. He was so tired. He buried his face in his hands.

He had thought himself guilty of only one betrayal while in prison. Now he realised that he had been guilty of two. He had betrayed Letitia. He had not been strong enough to withstand the perils of solitude. He had been in thrall to the monstrous lies of his own imagination: believing them to be the truth. That was the worst of it; that he had believed his mind secure.

"I'll go," he said bleakly, but could not bring himself to stir.

He felt Letitia's hand press cool against his neck.

"I'm not entirely perfect myself," he heard her say.

She too was very tired.

Her thoughts, so clear before his arrival, were now confused. She had always known him flawed. Was she going to allow the knowledge to assume undue significance now?

It was easy, she thought, to take issue with his faults now that he was here.

But what if he had confounded her expectations? What if he had not come? What then? And if she dismissed him now? What if he accepted such dismissal as final? Would his faults ever loom larger than her longing? Was she going to stand upon her slighted honour with such peevish solemnity when she only wanted to make her nest in his heart?

He should have been hanged for treason. Instead he was in the house of his enemy; his enemy was dead; the hand of his enemy's widow was on his neck. Letitia began to laugh at the perilous chanciness of events.

Danno's head remained buried in his hands. Her fingers crept inside the neck of his shirt. He gave, unwittingly, a sigh of pleasure. It was as though his skin itself had spoken.

"Celebration is surely due," she said, with an abrupt shedding of her qualms, "in place of such perverse gravity. You are, after all, alive and at liberty."

Another burst of sound escaped upwards from the funeral party as the dining room door was briefly opened.

"While Marvin is dead," she added, while her spirits rose irresistibly, like scraps of paper in a fountain of hot air. She was kneeling on the bed behind Danno. She wrapped her arms around him from behind and laid her head down on his shoulders. She blew gently on the skin behind his ear. She must not think of Caroline. Caroline was beyond harm.

Danno sat stiffly in her embrace.

He felt unexpectedly aggrieved.

He was expected to keep pace with each mercurial change of temper. Like a pianist following the dancing of a horse. She touched the lobe of his ear with her tongue and he shivered involuntarily. Her hands slid downwards to his groin. Friends were gathered below to mourn the deaths of Marvin and his daughter. Was she quite oblivious to the occasion? Or was ridicule her intention?

The rising of desire against his will was unbearable. He caught her hands in his to still them, but she began to bite his neck. She had bathed; she was wearing fresh perfume. What if Marvin had been still alive when she had returned to this house the night before? Could she have teased him thus for Danno's sake? Could she acclimatise to any situation? He found, to his annoyance, that he was playing with her fingers.

"I would rather have died," he said (easily, now that he was free), "than owe my liberty to such a sacrifice as you proposed on my behalf."

He turned his head sideways to look at her face on his shoulder. Her lips were damp and shining and her face was flushed.

"Could you really have suffered his attentions? Knowing his past?" he asked. The idea that she could have done so repelled him.

It seemed impossible. What had appeared as a small oasis of honour in her behaviour was now, in the light of his question, compromised. She shrugged. He felt her shoulders rub closely on his back.

"We'll never know," she said.

Her entire body was dissolving with desire: in defiance of its surroundings; in defiance of the occasion. Why would he not respond? Such defiance was not limitless.

She laid her cheek against his back and closed her eyes.

She could so easily have fallen asleep, slouched against his back. And then she felt him raise her hands to his lips, and heard him moan, as though defeated.

"Damn you, McKenna," she whispered at the sound. "I am not your soul's temptation, to be resisted at all costs."

Why did he always, by his resistance, make her feel a whore?

She pulled her hands away from his, climbed off the bed, and stood before him. Then she discarded her clothes, flinging them from her as though ridding herself of her besetting sins. She stood naked before him, her hands on her hips, her pelvis thrust towards his face.

"Now," she said. "Either act or leave."

For fully two minutes, neither one of them touched the other.

Finally, Letitia, desire turning to cold stone in her stomach, turned away. She bent to pick up a stocking from the floor.

He would leave her in this room. Another grievous memory to be overcome. She shivered; she was cold with grief.

She felt something fall across her back and shivered again at the unexpected touch. Danno's discarded silk shirt slithered to the floor beside her. She looked up. Danno had risen to his feet and was unbuttoning his trousers. He was aroused. She could not deny the evidence of her eyes.

He held out his hands to her; but she would not move. She had done too much already. Let him come to her. She began to roll her stocking up between her fingers.

And come to her he did.

He knelt down beside her, and ran his hands around the curves of her two buttocks. He kissed her mouth and still she made no move to touch him in return. He moved one hand to hold her head secure; with frettings of his tongue he teased her mutinous lips apart. His other hand he pushed between her thighs. A single finger slid creamily upwards.

She was well trapped.

He stood up and she rose with him. She hung her arms around his neck and he carried her to the bed. She lay on her back and he knelt above her, looking at her. She was so beautiful. He drew circles with a fingernail on her stomach. The fingers of his other hand slid slowly back and forth between her legs. Her stomach rose and fell against the narrow tracings of his nail. Her head began to twist from side to side; her tongue flicked at her upper lip and her breathing quickened.

Downstairs, the funeral party was breaking up. Voices of guests rose loudly up from the hall. The sudden eruption of sound caused Danno to pause.

He removed both hands from Letitia's body, and looked behind him nervously.

She groaned and wrapped her legs round his back.

"Courage, McKenna!" she whispered "They'll scarcely be coming up to say good bye!"

She pulled him flat on top of her. She was laughing helplessly, stifling the sound as best as she could in his shoulder.

"Wait!" he whispered back urgently, but her body could not be still. It pushed and rocked beneath him. Sliding into her, he felt anchored above a small but turbulent sea. The mourners below lost all significance.

"Oh Jesus!" he suddenly said, catching her rhythm. "Oh Jesus! Jesus! Jesus!"

He buried his tongue in her mouth to stifle all their sounds.

They had both reached a climax before the last of the mourners had left the house.

"Could even such a place as this be purged with love?" Letitia asked tentatively as they lay arm in arm on her bed.

It had been an exorcism.

He had misjudged her yet again. What he had taken for an act of brash frivolity had been, in reality, an attempt to render Sweetman harmless. But why could she not have said so in advance? Was he supposed to have known? Probably.

. . . Unless her remark had been no more than a justification invented after the episode had taken place.

It was while Danno was dressing that Letitia learned of Pansy's ravishment. "And so," Danno said, as he eased a glove over one wrist, "my mother believes my hopes of marrying Pansy revived."

Letitia looked at him. "Perhaps it is your duty. She was raped for love of you."

"I believe she would not have me if I asked."

"I should not imagine the choice is hers."

"The more reason for me not to push my suit."

"A most heroic self-denial."

Letitia spoke drily, but she caught his ungloved hand in hers and pulled it round her waist.

"Besides," he said, and his lips tickled her forehead. "My mother's view of the situation changed upon hearing of your unexpected loss."

"I am widowed, young and rich."

"Quite."

"And therefore highly desirable."

"My mother's precise reasoning."

Danno had been annoyed by the speed with which that thought had floated to the surface of his own mind. His infatuation was independent, he well knew, of Letitia's situation.

"But my desirability is more apparent than real," said Letitia, and in her voice amusement lurked. "There is a mortal flaw below the surface."

"Nothing could prove mortal to my desire," Danno murmured dreamily. His eyes were closed and his lips were touching her hair.

He was so quick with his taffeta phrases, silken terms precise. He was not being insincere, Letitia knew. He believed himself, at that moment, to be stating the truth.

Letitia smiled, unseen.

"Of course," she agreed silkily. "But we speak of your mother. To her, the flaw must appear mortal."

Danno removed his lips from her hair. He opened his eyes and looked at her, smiling.

"What is the flaw?"

"I remain rich only by avoiding marriage. On my remarriage, the estate reverts to Caroline . . ."

"Well then . . ."

"Should Caroline be already dead, then the estate reverts to Marvin's brother."

There was, he supposed, no reason why infatuation should render one immune to disappointment.

After he had gone, Letitia walked through the house, pulling back curtains, opening up windows. Air flooded into the house. He would ask her to marry him. He would be bound to do so. But she would refuse him and he, despite his protestations, would be relieved. Miss Wollstonecraft could almost have approved: except that Letitia's refusal would stem not from a desire for independence, but from the desire to prolong love for as long as possible.

***

Danno had been released from gaol and Letitia imagined herself free to speculate about the future.

She thought the danger past; but it had scarcely begun.

TWENTY FOUR

❧

Dear Sir, This evening, while at cards with my friends, I was summoned from the table by a servant at the request of my newest spy. I was, I will admit, reluctant to interrupt a game in which I had held the upper hand for an hour or more, knowing that my luck was unlikely to survive the disruption. However, the courting of these nervous young creatures cannot be underestimated; they must be wooed with attention and florid appreciation. I therefore went to speak to him with as good a grace as I could muster, expecting, for my pains, yet another rumoured landing by the French. Instead, he aroused my curiosity as it has not been aroused since the death of my dear wife (God rest her soul). You will judge the extent of my excitement by the fact that I have not returned to the card table, but am instead writing to you while the information is still fresh in my mind. He also roused my fears. I believe the matter sufficiently grave to bring to your attention without delay.

And yet I hesitate to commence: it concerns a matter which has already, and undeservedly, reduced my reputation at the Castle (though I must thank you for your personal support throughout this unhappy time). Were it not for the gravity of the matter, I might be tempted to keep the information to myself, for fear of further rebuff by your colleagues. Dear Sir, have the goodness to persuade those around you to treat me with the courtesy I believe I am, as a very loyal subject, due. I have, in recent weeks, been humiliated in the Castle corridors. Remember that it is for you that I proceed with my story.

It is now three months since the silk weaver lost his tongue. You will recall that, at the time, we thought him rendered perfectly harmless: both by virtue of his speechlessness; and by the fact that the mutilation had been carried out by his own alleged followers. It seems that we have badly underestimated Paradis' potential for mischief-making. Silence,

343

far from being a barrier to his popularity, has proved to be an asset. He
was, in tongue, so unremarkable that silence has enhanced his significance. Now his devotees can substitute, for his silence, their own desires.
You may wonder how it is that Paradis has come to be adopted as their
figurehead by those to whom his mutilation is due. The answer will amuse
you in its simplicity. Paradis is convinced that the mutilation was carried
out, not by his own colleagues, but by agents of the Crown itself. The faces
of his attackers were, apparently, at all times masked. The clothes were
unfamiliar. Most importantly, he anticipated Crown abuse. As for the
fresh and abject devotion of those so recently his attackers; well that is
easily explained. McKenna, upon his release, revealed to them the true
identity of the proposed Crown witness. The perfidy of Malachi Delaney
he also exposed. Remorse and breast-beating followed these revelations.
McKenna then revealed to them the news that Paradis had suffered
mutilation at the hands of government agents. They (not surprisingly) could
scarcely believe their ears. (I question, Dear Sir, whether McKenna
believes Paradis' mutilation to have been a government affair. I imagine
it merely suits his purposes to affect such a belief.) Their humiliation was
completed when McKenna turned up to the next meeting, accompanied
not only by Paradis himself, but with a note (heavy with gnomic authority)
in Paradis' own hand, saying: "There comes a time when rebellion, even
hopeless rebellion, is the only honourable response to oppression."
It seems that his dismemberment at government hands has been, for
Paradis, the final straw. He has been converted by the experience to
rebellion. Amongst his reprieved colleagues, euphoria has set in. Something
akin to adoration of a Holy Fool has ensued. His notes are fought
for by his followers (and thus, to his greater peril, preserved as evidence
against him). The unfortunately swift death of Delaney under interrogation has proved no deterrent (he had, according to my informant, long
complained of chest pains). Indeed, it has, if anything, added to their
euphoria by removing from them the fear of exposure at his suit. McKenna
and Paradis, I must impress on you, form a wickedly effective combination.
The cell now harbours an unprecedented fervour for rebellion; such fervour
is proving (according to my informant) alarmingly infectious to other
increasingly interconnected cells within the city.
I fear, Dear Sir (if you will pardon my presumption), that the Crown
has been too complacent; unless my news comes late to your eyes and

already this development ripens under surveillance. You, Dear Sir, are in particular danger, for with this resurgence of enthusiasm comes a revival of the plan to assassinate you as a signal for rebellion to begin; like the ringing of a bell to call a scattered congregation to matins. Again, these dastardly renegades do not plan to wait upon the French, but will proceed at their own convenience, relying on their own confidently-expected successes to draw French assistance to the cause.

I trust that this information will not be treated with the contempt meted out to the tip which I passed on to you a month back, concerning that gentleman who has since (I understand) escaped to France. Had my advice been followed, that same man would now be in custody. I realise, of course, that your faith in me has been unwavering; but there are others, Dear Sir, who have been quick to misjudge, whether through ignorance or malice, I cannot say . . . I remain ever your devoted servant . . .

***

Unknown to anyone else, Anton Paradis was disappearing.

Others assumed thoughts for him; they were never quite his own. But he had come to let them, for the most part, pass unchallenged. Challenge was too exhausting. His notes of correction so frequently merely puzzled the recipients. But that was what I said, wasn't it? There were things too ephemeral to write; there were thoughts too banal to write. Writing was too laborious; it defeated the subtlety of the spirit. The more his thoughts were misconstrued, the less important each subsequent misconstruction became. A protective dimness crept over his mind and Anton grew more peaceful.

Both Caitlín and Danno had the mistaken idea that they knew him better than before. They equated their more intense devotion to him with better knowledge.

Sometimes Caitlín felt she had taken Anton into the centre of her soul. Day by day she seemed to know him more absolutely.

"I can look into my own mind," she remarked to Danno once, "and see his thoughts as clear as though they were my own."

He had nodded in agreement.

"I find the same myself."

The fact that they both considered themselves privy to the same mind should have given them pause for thought.

Such thoughts of Anton's that survived were accorded a simplistic and quite alien clarity. A city reduced to a few brightly-drawn lines on paper.

He could no longer weave. His loom was in ashes, but that was no impediment. Other looms lay idle in the McKenna workshop. To weave required a fervour which he no longer possessed. Too tired, he wrote once, in answer to Caitlín's persistent questioning. He had been a weaver; he was still a weaver. He did not need a tongue, she told him savagely, in order to weave silk. Later he wrote a note which said, more biblically, more theatrically: weaving is not in season. Caitlín took the note to mean that the Castle season was almost at an end; the ladies were leaving Dublin for the provinces. It means, Danno explained to the rest of the cell (in the presence of Anton himself), that the occupations of peace cannot be pursued in a time of revolution.

***

In early March, Pansy called on Letitia Sweetman, clambering up the steps with a lap dog balanced on her stomach. The day was bitterly cold. Hail was jumping off the pavement like scalded water.

Pansy was six months pregnant. The condition was almost beyond concealment.

"My mother fears my father will not tolerate the condition."

Pansy's face had grown puffed with pregnancy.

"You don't exercise enough," Letitia had told her visitor, picking up one of Pansy's arms and examining it closely, as though admiring horseflesh. She knew precisely what the object of this visit was. "You have a layer of fat quite incidental to your condition." She held her arm against Pansy's for comparison. There was something to Pansy which brought out cruelty.

Pansy's eyes had filled with tears.

"Did you hear what I said?" she asked, quite snappishly.

Letitia pinched her own flesh up between her fingers, and then let it go. She nodded.

"He knows of the ravishment itself?"

"Yes. And forgives me for it."

"Were you not a victim?" Letitia inquired with curiosity. "What was there to forgive?"

"My folly," Pansy explained dully, as had been explained to her. "I behaved with folly and am therefore responsible for the consequences."

"However unexpected?"

"Yes."

"But you were forgiven," Letitia persisted.

"Yes," Pansy said again.

"Then surely he must forgive the expected consequences?"

"He depended on my mother to ensure that there should be none."

"And?"

"She would not risk my life."

"A poignant dilemma. But what has it to do with me?"

It was as she had guessed.

Pansy understood (from whom?) that Mrs. Sweetman did not intend to marry Mr. McKenna.

Letitia said nothing. Three times had McKenna asked her for her hand in marriage, and she had refused on each occasion.

"Mama says that you can offer Mr. McKenna nothing," said Pansy with nervous resolution.

"Apart from love."

"Which would not long survive such circumstances." Pansy knew more, now, of love. "You are astute, Mrs. Sweetman. Marriage to Mr. McKenna is clearly against your interests. You will not marry him."

Because she would not marry him, she should therefore urge him to marry Pansy instead. An agreement could surely be reached to suit all three? Pansy's swollen fingers tightened around her lap dog.

He was to be regarded as no more than a commodity.

What frightened Letitia was that she could imagine Danno McKenna agreeing to the arrangement. Why not, if love need not even be pretended?

The proposition was so material; so base. And yet, from whom else could Pansy seek protection?

"But I am pregnant too," Letitia told her visitor. "By Mr. McKenna," she added, in case there might be any doubt.

Pansy left, in tears.

***

She was pregnant (a fact not known to Danno). But still she did not think that she would marry him.

***

Two days later, the following notice appeared in the Freeman's Journal: The Castle has informed this newspaper that Daniel McKenna (the well-known Catholic silk merchant and dissident) and his weaver, the notorious Anton Paradis, were shot yesterday afternoon while attempting to resist arrest. It is understood that the arrests followed the discovery of arms on the McKenna premises. The incident in which the two men were shot took place in McKenna's courtyard.

Letitia and Caitlín had felt betrayed before their deaths. They had been harrowed once. Each had gone to the limits of their endurance to bring both men to safety. Each man might honourably have withdrawn. Instead they returned to danger with the inevitability of water running down a slope. What was there to duty which required the death of young men in the cause of hopeless rebellion? If rebellion was acknowledged to be hopeless, did not duty point to some duller path? They had both felt they were being abandoned for a chimera.

Each girl held the other's lover to blame for this abandonment. Their conflicting beliefs had caused a rift to appear between them.

Caitlín believed that Anton had been manipulated by the silk merchant. The merchant, she said, had taken Anton's slightest thoughts and had embroidered them until they hung dense with unwarranted significance.

Letitia, on the other hand, believed Anton to be the manipulator. There were times when she wished (guiltily) that he had died.

"Does he have to write such notes?" Letitia had asked bitterly. "You would condemn him to silence?"

But it was those gnomic notes which caused the damage. And he did not protest at their interpretation. It was the clarity of those notes which had revived Danno's enthusiasm for rebellion. McKenna said he loved her; yet he could not abandon the cause for love. She had offered to become his partner in the silk trade; yet he could not abandon the cause for silk. He was measuring his life in months, not years and Letitia knew that such measurement excited him. The prospect of death accentuated his pleasure in life. She had grown to dread the sight of Anton's writing.

"He would not write such notes did he not intend incitement."

Yet death was still untimely. It came before the outbreak of that rebellion for which they had been preparing with such assiduity.

In grief the young women grew generous: to one another; to the two dead men; even to the discarded Pansy. They also grew unknowingly deceitful. Unknowingly, they began to reconstruct the past. Slowly a stature worthy of their grief was accorded to the men they had loved for so little reward.

Dear Sir, It is more than a month now since the deaths of Paradis and McKenna took place. I have received neither payment nor favour for my part in bringing their dastardly combination to your attention. This is no way to treat your loyal friends. God knows that there are few the Castle can depend upon in such treacherous times as these. I stood in the corridors of the Castle two hours and more this morning, in great pain from my gout, but could catch no sight of you. I believe you to be sincere in your friendship for me and trust that my belief will not be shaken.

There is a curious postscript to the affair which, despite my present pique, I cannot but share with one I am so accustomed to thinking of as a friend. My wife, as you know, died some months ago. My household has been in disarray ever since and it occurred to me that I should marry again. I am not a young man, nor is my fortune (as you well know, Dear Sir) great. Wanting neither a fortune with no face, nor a face with no fortune, my problem has been to secure a marriage of well-balanced advantage. It was upon being told by one of my informants that three women, all close to parturition, now live in Sweetman's house (Sweetman's servants are up in arms, apparently) that a solution occurred to me. One of the young ladies is the jilted fiancée of McKenna himself (by whom, I am given to understand by the young lady's father, she is pregnant). She is, in the normal sense, unmarriageable. Her father, not knowing what else to do, has banished her. Hence her present situation. Yet her father is not heartless. When I put it to him that for a reasonable settlement I would be prepared to marry his daughter and legitimise the bastard, he fell upon my hand with both of his. She had been in happier times, he said, his heart's delight. I have not spoken to the young girl yet, but understand her to be amenable. She will do much, her father said (tactlessly, I thought) to avoid social ruin, and is grateful to be rescued from its brink. She stipulates only that she should be allowed to visit her parents, to whom she is devoted (a devotion ill-shown by her waywardness), once a week. So I am to be married this day fortnight; and some short time hence, to claim McKenna's child for my own. Strange indeed are the ways of the Lord.

I would suggest, Dear Sir, that you could give me no more fitting wedding present than prompt payment of the money owed to me for my tireless and singularly unrewarded efforts on behalf of the Crown.

I remain, as ever, your obedient servant . . .